John Marlay

The life of Rev. Thomas A. Morris, D.D., late senior bishop of the

Methodist Episcopal church

John Marlay

The life of Rev. Thomas A. Morris, D.D., late senior bishop of the Methodist Episcopal church

ISBN/EAN: 9783337263072

Printed in Europe, USA, Canada, Australia, Japan

Cover: Foto ©Raphael Reischuk / pixelio.de

More available books at **www.hansebooks.com**

OF

Rev. THOMAS A. MORRIS, D.D.,

Late Senior Bishop of the Methodist Episcopal Church.

BY

REV. JOHN F. MARLAY, A.M.

WITH

AN INTRODUCTION BY BISHOP E. S. JANES.

CINCINNATI:

HITCHCOCK AND WALDEN.

NEW YORK:

NELSON AND PHILLIPS.

1875.

PREFACE.

It was the wish of Bishop Morris that the story of his life should be written by his friend and colleague, the late lamented Bishop Clark, who had not only consented to undertake the work, but had made considerable progress in gathering material for it, when failing health, together with the incessant cares and exacting duties of the Episcopal office, compelled him to relinquish the engagement. At his request, and under his appointment, as literary executor of Bishop Morris, I have endeavored to carry out his original plan of the work as nearly as possible. I very much regret that Bishop Clark did not live to give the volume the careful supervision of his experienced and skillful pen. It is a satisfaction, however, to be able to state that the earlier chapters, completed about a year before his death, and submitted to his inspection, met his cordial and generous approval.

The materials used in the preparation of this memoir were, chiefly, a brief sketch of his early life written by Bishop Morris himself, coming down to the time of his election to the Episcopacy, with a mere outline of his subsequent history, and his volume, entitled "Miscellany," a book of essays and notes of travel. These traveling letters appeared originally, many years ago, in the *Western Christian Advocate*, and are among the very best specimens of their author's terse and vigorous style as a writer. In weaving them into a connected story of his life, however, it was found necessary to omit large portions altogether, and to exercise a good deal of editorial freedom in adapting the rest.

One or two discourses occupy larger space in the biography than seemed at first desirable; and yet, upon reflection, they were found to be so identified with the life and public services of Bishop Morris, that it was deemed best to insert them without much abridgment.

The life of the late senior bishop of the Methodist Episcopal Church was a remarkable one, not only for its eminent and extended usefulness, but for its early hardships, stirring incidents, and strange adventures; and if it were fully and adequately set forth, would make a much larger as well as more interesting volume than this. I have simply attempted to make the best possible use of the meagre material available. And it now only remains for me to submit the volume, with all its imperfections, to the charitable judgment of the public.

J. F. MARLAY.

CONTENTS.

5

" WOULD I describe a preacher, such as Paul,
  Were he on earth, would hear, approve, and own,
  Paul should himself direct me.   I would trace
  His master-strokes, and draw from his design.
  I would express him simple, grave, sincere ;
  In doctrine uncorrupt ; in language plain,
  And plain in manner ; decent, solemn, chaste,
  And natural in gesture ; much impressed
  Himself, as conscious of his awful charge,
  And anxious mainly that the flock he feeds
  May feel it too ; affectionate in look,
  And tender in address, as well becomes
  A messenger of grace to guilty men."

COWPER'S TASK : The Time-piece.

INTRODUCTION.

"THE righteous shall be in everlasting remembrance."
This passage of Holy Scripture expresses the mind of God
in reference to the remembrance of the good. It is his
will and purpose that their memory shall be perpetuated,
shall be everlasting. The sentiment and practice of mankind in all ages, and in all generations, has been in accord
with this divine declaration; with this difference, that
men have not been careful to confine their memorials to
the righteous, but have often sought to keep in the public
mind the names of wicked men. Men have often endeavored to insure their remembrance after their death by
erecting monuments to themselves while they were living.
Nations have frequently erected monuments to their most
eminent statesmen and illustrious heroes. The people of
this country are building one to Washington, and have just
dedicated one to Lincoln. Marble and brass and bronze
are, however, at a discount in this office of immortalizing
men. They are rendered comparatively useless by the
book. Monuments can only bear a name or briefly state an
event or two in the life of the person. The detailed history

of the man must be left to tradition, and soon become un-
reliable. The book gives a full statement of the character,
and a complete record of the actions of him whom it com-
memorates. The monument can be in but one place, and
be seen by only a favored few. The book can be carried
all over the land, and placed in the homes and hands
of the multitude. No man knoweth of the sepulcher
of Moses unto this day; yet no human name or no
human history is better preserved than is his. His fame
is still spreading as far and as fast as Christianity extends.
Dr. Coke found a grave in the Indian Ocean; no marble
column marks his resting-place, no brass tablet records
the incidents of his eventful life; yet the remembrance of
him shall endure as long as ocean waves lave the shore,
or ocean murmurs chant his requiem, for the book has
chronicled the nobleness of his character, and the devotion
and usefulness of his life. The book transcends in fitness
and efficiency all other memorials of the dead. Biography
is consequently one of the most important departments of
literature.

Bishop Morris was a man eminently worthy of such a
memorial. A well executed life of this distinguished
Christian minister can not fail to be edifying to the Church,
and especially to his brethren in the ministry. Such a
biography is contained in this volume; in my opinion the
work has been prepared with good judgment and much
skill. The portraiture of the Bishop's character is very accurately drawn. The incidents of his life are given in

sufficient detail, and make the volume exceedingly interesting and instructive; it will please the young as well as the experienced reader. The biographer could not give an account of Mr. Morris as minister, editor, and bishop, without giving something of the history of the Church during the period of his active official life. He was a prominent actor in many of the important events which occurred while he was holding these positions of trust and influence. The trials, triumphs, and progress of the Church for the last fifty years, thus incidentally given, are of great value. The memoir is worthy of a place in every Methodist minister's study, and every Methodist Sunday-school library.

Having been for more than thirty years associated with Bishop Morris in the general superintendency of the Church, I became most tenderly attached to him. During this time I had a good opportunity of learning his great worth. I often saw him in circumstances that severely taxed his wisdom, and sorely tried his Christian graces. I have known him at conferences, when greatly perplexed in making the appointments, spend nearly a whole night in prayer for divine guidance and help. At one of his conferences, when he was greatly distressed at the state of the appointments, he spent almost the whole of two nights in crying to God for his interposition. On the morning following this second night of prayer, before breakfast, the two brethren whose cases were the most troublesome, came to him, and proposed to take appointments which greatly relieved his embarrassments. The Bishop always believed they were divinely moved to do this in answer to prayer. In good judgment, prudence, and patience, and tender regard for both the feelings and interests of the preachers under his care, he was like his associate, Bishop Hedding. It grieved him deeply to disappoint the expectations or deny the wishes of either Churches or ministers He was a very loving and considerate colleague. His associates could always trust both his head and his heart. Notwithstanding his great age and long infirmities, we all felt deeply bereaved by his death.

> "O may we all like him, believe,
>   And keep the faith, and win the prize!
> Father, prepare, and then receive
>   Our hallow'd spirits to the skies,
> To chant with all our friends above,
> Thy glorious, everlasting love."

E. S JANES.

LIFE OF BISHOP MORRIS.

CHAPTER I.

INCIDENTS OF EARLY LIFE—AWAKENING AND CONVERSION—
CALL TO THE MINISTRY—ENTERS OHIO
CONFERENCE.

THOMAS A. MORRIS was born April 28, 1794, in Kanawha County, Virginia, five miles above Charleston on the west side of the Kanawha River. His parents, John and Margaret Morris, were both natives of Virginia—the former of Culpepper, and the latter of Augusta County. They belonged to the first band of heroic and enterprising pioneers who settled on the Great Kanawha River, about the year 1785, where, besides the ordinary difficulties incident to new countries, they passed through all the perils and excitements of an Indian war, in the progress of which many of the whites were killed by the savages. Wayne's treaty, in 1795, at length gave peace to the settlers. The house in which the Morris family resided stood on a beautiful swell of ground, near a never-failing spring of pure water, commanding a fine view of picturesque scenery for many miles up and down the river. It was a pleasant rural home, embowered in orchard and forest trees, far removed from the noise and unhealthy excitement of city life. Thomas belonged to a family of eleven children. His parents lived to a good old age, and at length, after a happy union of forty years, died nearly at the same time, in 1818, both possessed of a good hope of eternal life.

The early days of young Morris were happily passed amid the wild and romantic scenery of his mountain home. Late in life he was fond of relating how, in his extreme youth, he delighted to chase the butterfly over the hills, construct tiny boats to float down the rivulets that flowed through green pastures, to hunt with his rude bow and arrow through the forests, and, in Winter, trap the redbird and the quail. His father, however, being an industrious farmer, soon found other and more important work for the son. With his little hoe he was taught to labor in the fields, and in harvest time he was employed as a bearer of sheaves. During the Winter he assisted in the care of the "stock," and seems to have been especially pleased with the duty of a shepherd.

When Thomas was ten years old, the family removed from this beautiful home to a place about forty miles west, in Cabell County, on the State road leading to Kentucky. Here again they endured the hardships, toils, and privations inseparably connected with the settlement of a new country. Clearing away the forest, inclosing the ground and bringing it under cultivation from a state of nature, with the erection of the necessary buildings, required, of course, a great deal of hard labor; and having but a small force for carrying it on, they had for years to exert all their energies to improve and keep up the farm.

The means of education were very limited at that early day throughout the Western States and Territories, and especially in the north-western part of Virginia, where the Morris family resided. Teachers were few in number, and for the most part ill qualified for their work; nor were the most competent of them in very good demand, for many of the early settlers of that wild region cared little for books, so they could but obtain plenty of fresh land, good range for their stock, and an abundance of game. Still there were schools; not continuing, however, longer than "one quarter" of the year, and that always in the Winter, when boys could best be spared from the farm. By such limited means, the children of that day, on the frontiers, obtained what little knowledge of books they possessed; nor was it generally deemed important that the course of study be very extensive or thorough. To master Dilworth's Spelling-book, learn to read the New Testament, cypher to the "rule of three," and write a fair round hand, was regarded as quite an accomplished education, and ample for all the practical purposes of life. This "curriculum" Thomas had passed through creditably by the time he reached his eighteenth year. About that time he became a member of the first grammar-class ever organized in Cabell County. It was taught by Mr. William Paine, a native of England, a thoroughly competent teacher, and an earnest Methodist. This worthy old gentleman, besides performing his professional duties, gave his pupils many sound moral lessons, and, though gathered to his fathers long years ago, his memory is cherished fondly by all his surviving students.

When young Morris was about seventeen years old, his eldest brother, Edmund, who held the clerkship of Cabell County, made him his deputy, and he accordingly left the farm to enter upon the duties of his office. This position he held for nearly four years, except about six months spent in school. The clerk's office proved to be, in many respects, an advantageous position; here the young deputy acquired much useful information concerning business transactions, as well as an easy, rapid use of the pen. But the sudden transition from out-door labor to the confinement of an office seriously impaired his health. His nervous system became deranged, rendering him feeble and timid. When he left the farm, but few of his years in all the neighborhood were more athletic or courageous. It had been his habit for years to traverse mountains and valleys at all hours of the darkest nights, unaccompanied save by his faithful hunting dogs, unawed by the prowling wolf or the dangers of the forest. But after his health declined, he was not only nervous and feeble, but fearful and depressed in mind, losing all relish for his former exciting and adventurous sports and pursuits. A few months after his eighteenth birthday, and while in this feeble state of health, he was one of a company of drafted militia, to perform a six-months' tour in the North against the British and Indians. On the day appointed, the company assembled at the court-house, formed into "messes," shouldered their knapsacks, and started on the march to join a regiment forming at Point

Pleasant, and intended to re-enforce the main army near the Canada line. When they took leave of their friends, who had assembled at the court-house in great numbers to witness their departure, many of these raw recruits, as well as the lookers-on, were visibly and deeply affected. The father of Morris, though himself an old soldier, could not check his fast-falling tears, as he looked upon the emaciated form and youthful face of his child. But the farewells were spoken, and the march commenced. On the morning of the second day's march, however, great was the surprise of young Morris at being overtaken by his brother William with a substitute, whom his father had hired to take the son's place. To turn back so early in the campaign was not agreeable to his feelings, but, under all the circumstances, seemed a duty, and he reluctantly consented to the arrangement.

While connected with the clerk's office, it was part of his business to attend to all the lower and higher courts of the county, by which means he became well acquainted with the lawyers who practiced in these courts. This circumstance, together with an ardent ambition to occupy a position of usefulness and respectability in society, inclined him to choose the law as a profession. Three formidable difficulties, however, were in the way of carrying out that purpose,—imperfect education, the limited means of improving it in any of the schools accessible, and an extraordinary diffidence. The first two obstacles, he thought, might be overcome by industry and a systematic employment of his spare hours ; the last, his friends assured him, would soon pass away. In his later years he was often heard to say that the uncommon diffidence and timidity of his youth never wholly left him, and that, although a public speaker from his youth to an advanced age, he scarcely ever stood before an audience without embarrassment.

The parents of Morris were pious and devoted members of the Baptist Church, and had given much attention to the early religious training of their children. From the days of his childhood, Thomas had had occasional seasons of deep religious feeling, and many serious thoughts of death and eternity. His own record shows that he was scarcely ever without a conviction of his lost and sinful condition, and that from very early childhood he took a deep interest in every thing pertaining to the worship of God. But there were radical defects in his early religious training. His parents did not consider it their duty to encourage their children to make a public profession of faith in Christ. And, what was still worse, though they were unusually strict members of their Church, for that country and in that day, they allowed their children to go abroad on the Sabbath, and, to a great extent, select their own company and amusements, as did their brethren and neighbors generally. Young people thus left to themselves naturally grew up in the belief that, although they were bound to labor six days of the week, the Sabbath was their own day, a holiday, to be spent where and how they pleased.

Under these circumstances, young Morris stifled his convictions of sin, gradually lost his desire to become a Christian, and learned many evil practices while yet a youth. Being naturally of a sedate, thoughtful appearance, and always quite reserved in the presence of his seniors, he bore the reputation of being remarkably exemplary in his boyhood, while his own conscience assured him that he was far from the kingdom, abiding under the wrath of God.

So matters stood with him when he left the home of his youth, and passed from under the restraints of parental authority.

About this time, under the influence of older and more intelligent persons, his mind became poisoned with skeptical opinions, which he seems to have adopted rather as an apology for his impiety than as the result of careful investigation. His was a case of bewildered skepticism, and never of confirmed infidelity. He did not publicly avow his unbelief, or seek in any way to harm the cause of Christianity—for in his worst days the fear of God was not wholly removed from his mind—nor did he question the sincerity of Christians, or doubt their happiness, however much they might be mistaken.

In this state of mind he continued till his eighteenth year, when the terrible concussions of the earth which occurred during the Winter of 1811–12, aroused his guilty conscience, and he became greatly troubled about the future. There was, shortly afterward, a revival of religion in the neighborhood among " the people called Methodists," of whom he knew but little except through the misrepresentations of those who were prejudiced against them. To these meetings he went occasionally, and the general impression made upon his mind by all he saw and heard was

favorable. About that time—in the Spring of 1812—
he began to take the general subject of religion under
more serious consideration, and to form resolutions
to break off from his worst sins, particularly the use
of all improper words, but without any fixed purpose
of becoming pious at that time. For one year he
pondered this subject much, endeavoring earnestly to
reach a final conclusion on the main question ; that
is, whether it would be better for him, all things considered, to resolve on a religious life or not. On the
one hand, a Christian life appeared to be rational,
wise, and safe, and therefore desirable ; while on the
other hand he hesitated to make the necessary sacrifices of worldly plans and prospects, and feared to
forfeit the friendship of his gay and fashionable associates. But that which deterred him most of all was
the fear of failure, and the consequent disgrace of
apostasy. Moreover his religious training made him
slow to move under any power short of compulsion,
not then clearly apprehending the important distinction between coercive power and sufficient grace
freely offered to all men. Of this difficulty he was,
however, measurably relieved, soon after, by a conversation with the Rev. Samuel West, a Methodist
preacher, who convinced him that his crude notions
on that point were not sustained by the Word of
God. The last thing he gave up was the purpose to
be a lawyer, with the various plans which he deemed
necessary for the accomplishment of that object.

Finally, after much reflection on the subject, it
was made plain to his mind one day, when alone, that
it would be infinitely better for him to be " little and

unknown," or even despised and persecuted all his life, and then die in peace and be saved in heaven, than to carry out all his plans of worldly gain, and lose his soul. Whereupon he resolved, in the name and strength of Jesus, to halt no longer between two opinions, but to consecrate his service fully to the living God. As soon as this great decision was reached, he fell on his knees, and, for the first time in his life, tried to pray. This was in February, 1813, and in the nineteenth year of his age. To kneel occasionally in public worship, or at the family altar, as a matter of form or a mark of respect, had been his habit from childhood; but to kneel before God and ask for mercy, pardon, and salvation, was a new thing entirely. As he did so now, his feelings were peculiar and awful. His chief difficulty was the want of that pungent conviction which is so necessary in the process of conversion; nor could he exercise that simple trust in Christ as the only and sufficient Savior. For about six months he sought religion in secret, carefully concealing his purpose and state of mind from all his friends. But this method proved very troublesome, as well as unprofitable. When present at religious services he found it difficult to hide his emotion; for tears, unbidden, would often flow freely, as he listened to the fervent appeal or earnest prayer of the minister. It was still more difficult to mingle with his worldly associates without betraying the secret burden of his heart.

A frank avowal of his feelings and purposes would undoubtedly have been the wisest and safest course at this time; but, not having the moral courage to come out openly on the Lord's side, he was in constant temptation to stifle his convictions and disregard the monitions of his conscience. And now the conscious failure to carry out the resolution he had taken, and the impression that his sins were fearfully augmenting from day to day, came well-nigh driving him to despair, and for a time he seriously meditated upon giving up the struggle.

In the Summer of this year he attended a camp-meeting in the neighborhood, and there, under a sermon preached by Rev. David Young, on the " Parable of the Sower," his heart was more thoroughly broken up than it had ever been before. From that time he sought with increased diligence and earnestness; secret prayer was his constant refuge; conviction increased, godly sorrow was deepened, and the hope of final success began to revive. In a few weeks, however, he found himself threatened with the old difficulty, " the fear of man, which bringeth a snare." After much reflection on his unhappy condition and the best means of obtaining relief, he began to consider seriously the question of separating from the world, and choosing God's people to be his people, as the only probable method of obtaining what he so much desired,—peace of mind, and a sense of God's favor. But here, too, was a sore conflict to pass through. The influence of early religious training inclined him toward the Church of his ancestors, while the strong religious impressions ·received through the instrumentality of the Methodists seemed to suggest the propriety of uniting with them. The fact that the Methodists were then a feeble band, and much persecuted even by other religious denominations, may have somewhat increased the difficulty of settling this important question; but Mr. Morris determined to act deliberately, intelligently, and in the fear of God. He borrowed a Methodist Discipline, examined it thoroughly, and liked it well. He then began to compare it with the New Testament, reading them alternately. After considerable time thus spent, he said to himself, "The Methodists are the Lord's people, and his people shall be my people."

There remained, however, one more difficulty to be removed. In the early stages of his religious awakening he had concluded, in accordance with the views entertained by his parents on the subject, that it would be improper to unite with any Church until he had first obtained a clear evidence of the pardon of his sins. But the circumstances of his own case had nearly satisfied him then, and more fully convinced him afterward, that there is no period in the history of a man's life when he so much needs the help, encouragement, and protection of the Church, or receives greater benefit from it, than while, as a humble penitent, he is seeking the salvation of his soul. When at last young Morris felt that he would joyfully accept mercy on any terms, all his scruples on the subject of entering the Church as a probationer were gone.

Rev. Samuel Brown, the preacher on the circuit (Guyandott Circuit, Ohio Conference), had announced that he would preach his "farewell sermon" at his last appointment in the Morris neighborhood some time in August, 1813, and Mr. Morris resolved that he would on that occasion offer himself to the society for admission on trial, as a seeker of religion. The place of meeting was three miles distant from his home. At the appointed time he set off on foot and alone, choosing an unfrequented way through the forest, in order to avoid company and interruption. Fearing that his heart would fail him when the time came for decisive action, he three times stopped on the way, fell on his knees, and implored Divine assistance to do his duty. A large congregation had assembled; and Mr. Brown's text was, "Come, for all things are now ready." Mr. Morris felt that the subject of the discourse, and the manner of treating it, could not have been better adapted to his state of mind had the minister known all about his condition. At the close of the sermon, persons desiring to do so were invited to unite with the Church on trial. Unaccustomed to Methodist usages in such cases, and not knowing precisely how to act, Mr. Morris inquired of a class-leader, Robert Caseboult, as to the regular mode of procedure. "Go forward," said the leader, "and give your hand to the preacher, and your heart to God;" and immediately, while the congregation were singing the verse,

> "This is the way I long have sought,
> And mourned because I found it not;
> My grief a burden long has been,
> Because I was not saved from sin,"—

he stepped forward alone, and was enrolled among the followers of the Lord Jesus Christ, to the great surse and joy of the congregation, who gathered around the new recruit, and warmly welcomed him to a place in the Church. He was deeply affected, melted into tears of contrition and penitence, and felt that the unhappy wanderer had at last found friends, a home, and a resting-place.

Though he had not, at this time, an evidence of pardon, he had fully counted the cost, and resolved to perform every duty pertaining to the new life he had resolved, by God's help, to lead. This purpose was soon severely tested ; for on the evening of the day he united with the Church, he was called on to pray in a public meeting, which he did with much fear and trembling ; nor did he ever, from that day, refuse to pray when requested to do so, though his mind was often dark, and his heart heavy and oppressed, as he sought the Lord with strong crying and tears. In November following he obtained partial rest for his weary, sin-sick soul. But it was only a glimmering ray of heavenly light at first ; afterward it shone more and more, unto the perfect day.

It will be remembered that Mr. Morris's convictions were too slight, at first, to be satisfactory to himself ; but toward the last of a nine-months' struggle they became very deep and powerful. A sense of guilt as a sinner against God, and the fear of the wrath to come, caused him now many sleepless nights, spent mostly in an agony of prayer, sometimes in his chamber, and sometimes on the cold ground, in the dark and silent woods. This great mental distress, however, gradually subsided, as he, by faith, slowly apprehended Christ and the glorious provision he had made

for sinners.   One day, while in the clerk's office
alone, after a considerable struggle of mind to believe
and grasp the prize, and while singing the words,

> " O, that day when freed from sinning,
>   I shall see thy lovely face,
>   Richly clothed in blood-washed linen,
>   How I 'll sing thy sovereign grace !"—

his faith seemed to take hold on the bleeding Savior ;
he felt a strange emotion of love in his heart, and a
stream of joy seemed to be flowing in upon his
thirsty soul.   His first thought was, This is religion !
But alarmed in a moment lest he might be deceiving
himself, he drew back, his confidence failed, and all
was darkness again.   Two or three days afterward,
about the hour of midnight, this manifestation was
repeated, only a little stronger and of longer continuance, but followed by doubts and darkness for two
weeks.   The dark seasons through which he now
passed were attended with no special sense of guilt,
or fear of the future, but were like the night to a
traveler who waits and longs for morning, that he
may proceed on his journey.   A little instruction
from a competent spiritual guide, at that time, would
no doubt have lifted the cloud wholly from his mind,
and introduced him into the full light and liberty of
the Gospel.

About this time the class-leader having moved
away, and the little class in that neighborhood being
in a somewhat low condition, the new preacher, Rev.
John Cord, appointed Morris to fill the vacancy, and
handed him the class-book with the request that he
would convene the members once a week, and hold a

class-meeting. This appointment was received with much fear and trembling. During the week he retired into the woods, kneeled by the side of a fallen tree, spread out the class-book before him, read the first name, and prayed for him, and so on through the entire list, asking for grace and wisdom to say profitable words to them all on the ensuing Sabbath. The class was a small one, and the members, scattered over a wide territory, did not usually all meet together at one time; but on the following Sabbath there was a good attendance, and the Master was present with them to impart strength and comfort.

Besides his private religious duties, praying in his brother's family and leading the class, Mr. Morris was now much exercised on the subject of holding prayer-meetings, and offering the word of exhortation to his neighbors. Encouraged by the brethren to make the trial, he commenced on Christmas-day, by adding a few remarks to a public discourse delivered by an exhorter in the morning, consenting at the same time to address the congregation in the evening. In the evening the house was well filled, and he was favored with much liberty of utterance in delivering his message; at the close of which, he received a great and signal blessing, such as he never enjoyed before. For many days after, his soul was filled with holy joy, and often while walking alone, or sitting at his desk, musing on the goodness of God in delivering him out of all his troubles, tears of gratitude would flow from his eyes, and he rejoiced greatly in the Rock of his salvation.

Having made a few efforts at exhortation, on

verbal authority, he was, without any application on
his part, presented with a written license to exhort,
signed by the preacher in charge of the circuit, and
dated February 1, 1814, which he accepted and used
faithfully from that time forward.

In the mean time, an event transpired in his history which calls for more than a passing mention. In
the Morris family, early marriages had been universal;
and though Thomas once thought that his case would
perhaps be an exception to the general rule, it turned
out otherwise. That the married state, if prudently
entered into, was favorable to a life of piety, he was
thoroughly convinced, and his thoughts were a good
deal turned to the subject, not so much with a view
to any immediate steps in that direction, as to make
suitable preparation for the great event when the
more convenient season should arrive. In the little
class of which he was leader, there was a gentle and
lovely maiden, whose Christian graces and personal
charms so won his confidence and esteem, that his
mind became agitated with the question whether he
should ever be able to find a more worthy and suitable helpmeet than in the person of Miss Abigail
Scales. A little in advance of himself, both in years
and in Christian experience, this young lady, he felt
persuaded, would greatly contribute both to his usefulness and happiness in the path of duty toward
which God's providence seemed to be leading him.
As his interest ripened into a pure and ardent affection, he took counsel of his elder brethren, and with
their approbation, after much prayer and reflection,
"he ventured to name the subject to her," and she

became his affianced bride. "On the evening of January 23, 1814," in the words of Mr. Morris's brief diary, "the marriage ceremony was performed by Rev. Stephen Spurlock, in the presence of only a few serious friends, without levity or display of any sort."

The circumstances under which young Morris made his first effort at preaching, from a text, were somewhat peculiar. When his parents, who lived twelve miles distant, heard that he had given some public exhortations, they sent a message for him to come and preach at their house. In the neighborhood where they resided, it was not customary to hold meetings for prayer and exhortation in the absence of a preacher; and, not being familiar with Methodist phraseology, they announced that Thomas would "preach," whereas it was his intention to hold a meeting for prayer and exhortation. At the appointed time the house was crowded with his old neighbors and youthful companions, among whom he had spent the days of his boyhood. These old associates had come to hear a sermon, and would be greatly disappointed if the service should be a prayer-meeting; and, besides, on looking over his congregation, he perceived that it was not made up of the right sort of material for a profitable prayer-meeting. He remembered, furthermore, that the preacher on the circuit had voluntarily said to him: "If you feel like preaching at any time, it will be admissible to make the effort a few times by way of trial, without a regular license." So he resolved to make his first effort on that occasion. He sung and prayed, and read his text from Hebrews ix, 27: "And as it is

3

appointed unto men once to die, but after this the judgment," etc. Profound silence followed. There was probably more curiosity than prayer in the congregation. The preacher shook, as if in a paroxysm of ague. Before a word was uttered, the family, many of the neighbors, and the preacher himself, were in tears, while the rest seemed filled with amazement. But when he did begin to talk, it was like the letting out of water under the pressure of a strong head. For about twenty minutes word crowded word, as he often said afterward, "without emphasis, cadence, or period." Death and judgment were the topics, and however unsatisfactory the *manner* may have been to himself, there is reason to believe that solemn and lasting impressions were made on many minds.

His next effort was made at the same place three weeks subsequently, in which he endeavored to guard against the hurried manner of the first attempt, and got through with more ease and satisfaction to himself. Afterward he preached in several localities, as opportunity offered. Some time in March, Rev. Burwell Spurlock preached where Mr. Morris's class usually met, and requested Morris to preach also on the same day, which he did. After preaching, Mr. Spurlock met the class, and requested them to give Morris a recommendation to the Quarterly Conference for license to preach, which they promptly and cheerfully did. The quarterly-meeting was held at a preaching-place near the junction of the Guyandott and Ohio Rivers. The examination was conducted by Rev. David Young, Presiding Elder of Muskingum District, Ohio Conference. The Quarterly Conference being satisfied

as to his "gifts, graces, and usefulness," granted the
license ; to be retained, however, until he should receive the sacrament of baptism. The time selected
for the administration of this ordinance was immediately after the first sermon on the Sabbath of the
quarterly-meeting, when, kneeling at the water's edge,
Mr. Morris was solemnly baptized by the presiding
elder, who poured the water on his head. The influence of early education had somewhat embarrassed
him in his first attempts to investigate the subject
of water-baptism ; but he had now become firmly
convinced that *effusion* was the Scriptural mode, and
the baptism of the Holy Spirit which attended and
followed the application of water to him in that form,
was demonstration that he was in the path of duty.
The day of his baptism, and especially after the solemn
service was over, he was in the habit of referring to
as one of the happiest periods of his life.

Rev. David Young, under whose preaching the
heart of Mr. Morris was first thoroughly broken up,
who baptized and licensed him, and who was chiefly
instrumental in his becoming a Methodist itinerant,
was among the most distinguished men of his day.
He was born in Washington County, Virginia, March
9, 1779. His parents were pious Presbyterians, who
early taught their boy the Lord's Prayer, the Creed,
and the Catechisms. At the age of seven he was
taken by his parents to a prayer-meeting, where, during the first prayer, he was so deeply convicted of sin
that he wept bitterly. His father was a man of considerable wealth and culture, and possessed a good
library. This was David's delight ; and so well did

he avail himself of its advantages and other privileges
of an educational kind, that at the age of twenty-
one he was at the head of a grammar-school in Tennessee. Here, on the 19th of September, 1803, he
was converted under the instrumentality of the
Methodists. He immediately began to call sinners to
repentance, was licensed to preach, and in the Fall of
1805 was received into the Western Conference. In
person, Mr. Young was tall, straight, and well propor-
tioned; in movement, easy, dignified, and graceful.
His head was large and covered with a luxuriant
growth of golden hair, which he wore flowing from
his shoulders. His forehead was broad and high; his
eye full, and deep blue; and when he was aroused, it
flashed with the fires of genius. His manners were
those of a finished gentleman of the old school—with
probably a little too much sternness. He was a
man of great mental vigor, an acute thinker, and a
laborious student. As an orator, according to the
general testimony of those who knew him in his
palmiest days, he had few equals. In style he was
clear, chaste, and logical; occasionally his appeals
were grand and overwhelming. He was fifty-three
years a member of an annual conference, and six
times a member of the General Conference. He died
November 15, 1858, aged seventy-nine years.

For this eminent minister Mr. Morris entertained
the most profound respect and ardent affection through
life. His license to preach, signed by David Young,
and granted at the quarterly-meeting referred to
above, is dated April 2, 1814. From that date he
had plenty of opportunities to preach. The County

Court had, before he became a preacher, appointed
him commissioner of the revenue for that year in
Cabell County. This, in view of his feeble health,
he regarded as a very desirable office. It required
him to call on all the citizens of the county, who,
though comparatively few in number, were scattered
along the rivers and smaller streams over a wide extent of territory. As he passed around among the
people, in the discharge of his official duties, taking a
list of their taxable property, he received and accepted
many invitations to preach. The business assigned
to him was completed toward the end of Summer, and
it then became a grave and important question how
he should shape his future course. After much deliberation and consultation with friends, he concluded
to settle on a piece of unimproved land, given him
by his father, near the homestead. Accordingly he
addressed himself to the no easy task of building a
cabin, kitchen, crib, meat-house, etc. This work, after
four years of exemption from manual labor, taxed his
physical strength to the utmost. But perseverance
was crowned with success. Early in the Autumn of
that year he and Abigail took possession of "Spice
Flat Cottage," situated on a slight swell overlooking a
beautiful piece of table-land, embowered amid forest-
trees and spicewood shrubbery. The residence was
an unpretending one; but it was the abode of love,
happiness, and piety. To this humble dwelling in the
wilderness they invited the ministers of Christ, and
opened their door for preaching. Rev. Henry B. Bas-
com, whose fame as an orator became afterward so
great and wide-spread, was that year the preacher on

Guyandott Circuit, and preached at the residence of
Mr. Morris, where, also, he delivered weekly lectures
to such of the neighbors as cared to avail themselves
of the opportunity of hearing them. In the course
of that year a small Methodist society was formed
in the neighborhood, though most of the people in
that community who had any Church affinities were
Baptists.

In the mean time, Mr. Morris found that the work
of "clearing a farm," without help or the means to
procure it, was likely to prove a very tedious undertaking; and finally, at the solicitation of many of his
neighbors, he agreed to take a school, thinking that
he could apply the net proceeds toward the improvement of his farm. The school commenced for a term
of six months; but at the end of four the school-house
was destroyed by fire, and the enterprise was abandoned. This to the teacher was no cause of regret
so far as it concerned him alone; for teaching a school,
in that community at least, he had proved to be both
an unproductive and irksome business. At the close
of the first year in "Spice Flat Cottage," besides
teaching four months, and occupying his leisure hours
with the ax, maul, and grubbing-hoe, he had preached
and lectured about one hundred times, but had made
no great progress in the cultivation of the soil. It
was a difficult region, too, for successful operations as
a local preacher. The population was sparse, the
roads very bad, and the tax of time and money required
to meet the calls of remote appointments was very
heavy. In the Summer of 1815, at the request of his
eldest brother, Edmund, Mr. Morris made a tour of

exploration through the south-western part of Kentucky, for their mutual accommodation, as both had for some time entertained thoughts of moving further West. Edmund settled in Kentucky the next year after this trip, but Thomas still lingered at Spice Flat, until a very severe attack of chills and fever, that prostrated his wife upon a sick-bed, made him willing to leave the scene of his early married life. He finally determined to follow his brother to Kentucky, in the Spring of the ensuing year, and sold out his farming implements and stock, so as to be perfectly free to spend the Winter as might be thought most profitable for himself and the Church. About this time the Rev. John Dew, then on the circuit, solicited him to take employment as his colleague for three months; which proposition, having been submitted to Rev. David Young, Presiding Elder, and approved by him, was accepted. He entered upon the work in November, 1815.

There is abundant evidence that from the hour when Mr. Morris first felt it to be his duty to preach the Gospel, he was strongly impressed that he ought to give himself wholly to the work. From the very first he was seriously exercised on the subject of entering the itinerancy ; and with a view to such a probable contingency, he had studied as closely as his other employments permitted. When at his daily labor he kept his books with him, and, if compelled to rest a few moments, would read a paragraph, to be digested more fully while swinging his ax or mauls. His own consent to tear away from the world and enter the traveling ranks could easily have been obtained,

and some of his Methodist friends recommended
that course. But his nearest and best earthly
friend had a severe struggle before she became perfectly reconciled to go out and face the difficulties,
privations, and sufferings inseparable from an itinerant's life in those days. Her hesitancy was not
owing to any want of zeal in the cause of religion,
but grew mainly out of her delicate health; and
partly, perhaps, from the conviction that neither she
nor her husband was adapted, physically or otherwise,
to many of the duties and peculiarities of the itinerancy. There was little or no provision then for the
support of preachers' families on the circuits; their
own means were exceedingly limited, and, with the
prospect of an increasing family, the outlook, from a
worldly point of view, was rather dark and forbidding.
The opposition, also, of some of her near relatives, increased the embarrassment of the situation. Mrs.
Morris did not positively refuse to go into the itinerant ranks; but her feelings were so agitated by the
anticipation of it, that her husband deemed it prudent to waive the subject and await the indications
of Providence; nor had he long to wait. The Lord
brought her by a way she did not know, and led her
in a path she had not considered. During the illness
already referred to, she became deeply exercised on
the subject of her husband's traveling and preaching,
when no one else apparently was thinking of it.
Her own account of the manner in which her mind
was exercised, is somewhat remarkable. "The Lord
said to me," she related, "by his silent but intelligent Spirit, 'Let him go!' but my heart said 'No!'

In a moment I was siezed with an agony of bodily pain and mental anguish. For two or three hours I felt as if rolling on a bed of thorns, while the blackness of darkness and despair, comparable only to the torments of hell, seized upon my mind. The words were again applied with increased force, ' Let him go !' when I responded instantly, 'With all my heart ;' and in a moment all distress of body and mind were gone, and I felt exquisitely happy. " A wonderful change in her countenance was observed by her husband, to whom, as soon as she was sufficiently composed, she made the above statement, adding, " Now, if you feel it your duty to travel and preach, you have my full consent ; and, if you ever locate, no one shall ever say that it was at my request."

This was in the Fall of 1815, and she kept her promise faithfully to the end of her life. It was only a few weeks subsequently to the remarkable incident just related, that the proposition was made for Mr. Morris to become a colleague of Rev. Mr. Dew. Under all these circumstances he felt that he could not safely refuse. His itinerancy was an experiment ; he felt doubtful of success, and engaged in the work for one quarter only, with a view to satisfy his own mind whether it would be safe and proper for him fully to enter the itinerant ranks.

Those who best knew him will most readily believe his statement, recorded in his diary, that he was far from being sanguine of success. Many things caused him to fear a failure, and, among others, an enfeebled constitution, difficulty of supporting his family, want of suitable qualifications, and, last but not least, a temptation to doubt his Divine call to the ministry. Hitherto he had simply done as his brethren directed, in all cases where help was needed and he saw any prospect of doing good. Thus he had been made a leader, an exhorter, and a licentiate, without any solicitation on his own part, and had labored whenever and wherever those having rule over him advised. In accordance with this rule, when his services were called for on the circuit, he determined to make trial for one quarter at least.

The Winter of 1815–16 was severe. The cold was often intense, changes in the weather sudden, and traveling bad. Under these circumstances, in a sparsely populated neighborhood, the congregations were necessarily small, and the young itinerant would often, no doubt, be sorely tempted. The time, however, passed swiftly; for he was deeply interested in his work, and felt a growing desire to make a thorough trial of his fitness for it. The time for the quarterly-meeting having arrived, Mr. Morris was approached by his colleague, Dew, on the subject of a recommendation to the Annual Conference. "Do you feel, brother Morris," said Mr. Dew, "like selling yourself to the Church?" The characteristic reply was, "Yes, cheap!" After the usual examination, the Quarterly Conference granted the recommendation; but, as the Ohio Conference would not meet for six months, the presiding elder employed him as assistant on Marietta Circuit, with Rev. Marcus Lindsey as his colleague.

Before he left for his new field of labor, time was given him to fill a few outstanding appointments.

On his way to meet these engagements, Mrs. Morris accompanied him some distance, to visit a friend. The weather had suddenly become extremely cold, and the small streams were beginning to freeze over. Crossing these, as they were obliged to do many times, was both difficult and dangerous, for the ice was not quite strong enough to bear the weight of a horse. In one of these crossings, his own horse became frightened and unmanageable, and, after plunging through the ice, struck a bluff bank, where, in the attempt to rise, he fell back ; and Mr. Morris and his little daughter, whom he was carrying in his arms, were thrown into the stream, and the horse escaped. They got to the bank at last with difficulty, but not until his clothes were frozen stiff. Mrs. Morris took off her riding-habit and wrapped it around the child to keep it from perishing with cold, while her husband waded into the creek again to recover his saddle-bags. Then considerable time was spent in recovering the horse, and, when that was accomplished, they were obliged to travel two miles before reaching shelter or fire. This unpleasant episode cost both the father and child a severe illness ; but with such experiences the early preachers of Methodism, especially in the West, became familiar. The work to be done required heroic spirits, and, in the good providence of God, the right man was generally found in the right place.

Having partially recovered from this attack of illness, Mr. Morris set off, early in March, 1816, according to instructions, to meet Rev. D. Young at the quarterly-meeting in Athens, Ohio, which, at that

time, was an appointment belonging to Marietta
Circuit. Just before reaching Athens, while riding
down a muddy hill, his horse stumbled and fell, and he
was precipitated over the animal's head into the mire.
Almost literally covered from head to foot with mud,
to say nothing of a severely bruised ankle, he was
obliged to ride into the town ; and, to add to his mortification, just as he passed the church, the congregation was dismissed, and he was obliged to make
his first appearance before his parishioners in that
unhappy plight.

After passing around the circuit, and having secured a boarding-place for his little family, he returned for them to Virginia. With heavy hearts they
bid adieu to Spice Flat Cottage and the friends of
their youth, to take up their abode among strangers,
with the prospect of being homeless wanderers to the
end of their days. Still they were greatly strengthened and comforted by the thought that they were in
the path of duty, and under the guidance of Providence. There were times, however, when Mr. Morris
was in painful doubt about his call to the ministry ;
and when he engaged in the work on this circuit, it
was with the determination to test his health, qualifications, and call, until the session of the ensuing Conference, and then finally settle the question of continuing in the work.

The work of the circuit was heavy, and well-nigh
wore him down in six months. But he was full of
ardor, and labored indefatigably and not in vain in the
Lord. The Church was quickened, sinners were
awakened, and at many points on the circuit gracious

revival seasons were enjoyed. During the two quarters, Mr. Morris himself received sixty-six persons on trial, and his colleague a still greater number. This success, though it does not seem to have fully settled in his own mind the question of his call to the ministry, greatly encouraged and comforted him; and yielding to the entreaties of his brethren, and especially his colleague, he suffered his recommendation to go to Conference, which met at Louisville, Ky., where, in September, 1816, he was regularly admitted into the Ohio Conference on trial. The two years of his probation in the Conference were both spent on Marietta Circuit, and they were years of much prosperity to the Church, and of great spiritual enjoyment to Mr. Morris, who, before the close of the first year, had all doubts removed from his mind concerning his call to the ministry—a subject on which we purpose to give his well-considered views more definitely in the next chapter.

CHAPTER II.

CIRCUIT WORK—ORDAINED DEACON AND ELDER—TRANSFER TO KENTUCKY.

THE various denominations of the Protestant world agree substantially on the subject of a Divine call to the ministry. That it is the peculiar prerogative of the Head of the Church to designate men for the great work of preaching the Gospel, is admitted among Christians with very great unanimity. The Methodist Episcopal Church admits to the sacred office only those who "think they are moved by the Holy Ghost to preach." This principle was undoubtedly recognized in the appointment of Aaron and his sons, and the tribe of Levi, to the Jewish priesthood. In all ages of the world, and under every form of dispensation, the method of filling the priestly, prophetical, and apostolic office, has been the same. The mode in which the Divine will is now made known to the individual whose duty it is to preach the Gospel may differ, in some respects, from that employed in the first ages of the Church, or even in apostolic times. But all Christians who derive their opinions on this highly important subject from the New Testament, and believe that the Scriptures contain the only proper rule of faith and practice for the Church in all ages, must be convinced that men are set apart for the ministry by Divine appointment, and that none are true ministers of Christ "but they who are called of God, as was Aaron."

We give Mr. Morris's account of his call to the work of the ministry, in his own words:

"That some men are specially called of God to preach his Gospel, is a doctrine which I have always held as firmly as any other tenet of the Christian system, and for the reason that it is plainly taught in the Sacred Scriptures. It does not follow, necessarily, however, that God must work miracles to convince men of their duty in this respect, any more than in other respects. Men are convinced of their duty to preach, as they are of their duty to repent or pray,—1. These duties are taught in the Scriptures; 2. The Holy Spirit moves men to the performance of them; 3. They are encouraged to persevere in them by the blessing which follows obedience.

"Again, it is not contended that all the evidences of a man's call to the work of the ministry are conferred at once; for there are some evidences which never can be obtained, except by the test of experiment : as, for instance, gifts and fruit. No one knows whether he can preach until he tries, and much less does he know what will be the effect of his preaching. But there are some things he can know, respecting his call to the work, before he commences. First, he may know whether the providence of God opens the way, or not, for him to enter the field; and, secondly, whether he is moved by the Holy Ghost to go forward and preach the glad news of salvation. But to preach without some intimation of a Divine call, is the height of presumption. He who is a stranger to experimental godliness, and has no call to the work except that he has been educated for it by his friends, assumes an awful responsibility. He stands before the people claiming to be an embassador for Christ, when Christ has neither chosen nor sent him. And as to the authority supposed to be derived by what is called apostolical succession, in the sense in which that phase is now used and abused, it should be classed with the claim of the Jews to salvation on the ground that they were the natural descendants of Abraham. It is nothing worth. He who is soundly converted, called of God to preach, and has consequently the promise of Christ's presence and aid, belongs to the true Scriptural succession; and all others, no matter where, when, or by whom ordained, are intruders into the sacred office.

"I am far from believing that all the true ministers of the Lord Jesus Christ belong to any one denomination; and equally far from supposing that a Divine call supersedes the necessity of study, to show ourselves approved of God, workmen that need not be ashamed, rightly dividing the word of truth. With these views, which I have ever held without wavering, it has been my honest endeavor to look well to my own credentials.

"The evidences which satisfied me of my call to the ministerial work were chiefly these: 1. As soon as I began to enjoy the comforts of religion, I felt a desire to recommend it to others, which I did first privately. But this did not satisfy my mind; I desired to proclaim it to the multitudes, and this desire increased until it nearly engrossed all my thoughts by day and night, so that even in my sleep I appeared to be generally at some religious meeting, praying and exhorting. 2. Without any solicitation on my part the brethren urged me to go forward in the work of the Lord publicly. 3. The fear that I would be confounded in consequence of my extreme diffidence was overcome by the power of faith to a great extent. For years I had been doing business as a clerk of court, and to the last would nearly choke down in swearing a jury, or reading a paper, from which painful embarrassment I could by no means escape; but when I commenced speaking in public, though my natural weakness remained, the power of religious influence often raised me above it, so that I frequently spoke in the presence of multitudes with ease and pleasure. 4. My early efforts to exhort and preach were followed by a great blessing on my own soul. 5. My conscience bore me witness that I was in the path of duty; for if I improved every opportunity offered me to speak for Christ, in public as well as in private, I enjoyed peace of mind; but if I neglected to do this, or shunned the cross, my heart condemned me, and I was unhappy. 6. The pious part of the community thought I ought to proceed, and some of the people professed to be benefited by my labors. I formed some new societies, and received scores of new members into the old ones. Still, doubts of my call occasionally troubled me, attended with great despondency of mind, and sore temptations to desist from the work. It would often occur to me that the good accomplished might be accounted for without admitting my Divine call, and fears would arise that I might be in the way of others whom the Lord would delight to honor as the instruments of saving souls. 7. I wanted some responsible witnesses who could and would say, voluntarily, that under my preaching they were awakened for the first time, and from thence had turned to seek the Lord, and had been saved. The Lord gave me many such witnesses on the Marietta Circuit. 8. Satan still assaulted me by suggesting that all these might fall away and be lost, and my work go for nothing at last; but his mouth was soon stopped, for two of these witnesses, after living happily for some months, died shouting victory to the last. Since that time I have not doubted that God called me, unworthy as I am, to the work of the ministry, though I have feared often that, through unfaithfulness, my commission was forfeited. And my experience as a Christian has accorded with my experience as a minister. That I was changed by grace, and often blessed with the spirit of adoption, was with me no matter of uncertainty or doubt for many years; but afterward I sometimes feared, especially when low in religious comforts, that I had fallen from grace, as Paul said some of the Galatians did. Yet generally I have had peace and prosperity as a humble laborer in the Lord's vineyard, and have maintained a good hope, through grace, of everlasting life."

When Mr. Morris entered the regular work of the itinerant ministry he had almost every thing pertaining to his calling to learn, both as to his pastoral and social relations. He found himself in a school where experience and observation were, under God, his chief instructors. Being quite young, it would be strange if, under all the circumstances, he did not sometimes make mistakes. Of a very sensitive nature, a trifling error of judgment would occasion him great pain and mortification ; and although, with the ingenuous candor that marked his whole life, he often in later years referred to the mortifying blunders of his early ministry, we have reason to believe, from the testimony of his contemporaries, that these were very few and unimportant. On leaving his first field of labor in Ohio (the Marietta Circuit), he had every reason to thank God and take courage. His ministry there had been one of toil indeed, and even at times of sorrow ; but it had also been one of hope and joy and success. He had not labored in vain. Besides those reported by his colleagues, Cornelius Springer and Job Baker, he had had the pleasure of receiving about two hundred and fifty persons into the Church—a great and glorious work when we consider the wide extent of the circuit traveled, the sparseness of the population, and the many difficulties to be overcome. From a small diary kept by Mr. Morris during this period, extending from March, 1816, to August, 1818, we learn that, during these two and a half years spent on Marietta Circuit, he had traveled on horseback about seven thousand five hundred miles, and delivered about nine hundred and twenty public discourses, in the form of regular sermons, being a little over an average of one daily, exclusive of the labor of holding class and prayer meetings, and visiting among the sick and the serious. This amount of labor, which seems herculean to modern itinerants, he performed, too, it is to be remembered, in a feeble state of health, suffering severely at times from liver complaint, erysipelas, chills and fever, and last, though not least, constant weakness and pain in his eyes ; so that much of the time he was compelled to ride in goggles, and preach with spectacles on.

If the young minister of the present day inquires, When did he find time to study? we answer: The heroes of early Methodism did not require, for the preparation of their sermons, or the prosecution of their theological studies, a neatly furnished office, a handsome writing-table, and a large library ; nor did they claim their morning hours as sacred from intrusion, to be devoted wholly to study. They were generally men who religiously observed the rule, " Never be unemployed ; never be triflingly employed." Every scrap of time, every leisure hour and odd moment, was appropriated to study. Books were read through carefully on horseback, and whatever they contained of practical utility to the preacher was immediately called into requisition. When not reading or sleeping, or engaged in religious or social conversation, they were studying sermons, preparing new ones—thinking them out—and remodeling old ones. This process was carried on while riding, walking, sitting, or reclining. It was a necessity; but it also became a source of great enjoyment. The diversity of congregations would naturally suggest a variety of topics, and the remote positions of appointments from each other afforded opportunity for repeating sermons. Thus the early preacher could review, amend, and improve his discourses, until they were wrought into the most effective form.

Perhaps the most serious hardship encountered by the early Methodist preachers was the inadequacy and uncertainty of their support. The people to whom they ministered were poor, with few exceptions, and the full allowance for the support of a preacher (which was not always paid) was a miserable stipend. Often, indeed, must these devoted and self-sacrificing men have suffered severe tests of their faith as to what they should eat, and wherewithal be clad, while toiling in the Master's vineyard; but, trusting in God, and going forward, they were generally provided for— how strangely and providentially at times is illustrated in the following incident, which occurred during the first year of Mr. Morris on Marietta Circuit. Being in need of a pocket-handkerchief, he went into the store of James Whitney, Esq., of Harmar, to buy one. Before making the purchase, however, it occurred to him that his family might need the dollar more than he did the handkerchief, especially if they should get sick. He therefore left the store without making known the object of his call, or even hinting the matter to any one. After passing round his circuit he called at the store again, when Mr. Whitney handed him a small package, remarking, " It was left here for you by a gentleman from the country." It contained a silk handkerchief, just the article he wanted, and a silver dollar, both of which came very opportunely.

Methodism was not then the influential and popular cause which the growth of a century has now

made it. To unite with the Church then was no
slight cross, especially to such as had any connection
with influential and fashionable families. Several of
the converts under the ministry of Mr. Morris, at this
period, were disowned by their former friends; young
people were driven from home for becoming religious,
and joining the Methodists. One young lady of Marietta was whipped with a cowhide by her enraged
father for attending Methodist meetings. It was said,
at the same time, that Mr. Morris would receive a
like castigation as soon as an opportunity occurred.
The opportunity was not long delayed. Mr. Morris,
as soon as he heard of the threat, walked past the
door of the irate gentleman, who happened to be sitting on his portico at the time; but no violence was
attempted. Finding that he could not beat religion
out of his daughter, or hire her to leave the Church
of her choice, he adopted another plan to convince
her that the Methodists were not as good friends as
she thought them to be, hoping in that way to alien-
ate her affections from them. She was a minor, but
a remarkably intelligent young lady for her years.
He drew up a bond binding blank individuals for her
support until she became of age, and providing that
she should never apply to him for any thing as a
minor. Handing this paper to his daughter, he said,
" If Whitney and Dunlavy [prominent Methodists and
men of means] will sign this bond, you may go where
you please." She presented it to those gentlemen,
who immediately signed it. The young lady, thus
driven away from her own father's house, found a
pleasant home in the family of Mr. Whitney for the

time being, but soon sought employment and the means of self-support by teaching a country school. Her father was stricken down in about a year with a severe illness, from which he never recovered, and through which he was faithfully nursed by his persecuted child. This may serve as an example of the trials through which both the preachers and the people of early Methodism were called to pass.

When his full term of service on the Marietta Circuit was completed, Mr. Morris attended an annual conference for the first time. It was held at Steubenville, Ohio, where he was examined, admitted to full connection, and ordained deacon by Bishop George, in August, 1818. At that conference several things were witnessed by the young itinerant that made a deep impression on his mind. There he saw, for the first time, Bishops M'Kendree, George, and Roberts, all of whom were present. There, too, he saw first a body of grave divines in council, among whom were Quinn, Parker, Shinn, Crume, and others, all of whom have long since passed from toil to reward. The regular business of a conference was then very limited compared to conference business now ; but more time and attention were devoted to spiritual matters. Bishop M'Kendree, as he called the names of the elders, requested each to speak of his work and experience, converting the conference into a sort of class-meeting, which was at once interesting and profitable.

The Committee on Public Worship had notified Mr. Morris on Sabbath evening that he was appointed to preach at sunrise on Monday morning. With fear and trembling he rose in the pulpit at the appointed time, and commenced the service. As soon as he announced his subject, it became evident to him, from the looks of preachers and people, that something was amiss; but what it was he could not imagine. At the close of the meeting, one of the brethren observed to him that his task had been a difficult one—that is, to improve the bishop's sermon. It appeared, then, that Bishop Roberts had preached from the same text the day before, in the same house—a circumstance of which Mr. Morris was wholly ignorant, as he had attended service at another church the day previously. The occurrence was mortifying, of course, to a young man; but no harm came of it other than the pleasantry of his brethren, which, to a keenly sensitive nature, may have seemed a little cruel.

Another incident occurred at the Steubenville Conference not easily forgotten by Mr. Morris. On the recommendation of some of his friends, he was employed by Bishop M'Kendree as his private secretary. The bishop and his secretary occupied a large room with two beds at Mr. Haile's. Sabbath evening they retired early; but the responsibility of having to preach at sunrise next morning made the young scribe wakeful. At about two o'clock, on Monday morning, he awoke from his first uneasy slumber, and was surprised to see a light in the room, and the good bishop seated at his table, writing something in which he seemed deeply interested. He was stationing the preachers, and was doing it after the manner of Asbury; that is, according to his own judgment. Without consultation with his colleagues in office, or the presiding elders, he was calling over the list of appointments, and naming the man selected for each, in a soft, low tone of voice, as he wrote it down. Soon Mr. Morris, who was now wide awake, though perfectly quiet, heard the bishop say, "Barnesville, T. A. Morris." The young secretary did not understand then, what he had abundant opportunity afterward to learn, that necessity will sometimes arise for changes in the appointments after the first scheme is made out. He said nothing, but was well pleased with the arrangement, as Barnesville was one of the best circuits in the Conference. When at last, however, the appointments were announced at the close of the Conference session, he was somewhat surprised to learn that his destination was not Barnesville, but Zanesville!

From this Conference he returned to his family at Marietta, and with them set off to visit their friends in Virginia, after an absence of two years. On the way they received the sad intelligence of the death of his father, and of the serious illness of his mother, who died some days after their arrival. Their end was tranquil and peaceful; for they had both been, for many years, experimental, practical Christians. But desolation seemed to reign through all the walks of his once cheerful and happy home, and he soon hastened back to survey a new, and, to him, strange field of labor. Zanesville Circuit, when T. A. Morris and Charles Elliott were sent to it, in 1818-19, "included what are now called Zanesville Station, Cambridge Circuit, Putnam Circuit, and parts of others;" and, in the following year, when Samuel Brockunier and

James Gilruth were his colleagues, " it was so enlarged as to include Washington and Coshocton, and
the intermediate settlements.   Those familiar with
that region can easily see the extent of the circuit,
by running a supposed line from Zanesville to Dilan's
Iron-works, and curving round through the settlements on Jonathan's Creek to Wolf Creek, below
M'Connellsville;   thence up the Muskingum, on the
west side to Putnam and Zanesville ; thence south-
east by a zigzag route, past Chandler's Salt-works,
and on to the head of Wills Creek, and all the neighborhoods down to Cambridge ; thence to Washington,
Sugar Creek, Wagoner's Plains, Coshocton, and
Johnson's Plains ; and, finally, by numerous angles
and right-angles and acute-angles, back to Zanesville." (Morris's Miscellany, page 245)

For a family residence on this circuit, Mr. Morris obtained a one-story log-cabin, with two small
rooms, situated on the commons north-east of Cambridge, Guernsey County. This humble domicile he
fitted up in the cheapest and simplest manner. Of
his colleague the first year on this circuit, Charles
Elliott, it is unnecessary to speak at length here.
His name has since become a household word, and
his fame as an author and journalist has extended far
beyond the limits of his own denomination.   Dr.
Elliott's history is an important part of the history
of American Methodism, and must ever hold a high
place among the standard biographical literature of
the Church which he so long and so faithfully served.
It need hardly be said that T. A. Morris and Charles
Elliott worked together as true yokefellows, with the

utmost cordiality and in uninterrupted harmony during the year. They not only filled all the regular appointments, but struck out into the regions beyond, and, wherever a destitute neighborhood was found, the standard of the Cross was set up. Most of the country was new, the roads were very bad, the houses were open, lodging hard, fare coarse, and pay very inconsiderable. Indeed, it barely sufficed to keep soul and body together, and that only with the most rigid economy.

An incident that occurred about this time in the history of Mr. Morris, though unimportant in itself, may nevertheless serve to illustrate the times of which we write, and, also, the dealings of the Lord with his servants. It occurred at the beginning of the first year on Zanesville Circuit. Having passed around and arranged the plan of the work, returning home through Zanesville, Mr. Morris bought cloth for a coat, and left it with a tailor to be made up and ready for him the day previous to his first Sabbath appointment in that place, as he had no coat suitable to wear on such an occasion; Zanesville being even then a place of considerable culture and refinement. Punctual to his engagement the tailor sent the coat, and the bill also, to Mr. Morris's lodgings on Saturday night. It was paid for in full; but the preacher's purse was thereby utterly depleted—not a farthing being left. Still, he was well satisfied to have his new coat, and money enough to pay for it; and so he gave himself no anxiety about to-morrow. On Monday morning, however, he was obliged to make an early start for his next appointment. Soon after

setting out, he came in sight of a toil-bridge across
the Muskingum River, and over this bridge he must
pass in order to reach his appointment ; but how to
accomplish that without a cent of money in his
pocket, became now an embarrassing question. While
examining his pockets for a knife, comb, or something
that would be accepted as a pledge until his next
" round," he reached the gate, and a lady came to the
door to receive the toll.   After looking at him closely
for a moment, she remarked, " I believe you go free."
He thanked her, and rode on.   He said afterward,
in relating this incident, that he never saw that lady
before or after that day, and that during his two-
years' term on the circuit, this was the only time he
was passed free through that bridge.

Finding the affairs of the circuit generally in a
very unsatisfactory condition, he applied himself at
once to the work of restoring order, enforcing discipline, and organizing the societies. Boards of trustees
were convened, vacancies filled, and old debts paid or
provided for. Fifty nominal members were excluded—
some for immorality, but most of them for willfully
neglecting duty.   He and his colleague toiled hard
that year, and gathered some lost and wandering
sheep into the fold ; but in consequence of a rigid
enforcement of discipline, they were compelled, at its
close, to report a slight decrease.   In 1819 he
attended the session of the Conference held in Cincinnati, and saw for the first time the Queen City of
the West, containing at that date a population of
about eight thousand.   The sittings of the Conference
were held in the old stone church where Wesley

Chapel now stands. Mr. Morris soon learned that an annual conference was not an occasion either for idleness or recreation, but for constant and often perplexing business. At the first one he attended, the year before, and previous to his admission as a member, he was placed on the Book Committee; at this session he was placed on the Board of Stewards, a responsible and laborious position. After the appointments had been announced, Bishop George, who presided, pleasantly remarked to him at parting, "Well, Brother Morris, you made such a poor out on your circuit last year, we have sent you back to do your work over."

His colleague this year, by Conference appointment, was Samuel R. Brockunier; but at the close of the first quarter, the presiding elder, Jonathan Stamper, sent James Gilruth to their relief, and they then enlarged the circuit extensively, taking into their new "plan" many points that had never before been occupied. They labored incessantly in the work of organizing new societies and strengthening old ones, and had considerable success. More than two hundred were added to the membership of the circuit, and, at the close of the year, a net increase of one hundred and eighty-seven was reported. The support, however, was but little better than that of the year previous. Mr. Morris lived this year in Zanesville, occupying a very indifferent frame tenement, which the owner kindly tendered, free of rent, until he had other use for it. He then moved into the paint-shop of Mr. Thomas Moorhead, situated on the rear of his lot, near the old market-house. This dwelling also was furnished free of rent ; terms well adapted, no doubt, to the financial condition of the occupant, whose income did not amount to enough to buy food and clothing suitable for himself and family.

During that year, at a time when he and his family were in very trying circumstances, being in want of apparel and in debt for provisions, the Lord raised them up an unexpected friend in the person of Mr. Pierce, a merchant of Zanesville. This gentleman was not a professor of religion, nor even a stated hearer at the Methodist Church, and was, besides, a stranger to Mr. Morris, who had no acquaintance with him whatever. The weary itinerant, on reaching home one evening, toil-worn and depressed by the gloomy prospect before him, unable to see how he could much longer continue in the work with his feeble health and helpless family, was surprised to learn that Mr. Pierce had called on Rev. D. Young to inquire into his history, circumstances, and worldly prospects. As the result of his inquiries, he was soon seen on the streets with a subscription paper in his hand. Meeting a member of the Church, who was also a merchant, the following conversation ensued :

Methodist. What are you doing, Mr. Pierce ?

Mr. P. I am making an effort to relieve your minister.

Methodist. Well, I'll give something to help in that case.

Mr. P. No, sir ; your name don't go on this paper, nor that of any member of your Church, except T. Moorhead. You ought to be ashamed to let such a man suffer while laboring for your good; this effort is to be confined to poor sinners like myself.

Mr. Pierce headed the list with a subscription of ten dollars, and he succeeded very quickly in collecting about seventy-five dollars. This occurred near the close of the second year, and was regarded by Mr. Morris as a providential deliverance from a very distressing financial embarrassment. The amount of this donation may now seem small, and to many, perhaps, the incident will appear trifling; but in that day the support of Methodist preachers was so meagre, that seventy-five dollars would be a very great relief. During the first twelve years of the ministry of Mr. Morris, his salary averaged one hundred and sixty-six dollars and sixty-six and two-third cents, as his carefully-kept private accounts show. This was to pay house-rent, buy fuel, provisions, and clothing for the family, entertain company, educate the children, pay doctors' bills, public and private charities, books, horse, etc. During the two years of labor on Zanesville Circuit, though in feeble health, Mr. Morris rode on horseback about five thousand five hundred miles, and preached five hundred sermons. Of his colleagues this year, Rev. James Gilruth, after an active life in the pioneer service of the Church, died, a member of the Upper Iowa Conference.

Rev. Samuel R. Brockunier entered the itinerant ranks in 1818. The record of his long, active, and useful service extends thus far back into the heroic period of Methodism. Wise in counsel, earnest and

pathetic in the pulpit, affectionate and genial in the
social circle, he was eminently successful in his
various fields of labor.

In 1820, the Ohio Conference met in Chillicothe,
when Mr. Morris was elected to elder's orders, and
ordained by Bishop Roberts. His general health
was so now enfeebled, and his vocal organs so impaired by excessive labor and disease, that he
deemed it proper to make a full and frank communication to the Conference, leaving to their godly
judgment the question of his future relation to the
work. The result was, that he was placed in a supernumerary relation; but that relation was a far
different one then, practically, from what it has been
since. He was appointed to Lancaster, Ohio, just
constituted a station, and as such to be organized.
His labors that year included one hundred and sixty
sermons, visits to the country involving in the aggregate a thousand miles of travel, and a trip to
Kentucky. Yet he found the work comparatively
easy, and was much benefited by the change, both
as to his health and studies. The result of this
year's labors, however, did not show much apparent
success. Old difficulties of a personal character
among the members, and the unfinished state of the
church, were serious embarrassments; but under a
wise and prudent administration, peace and harmony
were restored, and the foundation laid for future
prosperity. Toward the end of this year, Bishops ·
M'Kendree and Roberts, on their way to the Ohio
Conference at Lebanon, spent a few days, including
a Sabbath, in Lancaster. During this episcopal

visitation, it was agreed and arranged that Mr. Morris should be transferred to Kentucky, and, instead of going to his own Conference at Lebanon, meet the Bishops at Lexington, the seat of the Kentucky Conference. The last Sabbath of his pastorate in Lancaster, the pulpit was filled, morning and evening, by ministers on their way to Conference ; but the people having learned of the proposed transfer, urged him to give them a farewell sermon. An appointment was accordingly made for such a service, to be held on Monday morning at sunrise. The house was well filled. He preached a tender, affectionate sermon from the words : " And now, brethren, I commend you to God and to the word of his grace, which is able to build you up, and to give you an inheritance among all of them which are sanctified." (Acts xx, 32.) At the close of the service he proposed that all who felt willing to enter into a solemn covenant to try to serve God and meet in heaven, should signify the same by giving him their right hand, in the presence of the congregation, while a hymn was being sung. Nearly the whole audience moved forward ; tears fell fast from eyes unused to weep ; a deep and powerful religious influence seemed to pervade the assembly, as, one by one, they bade adieu to a faithful minister of Christ who had taught them publicly and from house to house.

From Lancaster Mr. Morris went to Cabell County, Virginia, to visit his relations, among whom his family remained until his return from the Kentucky Conference. It may be well here to explain briefly the occasion of his transfer to that body :

When he sold his land in Virginia, to engage in the work of the ministry, he put the proceeds—about five hundred dollars—into the hands of his brother Edmund, then on the eve of removing to Kentucky, to be invested in land in that State, which was accordingly done. Afterward, owing to the unsettled state of the currency in Kentucky, and other causes, it was not deemed advisable to transfer this little pecuniary interest to Ohio. Edmund was the oldest brother, and had been chiefly instrumental in the formation of the business and social habits of the younger members of the family. By his advice, therefore, and that of other friends, Mr. Morris was led to believe that it would be the wisest course, upon the whole, to retain his temporal interest in Kentucky, transfer to that Conference, and pay what attention he could to the improvement of his property, while performing ministerial service as a traveling preacher. The results of the change, however, were disappointment, increased pecuniary embarrassment, and no little personal suffering. He always felt, nevertheless, that the dearly bought lessons received in that rough school of experience during a seven-years' campaign in the south-western region were providential and useful.

After a tedious journey, he and his family arrived safely in their new field of labor, Christian Circuit, in October, 1821. But their household goods, sent by wagon to Portsmouth, thence by boat to Henderson, Kentucky, and thence by wagon again to the circuit, did not reach them till the next June. This was, of course, very embarrassing. They were com-

pelled to procure board wherever they could, for the
time being, and get along without their Winter clothing as best they could. As for any reliable, regular
provision for the families of preachers by the circuits
of that day, and especially in that region, it was not
attempted; if, indeed, it was considered by the stewards any part of their business. At the first quarterly-meeting, the presiding elder, Rev. Charles Holliday, called attention to the rule requiring a committee
to estimate the amount necessary for house-rent,
fuel, and provisions for their preacher; and such a
committee was appointed, consisting of three of the
principal men of the circuit. But there the matter
ended; the committee never reported—probably never
met together on the business for which they were
appointed. And even if they had reported an estimate, it is extremely doubtful whether any attention
would have been paid to it. One brother on that
circuit, living at his ease on an excellent farm, being
called on by a steward for his quarterly contribution,
said: "Morris rides a larger horse and wears a finer
coat than I do. There would be more propriety in
his helping me, and I shall not give a cent."

Subsequently, wishing to lay in his supply of pork
for the year, Mr. Morris called on this same brother,
who was his near neighbor, to make the needful purchase. On being told that the price of pork was
$4.50 per hundred, he signified his willingness to buy
it at that rate; but the brother, fearing possibly that
the sale might not be a cash transaction, said: "The
market price is $4.50, as I told you; but *you* can't
have mine under $5." It is hardly necessary to

add that the preacher looked elsewhere for his pork. Very many people in those days seemed to think that it was conferring quite a favor on the preachers to listen to their sermons, and that any further compensation would be superfluous. But fortunately for the cause of religion, they were not all of that way of thinking ; otherwise none but wealthy ministers could have given their whole time and strength to the work of rescuing blood-bought souls from ignorance, sin, and ruin. As it was, some of them, with limited resources, were enabled to hold out, enduring many privations, and putting their trust in Him who said, " Lo, I am with you."

While a want of adequate support was common to the whole body of the Methodist ministry in that day, so that in this respect the experience of Mr. Morris was not at all peculiar, there was one difficulty under which he labored not so common among his brethren. Many of the people, it would seem, estimated a preacher's capability of usefulness among them by his lung-power—the strength of his voice— a rule which, if not universal, was far too general among all classes of hearers, the educated and the illiterate ; and, as Mr. Morris's lungs were at best comparatively weak, and now especially so in consequence of a diseased liver, his prospects for reaching a high standard of excellence in the pulpit were not the most flattering. However, he was encouraged by the declaration of the Bible, " Not by might, nor by power, but by my Spirit, saith the Lord of hosts," and felt resolved to do his duty, and leave results to Him who only can give the increase.

Following the written plan of his circuit the first

round of appointments, he found himself, on a week-day, at Colonel Edward Taylor's, in the north-west part of Montgomery County, Tennessee. The colonel was a wealthy planter; had a classical education; was a well-read man, and a devoted Methodist; but his notions of pulpit power and ministerial usefulness were those held by a majority of the people, especially in the South, at that time. Mr. Morris preached in the colonel's parlor to twenty or thirty neighbors, speaking in a moderate, conversational tone of voice. There was not an individual present the preacher had ever seen before, and fully half the congregation remained for dinner. At the table the following dialogue took place:

Colonel. Well, Brother Morris, was your preaching to-day a fair specimen of your manner?

Morris. Yes, on such occasions, to a small congregation.

Colonel. Well, such preaching may answer in Ohio, for aught I know, but it will never do any good in this country. We like to hear a man lay it on till the cries of sinners and the shouts of Christians are such that he can no longer hear his own voice, and then we are willing he should stop.

Morris. Well, Colonel Taylor, I do not know much about you here yet, and you do not know much about me; but if we all live, by the grace of God helping me, I will convince you, before all is over, that you are mistaken.

Here the conversation on that subject ended. The remarks of the colonel, however well meant, appeared to the preacher quite unseasonable; more

especially as there happened to be present at the
table a very intelligent physician from a neighboring county, who, though a courteous gentleman,
was a reputed skeptic, and Mr. Morris feared that the
table-talk would not contribute much toward the removal of his difficulties.   Yet, as the colonel was his
superior in years and culture, he endeavored to receive the rebuke in the spirit of meekness. After a
few visits there, his congregations greatly increased,
and early in the Spring of 1822 he dedicated Piney
Fork Chapel, erected by Colonel Taylor on his own
land, for the society of that neighborhood.   His text
on the occasion was, " In all places where I record
my name I will come unto thee, and I will bless
thee." (Exodus xx, 24.) As he was closing with some
practical remarks, one point was enforced earnestly ;
that is, that they should all pray in faith to the Lord
to record his name there that day by the conversion
of at least one soul. While speaking to the class
after preaching, he observed a lady present, who was
not a member, very much broken up in her feelings
and deeply penitent, whom he exhorted, and for
whom he and the class prayed until she was converted.   That lady was a near neighbor of Colonel
Taylor's, and a great favorite in his family.   The little
band who had struggled for years to keep up an organized class here were greatly encouraged by this
favorable start in the new chapel.

So far, the preaching here had all been done on
week-days, but believing now that the indications
required special and extra efforts, Mr. Morris appointed a two-days' meeting for his next round, so as

to include Saturday and Sunday. All the ministerial help he could obtain was brother John Y. Taylor, a local preacher from an adjoining neighborhood. The love-feast on Sabbath morning was a time of spiritual refreshing, and at eleven o'clock, though the day was somewhat inclement, the chapel would scarcely hold the people. According to usage on such occasions, in the country, they had two sermons in succession, and Mr. Morris preached last. Near the close of his discourse, as he made one of those eloquent and powerful appeals which move and thrill a whole congregation, there was a visible shaking among the dry bones. Penitents were invited to the altar. Quite a number responded to the call. Saving power came down, in answer to prayer, and in a few minutes five souls were born into the kingdom, and rejoiced greatly in the pardoning love of God. Among the happy converts of that day was Colonel Taylor's youngest daughter. As they passed out after the service was over, the colonel said to his son, "Well, Henry, our God is working all things about right here." Mr. Morris, overhearing this remark, said, pleasantly, "What do you think now, Colonel? Will this easy sort of preaching ever accomplish any good in Tennessee?" "Ah, I give it up!" exclaimed the colonel, warmly seizing his pastor by the hand; and no one was more urgent than Colonel Taylor to have Mr. Morris reappointed to the circuit for another year.

Christian Circuit at that time embraced all of Christian and Todd Counties, most of Muhlenberg, and parts of Butler and Logan Counties, in Kentucky; and parts of Montgomery and Stewart Counties, in

Tennessee—a territory almost large enough for a modern conference. It was a six-weeks' circuit, about three hundred miles round, with forty appointments. Certainly, the Methodist ministry was no sinecure in that day. It was considered but moderate work to preach and meet class once a day, on an average, and ride eight, ten, or fifteen miles. Preaching-places were not only far apart in general, but the way from one to another was extremely difficult, in many cases being only a dim path. Some of the Methodist preachers, in early times, carried a hatchet to mark the trees in a certain way, at each place where they had to turn off from the main track. And when they were favored with plainer roads, they were not well improved; and they had to contend constantly with mud, water, and quicksand, swamps, and pole-bridges. In the Winter season, when the weather was rough, the days short, and the roads in the worst state, it required great effort to keep up with the appointments. Sometimes twelve, fifteen, or twenty miles must be traveled to meet a morning appointment. Mr. Morris relates* that he had sometimes, when far from home, risen long before day, gone to the wood-pile covered with snow, and fished out the wood, a piece at a time, packed it on his shoulder, built a fire, and then roused the family to get him a hasty breakfast, in order that he might be off in good time.

In that day, too, preachers were expected to be punctual, and to preach, whether their hearers were many or few. During his second year on Christian Circuit, Mr. Morris rode nine miles, to a place called

---

* "Morris's Miscellany," page 248.

Dunham's School-house, where he had an engagement to preach. The school-house was among the Knobs, north-east part of Christian County, situated on the west point of a ridge, in an exposed position, being an open log building covered with clapboards. The north-west wind was piercing cold, so much. so as to prevent the people from turning out. However, four persons attended—three of them members of the society, and one a young woman, not a member of Church. These, the preacher found shivering round a small fire. Being very cold himself, he went to the woods, gathered as much dry wood as he could find, and made a large fire. The chimney was as broad as the end of the house. The preacher stood in one corner, an old brother sat in the other, and the three women in front of the fire. The hymn was sung, the prayer offered, and the sermon preached, just as if the house had been full; afterward they were examined as in class-meeting. They all wept, one shouted for joy, and the non-professor being seriously affected, a short prayer-meeting was held for her special benefit. She became from that hour an earnest seeker after salvation, and was soon converted. Mr. Morris then returned home, nine miles, without his dinner; and he tells us that, although he suffered some with cold, he did not regret going.

6

CHAPTER III.

ITINERANT LABORS—APPOINTED PRESIDING ELDER OF GREEN-
RIVER DISTRICT.

AN incident which occurred on this circuit in the
Winter of 1822–23, well illustrates the hardships through which our fathers in the ministry were
called to pass. Mr. Morris had added a new preaching-
place to his plan, near what was called the Ponny
Woods, in the southern part of Todd County. When
leaving that place the first time, before he had learned
the way across to Stemmond's School-house, he asked
for directions, and was told to pass around the farm
(on which he had just established the new appointment) to the east side, and there to take a dim track,
which he would find winding around the pond. It
happened, however, that before he reached the proper
one, another dim cart-road turned off, apparently in
the right direction, and he took that, supposing that
he was following the directions given. But it proved
to be a way leading into the pond, made for the purpose of hauling timber out of it in Summer, when the
pond was partly dry. He was mounted on a powerful horse called the "White Bear;" but, unfortunately,
his iron shoes had been on so long that they were
worn perfectly smooth. The snow lay six or eight
inches deep, the weather was unusually cold, and the

pond full of water from the heavy Fall rains. After
going some distance he came to ice in the road,
which, however, being formed on shallow water,
yielded readily to the horse's feet, and he passed
safely over it, congratulating himself that he was in
the right path, "edging the pond," as the farmer, at
whose house he had preached, directed him to do.
Soon he came to ice more difficult, tried in vain to
find some way around it, and was compelled at last
to dismount and lead "White Bear" across—a feat of
great difficulty for a smooth-shod horse ; but they
passed over safely. After firm road for a few hundred yards, he reached a point where there was
smooth, glassy ice for some thirty rods, and no possible way to avoid it. This, thought the preacher, is
"edging the pond" with a vengeance ; but beyond
this sheet of ice he observed that the ground rose
somewhat abruptly, and he concluded that, once safely
over here, his troubles would be ended for that day.
At all events, there seemed no way round the difficulty, and no time was to be lost, or he would fail to
reach his next appointment. Again he dismounted,
took the bridle-reins in his right-hand, flung his saddle-bags over his left shoulder, and started on the
perilous passage. In a very few moments the horse's
feet flew from under him, throwing him heavily upon
the ice. The noble steed struggled hard to regain his
footing ; when nearly righted, his feet repeatedly slipped,
and he got some terrible falls. At last, however, after
many unsuccessful attempts, he stood upright. Mr.
Morris fearing another accident of the same sort, and
understanding that the liability to a similar mishap

would be increased by leading the animal slowly, now pulled off his boots, and, leading the horse, ran before as fast as he could, in his stockings. They went with a rush, the preacher running and the horse skating, until they neared the shore, when the ice gave way, and let them both into the water. Fortunately it was not very deep, and they got to shore without much difficulty. But great was the surprise of Mr. Morris, on ascending the high point of ground which he had reached with so much difficulty and peril, when he discovered that for a quarter of a mile before him lay an unbroken expanse of smooth ice, and that, apparently, over very deep water! The truth then flashed upon his mind that he had, through careless directions, lost his way, and that he was entering the worst section of the " Ponny Woods." To go forward was impossible, and to retrace his steps would be at the risk of losing his valuable horse, without which he could not fill his appointments. First of all, he sat down on a fallen tree and put on dry stockings and his boots ; then, leaving " White Bear " alone, he returned on foot to the house whence he started, about two miles distant, the walk proving, in the deep snow, a very tiresome one. At the house he obtained the aid of two colored men, who went back with him, and by " roughing " the ice with an ax, got the horse safely out by the same way they went in. It was two o'clock in the afternoon when they got fairly out of the difficulty—too late, of course, to meet the appointment of that day. Next day Mr. Morris was attacked with rheumatism, from which he did not wholly recover for many weeks;

notwithstanding which, he remained on his circuit, and filled his appointments regularly, even when he required assistance to mount and dismount his horse, and was unable to stand long enough to preach.

It was during his first year on Christian Circuit that Mr. Morris, by an odd slip of memory, and the unskillfulness of his informant, preached the funeral sermon of a living man.* Funeral discourses in that country were not usually delivered on the day of interment, but often weeks or months subsequently. It was also the custom, especially of the more wealthy, to give a costly dinner to all the friends and neighbors of the bereaved family in attendance at the funeral; and some, who were not very scrupulous, had their funeral dinners on the Sabbath, so as to secure a large attendance. One of the Wednesday appoint-, ments of the circuit was at Shiloh, a country meeting-house, in Montgomery County, Tennessee. Among the members of the society there were Wesley Verhine and his mother-in-law, a pious old lady named Howell, who lived in his family. These individuals resided some twelve miles west of the place, in a neighborhood where they had neither class nor stated preaching nearer than Shiloh. One day, in the year 1822, after preaching and meeting class at Shiloh, Wesley Verhine requested Mr. Morris to preach a funeral sermon of his brother's child, in his own neighborhood, during the next round.

While Mr. Verhine and the preacher were talking over this matter and fixing a time for the service, the brethren and sisters of the Shiloh society, glad to see

* *Ladies' Repository,* 1853.

their pastor, were crowding around him with their
warm hand-shakings, and pressing invitations to dine.
He became somewhat confused by the superabundant
offers of hospitality, and from that moment the idea
of the funeral was entirely forgotten, till he had gone
round his six-weeks' circuit, returned to Shiloh,
preached and met class as usual, when Mr. Verhine
said to him, "We expect you at the funeral next
Sabbath."

"What funeral?"

"At my brother's, in our neighborhood. Brother
Gaines published that you would preach the funeral
sermon, instead of preaching at White's."

Now, the original conversation concerning the
funeral, which took place six weeks before, had passed
from the mind of Mr. Morris entirely. He therefore
hesitated a little about consenting; but knowing Mr.
Gaines to be a very prudent man, concluded that if
he had made the arrangement there must have been
sufficient reason for it, and so he agreed to go; at
the same time requesting Mr. Verhine to meet him
at White's on Sabbath morning, in order that they
might go together, the way being somewhat difficult
to find. Accordingly, at the appointed hour, on
Sabbath morning, the guide and some half-dozen
friends met the preacher at White's, and they all set
off together for the funeral. They moved along in
single-file, on horseback, by a dim path, much of
which was overhung with brushwood, and, of course,
unfavorable to the social arrangement of riding two
and two abreast. As soon, however, as an opportunity offered, Mr. Morris determined to learn some-

thing more definite respecting the case in hand, so
that he might not feel wholly unprepared for the
solemn duties of the day. He therefore rode along-
side of Mr. Verhine, and inquired:

"Was the man whose funeral sermon I am to
preach to-day, an old or a young man?"

"He is about forty-three years old."

"Had he a family?"

"He has a wife and three or four children."

"Was he a professor of religion?"

"He is not a member of any Church."

Mr. Morris observed that the replies were all
given in the present tense; but this he attributed to
the awkwardness of the speaker, not suspecting that
there could be any misunderstanding. The dialogue ended; he dropped back into the regular line
in a contemplative mood, thankful to have obtained
the material points of the whole case: The subject of
the funeral was past middle life; was the head of a
family, and not professedly pious. In view of this
information he selected a text, and shaped the outline
of a funeral discourse in his own mind, as the company rode silently toward the place. By and by they
came in view of "the house of mourning," surrounded
with numerous horses and quite a large concourse of
people for a sparsely settled country place. As there
was no church in the neighborhood, the service was
held in the house of the bereaved family. It was
tolerably large, but was very much crowded. With
some difficulty the preacher entered, and found his
way to a back window, where a chair and small table
were provided for his accommodation.

After marking the appropriate hymns and Scripture lessons, he cast his eye over the congregation, and seeing several ladies dressed in mourning, selected the one whom he supposed to be the sorrowful widow. In the first prayer some allusion was made to the lonely widow and disconsolate orphans, whose bereavement of their husband and father had occasioned the solemn meeting, etc. The text was: "But man dieth, and wasteth away; yea, man dieth and giveth up the ghost, and where is he?" (Job xiv, 10.) While enforcing the final interrogatory, "Where is he?" Mr. Morris dwelt pretty fully on the state of disembodied spirits, both righteous and unrighteous, and concluded the whole discourse in nearly the following words:

"Respecting the subject of this funeral occasion, I know but little, and therefore can say but little, as I never had the pleasure of any acquaintance with him, and, indeed, never saw him, to my knowledge. I have been informed that he lived to be a man past the middle of life, that he has left a companion and several children to mourn their sad loss, and that he was not a professor of religion. As to his moral and social habits and general character, they were, doubtless, much better known to his neighbors and friends here present than to me. It is not my prerogative or wish to pass sentence for or against any. I leave him where I leave myself and all others, in the hands of a just and merciful God. 'The Judge of all the earth will do right.'" •

While making these remarks, the preacher observed a man on his left, seated upon a chair, apparently much agitated. When the service closed, this gentleman invited Mr. Morris to remain for dinner; but he excused himself on the ground of a preengagement, and as soon as he could get out, started for the residence of Wesley Verhine, accompanied by that brother, his wife, and Mrs. Howell. By appointment previously made, he had agreed to dine with them that day. Nothing was said respecting the solemn occasion till they had proceeded some considerable distance, when the good old lady could hold in no longer. With a long-drawn sigh, she said:

"La me! brother; you made a great mistake to-day!"

"That is possible," said Mr. Morris, "I am liable to mistakes; but I did not observe it to-day. What was it, Sister Howell?"

"Why, you kept talking about the man whose funeral you were preaching, and the subject of the funeral was a little bit of a *baby* that got burned to death!"

"Baby! I preached the funeral sermon of the man of the house."

"Well, I thought so; but it was a mistake. The one that died was his child; and the man whose funeral sermon you preached is alive and well. He sat within six feet of you to-day, and heard all you said about him. It was he who invited you to stay for dinner."

The amazement and mortification of the preacher at this unexpected turn of affairs may be more easily imagined than described.

On this large circuit, Mr. Morris labored for some months, the first year, without a colleague; Rev.

Philip Kennerly, who had been appointed junior preacher, having died soon after Conference. Rev. Richard Gaines, brother-in-law of Dr. Cartwright, was employed finally as assistant preacher, and did good service. Rev. Major Stanfield was helper on the circuit the second year. During these two years Mr. Morris traveled about five thousand miles, and preached not less than five hundred times, besides performing all the other duties of preacher in charge.

The Conference in 1823 met at Maysville, Kentucky, more than two hundred and fifty miles from Christian Circuit. Mr. Morris's horse not being then in a condition to make so long and difficult a journey, it was reluctantly given up. Peter Cartwright called on his way home from Maysville, and informed Mr. Morris that he was stationed at Hopkinsville; and, also, that he was elected a delegate to the General Conference of 1824, to be held in Baltimore. For some months Mr. Morris had been residing at Elkton, county-seat of Todd County, and as there was no provision made for his family in Hopkinsville Station, it was thought best for them to remain at Elkton, for the time being, especially as they were living in their own property. Soon after the Maysville Conference, Bishop M'Kendree was a guest at their house. In the course of conversation, one day, the bishop said, "Have you bought this house, brother?" "Yes, sir." "Is it paid for?" "Yes, sir." "Then enjoy it while you can; but be ready to leave it at a moment's warning."

The last week of March, 1824, he set off on his journey to Baltimore, passing through Lexington; thence on

to Western Virginia; thence up the Kanawha Valley,
and on through Lewisburg, Harrisburg, Alexandria,
and Washington City.   This journey of eight hundred
miles was made on horseback, and that, too, when the
roads were in the worst condition.   At Lewisburg,
Virginia, he fell in company with Rev. Jesse Walker.
a delegate from Missouri, and a noted pioneer of
Methodism in what was then known as the Far West.

From an interesting biographical sketch of this
hardy backwoods preacher,* we learn that he was
about five feet six inches in height, of slender form,
sallow complexion, light hair, small blue eyes, and
pleasant countenance.   His dress was uniformly the
plain, drab-colored cloth in vogue among the Quakers,
white neck-cloth, and light-colored beaver hat, with a
very broad brim.

As to his mental furniture, he was without education, except the elementary branches of English,
imperfectly acquired.   He had, however, a good share
of common sense ; had read a good deal, and had
seen much of the world with keen, observant eyes.
His memory was stored with a vast fund of incidents
peculiar to a frontier life, which he communicated
with much ease and force, rendering him very
attractive in the social circle.   He was admitted as a
traveling preacher in the Western Conference in
1802, and appointed to Red-river Circuit, in Tennessee.   In 1806 he was appointed to Illinois.   The
work had no designation on the Minutes but Illinois.
Of course it was a mission, embracing the entire
population of that Territory, and it was under the

* " Morris's Miscellany," page 179.

superintendence of Rev. William M'Kendree, afterward bishop, but then presiding elder of Cumberland District. Between Kentucky and the interior of Illinois was then a wilderness, and to reach the mission was difficult. The enterprising M'Kendree determined to accompany the missionary through the wilderness, and aid him in forming his plan and commencing the work. They put off together on horseback, camped in the wild woods every night, roasted their own meat, and slept on their saddle-blankets under the blue canopy of heaven. No less than seven times they were compelled to swim swollen streams, which was often as perilous as disagreeable ; but in due time, by the blessing of God, they reached their destination safely.

Mr. M'Kendree remained a few weeks, visited the principal neighborhoods, aided in forming a plan of appointments for the mission, and then departed for Missouri, to visit a mission there. Jesse Walker, though left alone in his new field of labor, was not discouraged. After pursuing the regular plan of appointments until obliged, by the severity of the Winter, to suspend that mode of operating, he began to preach from house to house, or, rather, from cabin to cabin, continuing this method until the Winter broke. Shortly after this, a young preacher was sent to his relief. Being thus re-enforced, Jesse determined to include a camp-meeting in the plan of the Summer's campaign. Arrangements were accordingly made, and the meeting took place. It was a time of great religious interest ; and the open-air services were continued till, as Jesse Walker expressed it, " the last stick of timber was used up;" that is, till the last sinner left on the ground was converted.

Jesse Walker's next field of labor was Missouri, which, as may be supposed, was similar to that of Illinois. From that time he operated in the two Territories, till, in 1812, he was appointed presiding elder of Illinois District, which included all the ground then occupied in Illinois and Missouri.

In 1820, Mr. Walker formed the purpose of planting the standard of Methodism in St. Louis, where, up to that time, Methodist preachers had found no rest for the soles of their feet. He engaged two young preachers, of undoubted zeal and courage, to aid him in the difficult work. When they reached St. Louis, the Territorial Legislature was there in session, and every public place appeared to be full. The missionaries tried in vain to obtain private lodgings. When they announced the object of their visit, some would laugh, and others curse them to their faces. Thus repulsed and embarrassed, they rode into the Public Square, and held a council on their horses. The young preachers expressed strong doubts as to their being in the order of Providence. Their leader tried to rally and encourage them, but in vain; they took leave of Mr. Walker, and rode out of the city. It was an hour, no doubt, of sore disappointment, and perhaps despondency, to the pioneer. After sitting for some time alone, pondering the situation, he said to himself, " I will go to the State of Mississippi, and hunt up the lost sheep of the house of Israel." Suiting the action to the word, he turned his horse in that direction, and rode off alone.

Having proceeded about eighteen miles, constantly ruminating with anguish of spirit upon his failure in St. Louis, praying without ceasing for help and guidance, he came to a halt, and for a moment thus soliloquized : " Was I ever defeated before in this blessed work ? Never. Did any one ever trust in the Lord Jesus Christ, and get confounded? No : and, by the grace of God, I will go back and take St. Louis." Turning about, without seeking either rest or refreshment for man or beast, he retraced his steps to the city ; and, with some difficulty, procured lodging in an indifferent tavern, where the charges alone were first-class. Next morning he commenced a survey of the ground ; sought carefully for some suitable place in which to hold worship, and at length succeeded in obtaining the use of a temporary place of worship occupied by a few Baptists. But few attended his first service, and nothing special occurred. During the second effort, however, there were indications of deep religious feeling, and the Baptists closed their doors against him. He then found a large but unfinished dwelling-house, which he rented for ten dollars a month. Here he commenced preaching regularly, twice on the Sabbath, and occasionally on other evenings of the week. At the same time he gave notice that, if there were any poor parents who wished their children taught to spell and read, he would teach them five days in the week without charge ; and if there were any who wished their servants to learn, he would teach them of evenings on the same terms.

Being obliged to vacate his temporary chapel ere-

long, he resolved to build a church. A citizen gave
the necessary lumber, and very soon an unpretending
chapel was erected. From various unexpected sources
came donations of seats, pulpit, Bible, etc.; and, as
a result of Jesse Walker's first year in St. Louis,
he reported to Conference a snug little chapel erected
and paid for, a flourishing school, and seventy members. He was continued in charge of the mission
for another year, and enjoyed a good degree of prosperity. He afterward labored with great zeal and
success among the Indian tribes up the Mississippi.
His ashes now quietly sleep in Illinois, the scene of
his earliest missionary labors.

The General Conference of 1824 commenced its
session in the city of Baltimore, on the first day of
May. One hundred and thirty-three delegates, representing twelve conferences, were present. Bishops
M'Kendree, George, and Roberts alternately presided.
The first day of the session was taken up almost
wholly with the organization of the Conference, appointment of committees, etc. On the second day,
two delegates from the Wesleyan Conference, in
England, were introduced by Bishop M'Kendree.
These brethren—Rev. Richard Reece and Rev. John
Hannah—had been sent over with the fraternal greetings of their Conference, and were the bearers of an
address to that effect, which evinced the kindest sympathy with the Church in this country, and a strong
desire to cultivate more intimate friendly relations
with it.

The bishops presented their Quadrennial Address,
in which they referred to the general state of the

work, recommended an increase of the number of bishops, advised sundry changes in the boundary-lines of
several annual conferences, called attention to the
financial system of the Church, the necessity of providing the means of education for the children of the
Church, etc.

The subject of education seems to have claimed a
large share of the attention of this Conference, and no
wonder ; a great multitude of young people had been
gathered into the Church, and the duty of providing for
these the means of mental and moral culture could not
be ignored. The recommendation of the General Conference of 1820 was renewed, that each annual conference make an earnest effort to establish and maintain a seminary of learning within its bounds. It
was also recommended that each preacher should
obtain the names of the children connected with his
charge, and organize them into classes for religious
instruction. It is much to be regretted that this wise
provision for the moral training of the children has
not been more fully carried out.

The Missionary Society, now the glory of the
Church, was then in its infancy ; but it received its
due share of attention. Preliminary steps were taken
to establish a mission in Liberia.

Nathan Bangs and John Emory were elected
Agents of the Book Concern, and authorized to commence the publication of a weekly paper. The
Christian Advocate and Journal was accordingly
started, in 1826.

The most exciting discussion of the session was
on the subject of " Lay Delegation." Numerously

signed petitions, from various parts of the work, asked that the laity might be admitted to the legislative department of the Church. The Conference, however, after a full hearing and discussion of the question, declined to accede to the prayer of the memorialists.

The question of slavery also found its way into this Conference; and, after a somewhat protracted and heated debate, the "TENTH SECTION" was adopted, and incorporated into the Discipline.

Another very exciting discussion took place at this session on "the presiding-elder question." As early as 1808, the question of making this office elective was brought before the General Conference, thoroughly and ably discussed, and decided in the negative, by a vote of fifty-two in favor, to seventy-three against it. In 1812, the subject was again introduced, and the proposed change again defeated—forty-two voting for, and forty-five against it. In 1816, the question came up again. Speeches remarkable for ability were made on both sides of the question; but the proposed change was again lost— the majority against it being twenty-five. At the General Conference of 1820, the measure was again proposed, and again defeated; but such was the excitement occasioned by its defeat at that session, that a Committee of Six—three in favor and three against it—was appointed to confer with the bishops, and to report " whether any, and, if any, what alterations might be made to conciliate the wishes of the brethren upon the subject." This Committee, after consultation with the bishops, unanimously recom-

mended the adoption of the following provisions,
to be inserted in their proper place in the Discipline :

1. " That whenever, in any annual conference,
there shall be a vacancy or vacancies in the office of
presiding elder, in consequence of his period of four
years having expired, or the bishop wishing to remove
any presiding elder, or by death, resignation or otherwise, the bishop or president of the conference,
having ascertained the number wanted from any of
these causes, shall nominate three times the number,
out of which the conference shall elect, by ballot,
without debate, the number wanted ; provided, when
there is more than one wanted, not more than three
at a time shall be nominated, nor more than one at a
time elected. Provided, also, that in case of any
vacancy or vacancies in the office of presiding elder,
in the interval of any annual conference, the bishop
shall have authority to fill the said vacancy or vacancies until the ensuing annual conference. 2. That
the presiding elders be, and are hereby, made the
Advisory Council of the bishop or president of the
conference in stationing the preachers."

This report was adopted on the 20th of May,
receiving the decisive vote of sixty-one to twenty-five.

In the mean time, while both the advocates and
opponents of the measure were congratulating themselves that a vexed question was settled amicably, a
new and unexpected difficulty arose. The Rev.
Joshua Soule, who had been elected to the episcopal
office on the 13th, declined consecration in consequence of the adoption of this paper. He stated to

the Conference that, in his judgment, it was unconstitutional, and that he could not, consistently with his views, be bound by it. To add to the embarrassment of the Conference, Bishop M'Kendree, who had been too ill to participate in the deliberations of the Committee of six with his colleagues, three days after the passage of the resolutions came to the Conference room, and entered his objections against them as "unconstitutional, and, as he apprehended, subversive of the grand system of an efficient general superintendency and itinerancy."

It was finally proposed to suspend the operation of these new rules for four years, and that in the mean time the government of the Church should be administered as formerly. This compromise was adopted, and so the matter rested until 1824. The opponents of an elective presiding-eldership were not sufficiently confident of their strength at this Conference to attempt the repeal of the measures adopted four years previously, and they accordingly moved a continuance of the suspension for four years longer. After a protracted and earnest discussion, this motion prevailed. At this session Rev. Joshua Soule, who had declined the office in 1820 on the grounds already stated, was again elected bishop. Rev. Elijah Hedding was also elected bishop at this session.

At the close of the General Conference, Mr. Morris returned home, leaving Baltimore about the 1st of June, and making the trip in twenty traveling days, averaging forty miles a day. Soon after reaching home he had an attack of flux, which confined him to his bed for three weeks. So violent was the attack that his recovery was at one time considered highly improbable; but, by the blessing of God, he slowly recovered, after much and severe suffering.

His station that year proved to be rather a barren field to cultivate. He labored hard, but saw little fruit. The membership of the station were, many of them, very excellent people; but they were mostly poor, and however willing they might have been, were unable to support a pastor. Mr. Morris's salary on Hopkinsville Station was sixty-five dollars, on which he was expected to support himself, a wife, and two children. During the year he made about forty trips to and from the station, which was twenty miles from his home—making his traveling for the year, including the journey to Baltimore and return, about three thousand two hundred miles.

In 1824, the Kentucky Conference met at Shelbyville. Mr. Morris, with Thompson Holliman as his colleague, was appointed to Red-river Circuit, in Middle Tennessee. The circuit began at Clarksville, the junction of Red and Cumberland Rivers, extended to Neely's Bend, ten miles above Nashville, on the north side of the Cumberland, and curved round through Robinson County. The number of regular appointments was twenty-one, and the nearest one to his place of residence was twenty miles distant. These appointments must all be filled every four weeks, leaving four days each month to be spent at home. He found the people on the circuit kind and pleasant, and enjoyed with them some blessed seasons of revival. The total receipts for support that year, in money and clothing, footed up one hundred and eighty dollars. We shall not wonder to know that he was now sorely tempted to leave the work, and seek some employment by which to support his family. To be obliged every year to draw on his own slender resources to eke out a bare support, with no prospect of being able to provide against the wants of old age, must have been exceedingly depressing. After a long and severe mental conflict, the cloud was dispelled from his mind, light broke in upon his soul, joy returned, and he had, during the closing months of the year, unusual liberty and power in preaching.

In 1825, the Conference met at Russellville, fifteen miles from his place of residence ; but, though present at the seat of Conference, he was too sick most of the time to be in attendance upon the daily sessions. One day, while passing out of the Conference-room, his presiding elder, Rev. C. Holliday, whose term of four years had expired, whispered to him, " Arise, go down to Nineveh and preach ;" but he did not say where Nineveh was. This information, however, was imparted by Bishop Roberts at the close of the Conference, in reading the appointments, which embraced the following : GREEN-RIVER DISTRICT—Thomas A. Morris, Presiding Elder. Hartford—George M'Nelly, N. M. Talbott ; Greenville—Luke P. Allen, John Denton ; Henderson—George W. Robbins, Wm. Crane ; Livingston—George Richardson, Alex. H. Stemmons ; Christian—Wm. Peter, Benj. Ogden ; Hopkinsville—Rich'd Corwine ; Clark's River—John S. Barger, James Greenup.

This district was about one thousand miles round, including the journeys necessary to be made between quarterly-meetings in order to visit his family. His first quarterly-meeting was one hundred and twenty miles from home, though he resided within the bounds of the district. Some idea of the extent of this field of labor may be formed from the statement that one of the circuits—Clark's River—embraced that part of Kentucky west of the Tennessee River. The reader will gain the most vivid impression of the toils and heroic sacrifices of the early Methodist preachers in this wild region from Mr. Morris's own account of some incidents connected with his first district. We quote from his "Miscellany," page 241 :

"We were not the first on that ground after the Indians left. Brothers Crouch and Parker had been there forming a circuit the year previous ; and if they would speak out, they could relate scenes of suffering sufficient to cause the ears of the reader to tingle. Still, when we went, the settlements were 'few and far between,' and frequently without any road, or even path, from one to another. When we wished to visit a neighborhood fifteen or twenty miles distant, we ascertained, as near as we could, the general course, and struck off through the woods, without road or guide. If the sun was visible we steered by him, and if not, by a pocket compass. If a creek too deep to ford obstructed our course, we had our choice to swim or stay on our own side, having neither boat, bridge, nor canoe. Of the manner of overcoming these obstructions I will here furnish an example or two.

"At the close of a camp quarterly-meeting in Clark's-river Circuit, July, 1826, the small streams were much swollen, by reason of heavy rains. Soon after leaving the camp, we had to encounter a small stream, which was usually some three rods wide, but at that time spread over the banks and much of the adjoining low ground. However, we were told that by going to the Shallow Ford, above the forks, we could probably ride across without losing bottom; but where we expected a shallow ford we found a sheet of water about a hundred yards wide, it having overflowed its banks, with a rapid current in the middle.

"Our company consisted of George Richardson, John S. Barger, A. H. Stemmons, another young preacher whose name I have forgotten, and the writer. We were all sound except myself. I was sick—had been so for five or six days; and was much more fit to be in bed than on horseback. In consequence of this circumstance, the company objected to my swimming, lest the wetting, after taking medicine, might prove injurious. But by riding in midsides to the horse, I gained the large end of a great tree which had been cut down so as to fall across the main channel, just above the ford, for a temporary foot-bridge. Here they deposited me and the baggage till they should swim the horses over. In the mean time others came up from the meeting, forming a company of some fifteen in all. The coming-out place lay rather up-stream from us; and just below it, we were told, the bank, then under water, was too steep for the horses to rise when they should strike bottom.

To avoid this, and procure a sloping bank to rise on, they selected a place below, where the bluff changed sides. So that, after riding in till the horse was nearly covered, and arriving at the main channel, he suddenly and unexpectedly to himself, though not to his rider, stepped over a precipice, perhaps ten feet high, into a sweeping current, where horse and rider were violently immersed, but soon emerged some distance from where they first disappeared, and presently made safe landing. In this way the young brethren conveyed their own horses over ; after which, Richardson and Stemmons rode for the whole company, securing one horse and swimming back for another, making several trips each. This done, Richardson led me over the channel on the log, and, leaving still between us and the dry ground a sheet of water some thirty yards wide and three feet deep, he deliberately stepped in, took me upon his shoulder, and, notwithstanding much brush and driftwood were on the way, placed me safely on solid ground. The whole was accomplished in a few minutes. Here we parted with all but our own company with whom we first started from camp; and leaving the *Shallow Ford*, our way was clear before us to the next branch of the same stream, only a few miles distant.

"Our second crossing was like to prove more difficult than the first, having an equally rapid stream without the advantage of any log. Having appointments ahead, it was important to get on somehow or other ; and, after a short consultation, it was thought best, on account of my condition, to head the stream, or at least go far enough up to ford.

This being agreed on, we made the attempt, but were so much embarrassed by quicksand, especially where the ground had been overflowed, that we soon became weary of it, and determined to cross, if possible. Finding a place where the banks were dry on both sides, the water there being confined within its usual channel, we dismounted, and were consulting about the mode of crossing, when Stemmons concluded it was time to execute as well as plan. Fixing his large, laughing, blue eyes, on a tall, slim hickory, growing on our side of the creek, he deliberately began to ascend, which he did almost as easily and rapidly as a wild bear would climb a chestnut-tree in search of nuts. When he had left the ground about forty feet below him, and arrived where the sapling had scarce strength to support him, he turned on the side next to the stream, held on with his hands, letting his feet swing clear, and his weight brought the top down on the other side, and, with the assistance of another, who swam over to his relief, tied the limbs fast to the root of a tree. This bent sapling formed an arched bridge about forty feet long, six inches wide, and elevated in the center about twelve or fifteen feet, over the deepest of the turbid stream, on which we crossed—*astride*—safely, pushing our baggage before us ; and then we resumed our journey, leaving the hickory bridge for the accommodation of the public."

His first quarterly-meeting on the district was held in a log-cabin on Bayou Desha, a creek of the Mississippi. Here the Church was favored with a glorious work of grace. On Sabbath evening, particularly, the Word was quick and powerful, sinners were awakened, and the people of God rejoiced over returning prodigals. When the congregation was finally dismissed, many lingered, unwilling to leave the hallowed spot where they had found the pearl of great price. Among others were four young ladies, who had that evening been converted. They were neighbors' children and associates; three of them were grown, the other being about thirteen years of age. When about to separate for the night and return home, they flew into each others' arms, weeping and rejoicing. " I will praise the Lord while I live," said one. " I will praise him when I die," responded the second. " And I will praise him after death in glory!" exclaimed the third. " My soul is full of love," added the youngest. And with similar expressions of child-like faith and glowing zeal, did many others that night testify that Christ Jesus had power on earth to save.

In July, 1826, an important change occurred in Mr. Morris's health. On his way to the camp-meeting already referred to, in Clark's-river Circuit, he had turned aside a little from his own district to fill an extra appointment at Dover, Tennessee, on the west side of the Cumberland River. For some days there had appeared an eruption on his skin, in the form of watery pimples, to which he had paid little attention, not apprehending any serious result from so slight a cause. The meeting at Dover was held in the court-house. It was on Thursday, and but few attended. The first hymn and prayer were ended, and the congregation were singing the second hymn, when his left-hand began to shake, and he took the hymn-book in the other. Soon every thing about him became dark, and supernatural in appearance, and he felt like falling over, while his left hand sank down on the railing. When the hymn was ended, the shock was passing away, so that both vision and consciousness returned ; but a question now arose in his mind whether he should tell the strange congregation his condition, and ask to be excused, or try to proceed, saying nothing about it. After a short, and perhaps to them mysterious, pause, he determined to preach, and did so, as may be supposed, in a very solemn frame of mind, not knowing that he would ever be permitted to preach again. At the close of the service he discovered that his left-hand was very cold, the left-foot scarcely less so, and his left-eye strangely affected. That afternoon, so bent was he on meeting his engagements, he set off, alone and on horseback, to travel a distance of eighteen miles, over an entirely new route to him, and one very difficult to find. But, as he wrote in his little pocket-diary, he felt that he was on the Lord's business, and that he was in the Lord's hands, and would be as safe in the wilderness as at home.

As the day wore away, a fever came on ; so that he could scarcely remain in the saddle. At a late hour in the evening he reached a humble cabin, seven miles west of the Tennessee River, occupied by a widow lady and a large family of children, where he was kindly allowed to pass the night. So much exhausted had he now become, however, by the long ride in a July sun, and in a very feeble bodily condition,

that he could scarcely dismount and get into the cabin.
Next morning the good woman of the house sent
three miles for a schoolmaster to come and bleed
him. The amateur phlebotomist relieved his veins of
a quart of something resembling tar more than
healthy blood. That day he rode twenty-five miles,
reached the camp-ground at two o'clock, and preached
at three. He also preached on Saturday, Sunday,
and Monday, although hardly strong enough to walk
unaided. His Monday morning service was particularly exhausting, as he had agreed, some weeks previous, to preach at that hour on the subject of
Baptism, with special reference to the mode. His
sermon on that subject occupied an hour and a half
in its delivery, and was long remembered in that region as a powerful and convincing argument. But on
Monday evening, after this unusual and perhaps imprudent exertion, he suffered a second shock of paralysis, very similar to the first. It was fully a week
from the time of the first attack before any physician
could be seen or medical advice obtained. A man
of less courage and zeal would now have desisted
from active service long enough to repair the shat-
tered physical system ; but Mr. Morris pushed on,
holding his quarterly-meetings regularly, and dis-
charging all the duties of his office. For six weeks
he was not able to hold the bridle with his left hand.

While in this enfeebled bodily condition, he was
preaching to an immense congregation, at a camp-
meeting held on Henderson Circuit, some time in
August. Suddenly he became blind and deaf, and
all mental action seemed, for the moment suspended.

After a short pause he recovered, and finished his sermon. He felt that day that he was probably preaching his last sermon; that his body would be carried out lifeless, and his soul ascend from that pulpit to paradise. But God had other purposes concerning his servant, and more work for him to do. As soon as the sermon closed, he took to bed, and was confined to it for three days, when, by the blessing of God, he was permitted to resume his labors. Within three years of the first attack of paralysis, he had, as he estimated, not less than two hundred; but they gradually became lighter and lighter, after the first few weeks, until they subsided wholly. His memory was seriously impaired for a time, but recovered with improved general health. One of the most serious embarrassments resulting from this affliction was the interruption of his studies. He had been engaged for a considerable time in the study of the Greek language, in which he was making satisfactory progress; but now his physician positively interdicted all study beyond reasonable preparation for preaching.

CHAPTER IV.

STATIONED AT LOUISVILLE—GENERAL CONFERENCE OF
1828—RETURN TO OHIO—CINCINNATI METH-
ODISM—CHOLERA.

TOWARD the close of the second year on the district, Mr. Morris's family suffered much from sickness. His wife and daughter, especially, had a protracted and severe attack of fever. No help could be hired in the neighborhood to take care of them or superintend the affairs of the household. Mr. Morris sought diligently for a week, far and near, but beyond the volunteer aid of a neighbor, occasionally, could obtain no assistance whatever. His brother Edmund, who had preceded him there, and his brother Levi, who had removed to the same neighborhood subsequently, had both moved to Louisiana and left him among strangers. Besides all these things, which seemed to be against him, the property he owned when he entered the traveling connection, together with that which he had afterward received from his father's estate, had, during his six-years' campaign in Kentucky, been nearly all spent, necessarily, for the support of his family.

Under these circumstances, he came to the conclusion that it was his duty to seek a change of work, or rather a field of labor in which a reasonable support for his family could be obtained. The decision to leave Kentucky was not reached without a severe mental struggle. "Mount Olivet"—the name he had given to his cottage near Elkton—was now endeared to all the family, having been for six years a pleasant home. They had formed strong attachments to the open-handed and warm-hearted people of Kentucky generally, and especially regretted to leave their many kind and pleasant neighbors. When they first settled at Elkton, Methodism had no hold there—neither class, preaching, nor house of worship. Mr. Morris opened his own house for preaching, and soon a small class was formed; then a chapel was erected, toward which he contributed one hundred dollars, when his entire salary hardly equaled that amount. He had seen a good society grow up rapidly, and many of these were his own children in the Gospel, whom he loved with no ordinary affection.

Still, after prayerful deliberation, he felt satisfied that duty required him to make the contemplated change; and accordingly he disposed of his personal effects, except movable articles, and also sold the little farm he owned in the neighborhood; paid off all his debts; rented "Mount Olivet," and set off with his wife and children for Conference, which was held that year at Versailles. Expecting to be transferred to Ohio, his heavy boxes had been marked for shipment down the Cumberland and up the Ohio River. He and his wife and daughter rode in a light, covered Dearborn wagon, very comfortably; while his son, a lad ten years old, was mounted on a very small, gentle pony.

Mr. Morris had now been in the ministry twelve

years, including the one in which he was employed
by the presiding elder. During that time he had
traveled over thirty-three thousand miles, averaging two thousand seven hundred and fifty miles a year ;
and not one mile of it on railroad, steamer, or stage-
coach, and very little of it on wheels of any sort.
He had preached more than three thousand times—
about two hundred and fifty sermons annually—besides delivering numerous occasional addresses. His
aggregate salary for that period of twelve years,
including marriage-fees and private donations, was
about two thousand dollars, or one hundred and sixty-
six dollars per annum ! No marvel that his private
resources were nearly exhausted, and that the prospect ahead, with a sickly family and his own health
precarious, appeared somewhat discouraging.

During the two years of his presiding-eldership
in Kentucky, he had broken down two horses, traveled eight thousand miles, preached about five
hundred times, and received in all, for his services,
less than the cost of the two horses. When Mr.
Morris started to the Conference at Versailles, he
fully expected, as we have already stated, to be transferred to the Ohio Conference that Fall. He had received a cordial invitation from leading brethren of
Ohio to return to that State, and had sent a written
application to the bishop for a transfer. He was
surprised, however, on meeting Bishops Roberts and
Soule to learn from them that his letter, directed to
the seat of the Ohio Conference, had miscarried, and
that consequently no place had been left open for
him in the Ohio Conference. They assured him, at

the same time, that while it was impossible to make the desired change that year, it could easily be arranged a year later, and that, in the mean time, he would be obliged to receive another appointment in Kentucky.

This was a great disappointment. "Mount Olivet" was disposed of, his goods were *en route* for Ohio, and all his plans had been arranged in view of a removal to that State. Time proved, however, that a good providence was ordering all for the best; and he never regretted the unexpected change in his plans, after the first disappointment was over. That year he was again elected a delegate to the General Conference, although his brethren knew of his intention to leave them as soon as an opportunity offered. His appointment was this year Louisville, the leading charge in the Conference; a station, then, of two hundred and twenty white, and one hundred and seventy colored members, with two separate chapels. His reception by the brethren of this city was so cordial that he soon felt at home among them, and entered upon his work with zeal, preaching and visiting from house to house. He made out an alphabetical list of the names, street, and number, of all the members of the station, and visited every family once a quarter. As a result of faithful labors in the pulpit and among the people, the Church prospered; about seventy were added to the membership of the white congregation, which showed a net increase of fifty that year, after deducting deaths, removals, etc. The colored congregation also prospered. It was found neccessary to enforce discipline among this portion of his charge more rigidly than had been the practice of his predecessor; but, although a large number was excluded, others were gathered in, more than enough to make up the loss.

While stationed in Louisville, Mr. Morris had an engagement to attend a quarterly-meeting at Frankfort, distant some fifty miles. He set off one day, early in the Spring, to meet this appointment. It had been an open, rainy Winter; the mud was deep, and traveling on horseback very tedious. On his way up, having been kindly entertained by a family named Williams, at a place called Middletown, he accepted from them an invitation to leave a night appointment to preach there on his return trip, the next week. In due time, he called at the residence of his hospitable friends in Middletown, on his way home, and learned that the meeting was appointed to be held at "the old Faro-bank room," the usual place for preaching—there being no chapel in the village.

"But," added brother Williams, "there is no certainty of its being there; for we have a very singular brother here named Wallace, who assumes to manage every thing of the sort in his own way, and that is generally a way the rest of us do not approve; and I shall not be surprised to find that he has changed the place."

After tea they walked up to the faro-bank room, and found all dark.

"Just as I expected," said Mr. Williams; "Wallace has moved the meeting; but, as there is only one street in the town, we can easily find it."

They walked on, making inquiry, and learned that

the place was changed to Mr. Blackburn's school-house. This school-house had been a private dwelling, and consisted of two rooms and a front porch. They found the back room full of women, the other full of men, and the porch full of boys. The position assigned to the preacher was the door of the partition between the two rooms, where he could alternately see both sections of his strange audience, though the few tallow candles burned but dimly. Just by the door where he stood was the teacher's big chair; if placed in the door, it would have filled it, so that none could pass or repass. But as that was the only vacant spot, and Mr. Morris wished to occupy it himself, he pushed the chair to one side in the back room out of his way. The service commenced. The preacher was fairly launching out into his subject, when a man—afterward ascertained to be the officious Mr. Wallace—pressed through the crowd and through the door, pushing the preacher aside, and, laying hold of the big chair, made an attempt to force it through the crowd to its original place.

"What are you doing, my friend?" inquired Mr. Morris.

"I am getting this chair round to place before you for a pulpit."

"Please to desist; I do not need it, and can do better without than with it."

After waiting until the brother got out of the way, the minister proceeded; but he had hardly got fairly started again, when his attention was attracted to two men seated near him, engaged in conversation about their private affairs, in tones loud

enough to be heard through the house. Again he
desisted from preaching, and looked steadily at the
offenders, till all eyes were turned toward them, and
they at length became conscious that they were the
observed of all observers.

Perfect stillness being restored, Mr. Morris quietly
remarked, "We were only waiting for those two
gentlemen to finish their conversation, as that and
preaching at the same time did not harmonize well
together."

Again the sermon was resumed. Soon after, however, the boys on the porch commenced an entertainment of their own, of so noisy a character that the
voice within could scarcely be heard, and so another
pause was necessary. Mr. Wallace made a rush for
the porch, where he made more disturbance than the
boys had done; but at last the outbreak was quelled,
and partial quiet again secured. For the third time
the sermon was resumed. A few minutes only had
elapsed, when an infant in the back room became
restless and noisy; and though the amiable mother
resorted to all means usual in such cases to quiet the
little one, she failed, and was considerate enough to
leave for home. But, as there was no outlet from
the back room except through the door where the
preacher stood, he must needs stop the flow of his
talk again, step aside, and let her pass. When matters
again calmed down, he resumed for the fourth time,
but whether at the right or wrong place he could not
possibly determine.

Shortly after, a small boy in the back room,
who was perhaps five or six years old, produced a

ludicrous scene. He teased and worried his mother, who used her best endeavors to suppress his rising discontent, but in vain ; he whimpered on, waxing worse and worse. She finally shook him angrily, demanding, "What ails you?" when, in fretful tones, distinctly heard throughout the house, he exclaimed, "Scratch my back!"

The shock was sudden, the effect irresistible ; some hung their heads, but the majority broke into a loud laugh. The mortified mother, seizing the urchin, began to drag him toward the door, the preacher making way for her to pass. The enraged child had no notion, however, of leaving on compulsion, and he pulled back with all the strength he had ; but his efforts were overcome, and he was dragged through both rooms and across the porch to the street. After order was again restored, Mr. Morris attempted to resume for the fifth time, but could not recall the point at which he had stopped. He then aimed to reach the point by rapidly reviewing the general drift of the subject, but could not strike the trail. Finally, in despair he concluded to go back to the text, but could not even recall that ! He could remember neither text nor subject.

After a long pause, he remarked : "My strange friends, I make no great pretensions as a preacher, even under the most favorable circumstances ; and under such as now surround me, it is utterly impracticable for me to preach at all. Please excuse me, and receive the benediction."

Mr. Morris's salary in Louisville was five hundred and forty-eight dollars, the best year's support he had received up to that time. A short time after his arrival in the city, he went to a forwarding house to see if any thing could be done to recover his boxes of household goods, that had been directed to Ohio. To his surprise they were all lying in the warehouse at which he called, and in good condition, having, on account of various detentions, only just reached that point. He was still more surprised to find at the same place a box of books, worth ninety-five dollars, which had been charged to his account by the Book Concern at Cincinnati, the year before, and sent to his address at Mill's Point, on the Mississippi, but which had been given up as lost.

In the Spring of 1828 he started for Pittsburg, to attend the General Conference, and was accompanied by his family, who embraced this opportunity to visit their relatives in West Virginia. It was the first time any of them had ever been on a steamboat, and they greatly enjoyed the trip, especially as the *Marion*—in which they made the journey—was nearly filled with Methodist preachers.

The General Conference of 1828 convened, as usual, on the 1st of May. Bishops M'Kendree, George, Roberts, Soule, and Hedding were present. There were one hundred and seventy delegates, representing seventeen annual conferences. So great was the ratio of representation that Kentucky had eleven delegates, to-wit: Richard Tydings, Thomas A. Morris, Peter Akers, Benjamin T. Crouch, George C. Light, Marcus Lindsey, William Adams, Henry M'Daniel, Jonathan Stamper, George W. M'Nelly, and John Tevis.

The most exciting question before this General Conference grew out of what was called, in that day, the "radical controversy." A considerable party had been organized in the Church with a view to secure lay representation, and also to modify, in some way, the functions of the Episcopacy. These so-called reformers had two organs, the *Wesleyan Repository* and the *Mutual Rights;* in the latter of which appeared, some time in 1826, what purported to be a report of an address made by Bishop Hedding before the Pittsburg Annual Conference, on the duty of its members in reference to the discussion of Church reforms. In this report, sentiments were attributed to Bishop Hedding which he disavowed, as injurious to his character. Not being successful in his endeavor to obtain redress at the hands of the publishers of *Mutual Rights*, he brought the matter before the General Conference, and requested a full investigation. The result of the investigation was a complete vindication of Bishop Hedding.

At this General Conference a memorial was presented, from the Canada Conference, on the subject of establishing an independent Church in Upper Canada, asking that measures be taken with a view to such an organization. The matter was referred to a committee, and in due time a report was submitted and adopted, "dissolving, by mutual consent, the compact existing between the Canada annual conferences and the Methodist Episcopal Church." The desire for such separation, on the part of the brethren in Canada, did not grow out of any dissatisfaction with the conduct of their brethren in the United

States toward them, but chiefly from the opposition evinced by statesmen in Upper Canada to their being subject to the control of a foreign ecclesiastical head.*

In the Fall of 1828, Mr. Morris received official notice that he was transferred to the Ohio Conference, and appointed to Lebanon Circuit. He deemed it proper, however, before leaving for his new field of labor, to attend the session of the Kentucky Conference at Shelbyville, both to make his final report, and to visit his daughter, who was a student in Science Hill Academy, at that place. In severing his official connection with the brethren of the Kentucky Conference, with whom he had labored seven years in harmony, he now felt sincere regret. He said, on leaving them, that he did not know a body of purer men, of more faithful Methodist preachers, or more magnanimous spirits, than they were; that, so far as the ties of brotherhood and the pleasures of social intercourse were concerned, it was in his heart to live and die with them; but that considerations of private and family interest, or, in other words, duty to his family, indicated that the time for him to return to Ohio had fully come. And so, a day or two before the final adjournment of the Kentucky Conference, he took his departure for Lebanon, Ohio, by the same conveyance that took him and his family to Louisville the year before—a Dearborn wagon, his horse Samson, and the pony.

As Lebanon had just been cut off from Union Circuit, his first work was organization—no slight

* Bangs's "History of the Methodist Episcopal Church," Vol. III, page 388.

work either, on a field of such extent. At the end of his first year, in which he had no colleague, he reported five hundred and fifteen members. The stewards provided a small house for his occupancy, and collected about three-fourths of his quarterage claim, each of the two years he labored on the circuit; but provisions were plenty and cheap, and he lived through the term without any very serious financial embarrassment. Lebanon is situated in a remarkably fertile and beautiful section of Ohio, between the Little and Great Miami Rivers; and the circuit was, in many respects, a very pleasant field of labor. Still, that lovely region now conveys very little idea of what it was in its comparatively undeveloped state then. For a large part of the year the roads were very bad, and the congregations, except on Sabbath, very small. During his second year on this circuit, Rev. Joseph J. Hill was his helper, and a very useful, efficient one; they were favored with several gracious revivals, and reported an increase of fifty-one members.

While living in Lebanon, Mr. Morris was a near neighbor of Bishop Soule, who resided there for many years. Four of the bishop's children were received into the Church under the ministry of Mr. Morris and his colleague, one of whom became the wife of the latter. While here, Mr. Morris invested six hundred dollars, saved from the wreck of his Kentucky speculation, in town lots, with a small house on one of them. This property, six years later, he sold for twelve hundred dollars. This was his first successful effort at mending his broken fortunes.

At the end of two years on Lebanon Circuit, Mr. Morris was appointed to Columbus, which was that year (1830) made a station. On his arrival there to enter upon his work, the prospect seemed any thing but encouraging. The little chapel on Town Street was awkwardly constructed; the pulpit was placed between the two front doors; the house had a roof and floor, but no plastering; it had no seats, but loose, rough boards; there was the unsightly skeleton of a gallery, the naked timbers without flooring; while for a pulpit the preacher used a small, rough box, placed under the gallery at the rear end of the house, with the uncovered timbers overhead for a canopy. The house provided for the pastor and his family was a dilapidated tenement in the rear of the church, originally intended for the sexton. It was a one-story wooden building, consisting of two very small rooms, in which they lived the year out, received their company, and did their own work. As this "parsonage" was located in the vicinity of stables, on an alley, the inmates were greatly annoyed in Summer by flies. Mr. Morris, in his diary, speaks of the method he adopted to abate this nuisance:

"On the smooth surface of a broad board I poured a small stream of honey, so as to form a circle; immediately adjoining which, I formed an outer circle of gunpowder, with a connecting arm extending at right angles six inches, so as to ignite without frightening the enemy. When the whole circle of powder was covered with flies, two or three deep, with their bills in the honey, I applied a red-hot iron rod to the connecting train, blowing up hundreds at a blast. A few such operations each day left us in the quiet and peaceable possession of the field."

However unpromising the field of labor might seem, Mr. Morris felt that it was his business to make it better, by cultivating it diligently; and he went to work with a will—preaching, visiting from house to house, meeting classes, attending the Sabbath-school, instructing the teachers one evening each week, and holding prayer-meetings. It was hard toiling, and against many discouragements. As is generally the case about State capitals, there was in Columbus a great deal of fashionable vice and folly. Wine-parties, card-parties, and dancing-parties were alarmingly prevalent. Many efforts were made to draw off the young disciples from their religious course, and involve them in the guilt of these sinful amusements. In one instance, the managers of a public ball had the effrontery to send cards of invitation to some half-dozen young ladies, members of the Methodist Episcopal Church. The preacher regarded this as a deliberate insult to them, and through them to him and the entire Church. Accordingly, on the next Sabbath evening, when nearly all the offenders were supposed to be present, in a full house, he gave them such a rebuke as, in his judgment, the offense merited, and no more tickets to balls were sent to his young people that season. For a few weeks, some, affecting to take offense at his plain preaching, drew off from the congregation, and sought to take others with them, but they soon returned.

Extreme cold weather, when Winter fairly set in,

operated against them in their open chapel; but as
soon as moderate weather returned, the church was
more crowded than ever, and in the Spring they were
favored with a revival. During one week, while assisted by Rev. Joseph M. Trimble, the pastor received
over eighty persons into the Church as probationers;
but, in the very height of the religious awakening,
small-pox made its appearance in the city, causing a
great panic, and dispersing the congregations. For a
few weeks the revival influence seemed to subside;
but when the panic ceased, the people rallied again,
and the good work went on with greater power
than before. The first visitation was chiefly one of
awakening power, but the second was characterized
by converting grace. At their evening society-meetings for the benefit of penitents, it was not uncommon to have from six to eight clear cases of pardon
and adoption; and thus those who were received on
probation during the first stage of the meeting, and
many others, were soundly converted, and became
established believers and useful members of the
society. The number of members in the society
when it was organized as a station can not now be
ascertained; but at the close of that year Mr. Morris
reported three hundred and twenty, and the net increase was probably not far from one hundred.

As to the matter of salary, the stewards of the
station could only engage to pay what was then
called the "quarterage claim," amounting, in the case
of Mr. Morris, to two hundred and twenty-four dollars.
One of them, however—Mr. George M'Cormack—
undertook on his own responsibility to collect fifteen

dollars a quarter outside of the membership, for family expenses, and succeeded, making the total salary for the year two hundred and eighty-four dollars. On this small sum Mr. Morris and his family managed to live that year, and they did it uncomplainingly, believing that the brethren were not well able to do more ; and they always spoke of the year spent in Columbus as among the most agreeable, upon the whole, of their itinerant life. Before Conference, the brethren raised money sufficient to complete the church, and Methodism has never wanted a comfortable home in Columbus since.

In 1831, the Ohio Conference met in Mansfield, in the court-house. Among other items of important business, delegates were elected to the General Conference, to assemble the ensuing May in the city of Philadelphia. The delegation chosen was an exceedingly able one, consisting·of the following, now nearly all historic names : David Young, Russel Bigelow, James Quinn, John F. Wright, Leroy Swormstedt, Thomas A. Morris, William H. Raper, Arthur W. Elliott, James B. Finley, Zechariah Connell, Curtis Goddard, John Collins, William B. Christie, Charles Holliday, and Greenbury R. Jones. The Conference had ordered that certain papers should be put into the hands of the preacher who should be appointed in charge of Cincinnati Station, then including all our city Churches in one pastoral charge. A very short time before the final adjournment, these papers were handed by the secretary to Bishop Hedding, and by him to Mr. Morris, who was thus enabled to " guess " pretty accurately where his next appointment would be. For this, however, he was not wholly unprepared. Bishop M'Kendree had spent a few days at the parsonage in Columbus, a week or two before Conference, and in the course of a private conversation had said:

"I came through Cincinnati; the old stone church is taken down to make way for a new one, and services are held in the court-house. The congregation is in a scattered condition, and it will be difficult to gather them together again. I am not the responsible man at your Conference this year; but if I were, I should want you to go there."

The suspicion aroused in the mind of Mr. Morris, by this hint from the senior bishop, was fully verified at the close of the Mansfield Conference, when Bishop Hedding announced, among others, the following appointments: "CINCINNATI STATION—Thomas A. Morris, Nathan Emery, W. B. Christie, Edmund W. Schon."

This change was far from being a source of gratification to Mr. Morris. An overland move of one hundred and twenty miles of bad road was no holiday affair to a feeble, almost helpless family. They could have spent another year pleasantly in their humble domicile, and among their warm-hearted friends in Columbus. The new converts, many of whom knew little of Methodist polity, were sorely grieved to lose their beloved pastor, and could scarcely be reconciled to the arrangement. Among them was a poor but honest and industrious man, known in the community as Father M'Coy, whose great failing was a love for the decanter. Being pleased with Mr. Morris's preaching, he became first a regular hearer, then sober, then truly awakened and deeply penitent, and finally was happily converted. On learning that he was about to lose his pastor, he hastened to the parsonage, and with tears entreated Mr. Morris not to leave them. " I am a poor man," he said, "and can not do much ; but if you will only stay with us, I will give you all the potatoes you need next year." Father M'Coy lived a few years, a striking example of the power of saving grace, even in the otherwise hopeless case of a once confirmed inebriate, and then died in peace.

Mr. Morris sent his household goods by wagon to Cincinnati, while he with his family took Athens in their route, to visit his son, then a student in the Ohio University. On their arrival finally at the Queen City, they were doomed to meet an unexpected defeat of their previously determined mode of living. Having no suitable outfit for housekeeping in the city, Mr. Morris had written from Columbus to one of the stewards in Cincinnati to engage a suitable boarding-place for himself and family. To this reasonable request no attention was paid ; and, at the first official meeting, the stewards signified that it was their wish to have the parsonage occupied by the preacher in charge. He at once moved into the old house thus designated, on Broadway, near Fifth Street, and furnished it as comfortably as his means would allow. All this could have been borne cheerfully if his allowance had been adequate to meet expenses ; but in addition to the house, which was poor and uncomfortable, his salary was four hundred and fifty dollars, all told. The last fifty was added, he was

informed, in view of the fact that he would be expected to "entertain comers and goers"—visiting
brethren, lay and clerical.

Having but a limited supply of beds for the "comers
and goers," Mr. Morris found it necessary to buy a
cot, which he carried home on his own shoulders.
The first attempt to use it broke it down. He carried
it back for repairs, and, when mended, bore it along
Fifth Street as before, for the third time. It was hard
work, but saved the drayage. His wife's health was
very poor, and that of his daughter scarcely better ;
but to hire help without the means to pay for it was
a thing not to be thought of; and so, as the next best
thing, he procured a washing-machine, which, together
with his saw and ax, furnished him an abundance of
healthy exercise. His daughter had just strength to
prepare the clothes, change the water, and rinse them
when clean, while he was both able and willing—
under the circumstances—to turn the machine, by
far the hardest part of the job. Meantime, however,
the water-works were destroyed by fire, and "washing" became a more serious as well as more expen-
sive business, involving an outlay of twenty-five
cents a barrel for water, hauled from the river, for
laundry purposes. As for the ordinary daily supply
for drinking and cooking purposes, Mr. Morris carried
that in buckets from Spencer's well, a square and a
half distant from the parsonage.

Cincinnati Station at that time included Wesley,
Fourth-street, M'Kendree, Asbury, and New-street
Chapels, or the entire city and Fulton. The Confer-
ence year was marked by a succession of calamities

to the city, which were felt by all classes of citizens. River navigation closed very early, leaving the city so little fuel that wood, hauled into town from the surrounding farms, rose in price to eight and nine dollars a load. Then came numerous and destructive fires, consuming foundries, hotels, and steamboats, in which many lives were lost. The most embarrassing fire, and the one most generally felt by the community to be a great public calamity, was that which destroyed the water-works, leaving the people to obtain supplies from the river as best they could. Early in 1832, there was a great freshet in the Ohio River. Opposite to Cincinnati it rose sixty-four feet above low-water mark, flooding all that part of the city called " the Bottom ;" floating many houses from their foundations, and inflicting untold suffering on many poor families. These public distresses necessarily increased the toils and lessened the comforts of the preachers and their families. It was a year of hard labor, and of comparatively little fruit.

Mr. Morris was returned to the city in 1832, with George W. Walker and David Whitcomb for his colleagues. This was a most eventful year in the history of Methodism in Cincinnati. During the first week of the year, early in October, Asiatic cholera made its appearance so suddenly, and operated with such violence and fatality, as to produce general consternation among the people. Some shut themselves up at home, living abstemiously, and furnished with preventives and remedies ; others fled to the country, hoping by that means to escape from the deadly influence. Steamboats, canal-boats, stages, carriages, and market-wagons were crowded day and night with affrighted citizens, while many fled on foot, who could obtain no more rapid method of escape. Among these were many members of the Church, and several class-leaders. Such of the leaders as were obliged to leave with their sick families or friends, and notified their pastors of the fact, were borne with ; but such as fled precipitately, making no arrangements for substitutes, were deemed by the preacher in charge guilty of gross delinquency, and removed from office.

The preachers not only remained at their posts, and exhorted their brethren, publicly and privately, to do the same, but they labored more abundantly, attending the sick from house to house, encouraging the fearful, comforting the dying, and burying the dead. Indeed, for three weeks they scarcely took rest enough to sustain their physical nature, promptly obeying every call from the afflicted to all parts of the city and at all hours of the day and night ; not counting their lives dear unto themselves, so that they might finish their course with joy, and the ministry which they had received of the Lord Jesus, to testify the Gospel of the grace of God.

The city, during the prevalence of this dreadful epidemic, presented a mournful aspect. Thousands of citizens were absent in the country ; very many were closely confined by personal affliction or the demands of sick friends ; hundreds were numbered among the dead ; the transient floating population had entirely disappeared ; the country people, in terror, stood aloof; business was almost wholly suspended ; the tramp of hurrying feet was no longer heard on the streets; the din of the city was hushed, and every day appeared as a Sabbath. Instead, however, of the sound of church-going bells, and the footsteps of happy throngs hastening to the house of God, were heard the shrieks of terror-stricken victims of the fell disease, the groans of the dying, and the voices of lamentation. For weeks, funeral processions might be seen at any hour from early morning to late at night. All classes of people were stricken down in this fearful visitation. Doctors, ministers, lawyers, merchants and mechanics, the old and the young, the temperate and the intemperate, the prudent and the imprudent, were alike victims. Seventy-five members of the Cincinnati Station died that year, and fifty of them were marked on the Church records as cholera cases. Among these fifty were some of the choice spirits of the Church: Richard Dement, local elder; John Boyd, local deacon; Isaac Covalt, Esq., a steward, and a member of the City Council; Lewis H. Lee, exhorter and class-leader; besides many excellent private members, both male and female, all of whom, as far as could be learned, died in peace—many of them rejoicing to the last.

The first cholera epidemic passed away in October, with the first keen, frosty weather of the season; but the second attack, which commenced with the first warm weather in the Spring of 1833, continued till August, and destroyed more lives probably than the first, though not at any time apparently so violent.

Another great event of this year, and one far more pleasant to contemplate, was the extraordinary revival of religion in the Winter of 1832–33. During the epidemic of October, 1832, the churches of the city were open on Sabbath morning always, and sometimes in the afternoon, but closed at night, except the Methodist churches, which were open day and night, as usual, and, all things considered, well attended. As soon as the cholera subsided, our churches were filled; a work of grace began at once, growing in interest and power from day to day; so that, by the last of November, about one hundred and fifty probationers had been received. The Rev. John Newland Maffit now appeared in the city for the first time, and assisted the regular pastors for four weeks. His eloquent discourses drew very large congregations nightly, the work extended, and one hundred and fifty more were admitted on trial. A day or two after Mr. Maffit left, Rev. James B. Finley, the presiding elder, arrived in the city, to hold quarterly-meeting. The services began on Friday night, and were continued until Tuesday night, with most extraordinary manifestations of Divine power. During the quarterly-meeting, not less than a hundred souls were converted, and a hundred and twenty were received into the Church on trial.

The most remarkable demonstration of the Spirit took place in Wesley Chapel, at a watch-night service on New-Year's eve, when hundreds were prostrate at the same time, pleading for mercy—the joyful shouts of new-born souls mingling with the earnest cries of the penitent. The house was crowded above and below, and in every part of it the cry arose, "What must I do to be saved?" Not less than fifty were converted that evening, and fifty-six united with the Church on probation. Forty-seven were added to the Fourth-street Church the next night, and seventeen at M'Kendree. From that time the revival was regarded as general in all the congregations, and continued with very little abatement for months. During this great work of grace the official business of the Church was not neglected. The class-meetings were held regularly, and proved to be most powerful auxiliaries to the more public services; society-meetings were held often, to which none but members and penitents were admitted. Much care was taken to instruct penitents, and watch over those who had been admitted on trial as seekers of salvation; and, as a result of this judicious administration, they were nearly all converted, and became living and useful members.

Early in the Spring, the pastors held a series of meetings in the several charges, beginning on Friday and closing with a love-feast on Monday night. At these meetings they concentrated all the Methodistic forces in the city, day and night, except Sabbath, and the result in every instance was glorious. At the close of such an effort in Fulton, the very foundations of wickedness seemed broken up. Wives who had long prayed for their husbands, and mothers who had wept in secret over their prodigal sons and worldly-minded daughters, saw them fall down at the foot of the Cross to plead for mercy, and heard them rejoice subsequently in their glorious deliverance from the bondage of sin. The reformation of morals in that part of the city was very striking, and the Church grew and multiplied.

Upon the whole, this was a memorable year in the history of Methodism in Cincinnati. While hundreds were made sorrowful by the loss of dear friends, more still were permitted to rejoice over the salvation of relatives and neighbors. The whole number of applicants for membership on probation was thirteen hundred; but as some of these were transient persons, driven out of the city by want of employment, and others were swept off by the wasting epidemic, the numbered enrolled by the preachers, who were very careful not to admit improper persons, was but one thousand. The increase that year must have been very great but for the concurrence of unusual causes; especially emigration, caused by depression of business. At the close of the year, a careful examination of the records showed not less than six hundred and fifty removals by letter, while comparatively few had been received in that way. It is no matter of surprise, therefore, that the net increase was only a little over three hundred members. Still, the general result was in the highest degree encouraging and gratifying. At least one thousand souls, it was believed, had been "saved by the washing of regeneration and the renewing of the Holy Ghost," while old members were enabled to rejoice in the progress of the cause of Christ. The work was accomplished, so far as human agency was concerned, in a Scriptural and orderly manner. The means used were plain, practical preaching, exhortation, prayer, experience-meetings, and singing Methodist *hymns.* At all the night-meetings, the preachers remained till the service closed and the people dispersed. No irregularities or extravagant exercises were encouraged or permitted, every thing being done "decently and in order." Long will that time of refreshing from the presence of the Lord be remembered by many who participated in it, and by their children. Some few there were, indeed, who took exceptions at first to Mr. Morris's strict enforcement of discipline; but at the close of his second year the official members, by resolution, gave him a vote of thanks for the satisfactory manner in which he had administered the affairs of the charge.

CHAPTER V.

GENERAL CONFERENCE OF 1832—APPOINTED EDITOR OF
WESTERN CHRISTIAN ADVOCATE—GENERAL CON-
FERENCE OF 1836—ELECTED BISHOP.

THE General Conference of 1832, held May 1st, in
the city of Philadelphia, was composed of two hundred and twenty-three delegates, representing twenty
annual conferences. After the usual opening exercises, the appointment of standing and special committees, and the election of officers, the Address of
the Bishops was read. It congratulated the Church
on the general prosperity of the previous quadrennial,
on its happy deliverance from the internal dissensions
which had, at one time, seemed so threatening, and
on the increasing efficiency of the itinerant system.

The address then called the attention of the body
to the various benevolent, educational, and other enterprises of the Church, the care and enlargement
of which would call for wise and prayerful deliberation. The business of this General Conference seems
to have been conducted in great harmony, and with
unusual dispatch. No exciting question disturbed
the general good-feeling, or elicited angry discussion.
The presiding-elder question was considered settled,
and the radical controversy, after the withdrawal of
many of the leading malcontents, had ceased to

agitate the Church. On the twenty-second day of the session, two additional bishops were elected; namely, James O. Andrew and John Emory, both on the first ballot.

It was on his journey home from this General Conference that Mr. Morris, with a number of other delegates, met with a very narrow escape from a serious mishap. The company consisted of Bishop Soule, J. B. Finley, J. Edmondson, D. Young, A. W. Elliott, Jesse Green, and T. A. Morris. They were crossing the Alleghany Mountains on Stockton's fast line of passenger mail-coaches, from Baltimore to Wheeling. It was a very hot day, the 1st of June; but being homeward bound, and all on the best of terms with each other, the time was agreeably occupied with religious and general conversation. As they came down the west side of Polish Mountain, while passing a train of heavy wagons, the team took fright and ran off, dashing at full speed down the mountain. After running about a fourth of a mile, the coach was upset, and at the same time precipitated, with team, passengers, and luggage, down a rough and steep embankment, a distance of thirty-two feet. The driver saved himself by jumping off his box as soon as he saw that the coach must go over. Rev. Jesse Green, who sat with him, attempting to follow the driver's example, broke his arm. The coach brought up against a new and strong fence of oak rails, with such a terrible concussion that it was reduced to a wreck. The shock to the passengers was terrible, of course, and was soon followed by the outcries of the wounded. Bishop Soule was the first to extricate himself; he had received some slight wounds, and had lost part of one thumb. The next one who emerged from the *débris* was Rev. J. B. Finley, with his face cut and bleeding, and his whole system so shocked that he soon became quite sick and faint. Mr. Morris then crawled out uninjured. Rev. A. W. Elliott was heard calling for help, and was got out by the efforts of those who were least damaged—his shoulders being so wrenched by the fall that for years afterward he could not get his coat on without help. Rev. Joseph Edmondson was next recovered from the ruins, very much injured—his face being fearfully cut from chin to forehead, and the blood streaming down into his bosom. Last of all, they recovered Rev. David Young, whose unconscious moans were truly distressing; his collar-bone was crushed, several of his ribs were broken, and other injuries more or less serious received. They were on the south side of the hill, and the only shade available was the imperfect one afforded by the fence, in the corners of which the wounded were placed. There lay Finley, Elliott, Young, and Edmondson. As Mr. Morris was wiping the dust from the face of Young, Bishop Soule came up with Jesse Green in his arms, carrying him like a child from the hot and dusty pike where he fell; and he, too, was placed in the extemporized hospital in the fence corner. One of the company had a thumb-lancet, with which Bishop Soule bled Rev. Mr. Young pretty freely, and he soon revived. After waiting for some time, the accommodation stage came along, and carried all the passengers to Slicer's tavern, a mile or two distant, except

Morris and Elliott, who remained with the luggage until the driver returned with a farm-wagon, and hauled them, with the mail and trunks, to the tavern.

They had to send fourteen miles, to Cumberland, for a surgeon. Finally one arrived at midnight—Dr. Lawrence—who was kept busy until morning, setting fractured bones and dressing wounds. Next day, leaving Mr. Young in care of Mr. Finley, the rest of the party started for Cumberland, where Jesse Green was left with Dr. Lawrence, and, on Monday following, those who were able resumed their journey, thankful to have escaped with life.

The Ohio Conference met in Cincinnati in 1833, holding its sessions in the old Cincinnati College, on Walnut Street. Mr. Morris, having completed his term of two years as preacher in charge of the station, was that year appointed presiding elder of the Cincinnati District. He rented a house at Madison-ville, a small village about eight miles from the city, for which he paid three dollars a month, purchased a horse, a light wagon, and a cow, and felt quite at home among his rural and pleasant neighbors. The district stewards'-meeting allowed him one hundred and twenty dollars for house-rent, fuel, and provisions, which, with his quarterage claim, made a salary of three hundred and twenty dollars. He entered upon his work cheerfully and zealously, and was prosecut-ing it with his accustomed energy and success, when, in April, 1833, he was directed by the authorities of the Church to return to Cincinnati to take editorial charge of the *Western Christian Advocate.*

It may be well to pause here for a moment, and

invite the attention of the reader to a brief *résumé*
of the history of Methodist periodical literature. In
the language of the great American historian of our
Church, "Methodism began its march from the gates
of a university," and no man ever labored more indefatigably in the walks of literature for the elevation
of the popular mind than did John Wesley, who was
probably the very first to set the example of modern
cheap prices, sustained by large sales. In addition
to his own prose productions, constituting fourteen
octavo volumes, in the English edition, his "Notes"
and abridgments make a catalogue of one hundred
and eighteen prose works, forty-nine poetical publi-
cations by himself and his brother, and five distinct
works on music. In the year 1777, Mr. Wesley pro-
jected the *Arminian Magazine*, the first number of
which was issued early in 1778, and which is now the
oldest religious periodical in the world.

American Methodism has always been true to the
example of its illustrious founder; for, in 1789, only
five years after the organization of the Methodist
Episcopal Church, her celebrated "Book Concern"
was founded. Rev. John Dickins, then the only
Methodist preacher in Philadelphia, was appointed
"Book Steward" of the denomination. The capital
of the Concern was originally six hundred dollars,
lent to it by Mr. Dickins himself. In 1804, the Concern was removed from Philadelphia to New York.
In 1818, the *Methodist Magazine* was begun, which is
still published, under the title of the *Methodist Quarterly Review*. On the 9th of September, 1826, the
first number of the *Christian Advocate and Journal*

was issued, the success of which was very remarkable. "In a very short time," says Dr. Bangs, in his History of the Methodist Episcopal Church, "its number of subscribers far exceeded every other paper published in the United States, being about twenty-five thousand; and it soon increased to thirty thousand, and was probably read by more than one hundred and twenty thousand persons, young and old."

In 1820, at the earnest request of Methodists west of the Alleghany Mountains, the General Conference authorized the establishment of a branch of the Book Concern in Cincinnati, and in 1834 the publication of the *Western Christian Advocate* was begun. There were, in 1866, as we learn from a Centenary Sermon by Bishop Clark, two principal Book Concerns—one in New York and one in Cincinnati—with eleven depositories, accommodating different sections of the country, and located mainly in the large cities. The growth and enlargement of our publishing interest have been unprecedented in the history of similar enterprises. The six hundred dollars *borrowed* capital had resulted, in seventy-seven years, or at the period of the Centenary of American Methodism, in an *owned* aggregate net capital of $958,298.72. It kept in constant employment at that time about thirty-five cylinder-presses; issued twelve weekly papers, with an aggregate circulation of one hundred and fifty thousand copies; also a well-sustained quarterly, and a family monthly magazine circulating thirty-five thousand copies, a Sunday-school *Advocate*, and a German Sunday-school paper; together circulating about three hundred and twenty-five thou-

sand copies.   Some idea of the immense power and
influence of this great agency of the Church may be
gathered from the fact that in the Centennial Year—
1866—the actual business of the Methodist Book
Concern, in the East and in the West, amounted to
$1,303,966.95, for twelve months.

When, in April, 1834, Mr. Morris relinquished his
pleasant and congenial work on the Cincinnati District, to undertake the editorship of the *Western Christian Advocate*, he felt that he was making a new and
doubtful experiment.   The paper was to be made,
subscribers were to be obtained, correspondents secured, and, in short, every thing pertaining to the
business was to be learned *ab initio*.   At that day no
provision was made for an office assistant, or any
help whatever in the editorial management of the
paper.   One man was expected to prepare the editorials, make the selections from exchanges, condense
the current news, prepare the items, supervise all
manuscript, and attend to the correspondence of the
office.   The authorities of the Church had recognized in Mr. Morris the peculiar and rare qualities
that were demanded for such work.   He was even then
known widely as a writer who wielded a facile, chaste,
and ready pen; and also as a man of rare good
sense, wide observation, sound judgment, and great
practical wisdom.

Notwithstanding all the disadvantages under which
he was about to enter upon this new and untried
field, such were his energy and industry and ability in
cultivating it, that the paper entered upon its third
volume with over eight thousand subscribers; and it

is no disparagement of the many eminent writers
who have succeeded him to say, that the *Western
Christian Advocate* has never been more popular with
its patrons than when conducted by Thomas A.
Morris. As furnishing both a specimen of his terse,
neat style, and his views of the power and responsibility of the press, we subjoin the editorial entitled
" The Press :"

" That printing machine is a wonderful invention.
Nothing could supply its place in the dissemination
of knowledge. Through its agency one individual
may speak to millions, not only while he lives, but
when sleeping in his grave. Thoughts committed to
paper, and printed in books centuries ago, are still in
existence, and familiar to reading men of this generation. Thus, by the power of this simple engine,
distant ages are brought together ; and, with the aid
of translators, men of all languages may converse and
become acquainted with each others' laws, customs,
and religions, through the press. When the world
was dependent on scribes to multiply copies of manuscript, only limited scraps of history could be
preserved, and the knowledge of them was necessarily
confined to a few individuals who might obtain
access to the huge rolls of parchment on which they
were written.

" We are indebted to the press for the abundance
and cheapness of reading in this age. Had not the
art of printing been discovered, ' even the Word of
Life,' contained in the records of salvation, would still
be locked up in the archives of the university, and
read only by a few learned doctors of law. The

press, under a wise and gracious Providence, has
thrown the Bible among the multitudes of common
people, and made it at once the parent's companion
and the child's school-book. Thus the people generally in this favored land may have access to the
fountain-head of knowledge, which is able to make
them wise unto salvation, through faith which is in
Christ Jesus.

"So it is in all Protestant countries, and so it
should be throughout the world. To expect the
people to find their way to heaven without the holy
Scriptures, is as unreasonable as to require mariners
to navigate the high seas without chart or compass.
Whenever the people of any country shall be furnished
with the Bible, and sufficient knowledge of letters to
read it, they will soon understand their chartered
rights, both as Christians and citizens; and will have
courage to assert them, too, in defiance of popes and
tyrants. They, whose usurped authority rests upon
the slender foundation, 'Ignorance is the mother of
devotion,' have important reasons for withholding the
Bible from their deluded subjects. And to them
nothing is more troublesome than the press. It is
difficult for them to exclude from their limited do-
minions all the light which it sheds upon the world
around them. How important, then, is the press in
multiplying copies of the sacred writings, and removing obstructions to their circulation! Just in proportion as pure Christianity progresses and prospers in
the world, sound learning, civil liberty, and all the
blessings of social life will advance among the nations
of the earth, and no faster. 'Righteousness exalteth

a nation ; but sin is a reproach to any people,' is as true now as it was when Solomon wrote it.

"But the press, like all other benefits conferred upon man, is liable to be abused and perverted to improper uses. While 'the liberty of the press' is to be maintained by every Christian and patriot, care should be taken to restrain it within proper bounds. There is certainly a marked difference between the liberty of the press and the licentiousness of it, whether viewed in the political, literary, or religious department of its operations.

"The political press should teach the rights of man, expound international law, advocate the principles of our free institutions, keep the people advised of the state of commerce, and publish general intelligence. But it should never be enlisted in the cause of mobocracy, or demagogism, or such party measures as conflict with the general good of the country ; nor should it ever be degraded by dealing in slander, or personal invective, or any disgusting details of private scandal. This standard is evidently none too high. But if every political newspaper which falls below it were expunged from the catalogue, how few of them would be left ! How many political newspapers are there in the United States which do not evince more zeal for their respective leaders and parties than they do for their country ? Which of them will not abuse a political opponent to prevent his elevation, or flatter a political friend for the remote prospect of obtaining office ? Nay, which of them will not publish fulsome notices of a masquerade, a theater, a circus, a horse-race, or a tippling-house, for the paltry sum of a few cents? 'Straws show which way the wind blows,' and these objectionable items but too clearly indicate the spirit of the political press. In vain may it attempt to reform the people till it reforms itself.

"The literary press operates in a milder atmosphere, sustains a relation less exciting, and occupies a position less perilous, and consequently is, in a great measure, clear of the objections above named. That it has its toils, perplexities, and discouragements to contend with, is admitted ; but being free from the contaminating influence of office, and from the agitation of evil passions, it meets these difficulties calmly, patiently, and in hope of ultimate success. Besides, its toil is pleasant. What delightful labor to store the mind with knowledge, and then employ it in erecting monuments of science, and strewing the garlands of literature along the path of life for those who come after! Such employment, though it may promise little wealth and no sensual pleasure, has the advantage of being free from the corrupting influence of vicious associations, and threatens no remorse of conscience to be endured in the evening of life. Still, the literary press is only less liable to abuse than the political, and not wholly secure against it. The appetites of its readers are various, some of them quite vitiated by the use of improper aliment ; hence arises a temptation to indulge their perverted tastes to the injury of their judgment and general vigor of character. If proof be demanded, reference may be had to all the varieties of fiction, from the less offensive novel down to the commonplace love-tale, written by a novice for some would-be literary periodical, and to the debilitating and contaminating influence which they exert upon the minds and characters of their deluded readers. All tales of wild adventure, whether in war or love, are highly injurious to young readers of both sexes. They not only lessen the inclination to study and the desire for useful knowledge, but they fix in the mind erroneous views of men and things, by portraying characters which never existed, and recording events which never transpired, and thus introducing them to a world very different from the one in which they live. Walker's definition of romancer is, ' A liar, a forger of tales.' And yet thousands of young females, whose minds are naturally sprightly and amiable, spend their days and nights in poring and weeping over these forgeries, as though they were credible and useful histories. Such a young lady has received an erroneous education. It has led her in the wrong path ; and the sooner she retraces her steps, the better. She is in danger of becoming an object of pity in the estimation of intelligent people. They who have encouraged her to take this delusive course in the pursuit of knoweldge are justly censurable.

" But what should be said of the religious press ? Its responsibility is as much greater than that of all others as our spiritual and eternal interests are higher than those of earth and time. Mistakes here may endanger the everlasting welfare of deathless spirits ; yea, spirits redeemed by the blood of the Lamb, and already placed upon ground of possible salvation. The press which is professedly devoted to the interest of religion should never become entangled with any question of worldly policy, or of popular excitement, or of personal or party conflict, or angry controversy on any subject whatever. All such errors tend to weaken public confidence in the religious press, and to divert its patronage into other channels. It is worse than useless to teach religion in theory, while its teachers contradict their own principles in spirit and practice ; as the conclusion which naturally follows is, their religion makes them no better than their neighbors. The common sense of mankind will estimate the real value of every system and every enterprise by its practical results. If a press, though professedly religious, kindle the fire of contention, raise the storm of angry passion, and indicate a spirit of malevolence, it will be justly regarded as an engine of evil, sowing the seeds of discord and persecution. Religion would be far better off without any press than with one which only betrays her interests by practically renouncing her own principles, or with any number of presses which exhaust their energies by combating one another. What folly it is for those who are professedly aiming to accomplish the same great and good object—the conversion of the world— to turn aside from their high and holy calling, and wage a war of mutual extermination ! Every consistent Christian weeps and sighs over such an exhibition of human depravity.

"Let the religious press be restricted to its appropriate work, and it will find ample employment for all its time, strength, and resources, without assuming any needless responsibility. The main design of it should be to impart a knowledge of that religion

which brings 'glory to God in the highest, and on
earth peace, good will toward men.' And whatever
tends to the accomplishment of this result should be
encouraged by it. Here an almost boundless field
of useful enterprise opens to view. It embraces the
regular Christian ministry, with all of its intense interest, the progress of revivals under the ministration
of the Gospel, foreign and domestic missions, plans
for the instruction of youth and childhood, sanctified learning, and all benevolent associations which
have for their aim the glory of God and the happiness
of man. All of these interests are to be noticed, ex-
plained, defended, and encouraged, by presenting the
truth in love and in meekness of wisdom. Surely,
there is much land to be possessed and cultivated by
the religious press before the peaceful reign of Christ
shall be universally established and acknowledged. Besides, this press is expected to furnish the whole world
with all the religious reading which it needs, or may
need, in the form of books, duly assorted, distinguishing between the good and the evil. The work is vast
and increasing, both in extent and importance ; but
the means for its accomplishment, if not yet abundant, are at least accumulating. The gold and the
silver are the Lord's, and his treasury is increasing.
Presses are multiplying, and they are moving under
a full pressure of steam-power, so that a copy of the
Bible can be printed in a minute ; and missionary
ships are bearing off the Old and New Covenants to
heathen lands by the ton. Only let the religious
press not be turned aside from its own proper work,
and it will prove itself an invaluable auxiliary to the

Christian ministry in subjugating the world to the 'obedience of Christ,' and raising it to holiness, happiness, and heaven."

On the 1st day of May, 1836, General Conference assembled in the city of Cincinnati. It was composed of one hundred and fifty-four delegates, representing twenty-two annual conferences. The delegation from the Ohio Conference was a large and able one, as the following well-known names will show: Thomas A. Morris, Jacob Young, David Young, William H. Raper, Leroy Swormstedt, John Ferree, James B. Finley, Wm. B. Christie, James Quinn, John F. Wright, Augustus Eddy, and John H. Power.

Bishops Roberts, Soule, Hedding, and Andrew were present, and the first named opened the session in the usual manner. Two of the bishops—M'Kendree and Emory—had died in 1835, the former in the seventy-eighth, and the latter in the forty-eighth year of his age. Bishop M'Kendree entered the ministry at the age of thirty, labored some twenty-one years before his election to the episcopal office, in which he faithfully and efficiently served the Church almost twenty-seven years. Bishop Emory entered the ministry in 1810, and was elected to the episcopal office in 1832. On the 16th of December, 1835, he was thrown from his carriage, receiving such an injury in his head that he was insensible when found, and died on the evening of the same day.

Among other important questions presented to this Conference was the propriety of dissolving the Bible Society of the Methodist Episcopal Church. A separate denominational organization of this kind

had been found necessary in the early history of the
Church, and although it had answered its purpose
for a season, the time had now come when, in the
judgment of many, both in and out of the Board of
Managers, its continuance was no longer necessary.
After careful deliberation, the Conference recommended a dissolution of the Society, with a view to
unite the Methodist Episcopal Church with other
evangelical denominations in carrying forward the
objects of the American Bible Society. The harmonious co-operation of our Church with that great
national institution, since that period, abundantly
vindicates the course then adopted.

The rule respecting " laying aside " persons for
not meeting in class, which had been so interpreted
as to allow the acting preacher to drop the delinquent
without a trial, was so amended as to make it ob-
ligatory on the parties concerned to allow the accused
to be heard in his defense before a committee, the
same as in other cases of delinquency.

At this General Conference it was found necessary so to amend the Constitution of the Missionary
Society, as to provide for the election of a corresponding secretary, who should employ his whole
time in promoting the interests of that important and
rapidly increasing department of the Church. Hitherto the correspondence of the Society had been
carried on by the brethren connected with the Book
Concern ; but the increase of the business, both of
the Concern and of the Society, made the duties of
each so onerous that it was found impossible to
unite them longer without injury to one or both.

The Liberia Mission was this year erected into an annual conference, "possessing all the rights, powers, and privileges of other annual conferences, except that of sending delegates to the General Conference, and of drawing its annual dividend from the avails of the Book Concern and Chartered Fund."

Two additional weekly papers were authorized, and the one which had been established at Cincinnati by the Book Agents, on the recommendation of several annual conferences, was sanctioned and continued, making in all four religious weekly papers, besides the *Methodist Magazine and Quarterly Review*. In addition to these, however, there were four others, under the patronage of annual conferences; namely, *Zion's Herald*, in Boston; *Maine Wesleyan Journal*, in Portland; *Virginia Conference Journal*, in Richmond; and the *Auburn Banner*, in Auburn, New York,—making altogether eight weekly papers devoted to the interests of Methodism in the United States.

Among the important questions settled by this General Conference was one touching the right of an annual conference to locate one of its members without his consent. The question had been raised at several preceding General Conferences, and, although not decisively settled, the predominant opinion was that no such power existed. A rule was now adopted giving to an annual conference power to locate one of its members who had rendered himself "unacceptable as a traveling preacher," in their judgment, reserving to him, however, the privilege of an appeal to the next General Conference.

The Committee on Episcopacy recommended the election of three additional bishops, which, after some debate, was concurred in by the Conference. The election took place on the 23d of May. Mr. Morris's own account of this highly important epoch in his life is given in his peculiar style, briefly and pleasantly, as follows:

"During this General Conference I had to perform the double duty of delegate and editor, besides going to market and entertaining my guests. But all of these things put together embarrassed me less than one other trouble which my friends had brought upon me. For about four years they had been threatening me occasionally with the 'Big Circuit'— a proposition which I at first received as a joke, and joined with others in a little pleasantry over it. When, however, I became satisfied that they were really in earnest, I begged to be left out of the question, and did all that any prudent man ought to do to prevent myself from being nominated; but in vain. When I saw that my brethren were determined to bring me forward as a candidate, I consoled myself with the thought that when fairly beaten, as I was confident of being, they would drop the matter quietly, and that I should be no more teased on the subject.

"Apart from the fearful responsibility of the episcopal office, I had strong private and personal objections to filling it—not from any doubts as to the Scriptural authority for it, or of its fitness and utility in our Church polity, but from a consciousness of my own unfitness for the place, both as to experience and the necessary mental culture. I also felt that I lacked the courage to meet all the opposing influences and obstacles that must be encountered in the faithful discharge of the duties of the office.

"When the day for the election arrived, I was fully satisfied that I should be distanced on the first balloting, and felt comparatively calm ; but when the result was announced, Beverly Waugh and Wilbur Fisk were elected, and I lacked but one vote of being in company with them. I now became seriously alarmed, and requested my friends to withdraw my name from the canvass, as there was yet one more to be elected ; but they refused. As the balloting proceeded, I entreated them to excuse me ; but, as they still persisted, I finally arose and requested the Conference to consider my name withdrawn, and not vote for me any longer ; but my efforts were unavailing. On the fifth ballot I again came within one vote of an election, so that it was twice in my power to have elected myself; but from first to last I voted for other candidates. The result of the sixth balloting showed that I had the requisite number of votes, with a considerable number to spare, and I was declared elected. To make further resistance, I feared, would be unsafe and imprudent, and I submitted to the judgment of my brethren."

Dr. Fisk was at that time traveling in Europe, but provision was made for his consecration as soon as practicable after his return. The doctor, however, felt constrained to decline the office, both on account of his obligations to the Wesleyan University, of which he was president, and his failing health, which he felt to be unequal to the labors of the episcopal office.   Beverly Waugh and Thomas A. Morris, after an appropriate sermon by Bishop Hedding, on the 27th of May, were solemnly consecrated bishops of the Methodist Episcopal Church ; and on the same day the General Conference adjourned.

CHAPTER VI.

THERE were now twenty-eight annual conferences and six bishops. It was understood,
however, that the principal labor of the quadrennial
period commencing with the close of the General
Conference of 1836 would devolve upon Bishops
Soule, Andrew, Waugh, and Morris. Their colleagues, Hedding and Roberts, were now far
advanced in years, and too feeble in health to take
their full share of episcopal work. In view of his
health, Bishop Roberts had tendered his resignation
during the session of the General Conference at Cincinnati, but that body declined to accept it ; and a
resolution was passed that he should be required to
do no more service than he might find consistent
with his health and bodily strength. Afterward a
similar resolution was passed in relation to Bishop
Hedding.

In July and August, Bishop Morris attended the
Pittsburg Conference at Wheeling, and the Erie
Conference at Meadville, Pennsylvania, in company
with Bishop Soule. His own work for that year,
according to the episcopal plan, embraced the

sessions of the Tennessee, Arkansas, Mississippi, and Alabama Conferences ; and early in September he started from his home in Cincinnati on this extended Southern tour. We propose to let the bishop relate the story of this, his first episcopal circuit, himself. We quote from his volume entitled " Miscellany :"

" It appeared like a long, fatiguing journey to perform on horseback, and alone ; but there were points in view which could be reached by no other means of conveyance. There might be disease and danger in the course ; but I was on lawful business, intimately connected with the welfare of redeemed sinners ; and why should any man ever fear to go where duty calls, or remain till it is done ? More-over, I was well mounted upon *Nick*, a fine pacing gray. He moved as if on elliptic springs, and bore me onward with a strength of muscle and power of en-durance which excited my admiration. Far removed, not only from wife and children and friends, but from the crowds of strangers which usually throng the public lines of conveyance, it was a time for re-flection on the responsibilities and difficulties of my new position, and not wholly unimproved. Lonely reflection, however, was soon superseded by practical duties. While in council with the brethren of Ten-nessee Conference, at Columbia, a call was made for volunteers to supply the wants of the new Conference just set off in the State of Arkansas, and promptly responded to by some noble-hearted, self-sacrificing young ministers. Three of them were ready to bear me company thither, immediately after the final adjournment.   Their names were Randle, Duncan, and Simmons.

"Passing down through the Western District of Tennessee, we came on the fresh trail of fourteen thousand Creek Indians, just then removing from Alabama to their new home in the far-off West. At one of their camping-places, then vacated, was seen a standing hollow tree, out of the side of which had been taken a slab, by cutting above and below, and splitting it off, and which had been carefully replaced.   A citizen, whose neighbors had made examination, informed us that in the hollow of that tree was a deceased Indian, standing erect, with his gun, blanket, and hunting costume, as he appeared when living.   We subsequently saw several of these depositories of the dead.   As a matter of convenience, the Indians were separated into companies of fifteen hundred, and a sub-agent assigned to each.   We came up with the rear party in the vicinity of Memphis, were two days passing their extended line of companies, and slept three nights in sight of their camps.   No nation of men ever exhibited more powerful muscles than were developed in the persons of the Creek warriors.   Like other people, they bore the marks of inequality.   Some had the appearance of abject poverty.   Among this class, the men rode on ponies, carrying their guns and camp-kettles, while the women trudged on foot, bearing heavy packs on their heads, and small children lashed upon their shoulders.   A second class were better clad, had a better outfit, and presented more appearances of comfort.   The third class probably formed the nobility of the nation, were gaudily attired in silks and jewelry, and exhibited the insignia of wealth and office.

"After crossing the 'Father of Waters' at Memphis, we immediately entered the Mississippi Swamp, which, at that point, was forty-two miles across. The track was so worked up by the teams and pack-horses that we found it more pleasant to avoid it when practicable. For miles together our horses waded, but generally found firm bottom, except about the sloughs, where many tired Indian ponies stuck fast, and were left to perish in the bog, and where our noble animals had to struggle hard to escape the same fate. On the evening of the second day we emerged from the swamp, and crossed the St. Francis River. At a small, green bottom, two miles beyond the river, two companies of Creeks, numbering some three thousand in all, were camped for the night. We took lodging at a country tavern on the hill, about thirty rods from them. They had nearly as many ponies as people, and almost every pony wore a bell. The camp-axes were roaring; dogs and children appeared to be alike abundant and alike noisy. The whole, taken together, produced a singular confusion of sounds, and presented quite a novel spectacle.

"Next morning, about day-break, we rode out through the encampment, in a north-east direction, on the Batesville road. Having cleared the great swamp and reached an undulating surface, we congratulated ourselves that the worst of the journey was behind. For some twenty-five miles, our course led us over desolate pine and oak ridges, which nevertheless formed an agreeable contrast with the sludge from which we had escaped. At noon, rain began to fall, slowly at first, but steadily. In the afternoon we came by a small company of men engaged in raising a corn-crib near to a cabin, which seemed to be full, and presented no appearance of comfort, when the following conversation ensued:

"'How far is it to the next house?'

"'Twenty-one miles; and three more to the tavern.'

"'What sort of a road is it?'

"'Not very good, nor bad; just middling.'

"'Is there any deep water to cross?'

"'None that will swim, except Bayou de View, sixteen miles from here; and I don't reckon that will swim, quite.'

"Then, among ourselves, we held a conference on horseback, the rain still coming down. 'It is two o'clock; say four hours till daylight will be entirely gone. Can we reach the point of difficulty before dark?' 'Yes, I think we can.' 'If we fail to get through, we shall need our dinner by to-morrow.' 'Well, I have a little piece of corn-bread,' said one. 'And I have part of a sweet potato,' said another. 'That is as good fare as we can get here,' responded a third. It was suggested, if we had to camp out, there was no means of striking fire; but perhaps other campers might have left fire on the way.

"The case was finally summed up thus: 'Our time in which to reach Conference is short; there is no use staying here in the rain—come on.' And onward we went, ignorant of what was before us. In a few minutes our road disappeared under water. What does this mean? Why, the Black-river Swamp. 'They said last night that we should cross it, but it looks worse than we expected.' The sludge increased, and the horses sank more and more. Presently, while crossing a bad place, Nick, better acquainted with turnpikes than swamps, went down till he was nearly buried alive in quicksand and water. After a long and hard struggle, he came out, and brought me with him, but my saddle-bags were left behind in the mud. Having recovered them, we resumed the journey; but soon reached another slough, where, to prevent a greater evil, I dismounted, drove the horse, and followed on foot, through mud and water to the knees, by which we made a safe crossing. But the thought of its being twenty miles to the next house, wet and cold, my boots full of water, and the night approaching, was not very cheering. It was about the last of October. The climate was supposed to be unhealthy. We had fairly entered a dismal swamp, thirty-two miles wide, and, in consequence of heavy rains, unusually full of water. Instead of traveling four miles an hour, as we had expected, our horses were unable to make three. The beaten track was the least dangerous, as it always is over quicksand; but for miles together it was wholly under water, varying in depth from six inches to three feet, and the bottom little more than a continuous quagmire, as deep as the horses could struggle through.

"While daylight lasted we could follow the trace by the old 'blazes' on the sides of the trees; but night

closed in upon us long before we reached the main
point of difficulty, and the rain still increasing. We
lost the track, our feet dragged through brush-wood,
and the morass shook beneath us; but, giving the
affrighted horses loose reins, they returned to it.
Again we took the wrong direction, and went plunging
through water and alder-bushes, in danger every moment of being ingulfed in quicksand; but, after
some time, we found our road once more.

"A conference was then called to discuss the
question, 'Shall we give it up, or try to proceed?' It
was a solemn conference; and though darkness and
storm prevailed without, order and peace were maintained within. The sum of our conversation was
briefly this: To stay here all night, wet, cold, and
hungry, without shelter, without fire, or a foot of
dry ground on which to stand, is perilous; to proceed
was only perilous: and the conclusion was to try it
again. After losing and regaining the beaten way
a third time, at last coming to a bank of sand, and
then a rapid descent of some feet to a sheet of deep
water, we inferred that we were at the margin of the
much-dreaded Bayou de View. The direction was,
to enter near a large tree, bear up to the point of an
island; then, forming an angle downward, steer for a
projecting log on the opposite shore. But, alas! under the lofty trees and lowering clouds, the darkness
was such that we could not see the animals on which
we rode! What was to be done? To encounter the
turbid stream at random, was bordering on presumption; to wait for daylight, when the stream was rising,
was discouraging, and might defeat our whole enter-

prise. As it was a case in which life might be involved, a regular vote was taken, by calling the roll, and it was unanimous in favor of going ahead. It was also agreed that I should be commander. The line was promptly formed, as follows : Brother Randle, having a steady horse, and being a light rider, was to lead off; brother Simmons next; the writer third ; and Brother Duncan was to bring up the rear. It was further ordered to keep two rods apart, so that if we struck a swim, every man might have sea-room, and a chance for life. 'All ready?' 'Yes.' 'Proceed, then, and cry soundings.' 'Knee-deep ; up to the girth ; midsides ; steady ; over the withers, but still feel bottom ; more shallow now ; here is the point of the island.'

"'Very well ; now form an angle to the left ; down stream is easy.' The latter channel was no deeper than the former, and all made a safe landing, thanks to kind Providence !

"Our next direction was to leave the old trace here, turn down the bayou some distance without any road, so as to intersect a new way, which had been recently cut out, starting from a point lower down. Between the ford and the new way we tore through the brushwood, leaped over logs, and plunged into sloughs, at the risk of our limbs, but finally reached the road, when our horses gladly resumed the proper course. It was, to our great mortification, soon ascertained that the new way was more miry than the old. As we could see nothing, our quadrupeds had all the credit for keeping the road. Presently brother Randle's horse was heard plunging, at a

fearful rate, for some time, when he announced a
very dangerous place—'water up to midsides, and the
bottom very boggy.' Brother Simmons next put in,
and was glad when he got out. He advised me to
veer to the left. It might be better, and, he thought,
could be no worse. It proved to be unfortunate advice, as it threw me on a heap of logs that had been
rolled in to fill up a deep and dangerous bog, but
which were then all afloat. Nick had a terrible
scuffle over them. Once his foot hung fast; twice
the water rolled over him, and the rider was well-nigh
unhorsed. But finally he righted, and brought me
out unhurt. Taking a position, as nearly as I could
guess, opposite to where the others crossed, I called
to brother Duncan to steer by my voice and put
in. He came near sticking fast, but received no
damage. At a late period of the night, while groping
amid darkness that could be felt, mingled with
incessant showers, we were suddenly aroused by the
joyful note, 'A light! a light!' Approaching as near
as some unseen obstruction allowed, we hailed. An
old lady came to the door and demanded, 'Who is
there?'

" ' Travelers."

" ' Ah! I thought my sons had got back from
bear-hunting.'

" ' No, madam, we are strangers; have been be-
lated in the swamp, and wish to know if you will
shelter us the balance of the night.'

" ' Why, la me! I would n't turn off a dog such
a night as this.'

" Securing the horses to the tree, we joyfully

entered the cabin of poles, about sixteen feet long, and fourteen wide. The chimney was unfinished. There was a place for a hearth, but it was not filled up, and the fire was down in a hole, some eighteen inches below the puncheons. Four of us, with our wet baggage, added to the family, and two other strangers that were there before us, scarcely left us room to turn round. At midnight we made a comfortable dinner on pork and corn-dodgers; and, having dried off a little, we held our evening prayers at two o'clock in the morning, and quietly laid us down to sleep, grateful for our kind reception. About daylight we asked the old lady for our bill, which was two dollars. When we inquired if she meant two dollars each, she said: 'La me! I should be rich if I had that much. I mean two dollars for all four.'

"Having completed our preparations, we resumed the swamp; but the limbs of our animals were so lacerated by maple-roots and cypress-knees that they took it very reluctantly. We reached the Cash-river Tavern, with hard toiling, in an hour and a half, the distance being three miles, where the landlady, in the absence of her husband, first served us with breakfast, and then ferried us over the river. When the boat had crossed the rapid channel, she grounded on the bank, which was entirely inundated; so that we had no alternative but to mount in the boat, and leap over the bow into the water. Eight miles more of wading and plunging, which consumed just four hours, brought us out of the Black-river Swamp at Litchfield, thankful that we were alive.

"After reaching solid ground, and obtaining

lodgings, our first concern was to unpack our clothes, books, and papers, and dry them. This done, we preached, exhorted, and held prayer-meeting in the village of Litchfield, where the inhabitants received us kindly, and requested regular preaching, which was of course provided for them. Our little party felt toward each other like a band of patriot soldiers, who had endured a hard and hazardous campaign together, and we distributed among ourselves small presents, as mementos of our providential deliverance and mutual regard."

From this point the journey to Batesville was made with comparative ease and comfort, and the first session of the Arkansas Conference was held, November 2d, 1836, in the grand-jury room of the court-house. The secretary of the Conference, Rev. Wm. P. Ratcliff, in a communication to the *Western Christian Advocate*, under date of November 8th, says: "Bishop Morris was with us in good health, and manifested much interest in our infant Conference."

From Batesville, Bishop Morris continued his episcopal tour, traveling on horseback to the mouth of White River, and thence by steamboat to Vicksburg, where he held the Mississippi Conference, on the 7th of December. From Vicksburg he proceeded to Mobile *via* New Orleans, and presided over the Alabama Conference, January 4, 1837. Returning to New Orleans, he made a short trip to Catchoula Parish, in the western part of Louisana, to visit his brother Levi, where he preached several times to the "squatters," held a class-meeting, appointed a leader, and had a preacher sent to them the next year.

After a few days of rest and social enjoyment in the family of his brother, he proceeded homeward, reaching Cincinnati March 16, 1837.

During the Spring and Summer, Bishop Morris made many preaching excursions into Kentucky and Indiana, traveling for this purpose, wholly on horseback, not less than a thousand miles. In forming an estimate of this extra labor, we must never lose sight of the toilsome mode of travel which was almost the only alternative of the itinerant of that day. The weariness and exposure of a long journey on horseback, along rough and miry roads, can hardly be realized by the ministers of the present generation, accustomed as they are to the easy, pleasant, and rapid transportation of the steamboat and railway.

In the Fall, Bishop Morris again left home to resume his episcopal labors. He held the Holston Conference, at Madisonville, Tennessee, October 18th; the Georgia, at Athens, December 12th; the South Carolina, at Columbia, January 10, 1838; the North Carolina, at Guilford C. H., January 31st; the Virginia, at Richmond, February 21st; the Baltimore, in the city of Baltimore, March 14th; reaching home toward the close of the same month.

This year was one of marked prosperity in the history of Methodism.* Several of the conferences reported very large accessions. Among them, the Illinois had reported an increase of three thousand three hundred and sixteen; the Indiana, three thousand one hundred and thirty-eight; the Philadelphia, three thousand and forty-two; the New York, two

* Clark's "Life and Times of Hedding," page 464.

thousand six hundred and thirty-six; the Tennessee, two thousand eight hundred and forty-three; the Maine, two thousand five hundred and eighty-nine; the Troy, two thousand one hundred and thirty-two; the Erie, two thousand three hundred and thirty-nine; the Oneida, two thousand four hundred and ninety-two; and the Genesee, two thousand seven hundred and ninety-six. The total increase of members for the year, including local preachers, was forty-three thousand two hundred and seventy-five.

Remaining at home until the middle of May, Bishop Morris set out to perform his first tour of episcopal labor among the Eastern conferences. He first visited the New York Conference, held in the city of New York, where a meeting of the bishops took place by previous appointment. Among other items of business, they warmly approved the idea, which had originated in the West, of publishing a Methodist paper in the German language; and recommended the Agents at Cincinnati to commence its publication whenever they could do so without loss to the Book Concern.

Bishop Morris presided over the Troy Conference, at Keysville, June 6th; the New Hampshire, at Danville, Vermont, July 4th; the Black-river, at Fulton, New York, August 8th; the Oneida, at Ithica, August 29th; the Genesee, at Elmyra, September 19th; reaching home in October. On the 17th of that month he attended the Kentucky Conference at Danville, over which Bishop Waugh presided. On his journey home from this Conference, Bishop Morris passed a night at a public house in Nicholasville,

where his trunk was cut to pieces and plundered by
a thief, who was evidently in search of the trunk of
Rev. L. Swormstedt, the Book Agent, and which contained a large amount of money. Mr. Swormstedt,
however, had taken the precaution to have his luggage
removed to his room, and thus avoided a very heavy
loss. The thief, beyond a large amount of clothing
obtained from the trunks of Bishop Morris and several other travelers, got nothing to compensate him
for the six-years' confinement in the penitentiary,
which was the penalty he paid for his villainy. After
spending a few days at home, Bishop Morris started,
in November, as a substitute for Bishop Roberts, who
was unable to do full work, to hold the Mississippi
Conference, at Grenada, on the 5th of December, and
the Alabama Conference, at Montgomery, on the 2d
of January, 1839.

During this trip South, which was made chiefly
by stage-coach, the bishop was subjected to many
annoyances from the prevailing hostility of the baser
sort of people in that region to all who hailed from
the North, and who were, on that ground, denounced
as "Northern Abolitionists." At a point between
Holly Springs and Grenada, the stage passengers going south and those going north met at a country
tavern, and "laid over" part of the night. It soon
became known among the travelers from the south
that a Methodist bishop was among the passengers
of the other coach, and thereupon, as by common
consent, they began a series of petty persecutions
and insulting remarks. As the bishop paid no attention to their infamous conduct, they became more

wrathful, denouncing him to his face as a " Northern Abolitionist," and threatening, in the most violent manner, to drag him out of the tavern and hang him up without judge or jury. Some insisted that it ought to be done at once ; others declared that hanging would be too good for him, and that he ought rather to be drawn up to the top of a black-jack tree, and then dropped down through its craggy limbs, and thus " raked to pieces." The bishop's traveling companions had all retired, the landlord and his family were in another part of the house, and it was about ten o'clock. No one was in the public-room but the bishop and his assailants ; the former having stepped in to see that his baggage was properly cared for. He calmly and silently maintained his position in the room until the ruffians had exhausted their spleen in words of fury and threats of murder, and then quietly retired, treating the whole with perfect indifference. On his relating the affair afterward to Dr. Winans, that gentleman remarked : " You were in far greater danger of personal violence than you seem to have supposed. These Mississippi desperadoes have quite recently murdered several innocent and unoffending strangers, on the mere suspicion that they were 'Northern Abolitionists,' without waiting for any proof whatever."

At the close of the Mississippi Conference, at Grenada, Bishop Morris went to Vicksburg, and took a steamer for New Orleans, the captain having promised positively to land him in that city on Saturday. When the bishop, with his traveling companions—his own son and Rev. John F. Wright—entered the boat, on Thursday, they found a very large proportion of the passengers engaged in card-playing—a custom very general on Mississippi steamboats in that day. This was sufficiently annoying; but, to add to their grievances, Sabbath came on, and they were still steaming down the river. After breakfast, some of the gamblers waited on Bishop Morris with a request that he would preach a sermon to the passengers. He replied that preaching was his calling; and that, under all proper circumstances, he was very willing to preach; but that self-respect would not allow him to do so then and there. " You have," said he, " by your gambling, drunkenness, and profanity, in my presence, for days together, when I could not help myself, given ample proof that you are wholly destitute of respect for my religion and my profession as a minister; and now, having become weary of one kind of amusement, you seek another at my expense. I can not gratify you." Being disappointed, and probably a little mortified by this unexpected rebuke, they went away, and sent the captain with the same request, to whom the bishop made substantially the same reply, adding a severe reprimand of the profanity of which not only most of the passengers, but the officers of the boat, including the captain, had been repeatedly guilty in his presence. After that, the bishop did not see a card or hear an oath while he remained on the boat.

Arrived at length in New Orleans, the bishop immediately took boat for Mobile, Alabama, and had a safe, quick, and (save sea-sickness) pleasant passage. Passing up the Alabama River to Montgomery, the seat of the Conference, he again fell in with very disagreeable company. The river was low, the boat was small, and the crowd was extremely disorderly. Most of the passengers seemed to be on a "Christmas spree," and drinking, swearing, and gambling were the order of the day. Noticing finally that Bishop Morris avoided them, and that he could not be drawn into conversation with them, one of the party made an insulting remark to him ; but he held his peace. One of the company then suggested to another, in a voice loud enough to be heard by all, that no fleshy man could be intelligent, because he would be too lazy to be studious. This remark was assented to, with an oath, by the party addressed, and a general laugh followed. "Yes," said the first, "and we have a perfect example of the truth of my assertion on this boat," at the same time looking toward the bishop. Disagreeable as was the necessity, Bishop Morris was compelled to spend four days on this little water-craft in such company, in order to reach his Conference at the appointed time.

Apropos to the talk above recorded concerning fat men, we may here appropriately insert a brief article contributed to the *Western Christian Advocate*, in August, 1855, by the bishop, entitled,

"LEAN *vs.* FAT."

"IT is often said, 'Little men are generally sprightly,' and it is occasionally hinted that some of them are inclined to be 'saucy,' too. This train of thought was incidentally scared up by reading an editorial in the August number of the *National*

Magazine, on the lamented George G. Cookman, whose praise is deservedly in all the Churches, and whose reputation does not need for its defense detraction from the good name of others. In that article the editor, who is himself, physically, a mere pocket edition of humanity, holds forth in this wise :

"'Corpulency aggrandizes the body, but libels the soul. A gross, visible, self-obtruded libel is it amid the activities of this age, except where hereditary ; albeit reverend dullness and dozy dignity often wrap themselves in its soft integuments. Good-nature goes with it sometimes ; yes, and so it does with stupidity in general.' (Page 98.)

" Now, if it be admitted that the above extract expresses the true philosophy of man, we may well exclaim, Alas for Methodism ! that it should ever have been afflicted with such stupid drones as Thomas Coke, Adam Clarke, William M'Kendree, Enoch George, Robert R. Roberts, Elijah Hedding, and a host of others like them. These massive figures, with all their 'reverend dullness and dozy dignity,' must have compared but indifferently with the meagre dyspeptics of their times, and especially among dwarfish hypochondriacs. Moreover, if such compliments be awarded to the sainted dead, what may not be expected for the living ? Let such as have a good conscience, a good appetite, and plenty to eat, look out for proscription ; for in the light of the *National,* if I can understand it, to enjoy the flush of health, so as to 'aggrandize the body,' is at best to be a good-natured fool.

" Of course, the prospect for myself is not flattering.

Considering how much of the 'obese accumulation' I have to carry about me—an element, too, so obnoxious to the *National*—I can scarcely hope that, after the next editorial volley, there will be a grease-spot of me left, unless I reform, learn to drink hot-water tea, eat bread made of bran and saw-dust, half and half, and deplete fifty per cent. Let me calculate— yes, fifty per cent. That would reduce me to one hundred and twelve pounds ; so near the bulk and weight of the learned editor himself, that possibly I might recover my forfeited *caste.*

"At any rate, if this new philosophy had dawned on our benighted world forty years ago, there would have been a chance for me to make some show of activity ; but now I am doomed to the forlorn hope. I seriously apprehend that I am too old to adopt new habits of living, and conform to the new philosophy, so as to throw off the surplus 'accumulations,' and reform my 'reverend dullness.' Besides, I have some lingering scruples as to the propriety of dissenting from the Bible, which says, 'All they that be fat upon earth shall eat and worship.' (Psalm xxii, 29.) And now, after this spirited effort of the *National* to rouse the fathers in Zion from their 'dozy dignity,' and induce them to resume their youthful 'activities,' who can any longer doubt that we live in an age of progress ? I do not. But whether we are progressing upward or downward, forward or backward, is another question, and one I leave each reader to decide for himself."

At the close of the Alabama Conference, Bishop Morris took stage for Tuscaloosa, riding from Thurs-

day morning, before sunrise, until a late hour
Saturday night, without stopping, save a few minutes
for meals and changing teams. The stage was
crowded with passengers, mostly merchants and
other leading citizens of Montgomery; but their
conversation, for the most part, was so vile that it
was exceedingly painful to be compelled to hear it.
The Sabbath was spent pleasantly in Tuscaloosa.
On Monday morning, at two o'clock, the bishop again
seated himself in the coach, and was off for Nashville, a journey of four days' hard travel. Before
reaching Nashville, the stage capsized; but no one
was seriously injured, though Bishop Morris received
a sprain in one arm from which he did not wholly
recover for many weeks. Resting in Nashville until
Monday, he obtained passage home by steamboat,
and was landed in Cincinnati January 28, 1839, after
one of the most disagreeable trips of his itinerant life.

In February, Mrs. Morris was attacked with
spinal disease of a very violent character, producing
contortion of the face, from paralysis of the muscles
on one side, and attended with severe pain. The
bishop remained in her room almost constantly, day
and night, until in July, when confinement, anxiety,
and loss of sleep had so seriously affected his nervous
system that he was compelled to relax his efforts, and
commit her chiefly to the care of her nurse. She
was, however, at that time, in a hopefully convalescent
state, and was soon able to travel; when, by the
advice of his physician, the bishop took her on a
journey, by short stages, in a private conveyance,
which proved highly beneficial to her health.

September 11th, Bishop Morris presided over the Missouri Conference, at Fulton; thence to the Illinois Conference, at Bloomington, October 2d; thence to the Indiana Conference, at Lawrenceburg, October 23d, reaching home about the last of that month.

Very soon, however, it was found necessary for him to leave home again as a substitute for Bishop Roberts, who was still unable to perform active service. His route this time made it necessary to travel from Cincinnati to Augusta, Georgia, on horseback. After presiding over the Georgia Conference, which met in Augusta, December 10th, he proceeded in a "sulky" to Charleston, where the South Carolina Conference met, January 8, 1840. Finding his mode of travel inconvenient and embarrassing, he sold his horse and sulky in Charleston, and traveled by steamer to Wilmington, North Carolina, and thence by stage to Newbern, where the North Carolina Conference assembled, January 29th. From Newbern, he proceeded by steamboat and railroad to Portsmouth, Virginia; expecting to connect at that point with the steam-packet for Baltimore. But the expected packet failed to make the connection; and after waiting for its arrival several days in vain, it was finally determined to charter a small craft, a sort of a jobbing-boat, which was found lying idle at the wharf. Bishop Morris, and a few fellow-passengers as anxious as himself to get on, agreed to pay the captain of this vessel $600 if he would stipulate to carry them to Baltimore; they reserving to themselves the right of taking such other passengers as they could get, in order to reduce the expense as much as possible. The contract was made. Sixty-five persons took passage in the boat, early one morning, with the assurance of the captain that they should be landed safely in Baltimore the next morning. Soon the light craft was rolling like an eggshell. The passengers now discovered, what had before escaped their notice, that their boat had neither ballast nor freight, and that in the comparatively smooth water of the narrow channel, she was shipping water alternately on both guards. What, then, might be expected in a gale on the Chesapeake Bay? The passengers saw and felt the danger, and some went ashore at Hampton, and others at Old Point, leaving thirty-five to go through and pay the bill.

A dense fog prevailed during almost the entire trip ; and for two nights and a day no one on board could tell where the boat was, or in what direction it was going. Frequently they were fast on sandbanks, and twice without fuel, though fortunately, in both instances, a supply was soon obtained—once from a schooner, and once from the land. Finally, when the fog blew away on the third morning, they found themselves going southward along the eastern shore, exactly in the wrong direction. At last, after much difficulty in overcoming the floating ice in the bay above Annapolis, they reached a point twelve miles distant from Baltimore, where the ice was so heavy as to render navigation very hazardous ; and, to add to the general discomfort of the situation, the fuel gave out again. About dark, however, an ice-boat came along, and took off the passengers, and at midnight landed them in Baltimore.

"Never before," says the bishop, "was I so glad to feel the solid ground beneath me. Next morning I paid eighteen dollars for a seat in the mail-line to Wheeling. We were sent by rail to Frederick. The body of the coach which we took there, was full of mail-bags ; but a box for three passengers, was constructed before the mail, which we entered by climbing over the fore-wheels ; when once in that scuttle, it was like being confined in a dungeon. There I found myself packed in with two rowdies carrying a brandy-bottle, who were constantly drunk, and either singing vulgar songs, or engaged in obscene conversation, while the stench of their putrid breath was at once disgusting and sickening ; so that I was almost as glad to exchange my prison for a boat at Wheeling, as I had been to go ashore at Baltimore." From Wheeling the trip home was a quick and pleasant one, and toward the end of February the bishop found himself safely domiciled again by his own fire-side in Cincinnati.

CHAPTER VII.

GENERAL CONFERENCE OF 1840—VOLUME OF SERMONS PUB-
LISHED—EPISCOPAL TOURS.

THE General Conference of 1840 assembled in
the city of Baltimore, May 1st, and was opened
by Bishop Roberts. It was composed of one hundred and forty-three delegates, representing twenty-
eight annual conferences. The statistical exhibit of
the preceding year was as follows : White members,
650,357 ; colored members, 87,197 ; Indians, 2,249 ;
local preachers, 5,856 ; traveling preachers, 3,557 ;
total membership, 749,216. The Rev. Robert Newton was present as a representative from the Wesleyan Methodist Conference, and Rev. Joseph Stinson
as a representative from the Canada Conference.

Owing to the illness of Bishop Soule, in consequence of which he was unable to be in attendance
at the opening of the session, the Address of the
Bishops was delayed about a week. Bishop Clark,
in his " Life and Times of Hedding," says of this
address : " It is a document of great length, very
diffuse and circumlocutory, especially some portions
of it ; but it touches upon all the varied general interests of the Church, and especially the agitations
that had existed, and the new questions that had been

mooted, relating to the prerogatives of bishops, presiding elders, etc."

One of the most important questions of administration in the preceding quadrennium, and out of which had grown much discussion and no little ill-feeling, was in respect to the power of the bishops to decide points of law, and to refuse to put questions to vote which, in their judgment, involved an infraction of the Constitution of the Church. This question was considered at great length in the Episcopal Address, and the matter referred to a Committee. The following, which was adopted by the Conference, was the final report of the Committee: " 1. That it is the province of the bishop to decide all questions of law in an annual conference, subject to an appeal to the General Conference; but in all cases the application of law is with the conference. 2. That it belongs to the president of a quarterly-meeting to decide all questions of law in the quarterly-meeting conference, subject to an appeal to the president of the next annual conference; but in all cases the application of the law shall be with the conference."

The Conference also decided that the president of an annual or a quarterly-meeting conference had a right to decline putting a motion to vote if he considered it foreign to the proper business of a conference, or inconsistent with constitutional provisions; and also to adjourn a conference without a formal vote.

The questions of Slavery and Abolitionism were discussed, with the usual display of feeling on both sides; but no important action was taken on either subject. The time of the Conference was mainly occupied with the consideration of a variety of important interests, embracing Sunday-schools, Missions, Bible Distribution, Colonization, Temperance, Administration of Discipline, and other questions of minor importance.

"I went to that Conference," says Bishop Morris, " intending to resign my office, and submitted to my colleagues, and a few other intimate friends, a paper which I had drawn up in view of that determination." We find on the back of this paper the following indorsement :

"*Baltimore, June* 5, 1840.—By the advice of the bishops, and a few other brethren, this paper was withheld from the General Conference, for fear of producing excitement, without accomplishing the desired object ; but I retain it as a faithful record of my views and feelings. Whether the advice was good or not, time may prove. Lord help me to be faithful !

" T. A. M."

This document, much as the whole Church will rejoice that it was withheld, will be read with interest, as containing "a faithful record of the views and feelings" of its revered author. It is as follows :

"*To the Bishops and Delegates of the Several Annual Conferences, in General Conference Assembled:*

" REVEREND AND DEAR BRETHREN,—Unaccustomed to speak in General Conference, I avail myself of this method of addressing you on a subject which is to me of the utmost importance ; and although it is not to be expected that you will feel as I do respecting it, yet in view of the relations I sustain to the general work, about whose interests you have met to confer, I trust you will have the goodness to favor me with a candid and patient hearing.

"The object of this communication is to tender to you, in a formal manner, the resignation of my episcopal office, which I now do, not only in good faith and with the utmost sincerity, but also with an ardent desire and humble hope that it may be accepted.

"For taking this step, it will doubtless be expected of me to render some reason; with which expectation I will now most cheerfully comply. My course is not influenced by any doubt of the propriety of the office itself, by any conscientious scruples which interfere with the execution of its duties, or by any want of confidence in my brethren. My reasons may be briefly summed up thus: A conviction of mind that I am not qualified for the work, and therefore not in my proper place. My election to the office was contrary both to my wish and expectation. I had done all that seemed prudent, in order to prevent that election; it was, however, eventually effected. I regret now that I did not offer my resignation before my consecration.

"The reasons why I did not were these: 1. A fear of embarrassing the Conference by declining the appointment which was given me at a late period of its session. 2. A fear of breaking my ordination vow to 'to act in all things as a son in the Gospel.' For many years I had generally received the decisions of the Church in my case as indications of the order of Providence concerning me and my work,

and it was only in that view of the subject that my
conscience suffered me, on my examination, to answer
in the affirmative the first question proposed.

" Still the Methodist Episcopal Church sets up
no claim to infallibility; and I mean no disrespect
when I add, the General Conference may have erred
in the selection of an officer. Under all these circumstances of the case, I concluded, though with
much hesitancy, that it might be safe for me to make
a trial to do the work assigned me. I have done so ;
and the result of four years' experiment is a confirma-
tion of the conviction with which I commenced the
work, that I am not qualified for it ; that I have not
the knowledge, wisdom, faith, holiness, patience, moral
courage, and general weight of character, requisite to
fill such an office as the general superintendency of our
extended connection. And, more especially, I do not
feel competent to preside, so as to maintain proper
order in the conferences, and decide the numerous
questions of an intricate character which are referred
to me for decision, and often without time for reflection. It is true the brethren have shown me much
kindness, respect, and forbearance. In all these
virtues they have not only exceeded my expectations,
but commended themselves to my confidence and
gratitude.

" But these indications of goodness, however grateful to my feelings, have not removed the consciousness
of my own failures in performing properly many of
the duties of my responsible office. When I speak
of failures in this connection, I do not mean willful
neglect of work, but failures in performing it for

want of more skill and courage. My conscience bears me witness that in general I have done what I could, and as well as I could, under the circumstances, so far as my official acts are concerned. To accomplish the work given me to do, I have not only made a continual sacrifice of spiritual privileges and domestic comforts, but I have risked my life more than once, and in more ways than one. The reason of my doing so was, that I did not feel at liberty to throw off the responsibility which the General Conference had laid upon me; nor can I now, without your consent.

"You alone have authority to relieve me, and to you I appeal. I have borne the office of a general superintendent as a constant burden, under which I have sometimes well-nigh fainted. I now lay that burden at your feet, and pray you not to replace it upon me. Here I would not be misunderstood. For all I enjoy in this life, and hope for in the life to come, I am indebted, under God, to the Methodist Episcopal Church. She could always have done well enough without me; but I never could, and can not now, do without her; and in her communion I wish to live and die. Moreover, I have no wish to leave her itinerancy; for, however unworthy of the place, I am well persuaded the Lord has called me to the work of a traveling minister. But I do most respectfully request and humbly beg that you will accept my resignation as general superintendent.

"In making this request, I trust I am not criminally selfish; that I am not actuated exclusively by a desire to be relieved on my own account, but also for the good of the Church, being fully persuaded there are others who could do the work better, and do it, too, with less difficulty than I can. And if I did not believe that the General Conference could constitutionally and safely grant my request, I would not make it. I am no advocate of High Church notions ; nor do I think that, because a brother is appointed a Methodist superintendent, he must necessarily continue such during life or good behavior, whether he is adapted to the work or not. The appointment of an untried officer is an experiment, which may or may not succeed ; and when such appointment is found to be injudicious, it should be changed.

" My dear brethren, do not suppose that in this matter I have been hasty, for I am only executing a purpose of mind which has been maturing for more than three years ; though, from prudential considerations, I have said but little respecting it among the brethren. Finally, I do not wish to hurry the Conference in my case ; but nothing less than direct action on the main question of accepting my resignation, before the final adjournment, will satisfy my mind.

" Yours, in Christian bonds,

" THOMAS A. MORRIS.

" BALTIMORE, *May*, 1840."

In this paper the modesty, humility, and conscientiousness which were throughout his life characteristic of Bishop Morris, are very strikingly displayed. We may easily suppose that the conclusion at which he arrived was reached slowly and prayerfully, and that it must have required very cogent reasoning on the part of his colleagues and brethren to induce him

to relinquish a purpose which had been so long maturing in his mind. Probably no posthumous paper
of this honored servant of God will tend more to increase the admiration of the Church for his pure and
unselfish character than this "withheld resignation."

After the adjournment of General Conference,
Bishop Morris presided over the Pittsburg Conference, at Clarksburg, Virginia, July 15th ; the Kentucky, at Bardstown, October 14th ; the Holston, at
Walker C. H., Georgia, November 11th ; the North
Carolina, at Mocksville, December 23d ; the Virginia,
at Lynchburg, January 13, 1841 ; the Baltimore, in
the city of Baltimore, February 10, 1841 ; reaching
his home in Cincinnati in the latter part of March.

The Summer of that year was devoted to the
preparation of a volume of sermons for the press ; a
work which he prosecuted with such industry that it
was issued in the Fall of the same year. His reasons
for submitting a book of sermons to the public are
thus stated in the Preface :

"The want of a small volume of instructive discourses on various religious subjects, suited in matter,
manner, and cost to our people, and especially in the
West, has long been felt by them ; particularly as we
have no such work on the catalogue of books printed
and sold at our Book Concern. The Methodist Episcopal Church abounds in periodicals, biography, and
history ; but not in sermons of her own authorship.
Perhaps one reason of this is, Mr. Wesley's sermons
are supposed by many to supersede the necessity of
all others among us. I am perfectly free to admit
they are the best ever written, or that probably ever

will be written; still that work is too voluminous and costly to meet the case of those for whom this is more especially designed. Besides, it is not clear to my mind that all the sermons made in America, having a special adaptation to the state of society here, should die with their authors, without ever appearing in print, merely because superior ones for general purposes have been imported. There are in all communities some peculiarities which are best understood by the ministers who serve them. The Book Committee at Cincinnati, including the editors, have several times officially requested the preparation of such a work as this is designed to be, while the Agents of the Book Concern, and other brethren in the West, have for years kindly encouraged the undertaking; and hence, hoping it might do some good, I finally, though with much fear and trembling, consented to make the attempt."

The sermons, forty in number, and embracing a wide range of topics, are admirable specimens of the plain, pointed, and vigorous style of the author. In preaching, as in writing, he studiously avoids difficult and unusual words, adhering, as nearly as possible, to Scriptural phraseology. The volume has passed through many editions already, and will doubtless occupy a permanent place among the sermon literature of the Church.

On the 6th of August, 1841, Bishop Morris took stage for Indianapolis, Indiana; thence he journeyed in an open wagon through Logansport, Laporte, and Michigan City, to Chicago. Exposure to an August sun by day, and to the heavy dews of the night,

brought on a bilious attack, which delayed him in
Chicago several days. Having sufficiently recovered
his strength to resume the road, he proceeded to
Plattesville, Wisconsin, where he presided over the
Rock-river Conference, August 25th; thence to the
Illinois Conference, which met September 15th, at
Jacksonville; thence to the Missouri Conference,
which met October 6th, at Palmyra.

From the seat of the Missouri Conference, the bishop
proceeded to St. Louis, for the purpose of organizing
a party to proceed on to Texas together. The company consisted of Rev. John Clark, his wife and son
John, about nine years old; Rev. Josiah W. Whipple,
and Bishop Morris. Messrs. Clark and Whipple were
regular itinerant Methodist preachers, noble and
courageous spirits, who had, a year previously, volun-
teered to go as regular transfers from the Rock-river to
the Texas Conference, for the sole purpose of preaching the Gospel in that new and interesting Republic.
This little party had one covered wagon, hung on
elliptic springs, with baggage-racks, and all the necessary fixtures to render it a convenient and comfortable traveling wagon for a family. This wagon, drawn
by two stout horses, was occupied by Mr. and Mrs.
Clark, Mr. Whipple, and about five hundred pounds
of luggage. There was, in addition, a light buggy,
drawn by one horse, occupied by the bishop, the little
boy, and a quantity of light articles for every-day use
on the journey. The outfit for the trip—arranged by
Mr. Clark, who had labored some years as a missionary
among the Indians at Green Bay, and was accustomed
to journey through desolate regions—embraced a

marquee, or linen tent, glass lamp, ax, hammer, frying-pan, tea-kettle, coffee-mill, patent coffee-boiler, water-bucket, provision-basket, plates, knives and forks, spoons, etc.

The party left St. Louis on Tuesday, October 19th, passed the village of Carondelet, and, about fifteen miles from the city, crossed the Merrimack River. About ten miles further on they were kindly entertained for the night by a Mr. Hunt and family, whom the bishop had known on Marietta Circuit, Ohio Conference, in 1817. The next day they passed through Herculaneum, a village on the west bank of the Mississippi River, and above the mouth of a creek, which they crossed on an old ferry-boat. Passing on nine miles over a very difficult road, they reached the residence of Dr. Steel, where they dined ; and the bishop baptized a child of German parents, who resided in the neighborhood. In the afternoon they were able to make but seventeen miles, and were fortunate enough to meet a kind reception and find excellent entertainment for the night with a Mrs. Poston, a member of the Methodist Church, as were also her son and daughter. Our travelers found much difficulty in that part of Missouri in knowing what course to take from time to time, as there were seldom any guide-boards at the numerous forks of the roads.

The next day they hastened on to Farmington, thirteen miles, expecting to meet a congregation ; but, finding that the meeting had been postponed till night with a view to obtain a better congregation, they accepted the proffered hospitality of Mr. David

Murphy, a Methodist who had resided on his farm
adjoining the village about thirty years, and who, in
the afternoon, entertained his guests with many interesting anecdotes of Bishop M'Kendree and Rev.
Jesse Walker, who had often made his house a
resting-place after their excessive toils in that new
country. While waiting here, they also met Rev. Job
Lawrence, deacon elect, and the bishop consecrated
him to that office in due form. The evening proved
a stormy one, and the bishop preached a short
sermon to a small congregation in a very dimly
lighted Presbyterian church.

Leaving Farmington next day, Friday, October
22d, they pushed on to Fredericktown, Madison
County, where a "two-days' meeting" had been appointed in view of the expected episcopal visit.
Among the acquaintances made here were the Hon.
Judge Cook, Presiding Judge of the district, and Mr.
Davis, a respectable member of the bar, who were in
attendance upon the Circuit Court then in session,
and which adjourned Saturday night. They were
both Methodists, exerting a most salutary influence
in that region, and "affording additional evidence,"
in the words of Bishop Morris, "that gentlemen of
the green-bag profession may be experimental and
practical Christians." While many others who had
been in attendance at the court left for their homes
on Sabbath morning, these two gentlemen remained,
and worshiped all day, like Christians who knew
their duty and appreciated their privileges.

Leaving Fredericktown early on Monday morning,
our travelers pursued their journey without any

special or noteworthy incident, until Thursday night, when, for the first time, they had an opportunity to try how well they could entertain themselves over night. About dark they reached a beautiful tributary stream of Black River, and pitched their tent under a large cypress-tree growing on its bank. After taking off the horses and securing them to the trees, Mr. Clark, by means of his flint and steel, soon made a fire; and while the others were adjusting the tent and gathering fuel, Mrs. Clark prepared a good supper, which was served in genuine camp-style, and greatly enjoyed by the entire company. The ground was rather damp for comfortable sleeping, in consequence of rain that day; but they spread down buffalo-skins and blankets, using carriage-cushions for pillows, partitioned off the tent into two apartments, and at the hour of evening sacrifice had family worship, and slept in peace and safety until morning. Before leaving " Camp Cypress " next morning, curiosity led them to run a line around the trunk of the stately tree under whose branches they had rested, when it was found to be twenty-four feet in circumference.

While here they saw, for the first time on this journey, large flocks of paroquets passing over and occasionally lighting on the trees around them. They are a small species of parrot, something less than pigeons; with plumage mostly green, but exhibiting all the colors of the rainbow. Their greatest strength is in their yellow, hooked beak, with which they can sever small branches from fruit-trees. They are noisy birds, but their notes are not melodious. On account of their great beauty they are often domesticated, which is easily done.

On Friday morning, October 29th, our travelers crossed the Missouri line into Arkansas, crossed the Current River in a ferry-boat, and in the evening camped about fifteen miles beyond the river, on the bank of a large creek called Fourche de Mass. The evening was mild and calm, the full moon shone brightly, the camp-fire blazed cheerily, and all the party were in excellent spirits. Their bill of fare included warm corn hoe-cakes, fried ham, eggs, sweet potatoes, butter, coffee, and Boston crackers—an exhibit which certainly reflects great credit on the commissariat of the little party. Their design was to reach Jackson the next day, and preach there on Sabbath; but Providence ordered otherwise. About midnight the weather changed, and a gale sprang up, bringing with it clouds and rain, which pelted their thin habitation the rest of the night, and nearly the whole of the ensuing day, so that they could scarcely leave the tent at all without getting wet. Here, and in this condition, they expected to remain till Monday. Mr. Whipple started out on horseback to explore the neighborhood, with a view to collecting a congregation on the Sabbath. While he was gone, Mr. Clark chopped wood, to avoid the sin of gathering sticks on the Sabbath; but when, after much hard toil, he had secured an ample supply, Mr. Whipple returned, and with him came a Mr. Spikes, a Methodist, and a native of North Carolina, who lived in the neighborhood. At his urgent request, Camp Fourche de Mass was broken up, and the party, with some difficulty, made their

way through mud and darkness to the old gentleman's hospitable home, three miles off. The
incessant showers of rain on Sabbath made it impracticable to gather a congregation. On Monday it
was deemed prudent to lie by, in order to dry the
tent, and replenish the store of provisions. Mr.
Whipple went to mill, and bought flour, which Mrs.
Clark speedily converted into bread. Meantime
one of the party, with a rifle, which constituted a
part of the outfit, made a short excursion into the
neighboring woods, and soon returned with a fine lot
of squirrels, which, being parboiled for the convenience of carrying, made an acceptable addition to the
camp provisions.

Tuesday, November 2d, they crossed a small,
rapid river called Eleven Pines, and in the afternoon
passed through Jackson, a small town, formerly the
seat of justice for Lawrence County. A mile and a
half beyond this town, they camped, on the north
bank of Spring River. Next morning, some time was
lost getting the horses shod ; and when a start was
finally made, they had gone but a few miles when a
halt was called on the discovery being made that the
tea-kettle was missing. A messenger sent back soon
recovered that important piece of culinary furniture ;
but owing to these delays but seventeen miles were
gained by midday. Passing on through Smithville,
the new county-seat of Lawrence County, they
camped in the evening on the south bank of Straw-
berry Creek.

On Friday, November 5th, they reached Batesville, the seat of the Arkansas Conference, met a

warm reception, and found excellent accommodation among Christian friends.

The Arkansas Conference commenced its Sixth Session November 10th, in the court-house, the same building in which it first organized in 1836. Very few of the original members remained. In the short space of five years, most of these had disappeared from the roll by death, location, and other causes; but their places had been supplied, and the Conference had nearly doubled its numbers since its organization. Their geographical boundary was extensive; embracing the State of Arkansas, the Missouri Territory south of the Cherokee line, and a fraction of the north-east corner of Texas. The business of the Conference was conducted with great harmony and dispatch, and a final adjournment was reached on Monday evening.

On Tuesday, the 16th, at a late hour in the morning, our traveling party left Batesville, in a cold rain. After a detention of two hours at the White-river Ferry, they finally got safely across the turbid and rapid stream, made so by recent heavy rains. In the evening they sought and found a retired spot, off the road, for their camp, with a view to escape the pigs, which had been very troublesome on previous occasions. They found a suitable place on the north bank of the Sally Doe—a name suggested by a singular occurrence. Among the pioneers of the country was a heroine named Sally, who, observing a female deer in the water, stood on the bank, and with a gun killed it; from which achievement the settlers agreed to name the creek Sally Doe. Wednesday afternoon they crossed Little Red River, at Crolman's Ferry, thirty-two miles from Batesville. This is a deep, rapid stream, about ten or twelve rods wide. After leaving this stream, they inquired at every house they passed for corn, but could find no one who had any to sell until they reached the cabin of an old settler on Indian Creek, who furnished them a bushel and a half for a dollar. On Saturday they crossed the Arkansas River in a steam ferry-boat, and arrived at the capital of the State, Little Rock, where they met a hearty Christian welcome. On Sabbath, the bishop preached to a good congregation in the Methodist Church, and after sermon administered the sacrament of the Lord's-supper.

On Monday, the 22d of November, the party left Little Rock by the military road, leading off in a southwest direction. Very soon they entered an extensive forest of pitch-pine—the trees tall and straight, and many of them quite large. Six miles from the capital they passed the cabin in which Bishop Morris had slept in 1836, the night before he entered the forty-mile wilderness, on his way to the Mississippi Conference. On Tuesday they reached Benton, the seat of justice for Saline County, where the bishop preached to a small congregation, hastily collected, in the court-house.

Wednesday brought them to Washita River, a hundred and fifty yards wide, which was crossed on a ferry-boat, at about noon. After partaking of their luncheon on the south bank of this stream, they again resumed the road, and soon entered the "Twelve-mile Stretch," so called because for that distance the road passes over pine hills so poor that no one lives near it. Having penetrated this wilderness four or five miles, they found a running brook named Bayou de Sale, and pitched their tent. At half-past eight o'clock that evening a violent storm of wind and rain broke upon them, attended with sharp lightning and heavy thunder. For some time before this storm reached them, they heard its distant, awful roar among the pine-trees, and experienced something of the terrific grandeur of a hurricane at night in an un-broken forest. When, at last, it reached them, it "smote the four corners" of their tabernacle, the tent-pins gave way, and the cloth twisted up into a whirling heap around the occupants, and would doubtless have gone off with the wind, had not the men thrown their whole weight upon it. Before the tent could be readjusted, the entire company was thoroughly wet, and not till midnight were they sufficiently dried to lie down and sleep comfortably.

At the south end of this "Stretch" they came, on Thursday morning, to Bayou de Roche, which, as its name is intended to express, is remarkably stony in the channel and on either shore. A few miles brought them to another rapid little river, called Fourche Caddo, and, as it was turning cold, they stopped, started a fire by which to warm and eat, and then hastened on. That evening they turned off the road to the right, and after proceeding about one hundred yards down a small brook in quest of a suita-ble camping-place, the bishop's buggy, in which was the bag of corn, suddenly broke down. "The fore axle-tree, both wood and iron, gave way at the king-bolt,

and let me down softly," he says, "within one rod of.
where we judged best, upon thorough examination, to build our fire." As the buggy must of course
be repaired, they lost one day by the necessary detention, remaining for two cold nights at "Camp Mishap."

Saturday morning they again set out on their
journey. The weather had now become quite cold;
it froze all day, was windy, cloudy, and unpleasant;
but they pushed on, and reached Wolf's Creek by
night, where they had agreed to spend the Sabbath
and hold religious service. As the chapel here was
considered the best then in the southern part of
Arkansas, Bishop Morris's description of it will be
read with interest. "The walls," he says, "are made
of hewed logs, about twenty by twenty-four feet in
extent, with a wooden chimney in one end, and a
place cut out for a chimney at the other end, which
is partly closed up with slabs. In the front is a
large door, with a center-post and double shutters,
on the principle of a barn-door. Immediately opposite, on the other side, is a pulpit, which projects
some six feet from the wall, the forepart of which is
so high that when the preacher kneels to pray he is
nearly concealed from the view of the people. Behind this pulpit is a window without glass, the
shutter of which is neither long enough nor wide
enough to close it, and, consequently, it lets in a
double stream of air upon the preacher. The roof
is made of clapboards, between which and the floor
there is no ceiling, though there are some naked
poles laid across on the plates; and the cracks
between the logs are neither chinked nor daubed; and

though they were once partially closed by nailing on thin boards, these have been mostly torn off to afford light and a free circulation of air."

Here Bishop Morris preached in the morning. He says, "We had truly a chilly time, physically and spiritually." In the evening, the people kindled a large fire in the front yard, and when they got too cold to sit in comfort, they would go out to the fire, warm, and return.

Leaving Wolf's Creek on Monday morning, they crossed the Little Missouri River, and encountered nothing worthy of remark, except remarkably bad roads, until next morning, when they entered the town of Washington, Hemstead County, a place of neat appearance, compactly built, and one of the largest in the State. It contained, however, no Methodist Church at that time, and the bishop preached to a good congregation in the court-house. While the rest of the party tarried in Washington, Bishop Morris, Mr. Clark, and the presiding elder of the district, Mr. Gregory, made a visit to Columbus, a village about ten miles distant, and conferred deacons' orders on three local preachers—one of whom had carried a certificate of election twenty-two years without an opportunity of presenting it.

The following Sabbath was spent in Spring Hill. The village, though it numbered among its inhabitants several wealthy planters, and boasted an academy, had no church of any kind. Preaching services were conducted in the academy, where a fine, attentive congregation assembled to hear the Word.

Monday night they camped in the woods, and next morning entered a wilderness of about thirty miles without a house. They had proceeded but a few miles in this wilderness, when they were startled by the keen crack of a rifle. Soon a buck was seen flying across the road, as if wounded, and immediately after a young Indian, in hunting costume, attended by a well-trained dog, appeared on the scene. Presently his father and mother—it was supposed—with some younger children, came up with a train of small ponies, packed with skins and meat, in real hunter style. This was a family of Choctaws, returning from their Fall hunt. Had our travelers been men of leisure and fond of the gun, the temptation would have been strong to stop here for a few days ; but they had other and more important business in view than hunting deer, bear, or wild cattle. Indeed, they must pass the wilderness that day, or let their horses suffer for grain. After a hard day's drive, they reached Dorcheat, a bayou some forty yards wide, and camped for the night. An old settler was, with some persuasion, induced to part with a bushel of corn for two dollars.

On Wednesday, December 8th, they entered Claiborne Parish, Louisiana, and in the evening passed what was called on the maps Allen's Settlement, but they could see nothing of it except Mr. Allen's field and cabin. A mile and a half beyond this "settlement" they halted for the night, pitching their tent on a spot which afforded so many conveniences and comforts, that by common consent it was named Camp Felicity. The ground was handsome, water good, fuel abundant and convenient.

On Saturday, about noon, they passed a camp of Indian hunters. Their ponies, each with a tinkling bell about his neck, were grazing ; an old Indian was lying in camp on his stomach, resting his chin on his hands, while two squaws were hard at work, and a few children were playing around the fire ; the hunters being probably on the chase. Nine miles beyond this camp—which distance was passed without seeing a house—they reached a house of entertainment, kept by a Methodist, where they remained till Monday, preaching on Sabbath in a log chapel in the neighborhood, to about twenty persons. They could not complain, however, of the size of the congregation ; for it included, they were assured, the whole neighborhood.

The journey for the next four or five days was barren of incidents. On Friday, the 17th, they reached the Sabine River, at Gaines's Ferry, crossed over, and were within the limits of the "Lone Star Republic." In a short time they arrived at that interesting part of Texas called the "Red Lands," which was thickly settled and well improved. Their first night in the Republic was passed in their tent, near a pure fountain of excellent spring-water. Whatever they desired for themselves or horses was readily obtained here, and on reasonable terms, compared with the rates which had been exacted for similar articles in Arkansas and Louisiana. The night was cool, but clear, and so perfectly calm that the smoke went up from the hickory-log fire as straight as if it had passed through a chimney. After a first-rate camp supper, they spent the evening in their quiet habitation in the wilderness, in peace and contentment, singing occasionally the songs of Zion—though it *was* in a strange land—among others, the "Jubilee of the Israelites," and with some emphasis when they came to the words,—

"Though Baca's vale be dry, and the land yield no supply,
  To a land of corn and wine we'll go on, we'll go on," etc.

On Saturday evening they reached San Augustine, the seat of justice for the county of the same name, and one of the largest towns in Texas, though the population was then scarcely a thousand souls. Here the Texas Conference assembled on the 23d of December. Most of the members were present; two only being absent. There had been no deaths among them during the year; but some of the first band of missionaries were nearly worn out by hard work and exposure. The Conference was re-enforced by four transferred, one readmitted, and three young men admitted on trial. The whole number of names on the Minutes was twenty-three, including seven probationers. The Texas Mission had been instituted four years previously—in 1837; since when it had grown into an annual conference with twenty-three traveling preachers, thirty-six local preachers, and a membership of two thousand seven hundred and ninety-five. The missionary meeting was held on Monday night. The amount collected, in cash, was seventy-four dollars; after which, one gave four town lots; another, fifteen lots; another, one hundred acres of land; two others, three hundred and twenty acres each ; and another, a quarter of a league.

On the 30th of December, the bishop set out for Austin, distant from San Augustine three hundred and fifty miles. Journeying slowly along, partly from necessity, and partly with a view to preach wherever an opportunity offered, he reached the town of Washington, January 13, 1842, where he stopped to visit the grave of Dr. Ruter, the apostle of Methodism in Texas, who died at his post, May 16, 1838.

Rev. Martin Ruter, D. D., was born April 3, 1783, in Charleston, Massachusetts, of pious parents. When not more than three years of age, according to his own testimony, he had serious impressions, which increased with his years until 1799, when he resolved to become a Christian, and soon after experienced the forgiveness of sins, and united with the Methodist Episcopal Church. Impressed deeply that it would be his duty to preach the Gospel, he turned his attention to close and careful study of Divinity. In his fifteenth year he was licensed to exhort, and a year later (1801) was admitted on trial into the New York Conference, and appointed to Chesterfield Circuit. In 1818, the Asbury College, in Baltimore, conferred on him the degree of Master of Arts. In 1820 he was sent, by the General Conference, to conduct the business of the Western Book Concern, then established in Cincinnati. In 1822, the Transylvania University, of Kentucky, conferred on him the degree of Doctor of Divinity. He was re-elected to the Book Agency by the General Conference of 1824 ; but before the expiration of his second term he was

called to the presidency of Augusta College, which
office he held about four years. We find him next
stationed in Pittsburg, engaged in the more active
and congenial duties of the pastorate; whence, however, he was soon called to Meadville to preside over
the Alleghany College. This office he filled with
much credit to himself, and great advantage to the
University, until the Summer of 1837, when he resigned his chair for the purpose of undertaking the
superintendence of the mission just established in
Texas.

Dr. Ruter was no ordinary man. Though his
early advantages were only such as a common-school
education afforded, yet in the itinerant field he became a literary man, well versed in languages,
science, and history. In the pulpit he was solid,
grave, warm, and dignified.

"The mournful spot I sought for," says Bishop
Morris, "was easily found without a guide; the grave
being inclosed by a stone wall, and covered with a
white marble slab, three feet wide and six long, with
a suitable inscription. As we stood under a tree
which grew at the foot of the grave, reading the solemn epitaph, the sun was disappearing in the West,
while a thousand thoughts of the past rushed upon
our minds, and forcibly reminded us that our own
days would soon be past. With Dr. Ruter I had
often united in preaching the Gospel to crowded assemblies in Ohio and Kentucky. He now rests from
all his toil, enjoying the promised reward."

CHAPTER VIII.

ON leaving Washington, the course of Bishop Morris led him through Independence, a little east of which he gained the most commanding elevation, perhaps, in the Republic. Standing on a most lovely eminence, the eye rested on a landscape of surpassing loveliness, interspersed with clumps of evergreens, grazing herds, cultivated fields, and meandering streams ; the whole scene filling the mind of the beholder with sensations of admiration and pleasure. Near Independence he tarried two days with Dr. Hoxey, preaching in an academy, which was occupied in common by all the religious denominations, as there was no church in the village or neighborhood. The country about here the bishop pronounced the best he had seen in Texas.

Passing on westward from Independence, the route led him through scenery of great beauty, and even grandeur, for two days. Wednesday, January 19th, he reached Rutersville, in Fayette County— a village situated on an elevated prairie, five miles from the Colorado River, distinguished chiefly by the location of Rutersville College, in its immediate vicinity. The enterprise probably originated with Dr. Ruter, during his short but useful missionary career in Texas. A Preparatory Department was opened in 1840, and had, at the time of Bishop Morris's visit, about eighty students. On Sunday, January 23d, the bishop preached in the College chapel to a very large and attentive congregation.

Resuming his travels on Monday morning, he passed up the Colorado River twenty-five miles, and was kindly entertained by Mr. Middleton Hill. Next day it turned quite cold, and he set out in a drizzling rain, which made traveling extremely uncomfortable. But he was met, during the day, by Mr. Whipple, and together they crossed the river, and pressed onward, making the best of their untoward circumstances. By night they reached a delightful neighborhood, which had grown up around a small but lovely prairie, where they were handsomely entertained. That night the Indians, who had been for some nights collecting a drove of horses in a pen on Cedar Creek, visited a house in sight of the one in which they lodged, and stole five horses, besides a considerable number on the opposite side of the river. Next day, Bishop Morris preached at Bastrop, under the roar of artillery; the signal for collecting minute-men to go in pursuit of the Indians.

On Thursday afternoon, January 27th, they arrived at the country residence of Judge Webb, two miles from the city of Austin, a remarkably pleasant and inviting situation, in the midst of a grove of live-oaks, on a handsome eminence. Here

the bishop spent several days very pleasantly with
the judge and his family, and also had the pleasure
of meeting his own son, who had then resided in
Texas for three years.

In consequence of a severe cold which had settled on his lungs, he was unable to preach in Austin,
much to the disappointment of the society there.
In fact, he made but one visit to the city during his
stay in the neighborhood, and that was on Sunday
morning to hear a sermon by Mr. Clark, the presiding elder of the district. The location of the capital of the short-lived Republic, at Austin, did not
seem to strike the bishop as a very judicious one.
"The arguments in favor of the location of the
capital," he says, "must be chiefly drawn from considerations of beauty, romance, and solitude; for between it and the populated part of the country, there
is no connecting ligament, but a narrow string of
settlements along the Colorado. To reach Austin
City from Galveston requires a journey of two hundred and seventy-five miles; and to reach it from the
Sabine, on the east, requires a journey of about four
hundred. It may be geographically central, but it
certainly is not so to the inhabited parts of the
Republic."

On Monday, January 31st, the bishop turned his
face homeward, traveling in Mr. Clark's buggy until
he reached Houston, where he and his son took
passage on a steamer for Galveston. They reached
that city the next morning, whence, after resting a
few days, they steamed across the Gulf to New
Orleans, and with as little delay as possible

proceeded up the Mississippi River, reaching Cincinnati March 1, 1842.

From this long, difficult, and dangerous episcopal tour Bishop Morris returned to his home to find his beloved wife in rapidly declining health. At the time of his departure she was supposed to be improving, with a fair prospect of recovery; but during his absence the inflammation had gone from the spine to the lungs, and the disease baffled every attempt to arrest or remove it. She lingered until May 17th, when she joyfully entered that rest which remaineth for the people of God. From a sketch of this "elect lady," prepared for the *Ladies' Repository*, by Rev. Dr. (afterward Bishop) Hamline, we gather some particulars of her life and character.

Mrs. Abigail Morris was the daughter of Mr. Nathaniel Scales, and was born in Patrick County, Virginia, January, 18, 1793. Her early associates were not religious, but rather of that class who place a higher estimate on the gayeties of the world than upon a life of piety. When about twenty years of age, however, she became sensible of her lost state ·as a sinner, sought and obtained evidence of pardoning mercy, and united with the Methodist Episcopal Church. She was married to Mr. (afterward Bishop) Morris, January, 23, 1814. Very soon after this union, a great and unexpected trial came upon her. During the latter part of the first year of her married life, her husband began to feel that it was his duty to devote himself to the ministry in the itinerant ranks. Western itinerancy in those days presented so many difficulties, and threatened so

much privation to the family of the preacher, and
especially to one brought up as she had been, that
the prospect was not only disheartening, but to a
sensitive female overwhelming.   We have already
related, in the former part of this work, how, in the
Fall of 1815, while suffering under a severe attack
of intermittent fever, Mrs. Morris was led to yield a
hearty assent to her husband's desire to obey what
he felt to be a Divine impression.   This assent, fully
and heartily given, was never recalled.   When her
husband, discouraged by slender support for his
family, or want of success in his Master's business,
would talk of locating, she always dissuaded him from
it, lest some worse thing should come upon them for
deserting a work to which they had been so signally
called.

"For more than thirty years," says Bishop Hamline, "she was an orderly, living member of the
Church ; and for more than twenty-six years suffered
the privations incident to the itinerant work, patiently sharing its toils and anxieties, as they fall
upon the family of the traveling preacher.   While
health permitted, she was exceedingly active and useful in the work of the Lord, as a leader of female
prayer-meetings, visiting the sick, and exhorting all
with whom she had influence to flee the wrath to come.
When she had strength to speak in the love-feast,
the effect was often felt throughout the house, in an
unusual manner.

"Mrs. Morris was a great sufferer from sickness.
Few persons ever lived through greater afflictions
than she did during the last twenty-five years of her

life. Among the instances of her extreme suffering, the severest previous to her last sickness was in 1839, from spinal and neuralgic affection, whereby she was confined to her bed nearly six months, most of the time in extreme agony. This brought her apparently to the gate of death. But the grace of God was so manifested to her in that affliction, that the more she suffered, the more she rejoiced; and the nearer death seemed to approach, the more she triumphed through faith in Christ Jesus. Contrary to the expectations of herself, her physician, and friends, she was partially restored, and was able to go about for two years.

"In November, 1841, she took a severe cold, which fell on her lungs, followed with much pain, great soreness in the chest, a stubborn cough, night-sweats, and loss of flesh and strength; so that, by midwinter, she was confined to the bed. Bishop Morris was then in Texas, where he failed to receive letters from home, and knew nothing of her condition until he arrived at Galveston, on his return trip, in February following. He then got merely a verbal report of her illness; but on landing at New Orleans, he received letters of various dates up to February 15th, which created serious fears that he would see her no more on earth. When she embraced her husband, who had been absent nearly seven months, and her only son, whom she had not seen for three years, and never expected to see again, she exclaimed, with a tremulous voice, ' Now, Lord, I am ready to depart when it is thy will.'

"Much of the time during her last sickness her

17

faith was in lively exercise, producing the precious fruits of patience, meekness, resignation, gratitude, and love; all of which, from time to time, were abundantly manifested in her words and actions, to such an extent as could not be expected in any individual without a genuine work of grace upon the heart. Among the numerous friends that called to see her during an illness of six months' continuance, very few ever left her room without receiving from her a word of exhortation, admonition, or encouragement : and doubtless the good seed thus sown sprung up in many hearts. On one occasion, after a severe paroxysm of coughing, she said : ' O, that this might be the night of my deliverance ; that I might fly from earth and sin and sorrow, and be at rest forever !' Then, checking herself, she added, ' But I wait the Lord's pleasure.' On Saturday, the 9th of April, in the evening, she said, ' Such a sweet peace came into my mind this afternoon, that I trust never to doubt again that the Lord will sustain me to the end.' "

On the 26th of April, as the doctor retired from her room, she overheard him say that she had failed much since he saw her last. Referring to this soon after, she said, "It caused joy to spring up in my heart." A day or two later, she said to a friend, " I enjoy a sweet prospect of deliverence from all my sufferings." And again, " My soul is blessed of the Lord—it surely is ; and if I had a thousand souls, I would trust them all in his hands."

On the morning of the first Sabbath in May, she said, " I am feeble in body, but rejoice in spirit."

She then knew it to be the general opinion of her friends that she could not live more than a day or two longer; and, lest her strength should fail her, she that day had the family called to her one at a time, and gave her blessing to each, charging them severally to live for God, and meet her in heaven. This was probably one of the most moving scenes of the kind ever witnessed. She said, among other things, the Lord had often blessed her in health and in sickness, and he then blessed her in prospect of death; that for her death had no sting; that she had never felt such a sense of the goodness of God before; that she had often feared the affection she had for her family would render it difficult at last to give them up; but she thanked God that his grace that day had enabled her to do it willingly and cheerfully, and leave them in his hands, who would provide for them all needful blessings.

In the evening she continued in the same happy frame of mind. "Sweet heaven!" she exclaimed, "my happy home! O, how I long to be there! But my Father's will be done." On the 12th, at three o'clock in the morning, there was such a sinking, coldness, and difficulty of breathing, that she herself believed death had commenced his work; and when asked how she felt under the impression that she was so near her end, the reply was: "I feel delightful. Jesus is my everlasting friend, and will bear me safely through the dark valley of death."

On Saturday morning, May 14th, in the midst of great agony, she prayed for patience to suffer all the will of God. After severe coughing and strangling, she said, "It will soon be over; blessed be God for it! and I pray that the chariot of salvation may not delay." In the afternoon of that day, her physician, Dr. Judkins, to whom she was much attached, called to see her for the last time. She asked him if he did think the struggle would soon be over. On his making an affirmative reply, she said, with a smile, "That is good news." The next morning, it being the Sabbath, she was heard to say: "O Lord, thou art so good! Precious Savior! Blessed Redeemer! O, the rich fountain of redeeming love, in which I shall soon bathe my weary soul forever!" That night her mind became wandering; in which state, for the most part, she continued till Tuesday morning, May 17th, when she expired.

Impressive funeral services were held on Thursday, the 19th, in the Fourth-street Methodist Episcopal Church, Rev. Leroy Swormstedt preaching an appropriate sermon, from the words, "Into thine hand I commit my spirit; thou hast redeemed me, O Lord God of truth." (Psalm xxxi, 5.)

A wife, who for more than a quarter of a century shared in the toils and privations of a pioneer itinerant minister, contributing to his usefulness, and cheering him on when his own heart was dismayed by the trials and toils of his work, is entitled to occupy some space in the biography of her husband. We propose, therefore, to extend this sketch of Mrs. Morris further, by glancing at those traits of her character which seem to be worthy of special mention. As a wife and mother she was faithfully devoted to the interests of her family. She sought to promote the temporal comfort of her household. For public, obvious reasons, as well as for personal comfort, a minister's house should be well kept, and arranged with sober taste. No place, except the sanctuary, was so inviting to Mrs. Morris as home. There, with her children, her closet, and her Bible, she was happy.

She was *consistent.* Her manners, her conversation, her apparel, her conduct in every relation, and her treatment of all ranks and persons, bore the same stamp of humility, meekness, and benevolence. Probably no person ever succeeded better than she did in suiting her dress to her profession, and to the station she filled in the Church. There was a peculiar plainness and comeliness in her apparel ; and happy were it for the Church now, if, in this particular, all "women professing godliness" could imitate her.

Her *patience* was wonderful. To estimate it aright, one must remember how long and how severely she suffered, and in what circumstances. Her husband far away, her son in a foreign land, and she almost in despair of beholding either again on earth ; withal, possessed of the liveliest sensibility, and her affections gathered around these absent ones with a solicitude indescribable, while her bodily pains were excruciating. Yet she was patient. On one occasion, when a friend suggested the probability of her decease before the return of her husband and son, she was so overwhelmed with sorrow that for a moment she gave free vent to her uncontrollable grief. Soon, however, she became composed, and looking up, said, in a subdued tone, "Well, if Mr. Morris can do more work for the Church by my deprivation, I shall try to be resigned."

She was an *intelligent* Christian. She studied the Holy Scriptures. She not only gave the Bible preference over all other books, but made it a matter of conscience to read it every day in the year. If any thing unusual occurred, to prevent reading the ordinary lessons of the day, she made it up at night, frequently by curtailing the hours of sleep. This duty she performed with uncommon delight and profit. There are very few private Christians as familiar with the Bible as she was, being able to turn at once, without a concordance, to almost any prominent text in the Old or New Testament, and to quote hundreds of passages from memory. About seventeen years before her death, while agonizing for the blessing of perfect love, in her own chamber, she experienced that the blood of Christ " cleanseth from all sin." Though she never made a public profession of the grace of sanctification prior to her last sickness, in death her testimony was explicit, and she sent an affectionate message to her leader, urging her classmates to seek this full salvation.

Such were the prominent characteristics of a noble woman, wife, and mother, whose name deserves to be perpetuated with that of her husband.

In 1842, according to the plan of episcopal visitations, Bishop Morris presided over the Pittsburg Conference, at Wheeling, July 13th ; the Erie, at Cleveland, August 2d ; the Michigan, at Adrian, August 17th ; the North Ohio, at Delaware, September

7th; the Ohio, at Hamilton, September 28th; the Indiana, at Centerville, October 19th. On his return home from this tour he found his only daughter, Mrs. Jane B. Rust, apparently on the very verge of the grave, wasting away rapidly under the insidious and fatal disease that had so recently carried away her mother. By her bedside the bereaved and sorrowing father watched, until her sufferings terminated, November 30th.

Mrs. Rust was born at "Spicewood Cottage," Cabell County, Virginia, February 27, 1815, and was baptized the same year by Rev. David Young, of the Ohio Conference. Her constitution was naturally feeble, and her health delicate, all her life; but that did not materially injure her mild and amiable disposition. Her father says, in a biographical sketch published in his " Miscellany:"

"She was as steady and thoughtful in childhood and youth as most persons are at mature age. The most striking features of her character were meekness and kindness. When only five years old she read fluently and gracefully. She learned her lessons with great facility, especially such as were committed to memory, and being always diligent in preparing to recite them, seldom failed to stand first in her class; but was never known to take any credit or praise to herself on that account. When Jane left Science Hill Academy, at Shelbyville, Kentucky, in the fifteenth year of her age, she had acquired all the essential elements of a sound and useful education, and some of the ornamental branches, and bid fair to excel in literary attainments. The state of her health, however, about that time, rendered it necessary that she should exchange the sedentary habits of student-life for the more active employments of the domestic household.

"At the age of twenty-one she was happily married to Mr. Joseph G. Rust, of Cincinnati, who had been pious from his youth, and whose natural disposition and moral habits were congenial to her own. She became the mother of three children; and as she had been a most affectionate, dutiful child to her parents, so she proved herself to be a faithful wife, and tender-hearted but judicious mother.

"She commenced seeking a change of heart very earnestly, as near as I can recollect, in her ninth year, and for seven years missed no opportunity of going forward to be prayed for when circumstances were such as to allow it. She became a member of the Methodist Episcopal Church in her fourteenth year, but did not obtain a satisfactory evidence of the desired change of heart till about two years after. Though her piety was uniform, and her life highly exemplary, she never dealt much in professions of assurance till after the commencement of her last illness; but then her confidence in God seemed to gather strength in proportion to the increase of her affliction and prospect of death.

"The last letter which my daughter ever wrote was addressed to me at Delaware, Ohio, and was received during the session of the North Ohio Conference, from which the following is an extract: 'My hand shakes so, that it is with great difficulty I can hold a pen. I am very glad to hear that you are

well, and are sustained under your arduous labors. I
thank you kindly for all your letters, and especially
for the first one. . . . I have read it many times
over, and still it always interests me. I have been
very deeply afflicted since you left home, as you
know. The loss of our dear little babe was a great trial
to me, and for several days after I felt as if I could
not give him up; but, since that, I feel a sweet resignation to the will of the Lord, and would not have
him back for asking.' The trembling debility apparent on the face of that letter, fixed a deep and painful impression on the father's already sorrowful heart,
because it indicated too plainly that her feeble constitution was giving way under the influence of fatal
disease.

"Returning home September 12th, my worst fears
were fully confirmed. I found her prostrated, and far
gone in pulmonary consumption; but patient and resigned. She said to me: 'I have never felt like mur-
muring during my affliction. The Lord has been
good to me all my life. He blessed me wonderfully
at the late camp meeting. I there enjoyed the
preaching much, as I heard it while lying in my
tent. And such singing I never heard before.' In a
conversation with me a few days after, she remarked:
'I neither look back nor forward, but live a day at a
time. I am in the hands of the Lord, and am willing that he should dispose of my case. If I get better, I shall be thankful on account of my family; but
if not, the Lord will support me to the end.'

"On the following Sabbath, she was exceedingly
happy, and rejoiced aloud, exhorting her brother not

to be discouraged in seeking religion, for he had a kind, all-sufficient, and willing Savior to go to, who was ever willing to hear the cries of the penitent. The next day she told her physician she never expected to be much better; but she was resigned, for the Lord had supported her. She said it would be a trial to part with her family; but she trusted the Lord would give her grace to resign them all cheerfully into his hands. When I returned from the Ohio Conference, the first week in October, I found her still failing under the wasting influence of cough, chills, fevers, and night-sweats, and fully apprised of her certain approach toward the point of dissolution, but strong in faith, and joyful through hope in our Lord Jesus Christ.

"Monday, 17th, she said to me, 'I am determined to trust in the Lord, come what will; not that I feel fully prepared for heaven, but God is able to perfect that which is lacking, and I believe he will—bless his holy name!' As I had to leave next morning in the stage, at three o'clock, for the Indiana Conference, I went to her room at two o'clock, that I might spend an hour with her. At her request, I prayed with her once more. She was deeply affected, but rejoiced in spirit. In my absence the property of her father-in-law and husband was destroyed by fire; and while the fearful conflagration shed a glare of light upon her chamber-window, she thanked God she had a more enduring substance beyond the ravages of the destructive element, 'an inheritance which is incorruptible, undefiled, and that fadeth not away;' and exhorted those about her to lay up their treasure in heaven.

"When I returned from Indiana on the 27th, I found her disease greatly increased, and her strength so much reduced that she was never after able to sit up any; but she was still patient and resigned, professing to feel assured that the Lord cared for her, and that he could and would sustain her. When her affliction was extremely painful, she was willing to suffer all the will of God, and would not dare to ask her sufferings less, and prayed only for patience to endure, and grace to support her under them; and when they were mitigated, she would express much gratitude to her Heavenly Father for a little relief.

"Sabbath afternoon, November 13th, when I returned from church, she said to me: 'Pa, this has been a blessed Sabbath to me; I have enjoyed a sweet foretaste of that Sabbath which never ends. I was in a struggle all night and all morning for a blessing, and got rather discouraged; but it occurred to me the Lord could bless me here on a sick bed as well as if I was in the church. I prayed earnestly, and he did bless me in a wonderful manner. I never felt so happy in all my life. I felt that I could endure all my sufferings cheerfully, and that I should be a conqueror in death, through the blood of the Lamb. I used to feel so unworthy that I scarcely dared to call myself a follower of Christ; but he has forgiven me all, and I think I shall never again be tempted to distrust him. He will support me to the end.'

"Thursday, 17th, just six months from the day her mother died, she made this remark to me in the evening: 'Pa, I have been thinking to-day what a happy meeting I shall soon have with ma, where we shall range the blessed fields together, and on the banks of the river shout halleluiah forever and ever. O, what a blessed thing to be free from all suffering and sorrow ; and, best of all, to see Jesus as he is, and praise him as we ought !'

" On Monday, the 28th, she had several paroxysms of strangulation, in which we thought her in immediate danger of dying. While we were silently waiting the next paroxysm to come and hurry her into eternity, she calmly remarked, 'I know not · that I shall be allowed the privilege of speaking in my last moments, but I wish it understood that I am perfectly safe ; that God does and will accept me, not for any worthiness of my own, but for Christ's sake, and will save me with an everlasting salvation in heaven.' She then called her husband to her, and with many expressions of gratitude and love for his uniform kindness, and especially for waiting upon her so faithfully and cheerfully in her sickness, took leave of him, adding her blessing, and commending him to God. Next she called her father, and spoke to him in like manner ; then her mother-in-law, pouring out a full heart of grateful affection upon her ; and then another sister, whom she loved much,—giving to each suitable words of encouragement.

"About five o'clock that evening she passed through another extreme paroxysm of coughing and strangling, in which we fully expected she would expire ; but at last she revived so as to speak, and said : 'Jesus is with me ! Jesus is with me ! Jesus is with me ! Death has no sting ; the grave has no victory ! I have the victory through Jesus Christ,

and I view the grave as a sweet resting place for
my body, while my blood-washed soul will rest in
paradise !'

"Her ill turns continued, at irregular intervals,
through that night and the next day. In an unusually severe paroxysm, which occurred on Tuesday
evening about five o'clock, she appeared to be beyond
all hope of living through it, and the family were
called in to witness her departure. She, however,
revived again, after a very long and painful struggle,
and the first words she uttered were :

> " 'Yonder 's my house and portion fair,
> My treasure and my heart are there,
> And my abiding home ;
> For me my elder brethren stay,
> And angels beckon me away,
> And Jesus bids me come.'

"The longest and hardest struggle of the kind
occurred on the same evening, at half-past six
o'clock, and continued till we really believed her
spirit was in the act of departing; insomuch that,
when she finally recovered, it appeared similar to a
resurrection from the dead. If it were in my power
to give the reader a just idea of that agonizing and
heart-rending scene, I would not inflict it upon him ;
and, if it were practicable, would obliterate the recollection of it from my own mind. At the commencement of each of these attacks, she expected her
release, and with much apparent reluctance returned
again to life, praying most earnestly to be set free.
Indeed, her disappointment in not obtaining her final
deliverance when expected was the most difficult
thing to be reconciled to that occurred during the

whole of her affliction; but grace was afforded to secure the victory over this also. At one time she remarked: 'You thought that I should have got home before now; but I feared the news was too good to be true. However, I must wait patiently the Lord's time.' The last paroxysm so prostrated her strength, and was followed by such languor that she was never after able to hold a regular conversation, though she lingered till next morning, November 30th, at a quarter past eight o'clock, speaking a few words occasionally of her friends, and of the goodness of God, and frequently repeating the prayer, 'Lord Jesus, receive my spirit!' and then, without a groan, or any distortion of features, or any struggle whatever, calmly and sweetly slept in Jesus.'

About the 10th of December, Bishop Morris began an extra tour of episcopal visits, laboring in protracted meetings as follows: Madison, Indiana, ten days; Vernon, Indiana, three days; Louisville, Kentucky, three weeks; Jeffersonville, Indiana, one week; Bardstown, Kentucky, one week; Shelbyville, Kentucky, one week; Frankfort, Kentucky, one week; Lexington, one week; and Maysville, one week. Such excessive toil, added to travel and exposure in a very severe Winter, brought on vertigo of the head and palpitation of the heart in a form so severe that he was compelled to cut short the circuit of his visitations; and though he continued to perform his official duties, he did not wholly recover from the effects of the attack of that Winter for nearly a year.

On the 25th of March, 1843, he started for the East, and attended, with Bishop Hedding, the

Philadelphia Conference, at Philadelphia, April 5th; the New Jersey, at Trenton, April 26th; the New York, at New York, May 17th; the Providence, at Warren, June 7th; the New England, at Boston, June 28th; and the Maine, at Bath, July 19th,—sharing with his colleague in the labors and responsibilites of the work. While at the Philadelphia Conference, the sad intelligence of the death of Bishop Roberts was received. Bishop Morris returned to his home in August, and, after a few weeks of labor in camp-meetings, began his own tour of episcopal labor, presiding over the Kentucky Conference, at Louisville, September 13th; the Holston, at Abingdon, Virginia, October 4th; the North Carolina, at Halifax C. H., Virginia, October 25th; the Virginia, at Richmond, November 15th; thence by way of Baltimore and Wheeling to Cincinnati again, reaching home about Christmas.

Early in January, 1844, he made a visit to St. Charles, Missouri, where his son, Francis Asbury, was Professor of Languages in the St. Charles College. While on this visit he preached frequently, both in St. Charles and St. Louis. Returning from Missouri, he again left home, in the latter part of February, for the East, and presided over the Baltimore Conference, at Washington City, March 13th; the Philadelphia Conference, at Philadelphia, April 3d; the New Jersey, at Trenton, April 17th. At Trenton, he met his colleagues for consultation, preparatory to the memorable General Conference of 1844, and thus closed his second quadrennium of episcopal labor.

CHAPTER IX.

GENERAL CONFERENCE OF 1844—DISCUSSIONS ON THE SUB-
JECT OF SLAVERY—MARRIAGE—LOUIS-
VILLE CONVENTION.

THE General Conference of 1844 met in the city
of New York on the first day of May. It was
composed of one hundred and eighty delegates,
representatives of thirty-three annual conferences.
Bishops Soule, Hedding, Waugh, Andrew, and Morris
were present at the opening, and on the second day
of the session presented their Quadrennial Address.
Early in the session, the subject of slavery came up
in a way which seemed to preclude the possibility of
avoiding decisive action. A member of the Baltimore Conference, Rev. F. A. Harding, presented an
appeal from his Conference, which had suspended
him for refusing to manumit slaves which had become his property by marriage. For several days
this case occupied the attention of the General Conference, and was watched with intense interest
throughout the Church. Earnest and eloquent
speeches were made on both sides ; but the final vote
approved the action of the Baltimore Conference—
one hundred and seventeen to fifty-six.

The case, however, which caused the deepest
feeling on both sides of the vexed question, and

ultimately led to a division of the Church, was that
of Bishop Andrew, who had become connected with
slavery first by inheritance, and afterward by marriage. "The revelation of these facts," says Bishop
Clark, in his "Life and Times of Hedding," "produced
a profound and painful sensation. In other instances,
where the subject of Slavery or Antislavery came before this or preceding General Conferences, there had
always been some mode by which the matter could
be adjusted to the satisfaction of the great body of
the Conference and of the Church, and yet so as to
avoid sectional differences. But now a distinct
issue was made between the North and the South.
For the North to yield, and to give up the principle
which had always been preserved inviolate from the
organization of the Church—namely, that the Episcopacy should be kept free from any taint of slavery—
would have been not only disastrous to the Church
in all the free States, but also, in their judgment, an
unwarrantable sacrifice of moral principle. On the
other hand, the South, though they had yielded in
former years when only the election of men to the
episcopal office was concerned, were now equally
strong in their convictions that for them to yield to
the deposition of a bishop because he had become a
slaveholder, would be disastrous to the Church in the
slave-holding States. In fact, they had come to a
point where they must either boldly assert, or forever
surrender, the principle long maintained by most of
them,—that the mere fact of slave-holding should
constitute no impediment to any official station in
the Church."

The attention not only of the Church, but of the country, was arrested, and held through weeks of painful suspense, while the discussion of this great case proceeded. The excitement meantime increased day by day, as the full magnitude of the crisis became more apparent. A motion was pending expressive of the sense of the General Conference, that Bishop Andrew should desist from the duties of his office so long as the impediment of his connection with slavery remained. Speeches of remarkable ability were made for and against the adoption of this motion. On the 29th of May, the previous question was moved, but failed to obtain a two-thirds vote. Bishop Hedding, who was in the chair, suggested that the Conference intermit its usual afternoon session, in order to afford the bishops time to consult together, with a view to present a plan, if possible, for adjusting the difficulties by which they were encompassed. This suggestion was cordially received, and the discussion of the pending motion was postponed until the next morning.

On the following day, Bishop Waugh presented a communication from the bishops, stating that, in their judgment, under the existing circumstances, a decision of the pending question, whether affirmatively or negatively, would most extensively disturb the peace and harmony of the Church; and that they unanimously concurred in the propriety of recommending the postponement of further action in the case of Bishop Andrew until the ensuing General Conference. They further expressed the conviction that, if the embarrassments of Bishop Andrew should

not cease before that time, the next General Conference, representing the pastors and people of the
several annual conferences, after all the facts in the
case had passed in review before them, would be better qualified to adjudicate the case wisely and dis-
creetly than the body then in session. They also
suggested that, until the cessation of the embarrassment, or the expiration of the interval between that
and the next General Conference, such a division of
episcopal work might be made as would fully employ
Bishop Andrew in those sections of the Church in
which his services would be acceptable.

The bishops, in making this proposition, doubtless
felt assured, and perhaps had been assured, that all
impediments in the way of Bishop Andrew, growing
out of his relation to slavery, would be speedily removed if further proceedings in the case were stayed.
The question was laid over for one day. When the
subject came up the next morning, Bishop Hedding
withdrew his name from the document. He said he
had thought it would be a peace measure ; but facts
had come to his knowledge which led him to believe
that such would not be the case. Bishop Waugh
said he considered the proposed measure as a last
resort to promote the future peace of the Church ;
but he had not been very sanguine upon the subject ;
and if it failed, he should not be disappointed. Bishop
Morris said he wished his name to stand on that
paper, as a testimony that he had done what he could
to preserve the peace and unity of the Church. The
communication of the bishops was finally laid upon
the table, by a vote of ninety-five to eighty-four. On

Saturday, the first day of June, the pending resolution was passed, by a vote of one hundred and ten to sixty-eight. Against this action the Southern delegates presented an elaborate protest, which was entered upon the journals of the Conference. Subsequently, on the representations of some of the Southern delegates, a Committee of Nine was appointed, who reported a plan of separation, to take effect on receiving the sanction of the annual conferences, if the Southern brethren found it impossible to retain their ecclesiastical connection with the Methodist Episcopal Church. The final result, as is well known, was the dismemberment of the Methodist Episcopal Church, sixty years after its organization.

The General Conference of 1844 elected two additional bishops (L. L. Hamline and E. S. Janes), who were solemnly inducted into the episcopal office by the usual services, and by the imposition of the hands of Bishops Soule, Hedding, Waugh, and Morris, on the 10th of June. Bishop Soule eventually separated himself from the Methodist Episcopal Church, and became connected with the Methodist Episcopal Church, South.

At the close of this General Conference, Bishop Morris returned to his home in Cincinnati, and in a few days proceeded to Louisville, Kentucky, where, on the 25th of June, he was married to Mrs. Lucy Merriweather. After spending a few days with friends in Louisville and Cincinnati, he set out, accompanied by Mrs. Morris, for the seat of the Rock-river Conference, Milwaukee, Wisconsin. On reaching Milwaukee, he saw, for the first time, a newspaper article, which appeared originally in the *Commercial Advertiser*, of New York City, charging him with having become a slaveholder by marriage, and a slave-dealer, whereupon he addressed the following communication to that journal:

"MILWAUKEE, *July* 23, 1844.

"MR. F. HALL, *Editor Commercial Advertiser:*

"DEAR SIR,—I have just seen, in the *Albany Journal* of the 12th inst., an article headed 'Another Slaveholding Bishop,' and credited to the *Commercial Advertiser*, which is highly injurious to me and to the Methodist Episcopal Church, and which, I hope, you will have the goodness to correct. There is but one truth in the whole article; namely, that 'Bishop Morris has married a widow lady in Kentucky.' The statement that she is possessed of slaves is incorrect; and the report that I executed a contract, previous to marriage, relinquishing my prospective claim to her slaves in favor of her child by her former marriage, is wholly false. I made no such contract, no such relinquishment, and she had no child, as represented by the writer, to be a party in such transaction. The only connection she *had* with slavery was nominal, as trustee of her deceased husband's estate, under a will which secured, ultimately, the whole of it to her step-son; and, according to an express provision of the will, her marriage annulled the trust, and severed that nominal relation. Neither my wife nor myself has any interest in slave-property, direct or indirect, nor has either of us any connection with slavery, in fact or in form.

"Yours, respectfully,   THO. A. MORRIS."

This communication, which was published by the paper to which it was sent, and copied extensively, soon silenced the reports which had been put in circulation concerning the bishop's alleged connection with slavery. His wife's former husband, Dr. Merriweather, had acquired a few slaves by his first marriage, and they belonged to the first wife's son. Mrs. Morris had been Dr. Merriweather's second wife. She had no children, and claimed no ownership in the slaves ; nor had she any connection with them, only as the doctor's will made her one of the trustees to manage his son's property until he became of age. At the time of Bishop Morris's marriage to Mrs. Merriweather, that son was of lawful age, married and settled, having in his own possession all the slaves and other property left him by his father's will.

At the close of the Rock-river Conference, Bishop Morris proceeded to Iowa City, where the Iowa Conference met, August 14th. He also presided over the Illinois Conference, at Nashville, Washington County, September 4th, and the Missouri Conference, at St. Louis, September 25th. From St. Louis, Mrs. Morris returned home to Cincinnati, and the bishop commenced his journey to Tahlequah, in the Cherokee Nation, where the Indian Mission Conference commenced its first session, October 23d. The trip was commenced from St. Louis on the 4th day of October, on a steamer bound for Weston, far up the Missouri River. During the Spring and Summer, the whole of the vast table-lands adjoining the river, except a few elevated points, had been swept by freshets from hill to hill. Most of the fencing and many of the farm-houses had been destroyed ; and, instead of the expected crop being realized, the rich soil was washed away, or left covered with a layer of sand from twelve inches to two feet deep. The amount of property lost was, of course, incalculable. A few persons were seen attempting to repair their premises ; but most of the proprietors appeared to have abandoned them in despair.

The Missouri River now, however, presented a very striking contrast to what it had so recently been. It was so low as to render navigation extremely difficult and hazardous ; but, after the usual amount of sounding, grounding, floundering, sparring, backing off, and going ahead, a safe landing was made one mile below the mouth of the Kansas, and four hundred above the mouth of the Missouri, on the 10th of October, between sunset and dark. The ten or twelve preachers, who had started from St. Louis in company with the bishop, had all left the boat at different points for their circuits ; so that he found himself entirely alone, on the border of the Indian country, without guide or acquaintance, with lodgings to hunt, amid the deepening shadows of night. Shouldering his luggage, he ascended a steep hill, on the summit of which he found a new cabin, occupied by Colonel Chick, who, having been "washed out" by the late freshet, had sought a new home above high-water mark. The bishop was very cordially received, and kindly entertained by the colonel and his family until next morning. He then started, on horseback, to the Indian Manual Labor School in the Shawnee Nation, seven miles distant, where he had appointed to meet a party of missionaries, to proceed together through the Indian country to Conference.

The Indian Manual Labor School was patronized by several tribes ; but the largest number of scholars were children of Shawnees and Delawares. Since the establishment of this great central school, the small schools previously connected with each tribe had been discontinued, though their respective missionaries continued in the regular missionary work of preaching and visiting. The students varied in age from ten or twelve to twenty years, and numbered about one hundred and fifty. Bishop Morris witnessed part of the examination exercises at the close of the regular term. "Their performance," he said, "in spelling, reading, writing, geography, composition, and vocal music, was such as would do credit to any of our city schools in the United States." Besides obtaining a knowledge of books, the boys were taught practically the business of agriculture, while the girls were instructed in the domestic arts of knitting, spinning, weaving, and housekeeping generally.

The mission-farm was extensive and productive, embracing five hundred acres, inclosed, of which three hundred were well cultivated, and the balance in grass and pasture, the whole being well stocked with cattle, horses, sheep, hogs, and poultry. Three native buffaloes added to the variety, if not to the value, of the live stock. There was also connected with the Manual Labor School a steam flour-mill, capable of grinding three hundred bushels of wheat per day.

On Monday, October 14th, the bishop and his company started for the Indian Mission Conference. While some of the party on horseback steered through the border settlements of Missouri, Bishop Morris and three others, in two buggies, took the military road through the territory, which was once a comfortable road for a new country; but now the bridges were generally destroyed by freshets, and the sloughs very boggy, which rendered the traveling difficult. The company in which the bishop traveled consisted of himself; Rev. L. B. Stateler, Missionary to the Shawnees; Rev. Thomas Hulburt, late of the Canada Conference, and Missionary among the Chippewas; and Rev. E. T. Peery, Superintendent of the Indian Manual Labor School. They got a late start the first day, and, after traveling about twenty-five miles, camped for the night. Their tent was made of domestic cotton, circular, in the style of Northern Indian habitations, supported by one center-pole, and the base extended by cords and pegs. In this, with buffalo-skins for beds, and buggy-cushions for pillows, they slept comfortably and securely.

The next day they journeyed about thirty-eight miles, camping for the night on the south bank of the Mary de Zine, in a quiet, pleasant place, where the only interruption of their slumbers was occasioned by noises which arose, now and then, from a neighboring camp of Potawatomie Indians, who were sojourning there. The next day they overtook Rev. Thomas B. Ruble, Missionary among the Potawatomies, and a son of Chief Boashman, a young Indian who had been educated at the Manual Labor School, become a Christian, and was now acting as an interpreter. Thus re-enforced, the three carriages formed quite a respectable procession. Early in the afternoon they were caught in a north-eastern rain-storm, accompanied with high winds, which rendered their open buggies very uncomfortable for the time being; but they pushed on, and late in the evening reached the Mamita, near Fort Scott, where fuel and water could be procured, and where they pitched their tent for the night. Calling at the fort next morning, they laid in a supply of horse-provender, having been notified that this would be the last opportunity for the next fifty miles. That day the air was very chilly, and traveling across the prairies any thing but pleasant. When they finally reached the last skirt of timber, on the Drywood Fork, though early in the afternoon, it was too late to attempt to cross the Big Prairie, twenty-three miles across, and they halted for the night.

The next day they set out early, in a driving snow-storm, and encountered the first real suffering they had experienced on the journey thus far. On Saturday, the 19th, they passed through the Quapaw lands and the Little Shawnee Village, and in the evening arrived at Mrs. Adam's, in the Seneca Nation, where they were kindly received and spent the Sabbath. The religious services, held in the house of this excellent lady on Sabbath, were peculiarly impressive. The congregation contained about sixty persons only; but among them were Senecas, Stock-bridges, Shawnees, Cherokees, Africans, Canadians, and citizens from several of the United States. Here the Rev. N. M. Talbott, Missionary among the Kickapoos, north of the Kansas River, joined the party, and all proceeded together, Monday morning, to Conference.

On Tuesday, 22d, late in the evening, they reached Tahlequah, the capital of the Cherokee Nation, commonly called the Council Ground. They had not expected to find much of a city here, and were not disappointed. The National Council was in session. It consisted of a lower house, or popular branch, of twenty-four members, and a senate of sixteen members, occupying a very ordinary building. The impression made upon the mind of Bishop Morris, by what he saw and heard here, was, that the Cherokees were making progress in Christianity, civilization, and education, and that they might do well in their new country if they could permanently settle their internal difficulties. At Tahlequah, the party learned that the Conference was to meet in Riley's Chapel, two miles distant, and that the "headquarters" of the Committee of Reception were near the chapel, at the house of Rev. Thomas Bertholf. They reported accordingly, and were soon comfortably provided for in the neighborhood.

The Indian Mission Conference commenced its first session the next day, Wednesday, October 23d. The Conference included seventeen elders (all of whom were present but one), six deacons, and four licentiates, all tried men in the Indian work. About one-fourth of them were native preachers. As all the

work of this Conference was missionary, there was no
trouble about popular appointments or special transfers. The bishop stationed all the preachers in less
than two hours, and had no occasion afterward to
change a single appointment, nor did any one complain that his lot was hard. The little band of heroic
missionaries were living and working together in the
bonds of Christian affection. The religious exercises
at the opening of each day's session were conducted
in English, and at the close of the session in Choctaw
or Cherokee. The business of the Conference was
completed by Saturday evening, and on Sabbath the
ordinations took place, as usual; two of those ordained
being full-blooded Choctaws, one of whom was a fine
English scholar. Upon the whole, the bishop was
much pleased with his trip and visit among the Indians, and concluded that the missionary appropriation
employed to convert the Indians from sin and heath-
enism to Christianity and civilization was very wisely
used. From Tahlequah he proceeded to Little Rock,
where the Arkansas Conference met, November 20th.
Here, on Sabbath, Bishop Morris preached and
ordained ministers in the Representatives' Hall of
the capital, in the presence of the governor and most
of the members of the Legislature, which was then in
session. From Little Rock he returned home, closing up a year of extensive and perilous travel, and of
much exposure and toil.

During the months of March and April, 1845,
Bishop Morris made a special preaching tour through
the State of Kentucky, visiting Maysville, Lexington,
Frankfort, Louisville, and many intermediate towns.

This trip was undertaken with a view to promote harmony, allay sectional feeling, and do something, if possible, to prevent a division of the Church. Actuated by these feelings, he attended the Southern Convention, held in Louisville, in May, and which resulted in the organization of the Methodist Episcopal Church, South. His own somewhat despondent record concerning this effort to pour oil on the troubled waters is: "I accomplished nothing except, perhaps, to involve myself in suspicion on the part of my brethren of the Methodist Episcopal Church. Party prejudice proves often too strong for logic or facts. You may reason with a man's judgment, but not with his passions, either in the North or the South."

When the result of the Louisville Convention became known, the five remaining bishops in the Methodist Episcopal Church, at a regular meeting, held in the city of New York, July 2d, came to the conclusion, unanimously, that, under all the circumstances of the case, they would not be justified in presiding in any of the conferences thus separated from the jurisdiction of the Methodist Episcopal Church. Accordingly, Bishop Morris relinquished his Southern route in favor of Bishop Soule, and presided over the Fall conferences which had been assigned to Bishop Soule prior to his withdrawal from the Methodist Episcopal Church. By this arrangement, Bishop Morris passed over nearly the same ground as the year previous, holding the Rock-river Conference, at Peoria, August 20th; the Iowa, at Burlington, September 3d; the Illinois, at Springfield, September 17th ; and the Indiana, at Madison, October 8th.

In the Spring of 1846 he performed much extra labor, visiting and preaching in South-western Ohio and South-eastern Indiana. During this tour, which was made in a buggy, he met with an accident, which, but for a kind Providence over him, might have resulted very seriously, if not fatally.

He was driving on the National Road in Indiana, and had just passed through Lewisville, between Cambridge City and Knightstown, when he came to a creek, over which was a covered bridge. Having entered the bridge, he discovered, when nearly through it, a long, narrow gangway, thrown from the body of the bridge to an embankment, as a temporary means of passing, which looked dangerous. As it was too late to retrace his steps, and his horse had always appeared gentle, the bishop concluded to make the attempt to cross the dilapidated structure. When about half-way across, the horse became frightened, and, suddenly wheeling to the left, went over, carrying the buggy and driver along with him, a distance of some fourteen feet. Two men, who witnessed the accident from a neighboring field, ran to the spot immediately, and found, to their great surprise, that the occupant of the buggy was neither killed nor injured, having received neither bruise nor scratch on his person. The buggy, however, did not come off so well, being considerably damaged by the upset. Fortunately, the mishap occurred near a town, and the vehicle was soon ready for service again.

Bishop Morris's regular episcopal route for 1846

embraced Pittsburg Conference, at Uniontown, July
1st; Erie, at Akron, Ohio, July 29th; North Ohio,
at Ashland, August 12th; the Ohio, at Piqua, September 2d; and the Indiana, at Laporte, September
17th. He also visited the Ohio Wesleyan University,
at Delaware, during the year, and, at the earnest
request of the President, Rev. Dr. Thomson, delivered
an address to the students, the substance of which,
under the title of "Hints to Young Men," was published in the *Ladies' Repository*, in 1853. A few
paragraphs are selected:

"Whatever lessens our natural tendency to evil,
or increases our gracious tendency to good, should
be carefully observed and diligently practiced. Bishop
Taylor, in his 'Rules of Holy Living,' says, 'Manual
labor is one of the best means of driving the devil.'
Admitting the truth of this principle, which is
strictly philosophical, still I am persuaded that mental labor would answer the same purpose just about
as well. Perhaps both, alternately, would be still
better. While idleness is emphatically the school of
vice, close application of the mind to the study of
literature and science tends to sobriety and virtue.
Experience and observation both lead to the conclusion that the more one applies himself to mental
improvement, the more gravity of character he ac-
quires. Who ever knew a young man habitually
studious, and really desirous to become respectable
in after life, to violate his college rules? Plots of
mischief and insubordination may generally, if not
universally, be traced to the idle and vicious, whose
object in going to college is not to obtain an education

and prepare for usefulness in the world, but to indulge their evil propensity for frolic and mischief,
and, of course, to annoy and embarrass others whose
example of diligence and propriety of conduct is
a reproof to evil-doers. Thus, while it is truly
said, 'Idleness is the devil's workshop,' studious
habits promote good morals, and contribute to the
formation of an amiable character.

"Application to study is essential in another
point of view. Without it, no one ever becomes a
critical scholar, or a great man in Church or State.
All the books, teachers, and colleges in the world
can never make us learned or wise, without close,
persevering study. These may assist us, but the
work is chiefly our own. Every learned man, in this
respect at least, is self-educated. The greatest natural ability never supersedes the necessity of severe
mental discipline, unless we are content to be drones
in society. If any individuals ever rise to an elevated rank in the learned professions, or in the department of science or mechanism, who do not seem
to study, their cases are deceptive. Whatever they
may appear to be, they are, in fact, hard students,
and that, too, for a long term of years.

" Even such as have risen to distinction in our
country, without early advantages of education, have
done it by training their own minds, in after-life,
with unusual diligence and untiring perseverance.
Of course I do not allude to official elevation, which
the chances of party political conflict may confer on
unworthy candidates, but to meritorious elevation in
general estimation, on the broad ground of intrinsic

worth, so that he who possesses it needs neither prefix nor affix to the name his mother gave him to command respect from his contemporaries, or to perpetuate his fame on the pages of history. Whether our object, therefore, is to avoid evil principles and vicious habits on one hand, or to secure the most desirable objects of this life on the other, well-directed and protracted mental effort is all-important.

"Another and still more essential means of securing the greatest good is personal piety. This, above all things, gives proper direction to the mental and moral powers of man, and prepares him to govern himself and be useful to society. Whatever inducement an irreligious man has to restrain him from the way of sin and misery, and to lead him in the path of virtue and happiness, the Christian has likewise. Is he influenced by the desire of knowledge, the esteem of the wise and good, the love of home, competence, independence, self-respect, with the affection of friends and confidence of all? So is the Christian. But, in addition to all these, the religion of the Bible holds out to view moral considerations, such as are unknown in human ethics. It illuminates our dark understanding, dispels the natural ignorance of the human heart by the light of truth, removes its stubborn hardness, and conquers its sinful enmity against God by the soothing accents of mercy; inspires the most desponding with confidence, and relieves their needless fears; rolls off the burden of guilt and misery; sends the laboring conscience peace, and lights up in the soul the fires of heavenly love and joy.

" While 'newness of life' improves all the refined

sensibilities of our nature, it arms us with courage to endure with manly fortitude the numerous ills of this probationary state; while it warns us that death is near, it prepares us to die in peace; while it points us to the general judgment, it whispers in the ear of confidence that the Judge is our best friend, and that all is well. If the apostle of Christ showed us, in anticipation, the world on fire, dissolving the elements of this temporary abode of man, he, at the same time, assures us that we, 'according to his promise, look for new heavens and a new earth, wherein dwelleth righteousness,' to the exclusion of sin and misery, pain and death. Surely, that heaven-born religion that warns us against rebellion, with its present evils and fearful results hereafter, and that leads us in peace and safety through this world to endless bliss and glory, is of more value to us, even here, in self-government and the formation of character, than all of worldly wisdom and its delusive hopes."

In 1847, Bishop Morris left home in February, for Philadelphia, to attend, in that city, the regular annual meeting of the bishops. He afterward assisted his colleagues at the Baltimore Conference, in Washington; the Philadelphia Conference, at Wilmington, Delaware; the New England Conference, at Lynn; and the New York Conference, at Allen-street, New York.

His own episcopal circuit that year embraced the Troy Conference, at Albany, May 26th; the Black-river, at Malone, June 16th; the Oneida, at Binghampton, July 21st; the Genesee, at Geneva, August 25th; and the Michigan, at Ypsilanti, September

15th. He reached home from this tour late in September, and in a few days set out on an extra journey through Ohio, "holding forth the word of life" in Dayton, Piqua, Portsmouth, Chillicothe, and Hillsboro. Referring to his visit at the latter place, he says: "An extraordinary storm, freshet, and freeze blockaded me at Hillsboro several days, all roads being impassable. Finally, with much difficulty and peril, I returned to Chillicothe, where I was stopped nearly a week longer, because the bridges were swept away, and the streams impassable. At length I succeeded in reaching Portsmouth, where I sat up two nights watching for boats, which were laid up because the fuel was all swept off. On reaching home, I learned that my wife was water-bound in Louisville, and put off after her. We arrived there at two o'clock in the morning; could not land at the usual place, but made fast some distance below; got into a yawl covered with ice, and rowed to another boat; climbed up over her high deck, and thence, by a single plank extended from the boat to the window of a warehouse, we passed through a long, dark room, literally feeling our way to the street."

In view of the unhappy strife which had resulted from the "great secession" of 1845, and the importance of the action of the ensuing General Conference, the bishops, at their meeting in the Spring of 1848, unanimously and earnestly recommended that Friday, April 28th, be observed throughout the Church as a day of humiliation, fasting, and prayer. Bishop Morris preached a sermon on that day, in Alleghany City, Pennsylvania, from Matthew ix, 15;

"And Jesus said unto them, Can the children of the bridechamber mourn, as long as the bridegroom is with them? But the days will come, when the bridegroom shall be taken from them, and then shall they fast." This able discourse was afterward remodeled, and appeared in the *Methodist Quarterly Review* as an article on the "Duty of Fasting."

He also wrote the following, apparently for private and personal use, on that day:

"1. I am this day, April 28th, 1848, fifty-four years old. Millions born after have died before me, while my life and health are still perpetuated, a subject of distinguished mercy.

"2. All I have and all I am, except sin and misery, I owe to the Methodist Episcopal Church, under God. May I never prove recreant to her, nor ungrateful to Him!

"3. Having been a member nearly thirty-five years, and a traveling preacher more than thirty-two years, though much of the time unfaithful and unprofitable, I am fully satisfied there is no Church which affords more helps to piety in this world, or a better prospect of gaining heaven in the end, than the Methodist Episcopal Church.

"4. Since the separation of the Southern conferences, the peace of the Church has been much disturbed by angry controversy on both sides of the line. Many difficult questions remain unsettled; much trouble may be expected during and after the General Conference of 1848. O, for heavenly wisdom and Christian forbearance! Help, Lord! for vain is the help of man without thy blessing.

"5. The doings of the approaching General Conference will exert a powerful influence for weal or woe upon the interests of Protestant Christianity in general, and especially upon those of Methodism in the United States. To this crisis I have long looked as the day of conflict and trial, from which none but God can deliver us. May he deliver!

"6. To this end may we all confess our sins to him, and forsake them, and consecrate ourselves anew to the service and cause of Christ, that we may build up and not destroy the household of faith!

"7. It is a time that calls for firmness and moderation. 'United we stand, divided we fall.' No difference of opinion respecting Church polity should divide us, unless it be such as to involve conscience or a sacrifice of moral principle. Here I take my stand. The brethren may do what they will, provided they do not require me, against my conscience and principles, to participate in measures ruinous to the peace of the Church and dangerous to the country, and I am with them. Beyond this point, how could I go? May I not be put to the trial!

"T. A. MORRIS.

"PITTSBURG, *April* 28, 1848."

CHAPTER X.

GENERAL CONFERENCE OF 1848—DIVISION OF THE METHOD-
IST EPISCOPAL CHURCH—EPISCOPAL TOURS.

THE Tenth Delegated General Conference of the
Methodist Episcopal Church assembled in
Liberty-street Church, in the city of Pittsburg, May
1, 1848. Bishops Hedding, Waugh, Morris, Hamline,
and Janes were present. The Conference was composed of one hundred and fifty-one delegates, representing twenty-three annual conferences. The session was opened in the usual form by Bishop
Hedding.

On the second day, while Bishop Morris was in
the chair, the first complaint ever made against his
episcopal administration was formally presented by a
delegate of the Illinois Conference. It related to
the affairs of Ebenezer Church, in St. Louis, Missouri, and is substantially embraced in the following
extract from the memorial of the members of that
society :

"We complain that we were not only not protected, nor in any way recognized, but that the
episcopal influence and patronage were used against
us. We refer here to a private letter from Bishop
Morris to the then pastor of Centenary Church,

whose zeal for the new Church, since his affiliation with the South at Louisville, has been remarkable. This letter was read previous to the final vote being taken by the societies, and was brought to bear in favor of the Southern organization, deterring the timid from remaining in the Church of their choice; being assured, on the authority of said letter, that, if we did not join the Church South, we could not be Methodists, nor have any preachers sent us. We addressed a statement of our grievances to the above bishop, at the Rock-river Conference, in September, 1845; we reasoned and argued our cause with him, as peculiar and oppressive — that some two or three hundred members, lovers of the old landmarks of the Church, for no offense, should be sacrificed upon a Southern altar as a peace-offering. We only asked for relief or protection for the free exercise of the right of private judgment; to which the bishop replied promptly and peremptorily, calling our attention to the 'Plan of Separation,' and informing us that there was no provision made for minorities."

This memorial, after some discussion, was referred to the Committee on Episcopacy. As to the refusal of Bishop Morris to recognize and appoint a preacher to the minority of a charge, after the majority had voted to go into the Southern organization, it is plain that he could not have done otherwise under the then existing "Plan of Separation." The only point in the complaint that really impeached the administration, in the case of the Ebenezer Church, was the alleged letter " To the then Pastor of Centenary Church."

Now, it happened, providentially, that the pastor referred to—Rev. Joseph Boyle—was in Pittsburg, as a visitor, during the first days of the General Conference, and was present when the complaint against Bishop Morris was presented. His testimony, concerning the letter said to have been written to him, is contained in the following communication:

"BISHOP MORRIS,—*Dear Brother:* In reply to your verbal inquiry whether the pastor of the Centenary Church, in the city of St. Louis, Missouri, received a letter from you, in 1845, in relation to the division of the Methodist Episcopal Church, which was used by him to influence the members of said charge to adhere South, I would say:

"1. That I was pastor of the Centenary Church, in St. Louis, in 1845.

"2. That no such letter was received by me from you, either in 1845, *or at any other time.*

"3. That no letter, purporting to come from you to me, was read to the members of Centenary Church.

"Yours, affectionately,   JOS. BOYLE.
"PITTSBURG, *May* 11, 1848."

On the 18th day of May, the Committee on Episcopacy, through Rev. P. P. Sandford, Chairman, presented the following report, which was adopted:

"The Committee also had under consideration a complaint against the administration of Bishop Morris, and adopted the following as their opinion on the subject:

"The Committee on Episcopacy, to whom was referred so much of the memorial from adhering members of the Ebenezer Church, St. Louis, as referred to a certain letter said to have been written by Bishop Morris to the preacher in charge of the Centenary Church, St. Louis, have had the same under consideration, together with other matters connected therewith, and have been presented with a letter from said preacher in charge, dated Pittsburg, May 11, 1848, certifying that no such letter was ever received by him ; wherefore,

"*Resolved*, That there is no cause of complaint against the administration of Bishop Morris in that matter."

The General Conference of 1848 was regarded with profound interest throughout the Church. The ecclesiastical connection between the North and the South had been severed by the action of the Louisville Convention ; and much confusion, and no little ill-feeling, had resulted, especially on what was called "the border." As the first General Conference succeeding the organization of the Methodist Episcopal Church, South, its proceedings were every-where watched with the greatest anxiety. "Its deliberations," says Bishop Clark, in his "Life and Times of Hedding," "were conducted with universal care and discretion, and the results attained have tended powerfully to harmonize and strengthen the Church."

Bishop Morris's official tour, in 1848, included the Wisconsin Conference, just organized, which held its first session in Southport, July 12th ; the Rockriver Conference, at Belleville, August 2d ; and the Indiana Conference, at New Albany, October 4th.

Some extracts from the bishop's account of his

trip to the North-west, this year, will be read with interest:

"At eight o'clock, A. M., June 28th, our train cleared the narrows of Fulton, with its world of lumber and clattering machinery. In a few minutes we were gliding amidst the shadows of lofty forest-trees, along the fertile valley of the Little Miami River, enlivened by birds of various notes and flowers of every hue. How delightful the change! The stillness of the country contrasts pleasantly with the bustle of a crowded city. Riding in an elegant car, even at the moderate speed of fifteen miles an hour, is quite as agreeable as spinning street-yarn on foot, over burning hot bricks and stone, employing one hand in supporting an umbrella, and the other in relieving the eyes from dust and perspiration.

"We could not have selected a more pleasant time for our flight across the State of Ohio. The growing fields of Indian corn were spread out before us in richest verdure. The fields of golden wheat—some waving in the gentle breeze, some falling before the sweeping "cradle," and others arranged in clustering shocks; all indicating the greatest abundance—presented a cheerful appearance to the passing traveler. Farm-houses, factories, and fresh-looking villages were passed in quick succession, till we halted for dinner at Springfield, eighty-five miles from the city. From this to Urbana, fourteen miles, the railroad was not quite completed, but in rapid progress. Stages were ready to convey the passengers and their baggage. They put us through to Urbana in an hour and three quarters, where we slept comfortably at the house of our much-respected friend, Judge Reynolds, while the crowd passed on in the night-train.

"Next day, we took the morning train, affording us, among other pleasures, a full view of the wild meadows, or savannas, of Champaign County, interspersed with lucid streams and fragrant flowers, and swarming with horned cattle, colts, and lambs, contentedly cropping the luxuriant herbage. Another object of interest, that day, was the Wyandot Reservation. The dust of their fathers and noble chiefs slept there; but the remnant of their broken tribe were beyond the Kansas. What was recently their hunting-ground, and more recently a mission-station, is now visibly changing into cultivated fields and flourishing villages. How rapidly the aboriginals of America are wasting before the march of civilization! Already scattered and peeled, in a few centuries more they will be numbered among the nations that have been, and are not. Surely, as Christians and patriots, we owe them a debt of kindness.

"On Friday, a small steamboat brought us to Detroit in seven hours. The scenery on the lake, among the islands, and along the Detroit River, was imposing. At Malden, on the Canada shore, we landed to put some Indians out. They were from Missouri, and brought with them two young prairie-wolves, coupled together in leading-strings, which attracted as much attention as their owners. On reaching Detroit, we stopped at the National Hotel; but the Hon. Ross Wilkins soon called for us with his carriage, and removed us to his own quiet home.

He is the Associate Judge of the United States Court for the State of Michigan and a local minister of the Methodist Episcopal Church, and no drone in either office; for, after sitting all the week on the bench with Judge M'Lean, he preached twice in the country on Sabbath, met class, felt refreshed in spirit, and was ready to resume court business on Monday morning. The Sabbath brought us abundant privileges, and passed off pleasantly.

"After waiting the arrival of our boat all night, in a state of preparation to move on the shortest notice, our coachman called for us about four o'clock in the morning, and hurried us on board of the *Niagara*, just in from Buffalo, and bound for Chicago; but they soon got over their hurry, and did not slip cable till half-past six. That day, we took it leisurely through Detroit River, the Flats, Lake St. Clair, and St. Clair River, stopping two hours at one place for wood, and as long at another for coal, preparatory to the long runs ahead. Late in the afternoon, however, we cleared Gratiot, and bore northward on the broad bosom of Lake Huron. We had hoped to see the sun as he hid himself amid the waters, but a heavy bank of clouds, nearly stationary in the western horizon, obscured him, and changed the appearance of the lake from a bright sky-blue to that of a somber purple.

"As night fell upon us, grave thoughts intruded themselves,—three hundred souls aboard, with only a few inches of timber between them and a sheet of water two hundred and twenty miles long and one hundred and seventy-five broad, with the ordinary risk of collision, explosion, and fire. The visions of other years came up, and among them the Euroclydon with which Paul and his fellow-voyagers had to contend, on his way to Rome as a prisoner in chains for the faith of Christ. In that storm no sun, moon, or stars appeared for fourteen days, during which time they labored, prayed, and fasted, till Paul assured them there should be no loss of life, but only of the vessel and cargo, for which he gave a satisfatory reason : 'For there stood by me this night the angel of God, whose I am, and whom I serve, saying, Fear not, Paul; thou must be brought before Cæsar; and, lo! God hath given thee all them that sail with thee.' What a relief in their extremity! And how comfortable our condition in comparison with their perilous one,—all at liberty, all well, on board a noble steamer, well manned and provisioned, walking like a thing of life on the smooth surface, and affording all the luxuries of life! Of course we had much to comfort, and but little to render us discontented.

"The voyage of the lakes, from Buffalo to Chicago, is one thousand and seventy-five miles. The *Niagara* was a new boat of the line, on her sixth trip, and perhaps nearly equal in speed and strength to any other. On the lower deck were crowds of foreigners, with their piles of chests and movables, figuring in quaint costume, and making their first observations upon America, to whom every thing appeared to be novel, but not unpleasant. In the cabin were men of leisure and pleasure, with their families, seeking new sources of enjoyment—men of business, intent on its accomplishment; invalids traveling for health; peddlers of books and maps; tourists exploring new States; ministers and agents, on ecclesiastical business; and smoking, loquacious politicians—some promenading the deck in solitude, some clustered together in social chit-chat, others attracted by the sound of music and song.

"After the tea-table was removed, the headquarters of amusement seemed to be the ladies' cabin, where many assembled for the purpose of killing time, which hung heavily upon them. The moving agent of the whole operation was a son of Ham, patting his foot and drawing a horse-hair across a piece of cat-gut, which made a kind of screaking noise. He must have been a captain; for as soon as he commenced tossing his head about, and moving his right arm to and fro, though he gave no other signal or word of command, a number of individuals rose to their feet, commenced running past each other, and facing about, with a regular step to Sambo's violin. The characters under the influence of his enchantment were diversified,—boys and misses, dandies and flirts, men and women. But one who witnessed the affair declared that the commander of our boat beat them all; that he was the best dancer among them; and no one seemed disposed to dispute the fact.

"On the morning of Thursday, 6th July, near Thunder Bay, was witnessed one of nature's most beautiful exhibitions. It was a thin cloud, forming a regular arch, which spanned one-fourth of the visible heavens, the ends resting upon the north and the south, and the greatest elevation over the east. The

face of it presented every possible hue,—scarlet, deep
purple, golden yellow, silver white, pea green, and all
intermediate shades. It was apparently stationary,
and for one hour increasing in beauty and splendor,
till the luminary of day slowly emerged from the
"vasty deep," immediately under the center of this
triumphal arch, and threw his beams of light over
the sparkling waves toward the lofty peaks of the
Rocky Mountains. One such manifestation of infinite power and wisdom affords more real pleasure
than all the galleries of paintings this world contains.

"We reached Milwaukee on Friday afternoon,
where more than two hundred deck and cabin passengers were landed, to disperse through that new
country. Milwaukee is about twelve years old, and
contains about fifteen thousand inhabitants. It is
situated at the mouth of a small river of the same
name, which affords a safe harbor. The improve-
ménts are very respectable for so new a place, and
rapidly advancing. Its chief peculiarity is the color
of its houses. The bricks are all of a light cream
color, owing, probably, to some unusual substance in
the natural formation of which they are made, and,
when in the building, look as handsome as ordinary
bricks painted white, and are said to be very hard
and durable."

In 1849, Bishop Morris left home for the East,
February 14th, taking passage for Pittsburg on a
steamboat. The weather was intensely cold, and
river navigation was rendered both difficult and dangerous by the floating ice which met the steamer the
second day out. As the cold increased, larger and

heavier masses of ice were encountered, reaching sometimes from shore to shore, making the friction terrible, as the vessel plowed her way onward and upward against the strong current and all the massive obstruction which it bore. The hope of reaching Pittsburg was soon abandoned; but after four days of determined and persevering effort, the city of Wheeling was reached in safety, and here the bishop and his party remained over Sabbath. At that time, when river navigation was closed, there was but one way to reach Baltimore,—by stage to Cumberland, thence by railroad. The only point to settle was the time to leave. After a severe snow-storm, the weather became very cold on Sabbath night, and a journey by stage-coach over the bleak Alleghanies was a serious matter. But there were difficulties in the way of delay. General Taylor, the recently elected President, and his suite, with the usual army of office-seekers and pleasure-takers which pours into Washington on "Inauguration-day," were expected along in a few days; in anticipation of which, stage-fare was already on the rise. It was decided to push on, and thus avoid the crowd. The proprietors of the coach-lines were scattering flaming handbills, making large promises of superior accommodations, on a "splendid line of Troy-built coaches," so that crossing the mountains might have been regarded, by one not familiar with the practical operation, as a mere pleasure-ride. "Four coaches," says the bishop, "of the accommodation line, were loaded, of which ours was one. From appearance it had once been a second-class coach of its size, but had seen its best days, and bore evident marks of a veteran mountain pioneer.

"It was just large enough to accommodate six passengers of ordinary stature, and more should not have been required of it. But its unreasonable task-master piled on about a thousand pounds of baggage to begin with; and then about fifteen hundred pounds of humanity were stowed away inside, consisting of ten passengers, or, more technically, 'nine and a half;' one being under size, but not as much under as some of us were over. So that it was not respectful in our way-bill to call us 'nine and a half;' for, on an average, we compared respectably with any ten passengers on the train. Besides, we were favored with the usual supply of baskets, satchels, robes, etc. Our concern did not do a wayside business. We were all through passengers; and, when once crowded in and the door forced to upon us, we experienced the practical definition of a *squeeze.* I will venture to say that the same number of individuals were never before compressed within the same narrow space, and it is to be hoped they never will be again. The word was given, 'All set!' and we dashed off at a merry rate, but not in a merry mood. To endure the pressure we then felt, during a trip of one hundred and thirty-one miles, was a serious affliction, but one for which there was no remedy."

Finally, after much suffering from the cold, in that cramped, uncomfortable condition, they arrived at Cumberland, and gladly exchanged the hard seats of the rickety coach for the luxurious car which awaited them. About twelve hours' ride brought them to Baltimore, where the discomforts and fatigues of that "cold trip" were soon forgotten amid the cordialities of Christian friends.

Bishop Morris presided over the Baltimore Conference, Staunton, Virginia, March 7th; the New Jersey, at Burlington, April 18th; the New York, at Poughkeepsie, May 9th; the New York East, at Middletown, May 30th; the Philadelphia, in Philadelphia, March 28th; the East Maine, at Bucksport, June 20th; the Maine, at Augusta, July 11th.

He also attended a meeting of his colleagues at Newark, New Jersey, in April, where, after some consultation respecting our missions in the Missouri Territory, he was appointed to draft a memorial to the Home Department, at Washington, in relation to the expulsion of our missionary, Rev. James Gurley, from the Wyandot Nation. The material portions of this document are subjoined:

"The Wyandot Indians, formerly of Sandusky, Ohio, now of the territory west of Missouri, have for thirty years past been regularly supplied with missionaries from our Church, except a short interval since the organization of the Methodist Episcopal Church, South. When the Wyandots removed from Ohio to their present home, our missionary, Rev. J. Wheeler, who had been their pastor for years, accompanied them, and remained with them until 1846, when, the Indian Mission Conference having adhered to the Methodist Episcopal Church, South, he returned to his own Conference in Ohio. The Wyandots were much dissatisfied with their new position in Church affairs, and gave notice to the Church

South that they would look to us for supplies of ministers; and accordingly, in 1848, sent a petition to the Ohio Conference for a missionary. This was signed by the official and leading men of the society, as is usual in such cases. Rev. James Gurley, a minister long and favorably known among us, was selected, appointed, and sent, with a letter of instructions from T. A. Morris. That letter was obtained from Mr. Gurley by Major Cummins, United States Agent near Fort Leavenworth, and, so far as we know, is still in his hands; otherwise we would herewith forward to you the original.

"After Mr. Gurley's arrival at Wyandot, the official members of our Church there, in a communication to T. A. Morris, expressed their gratitude and pleasure on his reception among them, and, having heard an idle and false rumor of an intention on our part to recall him, remonstrated strongly against it. Subsequently, however, Dr. Hewitt, Sub-Agent of the Wyandot Nation, had Mr. Gurley arrested, and ordered him to leave the Nation. One fact, to which we beg leave to call your special attention, is, that no exception to the moral, Christian, or ministerial character or conduct of Mr. Gurley was alleged, even by Dr. Hewitt, as a reason for expelling him from the Nation; nor had Mr. Gurley any personal difficulty with any individual there. Yet he was driven off, to the great grief of the Christian society over which he was pastor, consisting of a large majority of the Church members in the Wyandot Nation.

"Now, what we wish is, to be informed whether

the act of Dr. Hewitt was authorized and sanctioned by the Government, or merely an assumption of power on his part. If the latter, we respectfully ask that the abuse of power may be corrected in such way as the Department may deem proper, the wrong redressed, and our Constitutional rights secured. We know of no reason why our missionaries should be excluded from the Indian Territory, while the missionaries of other Churches are tolerated and protected."

This communication, signed by all the bishops, was duly forwarded to Hon. Thos. Ewing, Secretary of the Interior. It caused the speedy removal from office of Dr. Hewitt, Sub-Agent at Wyandot, and the restoration of our privileges as a Church in the Indian Territory.

Bishop Morris, accompanied by his wife, traveled pretty extensively this year, through Maine, New Hampshire, and Vermont. While at Lebanon, New Hampshire, where he spent several weeks, he prepared for the press the funeral sermon of Rev. Dr. Levings, in compliance with a request made by the New York Conference. Afterward, he visited the White Mountains, of which he wrote a very entertaining account, which the reader will find in his volume entitled " Miscellany."

While filling an engagement at Paterson, New Jersey, in September, he heard of the illness of Bishop Hedding, and set off immediately as his substitute at the Genesee Conference, which met at Albion, New York, arriving there on the second day of the session.

On his return to Paterson, he found Mrs. Morris quite ill. Her symptoms grew worse, and for three or four weeks her case was regarded as extremely critical ; but, by the blessing of God, she slowly regained her health. As soon as Mrs. Morris was able to bear the fatigue of travel, they left Paterson, and proceeded to Philadelphia, where the bishop had secured board for the Winter. During his sojourn in Philadelphia, he preached more than forty sermons, mostly in the city.

His episcopal tour for 1850 embraced the Providence Conference, which met at Providence, April, 3d ; the New England, at Boston, April 24th ; the New Hampshire, at New Market, May 8th ; the Troy Conference, at Saratoga, May 29th ; the Vermont, at Bradford, June 12th ; the East Maine, at Frankfort, June 26th ; the Maine, at Kennebunkport, July 10th ; the Michigan, at Albion, September 4th ; the Indiana, at Jeffersonville, October 9th.

He also assisted Bishop Waugh at the Baltimore Conference, and Bishop Janes at the Ohio and North Ohio Conferences, besides attending the annual meeting of the bishops, held this year in Philadelphia, and the General Mission Committee Meeting in New York City. In less than eight months, Bishop Morris held twelve annual conferences, in the Spring, Summer, and Fall of this year, and, in addition, had charge of the Foreign Mission work, which involved a very extensive correspondence. Writing commissions and letters of instruction, however, was not the most serious part of this business. The chief difficulty was to find missionaries. During his term of service in this work, from May, 1849, to May, 1851, he appointed one missionary to Liberia, two to China, five to Germany, one to New Mexico, and not less than fifteen to California and Oregon. In view of such abundant labors, involving almost ceaseless travel and constant exposure, we do not marvel that his health had become so impaired by the close of this year that he felt obliged to discontinue holding or attending night services, and restrict himself to one sermon on the Sabbath.

Bishop Morris's first Conference in 1851 was the West Virginia, which met in Charlestown, June 4th. This was within five miles of the old homestead where he was born, and spent the first ten years of his life. At the close of the Conference he made a visit to this interesting spot, and thus records his impressions : "The fertile fields in which I first plied the hoe were there ; the Big Kanawha River, in which I was wont to fish and bathe, still flowed on as of old ; the towering mountains on the west still flung their evening shadows over the dear old place. But all besides was changed. The spring of purest mountain-water was neglected ; indeed, buried under masses of sand and gravel, washed down by the mountain torrent. The house that had inclosed it was demolished ; and the lofty forest-trees that, in my childhood, overhung the whole, were cut down. I turned toward the site of the venerable mansion that sheltered me in helpless infancy and happy child-hood, but naught remained except a heap of rubbish where the large stone chimney once stood. The old barn was gone ; the fruit-trees were gone ; and the

grass plot on which I played was plowed and cultivated, and new improvements at a distance of half a
mile on the river bank appeared. Most of the companions of my childhood were in another world, and
the few who remained in this were. far separated
from me, and all of us hastening to the end of life's
journey."

From Charlestown he proceeded to Alleghany
City, and presided over the Pittsburg Conference,
June 18th ; thence to the Erie Conference, which met
at Warren, Ohio, July 9th ; thence to the North Ohio
Conference, at Bellefontaine, July 30th ; thence to the
North Indiana Conference, at South Bend, August
20th. As he was going to the latter place, when
near Connersville, seated in a large nine-passenger
coach, alone, the team took fright, ran furiously for
some distance, and finally upset the coach. The
bishop was .pretty severely bruised by the fall, and
had a bone fractured in one of his hands, but was
thankful to escape with his life. From South Bend
he went to the Michigan Conference, at Monroe, September 3d ; and thence to the Ohio Conference, which
met in Springfield, September 17th, which closed the
official work of the year.

Since his second marriage, Bishop Morris had
been without a settled home up to this time ; and we
propose now to let him tell the story of his attempt
to secure one, in his own words :

" For many years we had no certain dwelling-place ;
but by traveling in Spring, Summer, and Autumn, and
boarding where we could during the Winter, we had
saved a little toward getting ready to keep house.

There were several objections to that migratory mode of living: my papers were deranged; it was sometimes difficult to procure suitable boarding; we had no spare room to accommodate a friend, and our health was suffering from confinement to one small room. Under these circumstances we concluded that the time had come for us to look out for some place where we might quietly pass the evening of life. Accordingly we bought and took possession of a residence on Mount Auburn. It was the estate of a deceased minister of another denomination, which had been mortgaged for the deferred payments, and had to be sold as the only means by which the liabilities of the estate could be settled.

"The Court, on the joint petition of the administrator and guardian, after due consideration, granted an order to sell the premises by public auction. After a month's notice, the sale took place, and the property was knocked off to M'Cullough and Morris, at its full value; they obtaining a bill of sale, a receipt for the first payment, and the promise of a perfect title as soon as Court should meet and ratify the sale. I bought the place of them, and gave it the name of 'Beulah.' In October, 1850, we took possession, put the entire premises in good repair, furnished the house as well as our means would allow, and congratulated ourselves on a pleasant settlement for the rest of our days.

"When the Court met, the administrator allowed weeks to pass without making any return of the sale; and when we inquired for the reason of the delay, we learned, to our surprise, that he had

employed a lawyer to have the sale set aside. And
our astonishment was still greater when we heard,
in a few weeks, that he had succeeded. The chief
reason assigned by the Court for this strange proceeding was, that the guardian was a non-resident
of Ohio—which, however, was as true when his
honor ordered the sale as when he set it aside. As
I was not inclined to endure the suspense and meet
the cost of litigation myself, M'Cullough and Morris
refunded what I had advanced, and released me from
my contract."

Notwithstanding the vexations and annoyances
attending this first attempt to settle, Bishop Morris
was disposed to regard the result as providential.
The situation on Mount Auburn, though very pleasant in many respects, would have been inconvenient
for himself and his family. He soon after purchased
a house on Smith Street, near Fourth, Cincinnati,
and, in October, 1851, took possession of "Home
Lodge."

On the 5th of April, 1852, Bishop Morris left
home to attend the New England Conference, as
substitute for Bishop Hedding. "Interested companies," he says, "had caused to be published a
notice that a boat was making regular trips between
Cleveland and Erie, so that passengers could avoid
staging. I concluded to risk it; but found, to my
sorrow, that I and many others had been imposed
upon. There was indeed a boat that kept runners
on the railroad to decoy passengers on board, with
the positive promise, verbal and printed, to land them
at Erie, but with the certain knowledge that it could

not be done, and had not been done that Spring.
This boat took our money on false pretenses, and,
after carrying us some distance, put us ashore to
take care of ourselves. Thus, after two nights and a
day on this vessel, ice-bound, and then two days and
a night contending with mud, riding where the team
could pull through, and walking over the worst
places, we reached Erie, at an expense four times
greater than the ordinary fare. I arrived in New
York, Friday evening, April 9th, and on the same
evening heard of the sad bereavemnt of the Church
in the death of the venerable senior bishop, Hedding.
On Monday, 12th, I attended the funeral services at
Poughkeepsie, saw this eminent servant of Christ
committed to his final resting-place on earth, and
read over him the burial-service of the Church. His
end was as peaceful and triumphant as his life had
been laborious and exemplary. He was among the
wisest and best of our race."   •

After the funeral, Bishop Morris proceeded to
Chickapee, where the New England Conference held
its session, commencing April 14th. He then returned to Poughkeepsie to meet the Episcopal Board,
now reduced to three in number. The principal
business of this meeting was the preparation of a
quadrennial address, which being accomplished, the
bishops proceeded together to Boston, the seat of the
General Conference of 1852.

CHAPTER XI.

GENERAL CONFERENCE OF 1852—ELECTION OF NEW BISH-
OPS—CONFERENCES HELD—TRAVELS.

THE General Conference of 1852 assembled in the Bromfield-street Church, in the city of Boston, on Saturday, May 1st, Bishops Waugh, Morris, and Janes being present. The Conference was composed of one hundred and seventy-six delegates, representing twenty-nine annual conferences. The Episcopal Address was read by Bishop Waugh on the second day of the session. It refers with much tenderness to the death of Bishop Hedding, and pays a deservedly high tribute to his pure and exalted character. "He sustained the highly responsible office of General Superintendent of the Methodist Episcopal Church," says the Address, "for nearly twenty-eight years. With a strong and discriminating mind, busily engaged for so many years in acquiring knowledge and wisdom from various sources of literature and science, of philosophy and religion, we shall not be regarded as extravagant eulogists when we say that he has left few equals in the church, and, take him all in all, no superior survives him. With all his greatness he had the simplicity of a child. His amiability, gentleness, and kindness endeared him to all with whom he had intercourse—from the prattling child to the youth, to the middle-aged, and to those of old age and declining years. All felt at ease in the society of this truly good man, and were delighted with his unpretending and attractive manners. As a preacher, he had many and great excellences. As an administrative officer, he was justly esteemed unrivaled in the soundness of his opinions, the correctness of his constitutional views and legal decisions, and the dignity and urbanity of his manner."

The address argues at some length against any such modification of the general superintendency as would be likely to result in the introduction of diocesan episcopacy, warns the body against ill-considered and radical changes in the system which had worked so admirably in the past, reviews the condition and prospects of the Church, recommends an extension of the probationary term of traveling preachers from two to four years, reviews the missionary, publishing, educational, and Sabbath-school interests of the Church, and recommends an increase of the Episcopal Board.

On Tuesday, May 25th, after a few moments spent in silent prayer, the Conference proceeded to ballot for four bishops. The result of the first ballot was the selection, by the requisite majority, of Levi Scott, Matthew Simpson, Osmon C. Baker, and Edward R. Ames, who were solemnly inducted into the episcopal office, according to the prescribed form, on Thursday, May 27th.

The General Conference of 1852 closed a quiet, harmonious session, on the first day of June. Its action on the great questions under consideration gave general satisfaction to the Church. After the final adjournment, Bishop Morris held the New York Conference, at the Bedford-street Church, June 9th; the Black-river, at Ogdensburg, June 23d; the East Genesee, at Honeoye Falls, August 18th; and the Genesee, at Lockport, September 8th. He also assisted Bishop Janes at the Cincinnati Conference, and Bishop Baker at the South-eastern Indiana Conference, reaching his home in Cincinnati about the middle of October.

In 1853, the Plan of Episcopal Visitation assigned to Bishop Morris the Baltimore Conference, March 2d; the Philadelphia, March 23d; and the New Jersey, April 13th. Of his trip East he gives, in the *Western Christian Advocate*, the following highly characteristic account:

"On Tuesday, February 22d, I walked to the Bookroom, post-office, ticket-office, and back to 'Home Lodge,' having journeyed on foot three miles through a cold rain to complete arrangements for getting myself and trunk on the morning express-train. During the night the rain changed to sleet and snow. Wednesday morning, before six o'clock, we heard the ponderous wheels of the omnibus rolling up to the door. As I dragged out my trunk, over stone steps and pavement all covered with ice, the unwelcome announcement came, 'You must hand it up, or I can not get it on.' It was a hard lift to stand on that ice and raise a heavy trunk to the driver's seat; but this was the condition alone on which it was to be taken. Great folks, these omnibus men! Being the first in, I had for a time plenty of room; but soon the driver was wheeling to the right and left, ringing door-bells, and hallooing for passengers, some of whom seemed to be in no special haste. After one hour thus employed, we reached the depot, obtained baggage-checks, and were ready to take seats; but, as usual, each car was secured by a lock at one end, and a rough specimen of humanity at the other, to keep out all but such as showed tickets, and to distribute passengers to his own liking. Your ticket may read, 'One first-class passage;' but if he says, 'Forward car, sir,' there is no remedy. So it is with all the crowded lines, as far as I know. Yet when one can congratulate himself that he is not left, but is rapidly leaving space behind him, he may well afford to endure these little inconveniences. Such as left without breakfast were fully ready for it in Columbus, where, for about ten minutes, they played a merry tune with knives, forks, and plates, during which time the substantials were evidently diminished, and good temper proportionably increased; for nothing earthly contributes so readily to the quietude of a hungry man as a good dinner.

"Leaving Columbus, I found myself in a car poorly furnished and much crowded. The stove resembled, both in size and form, an old-fashioned stone jug with a long neck. It contained but little fuel, and less fire, and was densely surrounded by standing passengers making curious observations upon its appearance and want of heat. The seats were hard, springs stiff, and motion irregular, sometimes giving us a vertical cant, and then a horizontal jerk, causing our heads to swing to and fro, as if staging on 'corduroy.' But on we drove, rattle and dash, clatter and crash, thunder and splash, at the risk of flying off the track and throwing the train into a confused heap. Yet no mishap occurred. In the afternoon, the kind-hearted conductor removed me one car back, where I found comfortable accommodations, for which I felt grateful. That day, between the south-western and north-eastern portions of Ohio, we realized changes, both as to cloud and climate, reminding us of the Scotch editor's weather-table: 'First it blewed, then it snewed, then it thewed, and then it friz.'

"On arriving at Cleveland, at seven o'clock P. M., we found the north-west wind sweeping over the lake, almost sufficient to congeal the blood and vitals. The steam of the locomotive was driven back into the depot, so as to obscure the lamps and render them of little use. In the midst of darkness, there was quite a scramble for baggage. After a detention of three-quarters of an hour, my own was secured, and I was taken to the —— Hotel, which had been represented as a first-class house. I was sent to a room in the fourth story, which I found to be a very contracted affair, without fire-place or stove. To spend the evening there was out of the question, and I returned to the office, filled with clouds of tobacco-smoke, which I endured as long as I could, then flew to the door for a breath of fresh air, till the cold would drive me back into the smoke again. Thus I alternated between frost and sickening fumes till ten o'clock, when I ascended to the elevated scuttle where

I was to pass the night, and which I did as well as I could, in a very dirty bed.

"Thursday, the ride to Pittsburg was rather cold for comfort, except to the nice young men who secured all the choice seats near the stove, leaving the rest of us to contend with the severity of the weather as best we could, by striking our feet together to keep up a free circulation. Friday, at a quarter to twelve, I left Pittsburg on the Pennsylvania Central Railroad, traveled all night, passed the seven inclined planes safely, and reached Harrisburg on Saturday morning before sunrise; and the same day went down on the Cumberland Valley Railroad to Chambersburg, where I spent the Sabbath very agreeably, and preached in our excellent and well-filled church. Monday evening, I passed on to Hagerstown in a horse-car, and was ready for the opening of the Baltimore Conference, March 2d."

After a protracted and laborious, but, on the whole, pleasant, session of ten days, Bishop Morris spent a week in Baltimore, enjoying the hospitalities of the "Monumental City." He devoted a day to visiting among the fathers and their families, of whom he makes this pleasant record:

"Accompanied by a friend, I rode to Hookstown, and called at 'Pilgrim's Rest,' to see the venerable and Rev. Henry Smith, now, I believe, about eighty-four years old. We found him out, with his coat off, trimming pea-sticks; for he has an acre lot which he cultivates with his own hands, the products whereof, together with conference dividends, are his living for himself and family. He informed us that, while the

weather allowed him to take out-door exercise, he
ate, slept, and felt comfortably ; but when confined to
the house he felt the worse for it.   He still preaches
occasionally, appears to be quite cheerful, enjoys the
society of Christian friends, and is patiently waiting
for his Lord to call him home.   While we prayed
together, the Divine presence was sensibly felt among
us.   He is a Methodist preacher of the original
stamp, both in appearance and spirit.

"From thence we rode to the residence of Rev.
Joshua Wells, a snug little place of several acres, a
mile or two north of Baltimore.   He is nearly eighty-
eight years of age, if I remember right, and has been
a traveling preacher sixty-four years.   Though unable
to preach now, he still recites with precision and
animation the stirring incidents of his early ministry,
as well as the oppositions and triumphs of American
Methodism in his day.   His personal appearance is
such as to command respect from all.   His protracted
ministerial service calls for gratitude, and his conciliatory manners plant him firmly in the affections of
the Church.   His pious companion, only a few years
younger than he, was suffering severe pain, without
hope of relief here ; but suffering joyfully, in prospect
of being soon removed to the heavenly rest, where
there is no pain forever."

Leaving Baltimore, Bishop Morris proceeded to
Harrisburg, in which city the Philadelphia Conference assembled, March 23d.   The session was a very
pleasant one.   "Immediately after," says the bishop
in one of his letters, "I went to Philadelphia, thinking that, if any storm should arise over the city

22

appointments, I should be in the place to meet it; but none came. Indeed, it was the calmest time I ever witnessed there at the close of the Philadelphia Conference."

After a visit of several days in the city, he took boat down the Delaware River to Salem, New Jersey, one of the oldest and most pleasant towns in the State. Adjoining the church, in Salem, is a cemetery of great interest on account of some honored names there inscribed; and, among others, that of Rev. Asa Smith, formerly of the Philadelphia Conference, who died in 1847, aged seventy-five years. Near the top of his head-stone is the device of a Bible, open at John xi, 25: "I am the resurrection and the life." Three rods east of this grave is a plain, handsome monument of marble, over the remains of Rev. Thos. Ware, one of the patriots of 1776; converted in 1781; entered the itinerant ranks in 1783; witnessed the organization of the Methodist Episcopal Church in 1784; was a member of the First Delegated General Conference in 1812; was one of the early Book Agents; and died, in 1842, aged eighty-three years. About two rods from his monument stands a very ordinary slab, to indicate the resting-place of a very extraordinary man—Rev. Benjamin Abbott—who, after distinguishing himself in his youth as a fighter, became converted, and was twenty-three years a member, sixteen years a local preacher, and seven years a traveling preacher in the Methodist Episcopal Church. He was a revivalist of marvelous success, "a son of thunder," who accomplished vast good in his day, by the strength of his faith, and the power of the Holy Spirit which attended the word spoken by him. He died in 1796, aged sixty-four years.

After a pleasant Sabbath in Salem, Bishop Morris proceeded to Bridgetown, New Jersey, where the New Jersey Conference met, April 13th.

Returning from the East, he attended the Commencement exercises of the Ohio Wesleyan University at Delaware, and dedicated the new university chapel, preaching on the occasion with unusual power and effect. A few weeks later, he was present at the graduating exercises of the Wesleyan Female College of Cincinnati, and, as President of the Board of Trustees, presented the diplomas to the young ladies, with the following remarks :

"LADIES,—Long-looked-for has come at last ; the hour of your release is here. To-night you escape from college confinement, and to-morrow celebrate your jubilee. To gain the point of graduation has cost you years of toil and solicitude ; but that anxious toil is passed, and you do not regret it. With nimble step and merry heart you return to your parental homes, exchanging college halls for domestic retreats, and classmates for the companions of your childhood. You will, however, not be wholly dependent on friends ; for you carry with you the means of self-entertainment—though considerations of usefulness will suggest contact with society. Disappointment may be expected ; for the theory of life as you study it in books, and practical life with its stern realities, are different things. To succeed, practically, you will need the grace of perseverance, of patience, of forbearance, of resignation. For the ills of life, the best antidote is the love of God in Christ. Other friends you may have; but Christ is a friend that sticketh closer than a brother. As you proceed in life's pilgrimage, carry with you these deeds of privilege; and when, in after years and in scattered positions, you look upon them, you will remember your protracted sojourn at the Wesleyan Female College, and the many friends who now cluster around you in the Queen City. When life and its perils are passed, may we all meet in heaven!"

His next appointment was to preach the annual sermon to the students of the Indiana Asbury University at Greencastle, during the exercises of Commencement-week, which occurred in July. We find an amusing account of his journey to fulfill this engagement, in the *Western Christian Advocate*, August 3, 1853:

"On Wednesday, July 13th, my wife, granddaughter, and I enjoyed a ride of two hours to Dayton, where we passed the afternoon and evening pleasantly with our friends. The cars for Greenville—headquarters of Dr. Durbin's first circuit—left Dayton at five o'clock in the morning. To gather up the family from different rooms, get the baggage removed to the depot, and all stowed away in time, was a hard scuffle. This over, I hurried to the ticket-office, and found it locked, the functionary of that department being averse to early rising, doubtless; but soon after getting under way I drove a bargain with the conductor. For nine dollars he furnished us with three oblong squares of pasteboard,

on which was printed, 'Dayton, Greenville, and
Indianapolis.' Our iron pony, though a sprightly
little fellow, was rather too weak in the back for the
load he had to carry. On a level plain he could jog
fifteen miles an hour, and on a descent twenty ; but
on an ascending grade he could scarcely make five.
When we reached Union, where we should have connected with the train from Bellefontaine to Indianapolis, that train had passed on ; and ours gave
chase, but failed to overtake it. We passed through
Winchester like a whirlwind. In vain the passengers
for that place remonstrated against being taken beyond their destination—resistance to the authority
of a conductor is fruitless. On reaching the first
watering-stand west of Winchester, the iron horse
was unhooked from the train, and, single-handed,
went careering over the plain toward Muncie ; but
for what purpose we were left to guess.

"In about half an hour, by a retrograde motion,
he returned and resumed his burden. The signal to
reverse the wheels was given, and we found ourselves
crawfishing. Having previously learned from the conductor that our car would go through to Indianapolis,
and that we would breakfast at Muncie, we now supposed that, after returning to Winchester to leave the
passengers for that place, we would resume our course
westward. It was a mistake. Our baggage was all
pitched out on the platform at Winchester ; and
though no proclamation was made, or word of explanation given in the cars, it became evident that the
contract was violated, the trip abandoned, and we left
to provide for ourselves. There was no remedy but

to wait patiently for the evening train. Adopting the maxim, 'What can not be cured must be endured,' we went to a public house, where, at ten o'clock, we breakfasted. The evening train was due at five o'clock and forty minutes, but did not arrive until seven. In the mean time, Mrs. Morris became so sick that, to proceed that night was impossible, and we remained till morning. The morning train was due at seven o'clock. We were punctual. After waiting an hour and a quarter, we saw smoke; then heard the quick, heavy breathing of the metal horse, 'faint, but pursuing.' We hurried aboard the train, which moved forward a few paces, backed on a side-track, and stood still till nine o'clock, when, having obtained a clear track, we resumed our course, and on the third day completed the trip from Cincinnati to Indianapolis.

"On Saturday morning I had the pleasure of preaching the opening sermon of a quarterly-meeting, at the Depot Charge, Indianapolis, where the brethren are favored with a pleasant revival of religion. In the afternoon we rolled down to Greencastle, where, on the following day, I was to preach to the students. By remaining in-doors Saturday evening I missed hearing Rev. Aaron Wood's lecture on 'Progress,' which, from the many allusions made to it, I judged to have been a rare treat. Indeed, it was more than hinted by some who heard it, that the elements of popular elocution and power still lingered among the Alumni of old 'Brush College,' the school of itinerant prophets in the west. On Sunday afternoon I gave the young men a plain, simple talk on

'Wherewith shall a young man cleanse his way? by taking heed thereto, according to thy word.' (Psalm cxix, 9.) As the discourse was not written, and I had never learned the refined art of reading sermons, they had to take it after the old Methodist fashion, off-hand."

On the 20th of September, Bishop Morris left Cincinnati for Missouri and Arkansas. Being detained a day in Louisville on private business, he missed the regular packet, and was obliged to take passage on a small transient boat, much crowded and poorly provided with accommodations. "The captain," says the bishop, "was exceedingly accommodating to all under his care. When stewards and cabin-boys chose to swear and act the rowdy, they did so without rebuke. One printed rule of the boat required all games to cease at ten o'clock, yet the blacklegs gambled for money from dark to sunrise, then went to bed, and had breakfast sent to their rooms at ten o'clock. When preaching was proposed, the captain was not only willing, but placed the table, books, and chairs, went all through the boat and called in the hearers, got them seated in due order, and then retired. To every one he had a pleasant word, was especially kind to ministers, and had we not been witnesses to so much wickedness, our time would have passed pleasantly.

"After a tedious voyage of five days we reached St. Louis, and immediately went aboard a Missouri-river packet. On that craft also we had the usual variety of good, bad, and indifferent people. They kept an excellent table, the officers were civil and kind, but the crew was of the worst material. It is a long time since we heard as much profanity in one week as we did among those firemen, deck-hands, and cabin-boys. The Missouri River was very low. Our boat was large, carrying about one hundred and fifty tons of freight, and a large number of passengers, and had hard work to cross some of the bars, especially one at the mouth of Osage River. In six days we made fast at St. Joseph, five hundred and sixty miles, by water, from St. Louis.

"Nebraska Territory presented a wild appearance. The Kickapoo village, consisting of wood huts, is on a commanding elevation, in full view from the river. White squatters are also occasionally seen in the Indian Territory. Should the Government effect a treaty for it, there will soon be people enough there to form a State. Missionaries will soon be needed among them. St. Joseph is a growing town; and would be more so, only for the encroachments of the river, which has already swept away one corner of it. A plan is now devised to stay this work of destruction. From thence to Newark, *via* Savannah, we passed over an undulating region of exceedingly fertile land, some prairie, but most of it covered with forest-trees of ash, linn, walnut, oak, etc., with undergrowth of sumach and hazel. It is thickly settled by enterprising families from most of the Western States."

The Missouri Conference commenced its session at Newark, October 5th. There were, at that time, about fifty preachers in the body, including those on trial. The session was a harmonious and pleasant one, and closed on Monday.

In company with Rev. J. M. Chivington, Missionary to Wyandot, the bishop left Newark on Tuesday, October 11th, for Fayetteville, the seat of the Arkansas Conference. Their vehicle was a sort of stage-wagon, and their team consisted of two horses, one well "broke," and the other not, so that they set off on the journey with some misgivings. The first day's drive, however, brought them, without any serious mishap, to St. Joseph, where they completed their outfit by adding a lantern, matches, and tin cup. On Thursday they crossed the Missouri River at Weston Ferry, and entered Nebraska Territory, passing Fort Leavenworth, and traveling through the lands of the Stockbridge Indians. On Friday they reached Wyandot, and visited Mrs. Armstrong, a daughter of the lamented Rev. Russel Bigelow. They found her living comfortably in a good home, supporting herself, in part, by teaching. Saturday they went to the mission premises, then occupied by Dr. Klepper, late missionary, and remained with him over the Sabbath. The bishop made his first effort at public speaking through an interpreter, on Sunday, and was not very much pleased with the method.

Leaving the mission-house on Monday, October 17th, they pursued the difficult and tedious journey to Arkansas. Over dim prairie-roads, through dark and gloomy forests, through rain and mud, they pushed on by day, obtaining such accommodations as they could find by night; and on the seventh day reached Fayetteville. On Wednesday, October 26th, the Conference was opened in the usual manner. The sessions were held in a public hall. The first day four members were present, besides sixteen probationers. The next day six brethren were admitted into full connection, and one was received by transfer. Fifteen were subsequently admitted on trial; and ten were continued on trial. At the close of the session the roll stood thus: Eleven members, and twenty-five probationers; total, thirty-six. The preachers reported one thousand two hundred and eighty-nine members, four hundred and sixty-five probationers, thirty local preachers, and twenty-two colored members,—making a grand total of one thousand eight hundred and forty-two.

Bishop Morris found the Arkansas Conference about as large as when he originally organized it in 1836; but, in the mean time, the great secession of 1845 had swept into the Church South most of the preachers and people. It was deemed practicable and advisable, under all the circumstances, to close the session on Saturday night, which was done, with the understanding, however, that all the brethren would remain over Sabbath, to witness the ordinations and assist in the religious services.

This long and fatiguing trip of three thousand three hundred miles was safely accomplished, and the bishop found himself again in "Home Lodge," about the middle of November.

During the Winter, besides preaching often in Cincinnati, he visited several of the interior towns of Ohio, preaching with great acceptance and profit always, and encouraging the pastors in their work. He also wrote several valuable articles for the Church press. We subjoin a few passages from a very interesting sketch of a remarkable man, Rev. James Axley:

"Long as I had been crossing the path of that notable man, and much as I had heard of him among the people, my first sight of him was not obtained until the Autumn of 1837. That year the Holston Conference met at Madisonville, eastern part of Tennessee, some ten miles from which Mr. Axley, then in a superannuated relation, resided. The first day of the session, after the adjournment, I was walking to my lodgings alone, when I heard a brother some forty steps behind me say to another, 'Yonder comes brother Axley.' Looking ahead, I observed a man advancing toward me whose person was imposing. He was perhaps five feet eight inches high; not corpulent, but very broad and compactly built, formed for strength; his step was firm, his face was square, complexion dark, eyebrows heavy, appearance rugged; dressed in the costume of his fathers, with straight-breasted coat, and broad-brimmed hat projecting over a sedate countenance. His wide-spread fame as a natural genius, without any early education, and especially the numerous incidents I had heard of him as a Western pioneer, had excited in me a greater desire for his personal acquaintance than that of any other living man I had ever seen, except Jacob Gruber. The sound of his name falling on my ear, involuntarily quickened my pace, and we were soon together. As I neared him I held out my right-hand, and received his, when the following salutations were exchanged:

"'How are you, brother Axley?'

" ' Who are you ?'

" ' My name is Thomas A. Morris.'

" Then, surveying me from head to foot, he replied :

" ' Upon my word, I think they were hard pushed for bishop-timber when they got hold of you.'

" ' That is just what I thought myself, brother Axley.'

" ' Why, you look too young for a bishop.'

" ' As to that, I am old enough to know more and do better.'

" I never heard brother Axley preach ; but, according to popular fame, his pulpit performances were practical, forcible, and left a deep and abiding impression on the multitudes that thronged to hear him. To this day, we occasionally hear allusions made to a sermon he preached in Baltimore, during the General Conference of 1820, of which he was a member. It must have been a potent sermon, to be remembered so distinctly for the third of a century. I have heard also, very frequently, allusions to his pulpit performances in different parts of the Western country, where he had operated to good purpose as a traveling preacher, more particularly in Kentucky and Tennessee. But perhaps the effort which occasioned the most talk, and obtained the greatest notoriety, was the one said to have been made in his own section of the country, and was commonly known as ' Axley's Temperance Sermon.' It should be known that East Tennessee, in those days, was regarded as a great country for producing peach-brandy, and for a free use of it ; also that the

'New Lights' abounded there, familiarly called Schismatics, and that Church members who rendered themselves liable to a disciplinary process would occasionally go over to them, as a city of refuge, where they felt safe from its restraints. With this preliminary, I proceed to give a passage from the sermon, on the authority of a highly respectable Methodist minister:

" 'TEXT: "Alexander the coppersmith did me much evil: the Lord reward him according to his works."—2 TIM. iv, 14.

" 'Paul was a traveling preacher, and a bishop, I presume, or a presiding elder at least; for he traveled extensively, and had much to do, not only in regulating the societies, but in sending the preachers here and there. He was zealous, laborious, would not build on another man's foundation, but formed new circuits, where Christ was not named; "so that from Jerusalem, and round about Illyricum, he had fully preached the Gospel of Christ." One new place that he visited was very wicked — Sabbath-breaking, dancing, drinking, fighting, and swearing abounded; but the word of the Lord took effect, there was a great stir among the people, and many precious souls were converted. Among the subjects of that work, there was a certain noted character, Alexander by name, and a still-maker by trade; also one Hymeneus, who was his partner in the business. Paul formed a new class, and appointed brother Alexander class-leader. There was a great change in the place; the people left off their drinking, swearing, fighting, etc., and the stills were worked up into bells and kettles, and thus applied to useful purposes. The settlement was orderly, the meetings were prosperous, and things went well among them for some time. But one year they had a pleasant Spring; there was no late frost, and the peach-crop was abundant. I do suppose, my brethren, that such a crop was never known before. One Sunday, when the brethren met for worship, they gathered round outside of the meeting-house, and got to talking about their worldly affairs—as you know people sometimes do, and a very bad habit it is—

and one said to another, "Brother, how is the peach-crop with you this year?" "O," said he, "you never saw any thing like it; they are rotting on the ground under the trees; I do n't know what to do with them." "How would it do," inquired another, "to *still* them? The peaches will go to waste, but the brandy will keep; and it is very good in certain cases, if not used to excess." "I should like to know," said another, "how you could make brandy without stills?" "Why, it was answered, "brother Alexander is as good a still-maker as need be, and brother Hymeneus is another; and rather than see the fruit wasted they would, no doubt, make us a few."

" 'The next thing heard on the subject was a hammering in the class-leader's shop; and soon the stills in every brother's orchard were smoking, and the liquid poison streaming. When one called on another, the bottle was brought out, with the remark, "I want you to taste my new brandy; I think it is pretty good." So they tasted, until many of them got about half drunk, or perhaps three-quarters. Soon the society was all in an uproar; and Paul was sent for, to come and settle the difficulty. At first it was difficult to find sober, disinterested ones enough to try the guilty; but finally he got his committee formed, and the first one he called to account was Alexander, who pleaded not guilty. He declared that he had not tasted, bought, sold, or distilled a drop of brandy. "But," said Paul, "you made the 'stills,' otherwise there could have been no liquor made; and if no liquor were made, no one would be intoxicated." So they expelled him first, then Hymeneus; and went on until the society was relieved of all still-makers, dis-tillers, dram-sellers, and dram-drinkers, and peace was once more restored. Paul says: "Holding faith and a good con-science; which some having put away, concerning faith have made shipwreck; of whom is Hymeneus and Alexander, whom I have delivered unto Satan, that they may learn not to blaspheme." ' "

In the early part of 1854, Bishop Morris visited Urbana, Oxford, Dresden, Roscoe, Coshocton, Cleve-land, and New Richmond, preaching at all these points greatly to the edification of the Churches. He presided over the Black-river Conference, at Camden, New York, May 31st, and on his return home immediately arranged a plan of extra appointments for the Summer, embracing a large number of charges, chiefly in the State of Ohio. His official tour of conferences for this year embraced the Wisconsin, at Janesville, August 29th; the Rock-river, at Lewistown, Illinois, September 13th; the Iowa, at Dubuque, September 27th; the Illinois, at Springfield, October 11th.

About the first of December he left home to attend the annual meeting of the bishops in the city of Baltimore. The entire Board—Waugh, Morris, Janes, Scott, Simpson, Baker, and Ames—were present, and the meeting was continued for six days. While together, they reviewed the administration of each, revised the Plan of Episcopal Visitations for the ensuing year, surveyed the whole field of the home and foreign work, and made a distribution of the latter as well as of the former. The foreign work assigned to Bishop Morris was Western Europe, including Germany, France, Sweden, and Norway. It was not expected that he would personally visit these foreign missions, but select, commission, and send forth laborers, as the exigencies of the work might demand, and superintend them by correspondence.

In 1855, Bishop Morris presided over the West Virginia Conference, at Wheeling, May 30th; the Pittsburg, at Johnstown, June 13th; the Erie, at Newcastle, July 11th; the Ohio, at Athens, September 5th; the Cincinnati, at Urbana, September 26th; and the Kentucky, at Maysville, October 11th.

In addition to his ordinary official duties this
year, Bishop Morris made many extra visits to the
Churches within easy reach of his home, every-where
preaching the Word. He also wrote several articles
for the periodical press, the chief of which were:
" My Pocket Bible," " State of Religion," and " Fast
People," published in the *Ladies' Repository*."

CHAPTER XII.

THE General Conference of 1856 assembled in
the Representatives' Hall of the capitol in the
city of Indianapolis, on the first day of May, as usual.
Bishops Waugh, Morris, Janes, Scott, Simpson, Baker,
and Ames were present. The opening religious services were conducted by Bishop Waugh. The Conference was composed of two hundred and twenty
delegates, representing thirty-eight annual conferences. The Episcopal Address was read on Saturday,
the third day of the session, by Bishop Janes. As
the original draft of this document was prepared by
Bishop Morris, at the request of his colleagues, a
brief *résumé* of its contents may be appropriately
given here. After the usual congratulatory opening
sentences, and a tribute to members of the preceding
General Conference, who had died since its session,
the address refers, with gratitude to the great Head
of the Church, to the prosperity enjoyed during the
last quadrennial period. The increase of traveling
preachers in that time had been 958; of local peach-
ers, 910; of members and probationers, 77,627. But
the numerical table did not exhibit all the fruit of

that four years of labor. Very many new houses of worship had been erected, better provision had been made for the support of the ministry than ever before, and the contributions of the Church for missions and other benevolent objects had been largely augmented.

The address suggested certain changes of Discipline; namely,—1. The rule requiring the concurrent advice of all the annual conferences, to authorize the bishops to call an extra session of the General Conference. 2. The ratio of representation, now so great as to render the body too large for the rapid and convenient transaction of business, should be reduced, so as to authorize not less than one representative for every thirty members of annual conferences. 3. A change was recommended in the section defining the method of proceeding against accused traveling preachers. The tribunals were too large to hope for the undivided attention of all the members during the progress of a complex case, and the loss of time to a large body of pastors was a serious one, to be obviated, if possible. It was recommended that such cases be referred to a select number, not exceeding fifteen.

The address then reviews, in detail, the various interests of the Church—Educational, Publishing, the Tract Cause, Sunday-schools, and Missions—accompanied with such suggestions as the exigencies of each department seemed to call for. The General Conference was also informed that, in compliance with the request of the Troy, Erie, North Ohio, and Wisconsin Conferences, different resolutions, asking a change in the General Rule on Slavery, had been laid before all the annual conferences for their concurrence, but that no one of these resolutions received the constitutional majority of the members of the annual conferences.

The modifications of Discipline recommended in this Address were all adopted. The session was a protracted one, the final adjournment taking place on the fourth day of June; but the proceedings generally were harmonious, and the results satisfactory. Rev. John Hannah, D. D., and Rev. Frederick J. Jobson, were present as delegates from the British Wesleyan Conference, and, by their personal intercourse and admirable public addresses and sermons, greatly strengthened the bonds of union between two bodies of a common origin. Bishop Simpson and Rev. John M'Clintock, D. D., were elected delegates to the British Conference.

After General Conference, Bishop Morris presided over the Troy Conference, at Burlington, Vermont, June 18th; the Wyoming Conference, at Binghampton, New York, July 2d; the Genesee Conference, at Medina, New York, September 3d; the Detroit Conference, at Adrian, September 17th; and the Michigan, at Coldwater, October 1st.

Soon after reaching home from this tour, he and Bishop Ames were summoned to Chicago, to attend a meeting of the Western Book Committee, held for the purpose of appointing an editor to the *Northwestern Christian Advocate*, a place made vacant by the death of the brilliant and lamented Rev. J. V. Watson. Rev. Thomas M. Eddy was chosen, and was twice subsequently re-elected to the position by the

General Conference. On the journey home from Chicago, the train on which Bishop Morris was a passenger was thrown from the track, but very fortunately no one was injured by the accident. A cold and cheerless night, passed in the forest while the train was being righted, was better than broken bones—a result from which all were glad to have escaped.

On the 8th of November he left home for New York, to attend the meeting of the General Mission Committee, the Missionary Anniversary, and the annual meeting of the bishops. On his way east, he spent a Sabbath in the city of Cleveland, and preached to a large congregation. While in New York, he preached several times in that city and in Brooklyn.

In 1857, Bishop Morris attended the New Jersey Conference, which met at Trenton, April 8th, Bishop Scott presiding, and, after assisting his colleague three days, proceeded to fill his own appointments, which were, that year, as follows: The New York Eastern Conference, which met in Brooklyn, April 15th; the New Hampshire, which met in Lawrence, Massachusetts, April 30th; the East Maine, which met in Camden, May 20th; the Ohio, which met in Chillicothe, August 26th; the Cincinnati, which met in Piqua, September 9th; the South-eastern Indiana, which met in Aurora, September 23d; and the Indiana, which met in New Albany, October 1st.

About this time Bishop Morris wrote, and published in the *Ladies' Repository*, an article entitled: "My Father in the Gospel," a sketch of Rev. David Young, which, both on account of the writer and the subject, is entitled to a place in this biography. We make room for the material parts of the sketch :

"Mr. Young was one of the few Methodist preachers whom I knew prior to my becoming a Methodist. Our acquaintance began in the Fall of 1812, when he was presiding elder on Muskingum District, then including, in its ample range, Zanesville, Marietta, and North-western Virginia, where I resided, and where he was perfectly at home, being himself a native of Washington County, Virginia, born March 9, 1779. Most of my early views and impressions of Methodism were derived from him. It is true, I had felt conviction for sin from childhood, and that Robert Caseboult, then a class-leader, had taken interest for me, and talked with me, before I heard Mr. Young, and I was seriously inquiring for the way of life. But in July, 1813, while I listened to David Young preaching at camp-meeting, on the Parable of the Sower, I was brought to form a solemn purpose to seek earnestly for salvation till I should obtain it. In August I joined a small country class as a penitent seeker on trial. I had prayed in secret for months, but made little progress till I took this decisive step, and thus drew a separating line from my irreligious associates. The conflict with sin thus renewed, continued till some time in November, when I obtained some relief and comfort, and on Christmas I received a clear sense of pardon, and a full "spirit of adoption." In the mean time, I missed none of Elder Young's quarterly-meetings. At one of them he baptized me in the presence of a multitude ; and the same day on which he poured the water on my head, the Lord poured plentifully his Spirit into my heart. When I was recommended by the society for license to preach, Elder Young examined me before the Quarterly Conference. He also wrote and signed my first license to preach, dated April 2, 1814. In 1815 he employed me as junior preacher on a circuit, and in 1816 I was admitted on trial by the Ohio Conference. From that till 1818, being separated in the work, our acquaintance was perpetuated by free correspondence; but from 1818 to 1820, he, being superannuated, was my constant hearer in Zanesville, where he resided. He continued his efforts in every practicable way for my improvement, and, indeed, till I graduated to elder's orders, he took as much interest in my ministerial education as if I had been his natural son.

"In person, Mr. Young was tall and slender, but straight and symmetrical. His step was elastic. He wore the straight-breasted coat and the broad-brimmed hat usual among early Methodist preachers. His yellow hair, all combed back, hung in great profusion about his neck and shoulders, giving him an imposing appearance. His deep-blue eyes were prominent, and exceedingly penetrating. I heard a Virginia lawyer say 'he could withstand the direct contact of any preacher's eye in the pulpit he ever saw, except David Young's; but his always made him quail.'

"In manners, he was a finished gentleman, well raised, and familiar with the rules of polite society. The social element was not largely developed in his composition; at least, not apparently so in general society. When with his personal friends, there was no more pleasant companion than he was; and to strangers he was civil and very respectful, except they took improper liberty, or asked an impertinent question, when they were pretty sure to receive a stern rebuke. Any individual, however weak or obscure, approaching him as an inquirer after truth for its own sake, never failed to profit by his ample instruction; but woe unto the captious fault-finder who rudely attacked him or his creed. With such a man he did not stop to argue; but demolished him with one withering sarcasm, and passed on. When a weak but conceited predestinarian attacked him on perseverance, saying, 'So, Mr. Young, you believe in falling from grace, do you?' he promptly replied, ' I believe in getting it first.'

"Mr. Young was a man of respectable erudition. Prior to his entering the ministry, he taught a grammar-school for young men. Subsequently he read as many books, as well selected, and understood them as thoroughly, as any man of my acquaintance. He was possessed of extensive knowledge on general as well as on theological subjects. Philosophy, general history, laws of nations, systems of government, and our own Federal and State affairs, were with him familiar topics. He was particularly well versed in Church history and Methodist jurisprudence. Whoever enjoyed a free conversation with him was enlightened by it. He abounded in incident, and had a rare talent for narration, both in the pulpit and in social life; yet, as a minister, he was grave and dignified. No man conducted a public religious service

more solemnly or impressively than he did, especially
in reading the Scriptures and in prayer. He was
deeply experienced in the work of saving grace. I
heard him say in a love-feast, before a large assembly
of Christian friends, 'he knew where and when he
was converted, and where and when he was sanctified.' And, allowing for his constitutional peculiarities, he honored his profession. His deep religious
emotion was always apparent in his prayers and sermons. While preaching, his eyes were generally
suffused with tears of sympathy; and occasionally
they fell like drops of rain, as if the great deep of
his heart was broken up. On special occasions,
while applying the momentous truths of the Gospel,
he stood on his knees in the pulpit, and with many
tears entreated sinners, as in Christ's stead, to be
reconciled to God. Such appeals were not easily
resisted; for at such times he spoke and exhorted 'in
demonstration of the Spirit and of power.'

"Among the most noted Methodist preachers of
their day, were William Beauchamp, Samuel Parker,
and David Young, each of whom excelled in his own
way. Beauchamp was the most instructive, Parker
the most persuasive and practical, and Young the
most overpowering. It was my good fortune, when
young in the ministry, to hear them all. Under the
preaching of Beauchamp, light seemed to break on
the most bewildered understanding; under that of
Parker, multitudes of people melted like snow before
an April sun; while under the ministry of Young, I
knew whole assemblies electrified by one paragraph,
as suddenly and sensibly as if coming in contact

with a galvanic battery. I have myself, under some
of his powerful appeals, felt cold tremors coursing
down both sides of my spine, and the hair on my
head apparently standing on end. On some camp-
meeting occasions, where the surroundings were
unusually exciting, under his preaching whole multitudes simultaneously sprang from their seats and
rushed as near to the pulpit as they could stand together, seemingly unconscious of changing positions.
His force was not in imagination or declamation, but
in the proper combination and earnest presentation
of Gospel truth. And the deep impressions thus
made were generally lasting; for the truth was
applied to many hearts by the Holy Spirit. While
he greatly excelled as a preacher, he was a man of
mark, wherever known. In his own Conference, he
was among the few acknowledged as leaders; and in
the General Conference his weight was felt and
admitted, as a business man and a leader."

In 1858, the death of Bishop Waugh, which occurred on the 9th of February, and the impaired
health of Bishop Simpson, made necessary a revision
of the Plan of Episcopal Visitations. The year was
one of extraordinary labor to such of the bishops as
were able to perform service, especially to such as
began to feel the weight of years. In the Spring,
Bishop Morris presided over the Kentucky Conference, at Covington, March 25th; the Minnesota, at
St. Paul, April 15th; the West Wisconsin, at La
Crosse, April 29th; and the Wisconsin, at Beloit,
May 12th. Of his trip home from Beloit, the bishop
gave an interesting account to the readers of the

Northwestern Christian Advocate, from which we take
a few passages :

"The Conference at Beloit terminated a pleasant
session, May 18th ; and, at half-past six next morning,
I left for home. About noon I reached Chicago ;
and, after surveying the new church-edifice on
Wabash Avenue, and enjoying the hospitalities of
Dr. Eddy, I got off at half-past nine o'clock at
night, amid falling showers and darkness profound,
all which availed nothing to arrest the progress or
depress the spirits of one homeward-bound.

"While my strange fellow-passengers were mostly
nodding or snoring, and my afternoon nap had relieved me of all sense of drowsiness, it became a
question, 'How shall I pass the night?' Now, riding
in the cars generally revives in me the spirit of song,
especially when returning home from a hard campaign ;
but only the spirit. My singing days for the entertainment of others are past ; but I often hold a
concert with myself, as I did that night. My plan
of self-entertainment was soon arranged—the programme being as follows :

"1. 'I am weary of straying,
        O, fain would I rest,' etc.

2. 'O thou God of my salvation,
        My redeemer from all sin,' etc.

3. 'How sweet the name of Jesus sounds
        In a believer's ear,' etc.

4. 'O, sing to me of heaven,
        When I am called to die,' etc.

5. 'Joyfully, joyfully, onward I move,' etc.

6. 'Have you heard, have you heard,
        Of that sun-bright clime,' etc.

"Now, whatever be thought of the performance, the programme was excellent. These pieces are some of my favorites. I found I could repeat them all from memory. It was a free concert,—went off well. The effect was delightful, and the performance filled most of the time from Michigan City to Lafayette; my manner being to hum the tunes, repeating the words in a subdued voice, so that when the train is under way I am heard only by myself.

"Arrived at Lafayette, at about five o'clock in the morning, we were all roused by the proclamation of the conductor, that 'the passengers for Indianapolis and Cincinnati remain over here till three o'clock this afternoon.' On this unwelcome intelligence, we held a colloquy with the conductor, which elicited the fact that the detention was caused by a broken bridge, and that those who preferred it could continue on the New Albany and Salem Railway to Greencastle, and thence to Indianapolis. Thinking that better than waiting ten hours, I determined to try it, and was soon off again.

"As we neared the deep chasm at Crawfordsville, the train came to a stand-still, when we were politely informed, 'The passengers will have to do a little walking here.' We all promptly obeyed orders. To our right was a bluff not to be passed. On our left, from the lowest step of the car, we had to let ourselves down some two or three feet. The platform to land on was a hill-side falling off at an angle of about forty-five degrees. For some distance, we clambered along as we could without slipping down; then, through sludge and over logs, till we found a sloping point leading down toward the ravine. The ladies' dresses got well varnished with Hoosier loam. When down, our next feat of activity was to leap over a narrow stream of water. Then came the hard pinch,—to ascend the bluff beyond. It was nearly perpendicular; but the grade was reduced by excavating steps obliquely, at intervals of two feet or more, on which to rise. The young and light passengers went up quickly; but with my heavy overcoat, covering two hundred and thirty pounds of humanity, locomotion was difficult, as the muscles of my lower limbs testified on gaining the summit, where we found another train waiting. This tedious and painful transfer was made necessary by the destruction of the bridge which had spanned that fearful chasm, but had been carried away by a recent freshet.

"On reaching Indianapolis, and finding I had two or three hours to wait, I called on my faithful friend, Rev. Augustus Eddy, and baptized my namesake, his grandson, Zara Morris Edwards, of Red .Wing. That evening, May 20th, I reached my quiet 'Home Lodge.' One circumstance connected with this trip was remarkable: Between Clinton, Wisconsin, and Cincinnati, I did not see in the cars a man, woman, or child I had ever seen before, to my knowledge. This suited me exactly, as then situated. I love the society of friends when in a condition to enjoy it; but when I have been talked to one week right straight along, day and night, in the chair and out of it, I am so worn out that solitude becomes at once a luxury and a medicine."

Bishop Morris next presided over the Upper Iowa

Conference, at Lyons, August 25th; thence to the Iowa Conference, at Fairfield, September 8th; thence to the Illinois Conference, at Griggsville, September 22d; thence to the Southern Illinois, at Olney, October 6th; and thence home.

The annual meeting of the bishops was held in Chicago, December 2d. Present, Morris, Janes, Baker, and Ames; absent, Scott and Simpson. The plan made out at this meeting was subsequently remodeled, to enable one of the bishops to visit the Pacific Coast, and preside over the California and Oregon Conferences. On account of family affliction, Bishop Morris was assigned to such work as would require the least travel and absence from home. He presided at the Kentucky Conference, Alexandria, March 20, 1859; the North Indiana, at Logansport, April 7th; the West Virginia, at Parkersburg, April 20th; and the Pittsburg, at Alleghany City, April 27th. Leaving home on Tuesday, April 19th, he arrived at Parkersburg on the same evening, and opened the session of the West Virginia Conference next morning. Closing this Conference session on the following Monday, he had one day in which to reach Alleghany City. Taking the Baltimore train on Monday night to the Grafton Junction, he there waited for the early morning train for the West, by which means he reached Wheeling on Tuesday in time to connect with the train from Bellaire through Steubenville; and thus, by traveling day and night, reached the seat of the Pittsburg Conference on Tuesday evening.

Early in June the bishops met in Pittsburg to revise their Plan, with a view to send one of their numoer to the Pacific Coast, as before stated. Bishop Baker was designated for that service. Bishop Morris's Fall conferences this year were the Delaware, at Fremont, Ohio, September 14th; and the Northwest Indiana, at Greencastle, September 28th. In addition to his regular official duties, he wrote out for publication "A Discourse on Methodist Church Polity," a sermon which he had delivered in the Spring at the sessions of the North Indiana and Pittsburg Conferences, and which had been requested for publication by both those bodies. As this sermon embodies the bishop's mature thoughts on our Church polity, the substance of it seems well entitled to a place in his biography. We begin with the paragraph entitled, "The Starting-point," on the sixteenth page:

"In Methodism, the starting-point is the love of God as developed in redemption, in the gift of the Spirit, and the Divine call to the work of the ministry. Without redemption, there is no possible salvation for sinners; without the Holy Spirit, there could be no personal application of the benefits of redemption; and without some one be called to teach us, we should remain ignorant of our blood-bought privileges, as Paul said to the Romans: 'For whosoever shall call upon the name of the Lord, shall be saved. How, then, shall they call on him in whom they have not believed? and how shall they believe in him of whom they have not heard? and how shall they hear without a preacher? and how shall they preach except they be sent?' Now, suppose a nation in which there is not one experimental, practical Christian: how would the saving knowledge of the truth first be communicated? To convert souls is God's work; but he usually employs human instrumentality to teach them their lost condition and their remedy. We say, usually, but not necessarily; for he can work with or without outward means. He, however, so far as we know and believe, employs only such as possess the knowledge necessary to be imparted to others. Sinners can not savingly enlighten each other. It requires a converted man to get other men converted, or they must be operated on by the Holy Spirit, independent of human interference. Then, to originate a work of saving grace, we may rationally conclude, where there are no examples of it previously, God must do one of two things,—first, he would send a converted man from some Christian country to teach, warn, and invite souls to Christ; or, secondly, he would, by his Word and Spirit, awaken, enlighten, and call some sinner, grant him repentance, faith, pardon, regeneration, and adoption, and then send him out among his neighbors to tell them what the Lord had done for him and was willing to do for them. In either case, there is a missionary in the field. And when he gets one soul converted, he has one witness and one helper. Their united influence will prevail with others, and the work will enlarge itself till the number will require an understanding as to the terms of fellowship.

"A Little Organization.—When converts are multiplied from units to tens, some kind of organization becomes necessary to maintain unity and peace. They may begin with a record of the names of all the converts or persons proposed for membership.

These form the nucleus of the Church. The missionary pastor and his children in the Gospel are of one heart and mind. To remain so they must adopt some simple code based on the Bible, defining their faith and practice. They must agree on the Scriptural standards of morality and godliness, to prevent future difficulty; also the respective rights and duties of pastor and members, when and where they will meet for religious worship, and what shall be the order of their public and social exercises. They will likewise need certain officers to promote the interests of the society in its various departments, and strengthen the hands and hearts of pastor and people. They who are strong in faith, gifted in prayer, and apt to teach, are appointed leaders of prayer-meetings and class-meetings. Active and pious sisters may be highly useful among the serious, the sick, and the poor. Such brethren as may possess deep piety, sound judgment, and business habits, are elected stewards to take charge of the secular affairs of the Church. They who have financial skill and general influence in Church extension are chosen as trustees. And such as have aptitude to teach and manage children and youth are assigned to the Sabbath-school department. Thus they proceed to perfect the little organization so as to bring their entire forces into requisition.

"Again: as such local societies or Churches come up in other places, attention becomes necessary to connectional arrangements. All the societies wishing to belong to the ecclesiastical confederation, and come under the same general jurisdiction, must adopt the same articles of faith and rules of discipline; for 'how can two,' or more, 'walk together, except they be agreed?' By such union the societies mutually strengthen and encourage each other. In an early stage of the process of organization, it becomes indispensable to settle fully and securely the

"TERMS OF MEMBERSHIP.—As the work progresses and prospers, many persons may desire admission; and some, perhaps, not regarded as suitable to be received; and others, already received, not profitable to be retained. Mere personal preference is not a safe rule. Religious experience and moral deportment must be regarded as the standards of qualification. Our fathers, who gave us the outline of the present system of Methodist discipline, made a capital hit when they adopted the rule requiring a probation of at least six months prior to regular membership—a rule still enforced in all cases, excepting such as bring letters of recommendation from orthodox sister Churches as worthy members. The condition of admission on trial is, 'A desire to flee from the wrath to come, and to be saved from sin.' But this desire, to become available, must be evinced in three ways,—1. By doing no harm, by avoiding evil of every kind, etc.; 2. By doing good, etc.; 3. By attending upon all the ordinances of God, etc. If the pastor knows the candidate to come up to this standard, he can admit him on trial at once. But in the absence of such personal knowledge the rule is, 'Let none be admitted on trial except they are recommended by one you know, or till they have met twice or thrice in class,' so as to form some opinion of their fitness. The wisdom of this rule is apparent on the face of it. To profess a change of heart, and to make some show of outward reformation, are easy ; but a probation of six months, subjecting the candidate to weekly class examinations, both as to his religious exercises and daily deportment, is a much safer test of sincerity and consistency than a single profession at any one time.

"The conditions of full membership after probation are three,—first, a recommendation by a leader with whom the candidate has met at least six months on trial, who has every opportunity to know his religious state, daily walk, and general bearing ; secondly, he must be consecrated to God in baptism, either in infancy or adult age, this being the initiating ordinance into the visible Church of Christ ; thirdly, he must, 'on examination by the minister in charge, before the Church, give satisfactory assurance both of the correctness of his faith, and his willingness to observe and keep the rules of the Church.' These conditions are few and simple, but indispensable ; and, taken altogether, they show conclusively that our Church is at least as well guarded against imposition in the reception of members as any other Church. When any one has fully complied with them, the pastor, in the name and on behalf of the whole Church assembled, extends to him the right-hand of fellowship, and pronounces him a member.

"ACQUIRED RIGHTS.—By becoming a member of the Methodist Episcopal Church, you acquire rights which you never had before, and never could have possessed without such membership. And, first, you secure an interest in all the Church property, which, in houses of worship, parsonages, cemeteries, and institutions of learning, amounts to at least twenty millions of dollars. There may be a few houses of worship occupied by our preachers and people which are not regularly conveyed to the whole Church, but are held in trust for the use of the local societies connected therewith; in these your connection with the Church at another place gives you no title. Such deeds of conveyance are unfortunate. They are not according to our Discipline; and we may hereafter be turned out of such houses, if the local authorities holding them should become disaffected toward our Church. Now, we do not say that brethren holding and occupying such houses are not good Christians or good Methodists; but we do say that their title to the property is not Methodistical. Secondly, by becoming a member of the Methodist Episcopal Church you have acquired a full share in all her privileges. This includes an interest in her sympathies, her prayers, and her ample means of religious instruction and encouragement; in her ordinances, including the holy eucharist; and in her powerful ministry and pastoral oversight. You have secured a right to attend and participate in all her religious meetings for public and social worship, whether for expounding and hearing the Gospel, for prayer and praise, or for mutual edification by reciting personal experience. You have all the privileges found in any other evangelical Church, with class-meeting and love-feast into the bargain,— two choice means of religious improvement at once profitable and delightful. Without intending any offense to others, we here say there is no Church in this country blessed with a more spiritual living membership than ours is, though there is much room for improvement among us ; no Church affords more helps or better encouragement to a godly life than ours does. And as to our doctrinal views, we have never had occasion to waste much time or strength in adjusting them ; for our unity in this respect has been unparalleled from the beginning of our history to the present time. None of our losses by secession were occasioned by doctrinal controversy ; but always rose out of conflicting views on questions of expediency—views intemperately urged by brethren of a restless spirit and a reckless purpose. Certainly, our doctrinal unity is cause of devout thankfulness to the whole Methodist family. Thirdly, these acquired rights are secured to you on such a firm constitutional basis that no earthly power can deprive you of them till you willfully forfeit them by disobedience to, or some personal violation of, the rules of the Church. The idea of some, that a Methodist preacher has power in himself to dispossess a layman of his membership in any case, is entirely groundless. That he had such authority once, in the infancy of Methodism, is admitted ; but it was found to be unsafe for the members, and was therefore taken from him at an early period. Nothing that a member can do authorizes a pastor to exclude him till he is regularly tried and found guilty by his fellow-laymen. And if any preacher in charge were to exclude a member without a Disciplinary trial, such preacher would receive severe censure by the Conference where he is amenable, and justly too.

"THE MINISTRY.— Between the members and pastors there are active agents for good,—class-leaders, exhorters, and local preachers. The leaders are appointed by the preacher in charge, to aid him in his pastoral work of visitation and prayer and instruction. Exhorter's license is granted by the pastor on recommendation of the members, and renewed annually on that of the quarterly conference. Local preacher's license is granted by the quarterly conference on the recommendation of their respective societies, and renewed annually when their gifts, grace, and usefulness will warrant such renewal. Local preachers are eligible to deacon's orders in four years, and to elder's orders in eight years. There are in our Church over seven thousand local preachers, deacons and elders. Among so many, there may be some drones; but in general they are worthy brethren, co-operating with the regular pastors to extend the kingdom of Christ.

"The pastors proper, in our Church, are regular traveling preachers. How they become such, is a question worthy of special consideration. There are two general systems of preparing men for the Gospel ministry. One is, to select boys who may or may not be converted, and who subsequently may or may not be called of God to preach, and educate them *for* the ministry. But our system is, to select young men who are both converted and called, in the judgment of their brethren, and train them *in* the ministry, uniting the study and practice of theology all the way through. This we have proved to be a successful system of training ministers. The details of our system are briefly these: A young man feels himself moved by the Holy Spirit to the work of the ministry. His brethren, where he resides, being acquainted with him and his gifts and graces, . . . recommend him to the quarterly conference for license. Here he is examined as to his belief of our doctrines and Discipline; also his experience and call to the work. This examination is conducted by the presiding elder in presence of the conference; and, if approved, he is granted license to preach. Next, after a proper trial of him as a preacher, he is recommended by the quarterly to the annual conference for admission on trial as a traveling preacher. If received, he is assigned to a field of labor, usually as the colleague of a more experienced minister. Then there is given him a course of study, embracing science and theology, and extending through four years.

PRESIDING ELDERS.—The office of presiding elder is simply one of appointment by the bishop for executive purposes. A presiding elder's district includes about twelve pastoral charges, more or less, each of which he visits four times a year, to preach, administer the ordinances, and hold quarterly conference. He takes charge of all the elders and deacons, the traveling and local preachers and exhorters, in the district, and is required to see that every part of the Discipline is carried out; that the interests of the missionary, Sabbath-school, and tract causes are properly cared for. He presides in the appeal trial of

excluded members, and decides all questions of law
in the quarterly conference. He also directs young
men to their course of studies, and examines the candidates for orders ; he receives, employs, and changes
preachers in the interval of conference and absence
of the bishop ; and such as are disorderly he brings
to account by committee, or reports them to conference. He also is consulted by the bishop as to the
arrangement of the work and appointment of the
preachers to it, etc. It will be seen readily how important this office is to the great itinerant system.
If this part of the machinery be removed, the whole
is in confusion. An error in selecting the officer is
no argument against the office. The people might
prefer a popular preacher on the district, but sound
judgment and executive skill and administrative ability are much more important in a presiding elder than
popular talent in the pulpit; at least, this is the
opinion of such as have most experience.

"The office first appears on the Minutes of 1785,
where an elder's name stands at the head of each
district, but without the prefix 'presiding,' till 1789,
since which period the Minutes in this respect have
been uniform. A usage of so long standing is entitled
to respectful consideration. It has, however, higher
claims than age confers on the score of utility. The
experiment has proved itself successful. No prudential regulation in our Church has done so much to
render our itinerant ministry effective, except the
general superintendency, as the office of presiding
elder.

"THE APPOINTING POWER.—This pertains to the

general superintendency. We have now—1859—six bishops, neither of whom claims any local diocese. They are jointly responsible for the oversight of the whole connection; they divide it into six parts, each taking his route for one year, and then changing, so that each in his turn presides in all the conferences. One of our official duties is 'to fix the appointments of the preachers' under certain rules of limitation well understood among us. In our peculiar organization, many individual rights are relinquished for the general good. Ministers relinquish any real or supposed right of preference for places, with an understanding that the members are not to choose their pastors, but to receive whomsoever are sent. This is as fair for one party as the other. Of course, the execution of such a system requires the agency of a third party, the bishops. Now, the Church has confidence in the appointing power, or she has not. If she possesses confidence in us, why complain of our action in the premises? If confidence be wanting, why not remove the appointing power into other hands? By a certain constitutional process, the power to appoint the preachers might be transferred from the bishops to a committee of preachers and laymen; or, what would virtually amount to the same thing, abolished entirely, leaving ministers and members free to make their own arrangements. But what, then, would be the fate of the itinerancy?

"THE GENERAL CONFERENCE.—Thus far we have discoursed chiefly on the executive affairs of our Church, but now turn our attention, for a few minutes only, to her rule-making department. The General

Conference is composed of delegates from all the annual conferences, who collectively represent and act for the entire connection of ministers and members. They meet quadrennially, and remain in session about one month. . . . Besides revising the Discipline, they elect bishops, book agents, editors, corresponding secretaries for the Missionary, Sabbath-school, and Tract Societies, and regulate the publishing interests of the whole Church ; they fix the boundaries of all the annual conferences, try appeals of expelled or censured traveling preachers, adjust the general finances of the Church, and examine carefully the administration of the annual conferences, as recorded in their respective journals. They also are the tribunal to which the bishops are amenable, and hold them to strict account, both for their personal conduct and official administration,—all of which is right and proper. As to their legislative authority, the Discipline declares : 'The General Conference shall have full power to make rules and regulations for our Church, under the following limitations and restrictions.' We name some of the things which it can not do : 'The General Conference shall not revoke, alter, or change our Articles of Religion, nor establish any new standards or rules of doctrine contrary to our present existing and established standards of doctrine.' Again : 'They shall not revoke or change the General Rules of the United Societies.' Again : 'They shall not do away the privileges of our ministers or preachers of trial by a committee, and of appeal.' Yet any of these restrictions, except the one covering our Articles of Religion, may be removed

by the concurrent action of three-fourths of all the
voters of all the annual conferences and two-thirds of
the General Conference. In all things not thus restricted, the delegates are free to act for the whole
Church."

The discourse then goes on to answer a few
popular objections to Methodist polity; the first being
that "the membership have no check upon the
ministry." To this the bishop replies, first, our dependence upon them for men to keep up the ministerial force to carry on the work is a check. All the
conferences, both annual and General united, could
not make one traveling preacher without the pre-
action of lay members recommending him for that
purpose. And, secondly, the members hold a check
over their ministers in the form of material aid. We
are as dependent on them for the means as we are
for the men to carry on the work.

To another objection, that "the members are not
allowed any representation in the conferences," it is
replied that "we may concede, first, that the present
representation of members is indirect, more so than
would be satisfactory in civil affairs;" and "we concede, secondly, that if the members of our Church
really desire a direct representation in the conferences, with all its expense, trouble, and responsibility,
they should have it. . . . If the members generally ever do request it, the General Conference will
respond with fraternal kindness, as they always have
done." "As to what would be a safe and suitable
plan of lay representation, I acknowledge myself
unprepared to suggest, and would rather wait for

time to develop our wants, and the indications of Providence for the best method of supplying them."

In 1860, Bishop Morris presided over the East Baltimore Conference, at Lewisburg, Pennsylvania, February 29th; the New Jersey Conference, at Salem, March 14th; and the Providence Conference, at New Bedford, Massachusetts, March 28th, which closed the official labors of another quadrennial period.

CHAPTER XIII.

GENERAL CONFERENCE OF 1860—AN INTERESTING OCCA-
SION—REMOVAL TO SPRINGFIELD.

THE Thirteenth Delegated General Conference
assembled at St. James's Hall, in the city of
Buffalo, New York, on the 1st of May, 1860. Present—Bishops Morris, Janes, Scott, Baker, Ames,
and Simpson.

Bishop Morris called the Conference to order, and
conducted the opening religious services. This Conference was composed of two hundred and twenty-
one delegates, representing forty-seven annual conferences. The session continued until June 4th, and
was occupied largely with the discussion of proposed
new rules on the slavery question, the Committee on
that subject having recommended the amendment of
the General Rule, so that it should read: "The
buying, selling, or holding of men, women, or children, with an intention to enslave them." To carry
this resolution required a two-thirds vote, which it
failed to receive. There were one hundred and
thirty-eight votes for it, and seventy-four against it.

The subject of Lay Representation also called
forth an animated discussion, and was finally disposed
of by providing for the submission of the question to

a vote of the "male members over twenty-one years
of age, and in full connection," between the sessions
of the respective annual conferences in 1861 and
1862 ; and further providing that the bishops should
lay the same question "before the annual conferences, at their sessions in 1862."

On the 11th of May, solemn and impressive
services were held in commemoration of Bishop
Waugh, the senior member of the Episcopal Board,
who had died February 9, 1858, and to which appropriate and affectionate allusion was made in the
Episcopal Address at the opening of the Conference.
Bishop Morris, at the request of his colleagues, conducted the services, selecting for his text the twenty-
eighth verse of the eleventh chapter of Second
Corinthians : "Beside those things that are without,
that which cometh upon me daily, the care of all
the Churches."

The Christian ministry, he remarked, is a subject
of paramount importance. It is enough to fill the
head, hands, and heart of any man for life. Two
things should be kept in view in executing this high
trust,—first, we should aim to come up to the Gospel
standard as nearly as possible ; and, secondly, we
should never presume to go beyond it. In the New
Testament we have ample instruction in regard to
the practical duties of the office, and also illustrious
examples of their observance. Paul says, "Be ye
followers of me, even as I also am of Christ." Now,
while we are to imitate Paul in regard to his self-
sacrifice, his ardent zeal, and his persevering efforts
to save souls, it does not follow that we may be his

successors in all respects. The general theme of the discourse would be, Paul and his Successors; and on this subject the bishop proposed to discuss three propositions,—1. There are some things pertaining to the ministry of Paul, with regard to which we can not be his successors; 2. There are some things, in which we do not desire to be his successors; 3. There are some things, in which we may and ought to be his successors.

I. On the first point, it was remarked that Paul possessed the gift of tongues; that is, in the sense of speaking many languages. Paul, no doubt, had the knowledge of some languages acquired in the usual way,—by persevering application to study. But he also possessed the knowledge of many languages by direct inspiration. He said, "I speak with tongues more than you all," etc. Secondly, Paul was endowed with the spirit of prophecy. He spoke as he was moved by the Holy Ghost. He very distinctly, in his letter to the Thessalonians, prophesied the apostasy of the Romans, under the personification of "the Man of Sin." He also prophesied the downfall of that corrupt power: "Then shall that Wicked be revealed, whom the Lord shall consume," etc. He also said, "The Spirit speaketh expressly that, in the latter days, some shall depart from the faith," etc. These passages are sufficient to show that St. Paul was an inspired prophet. Thirdly, he was endued with the gift of miracles. He rebuked Elymas, the sorcerer; and there fell upon him a mist of darkness, and he went about seeking some one to lead him by the hand. When the damsel, possessed of the spirit of divination, became an annoyance to the apostles, Paul turned and said to the spirit, " I command thee, in the name of Jesus Christ, come out of her ;" and the spirit did so the same hour. When Paul was shipwrecked, and the viper came out of the fire and fastened on his hand, and when the barbarians looked for him to have fallen down dead, he shook off the viper, and it did him no harm ; and they changed their minds, and thought he was a god. In the same island was Publius, whose father was sick of a fever ; and Paul went in to him, laid his hands upon him, and prayed for him, and he was instantly healed. In one instance—that of Eutychus—he raised the dead.

Again : he was an apostle, and in that office has no successors. The apostles were a peculiar class of ministers, instituted for a special purpose, to be perpetuated for a short time. Their mission was to establish Christianity by appealing to the facts of the Gospel history from personal knowledge ; and, when necessary, confirming their statements by working miracles. This was sufficiently done in one ordinary life-time. Then they disappeared from the stage of life, mostly by deaths of violence, and have no successors.

II. There are some things pertaining to the ministry of Paul, with regard to which we do not want to be his successors.

The bishop spoke here of the privations, opposition, suffering, personal violence, and abuse which St. Paul endured. But, besides these things, he had the care of all the Churches. The work was great, the opposition powerful, and there was a continual influx of difficult questions upon the apostle, respecting doctrines and practical duties—questions of experience, of discipline, and of dispute—all pouring upon him at once; insomuch that Dr. Clarke calls them an "insurrection of cases," and gives it as his opinion that the difficulties from within were a greater burden than all the pressure from without.

III. Concerning the things in the ministry of Paul, with regard to which we may and ought to be his successors, Bishop Morris said that, while the apostle was endowed with extraordinary gifts, he practiced all the ordinary duties pertaining to Christian life, and exercised all the ordinary functions of the ministry, and in these things we should be his successors. First, he was a converted man. So, we trust, we are converted, and have felt the power of Christ's resurrection and the fellowship of his sufferings. Again: he believed in a progressive spiritual life. He did not teach that when men and women are born again they are born full-grown, but that they are "babes in Christ." He exhorted Christians to "grow in grace," and to "learn the principles of the doctrine of Christ, and go on unto perfection." And what he taught he practiced: "This one thing I do, forgetting those things which are behind, and reaching forth unto those things which are before, I press toward the mark for the prize of the high calling of God in Christ Jesus." We believe in these doctrines: Pardon, regeneration, the witness of the Spirit, and holiness. In these regards we claim to be the successors of the apostles.

In the next place, Paul was called of God to preach. He is very specific on this point. Necessity was laid upon him to preach the Gospel. We have the same feelings. We do not regard the ministry as a mere profession. All our ministers have professed to be moved by the Holy Ghost. Paul was a traveling preacher. Round about from Jerusalem to Illyricum, he fully preached the Gospel of Christ. When we read his journal in the New Testament, we are led to inquire, Is there any thing analogous to this in modern Church annals? Something very similar we find in the career of Wesley in England, and Asbury in America; and we rejoice to know that many of their sons strive to follow them. Paul was also a pastor; he had the care of all the Churches, and was, officially and practically, a pastor as well as a preacher and an apostle. Bishop Morris then sketched the duties of a bishop in the Methodist Episcopal Church, embracing the supervision of the temporal and spiritual interests of the Church, the immense amount of travel necessary in the discharge of these duties, ranging from five thousand to twenty thousand miles per annum, the heavy official correspondence required, and the responsibility of appointing the ministers to their several fields of labor. He said that, to do the work of a Methodist bishop, "as we are expected to do it, requires the faith of Abraham, the patience of Job, the courage of Paul, the meekness of Moses, the wisdom of Solomon, the eloquence of Apollos, and the paternal love of John." He then added a remark which produced a general smile, notwithstanding the solemnity of the occasion;

and we reproduce it as illustrative of the quiet humor
for which the bishop was always noted : " Notwithstanding all the responsibilities and privations and
sacrifices and labors it will bring upon them, there
are competent brethren who are willing to accept the
office rather than that the good cause should suffer."

The sermon closed with a full and interesting
biographical sketch of Bishop Waugh, and reflections
and lessons suggested by the sad bereavement of the
Church. It occupied an hour and a quarter in the
delivery, and was listened to with profound interest
by an audience of more than two thousand persons.
Our brief abstract of the discourse is taken from the
notes of the General Conference reporter, published
originally in the *Daily Christian Advocate.*

On the sixteenth day of the session, Rev. J. K.
Gillett rose to a question of privilege, and stated that
there was in the house a member of the Michigan
Conference who had something to present to the
body which would interest every member. He moved,
therefore, that Rev. Mr. Morgan be introduced. On
being introduced to the Conference, Mr. Morgan exhibited a plain silver watch, once the property of
Bishop Asbury, and which he desired to present to
Bishop Morris, with the understanding that at his
death it should be given to the senior of the remaining bishops, and thus always be in the hands of the
oldest incumbent of the episcopal office. On receiving it, Bishop Morris said : " This is the first watch
that was ever presented to me. But I would rather
own it than the finest gold repeater ever made. I
perceive that its voice [holding it to his ear], like

my own, is feeble; and I am told that its mainspring is weak. Probably, like myself, it is nearly worn out. I accept it with earnest thanks, and will soon transmit it to my successor, and go, I trust, to meet its former venerated owner in the house not made with hands."

On the 28th of May, the following resolution was adopted:

"*Resolved*, That in view of the advancing age of Bishop Morris, the senior superintendent, he be not required to travel at large through the connection, but be left at full liberty to perform only such official labor as he and his colleagues may judge proper."

On the adjournment of General Conference, Bishop Morris returned to Cincinnati to make arrangements to remove to Springfield, Ohio, which he had fixed upon as his future home, and where, early in the Spring, he had made a purchase of property suitable for a residence. His new home was occupied June 20th, and a highly characteristic description of the "place," which he named "Salubria," appeared soon after in one of the Church papers, as follows:

"The house, though not elegant, is substantial, roomy, and comfortable. The inclosed ground is an oblong square, at the angle of Mill and Harrison Streets, measuring two hundred feet on the former, and four hundred and fifty on the latter. It embraces the buildings, yard, garden, 'truck-patch,' and cow-pasture, and contains a fraction over two acres, exclusive of an outside strip left for a pass-way. There are a few apple, peach, cherry, and plum trees on the ground, with a limited number of ornamental shade-trees, and a good supply of natural forest-trees, of which the most noted is a sturdy oak in the north-west corner of the yard, about nine feet in circumference at the base, and nearly one hundred feet high, which, with other trees, affords a pleasant afternoon shade.

"The live-stock on the premises is as follows: 1. Job, our favorite family horse, looks pleased with his new apartments and supply of provender, and moves gracefully in harness. His character is decidedly good. Ladies drive him, and feel secure. He is as indifferent to the whistle of a locomotive or the report of cannon as to the hum of a bee; gentle as a lamb, and patient as the man of Uz. 2. 'Belle,' our present dependence for milk and cream. 3. Two white pigs, which willingly relieve us of the kitchen-scraps. 4. One dozen pullets, white, yellow, brown, and speckled. The leader of this feathered tribe is Peter, a very pompous bird, dressed in fancy colors, moving around with an appearance of self-gratulation. In one respect, he is useful; by his stentorian voice he lets us know how the night-watches pass, and when the day dawns. 5. Clarinda, with her family of black, brindle, and spotted kittens. 6. Snap, our terrier-pup, full of life and mischief, yet a favorite of the family. In addition to this show of life and comfort, the people are kind and agreeable, treating us more like old friends than new-comers. So far, we enjoy the change from city to country as well as we expected; and if we can pass the Winter pleasantly, will be fully satisfied here. My calling has occasioned frequent removals. I have been a citizen of four States; but have probably found my last camping-place this side of Jordan."

The bishop's Fall tour of conferences embraced the East Genesee, at Lima, August 22d; the North Ohio, at Ashland, September 12th; and the Détroit, at Dexter, Michigan, September 26th. At the East Genesee Conference, Rev. D. D. Buck, on behalf of Mrs. Chapin, of Geneva, New York, presented Bishop Morris with a pair of spectacles formerly owned and worn by Bishop Asbury,—the donor being the same lady who, at the General Conference, presented Bishop Asbury's watch to Bishop Morris. On receiving the spectacles Bishop Morris said:

"I am very much obliged to the good lady for her interesting gift. I will carefully preserve it, and, if I live to return home, I will deposit the spectacles in the drawer with the watch which was given me by the same lady at the General Conference in Buffalo. I never saw Bishop Asbury; but, as nearly as I can recollect, I reached my first circuit in Ohio on the day on which he died. I am glad to receive the glasses through which he read the Word of Life. I have long esteemed Bishop Asbury as the great apostle of American Methodism. By these glasses I am forcibly reminded of my own infirmities. When I was about eighteen years of age I received injuries in the optic nerves. For three years I had to wear goggles out of doors, and spectacles within. It was to many a matter of great doubt whether I should have eyes or not. At last I quit doctoring, and my sight mended more in the next three months than it had in the previous three years. My eyes continue better till to-day; nevertheless, I still have to use two pairs of glasses. I change during divine service, as I can not read with the same with which I look out upon the congregation. So I work along. Bishop Asbury has got beyond the need of glasses. I presume his eyes are like 'apples of gold in pictures of silver.' I hope to reach that happy place. Brethren, pray for me, that I may hold faith and a good conscience to the end."

Bishop Morris met his colleagues and the General Mission at New York in November, but was hastened home by news of his wife's illness. Soon after his return, he addressed a communication to the editor of the *Western Christian Advocate*—Dr. Kingsley—from which we make an interesting extract:

"Perhaps, Doctor, some of my friends would like to know how I am passing my sixty-seventh Winter. If so, I am happy to say, Rather pleasantly, all things considered. In the early years of my ministry I knew no vacation. Winter and Summer, Spring and Autumn, were alike busy seasons. Then I preached once a day, on an average, the year round; but now my average is about once a week. As our work is now arranged, we have no conferences in Winter, and but few in Summer. Our press of official duties is in the Spring and Fall. So I am keeping close Winter quarters here; but with a good grate, and plenty of bituminous coal, I am able to maintain a temperature of sixty-five degrees, thanks to kind Providence. Moreover, in my quiescence I enjoy some communion with my brethren, and learn a little of the affairs of our Church, our country, and the world,—in all of which I take a deep interest. As to my means of information, exclusive of my library, I receive four monthlies, ten weeklies, one tri-weekly, one daily, and numerous pamphlets. These afford daily employment. My evenings, however, are tedious ; for, with eyes habitually weak, and now becoming quite dim, I do not attempt to read at night. To worry through by daylight, I read many of the newspaper articles as Congressmen read their bills the first and second times, 'by their titles.' To be more exact, there are some things in the papers which I generally read, and some which I generally do not read. Among those which I usually read are leading editorials, contributions on proper subjects over responsible names, well-timed articles on the state of the Church, the country, and the world, and items of general news. Among the things which I generally do not read are poetry, anonymous articles, long lectures, political speeches, speculative theology, and all matters involving personal quarrel or violent political conflict. When in middle life, I dreaded two things which I saw might overtake me,—1. The necessity of curtailing my ministerial labor, and becoming partly inactive and inefficient ; but by a gradual process I have gotten over this difficulty, and am content to do what little I can. 2. I dreaded old age. I expected to see the world appear murky, and the Church appear as a moral desolation, and that life would become a burden. But I experience nothing of all this. My health remains comfortable, my mind cheerful and spirit buoyant, and I am pleasantly passing the evening of life. In reviewing the past I see some things to regret, and some from which to draw consolation. Upon the whole, I have no wish to repeat life's campaign, lest, instead of making it better—of which there is much need—I should make it worse. Wishing to be thankful for the past, and hopeful for the future, I leave myself and my family, my Church and my country, in the hands of God, praying him, through Jesus Christ, to hasten the world's conversion."

In 1861, Bishop Morris commenced his official labors by presiding over the Missouri and Arkansas Conference, at St. Louis, March 7th; thence to the Kansas Conference, at Atchison, March 21st; thence to the Nebraska Conference, at Nebraska City, April 4th. Of the first he says:

"The Missouri Conference closed a pleasant session on the 13th of March. The religious exercises were refreshing. This body embraces some able and earnest men, not easily diverted from their good purposes. Under the financial pressure of the past year, the work indicated more signs of contraction than expansion, but without much loss in the membership. The ministers there had not only the difficulties common to new countries, such as hard work, rough fare, and poor pay, but also such as pertain to their peculiar position in a slave State; of which I need here say nothing, as the particulars have been sufficiently detailed in the *Central Christian Advocate.* If the Government rights up, and its political affairs become settled, they expect to live and prosper in Missouri; but if not, they intend to do as well as they can. No more should be required."

He left St. Louis, March 15th, on the steamboat *Warsaw*, and reached Hannibal the next day. Here he found the St. Joseph train waiting; and by it arrived at Macon City the same evening, Saturday, where he spent the Sabbath. On Monday morning he resumed the journey, reaching St. Joseph late that night. Next morning, taking the Platte County Railroad, he arrived in good time at Atchison, the seat of the Kansas Conference. He says:

"Atchison is a young city, rising up in a location resembling an ample theater. Here is the depot of the Kansas Relief Society. The streets were daily crowded with wagons and teams from the interior, so that it was difficult to pass. The facts heretofore published respecting the destitution of Kansas were confirmed by the preachers from every part of the State as substantially true. These ministers are sunburned, hardy men, who have endured much hard service, and look as if they were ready for more. They did up the business of the Conference with order and dispatch. The work is arranged into six districts, one of which embraces Pike's Peak, and is called the Rocky Mountain District; Rev. J. M. Chivington, Presiding Elder. This brother is sometimes called the Rocky Mountain infant. His physical dimensions are those of a giant, with a soul large in proportion. He wears a robe made of wolf-skins, with the tails for tassels. I told him that I had read of a wolf in sheep's clothing, but never before saw a sheep in wolf's clothing.

27

"The dust in Kansas was nearly suffocating whenever a train moved. Whether in the street or on the common, it rose like a cloud, and was whirled in every direction by the wind; which is more furious there than I have witnessed elsewhere, except in Minnesota. If they have there a calm day or night, it is an exception to the general rule. The wind whines, growls, yelps, howls, bellows, and thunders; and then comes a blast, the effect of which resembles the tread of an earthquake. If a brief lull ensue, it is only to gather strength for another onslaught; and so it goes on, day and night. One good effect is, the malaria is dispersed, and the country is mostly free from bilious disease. The people generally look very healthy."

On Wednesday, March 27th, the bishop, accompanied by Dr. Hitchcock, one of the Western Book Agents, crossed over to St. Joseph, Missouri, a city at that time of twelve thousand inhabitants, on the Missouri River, and in the midst of a country of great beauty and fertility. They remained here over Sabbath, preaching to the feeble society in their humble chapel. It was, however, a day of rest and refreshment to both preachers and people. On Monday evening they took a steamer for Nebraska City, and, with some unavoidable delays, accomplished the journey by Wednesday night, arriving at about eight o'clock in a drenching rain-storm. "Being informed that the boat would proceed on a few miles to a wood-yard before lying up for the night, we went ashore as soon as she landed, hoping to find a hack; but there was none there, and we had no alternative but to take it on foot. The night was very stormy. The first step from the gangway was into mud, and every subsequent step from that to the hotel was into mud. It was very adhesive mud; our feet went in easily enough, but the trouble was to get them out. The darkness was such as to be felt. To find the way without a guide was simply impossible; but a fellow-passenger who resided in the city kindly offered to pilot us to a hotel. He went before, reported progress, and we followed by the sound of his voice. Our way led over hills and hollows, which made it exceedingly tiresome. The rain, driven by a fierce wind, struck us obliquely, and with great force. When we reached the hotel, distant about half a mile from the landing, my outer garments were wet with rain, and my under ones equally so with perspiration."

The Nebraska Conference commenced its first session April 4, 1861, and adjourned on the following Monday evening. It was a small body, embracing but little over twenty preachers, and the work was arranged into two districts, covering the inhabited parts of the territory. The prospects, however, were encouraging, and the Nebraska has grown to be a large and flourishing Conference.

In the Autumn of this year, Bishop Morris presided over the Cincinnati Conference, at Springfield, September 4th, and the South-eastern Indiana, at Jeffersonville, September 18th. In consequence of a long and severe illness of Mrs. Morris, he did not attend the Fall meeting of the General Mission Committee, at New York, and the annual meeting of the bishops took place at "Salubria," December 12th.

In the early part of this year, the great rebellion against the civil government of the United States was inaugurated in the slave-holding States of the Union, and the people were profoundly agitated in view of the alarming prospect. Fort Sumter had already been fired upon, and armed treason was boldly flaunting defiance in the face of the national authorities. It will interest the reader of this biography to know the views of the senior bishop of the Methodist Episcopal Church at this critical and trying period of the country's history. On the 17th of May, 1861, he addressed a communication to the *Central Christian Advocate*, St. Louis, Missouri, from which we quote a few paragraphs:

"All party strife about Republicanism and Democracy, about Abolition and Pro-slaveryism, should be suspended. The choice now is between law and anarchy. The question at issue before the American people is, Government or no Government. It has but two sides, and we can employ but two parties. Let all the friends of God and their country take the affirmative side of this question, and the rest may take the negative side or no side at all, as they like. He that is not for us is against us. There is no middle ground. Every friend to his country can render her some aid. Some can take the field, and others can contribute toward defraying the expense; and they who can neither give nor fight can pray.

" No attempt is, or has been, made by the Federal Government to deprive the secessionists of any right secured to them by the Constitution of the United States. On the contrary, the favors of the Govern-

ment have been lavished upon them in undue proportion. Secesssion, therefore, is rebellion without any
plausible excuse, and will result in the destruction of
its authors and leaders, and many of those engaged
in it. One thing is cause of deep regret; that is,
many innocent persons will suffer with the guilty.
This is unavoidable from their involuntary relation to
the revolutionary movement. As for us who adhere
to the Union, we have little to fear, and can say with
David, 'Though a host should encamp against me,
my heart shall not fear: though war should rise
against me, in this will I be confident.' It remains
for Christians to watch, pray, trust in God to save
the country, and calmly wait for the result."

Bishop Morris never faltered for a moment either
in his patriotic devotion to the cause of the Union,
or his faith in the ultimate triumph of the Federal
arms; and in the darkest days of the Rebellion, when
many friends of the Government were filled with
gloomy forebodings, the national flag, the banner of
beauty and the emblem of freedom, was always seen
floating from the outer wall of " Salubria."

In 1862, the bishop's Spring work began with the
Philadelphia Conference, which met in the city of
Philadelphia, March 19th. The session lasted ten
days, and the pressure of responsibility and toil was
so great that symptoms of his old disease—paralysis—
revived, insomuch that he faltered and reeled. On
the last day of the session—the appointments having
been all arranged, ready for announcement—finding
himself in constant danger of prostration, he called
Rev. T. J. Thompson to the chair, and, putting into

his hands the business of the Conference, left the city for Elizabeth, New Jersey. Exemption from all care, with a few day's rest, so far restored him that he was able to preach in Elizabeth on the following Sabbath.

He next presided over the Newark Conference, at Newton, New Jersey, April 2d, and on the final adjournment of that body, on the 9th, left for home in a severe snow-storm, which had so increased in fury by the time he reached the high mountain range west of Altoona, in Pennsylvania, that the train was detained by the snow-drifts for ten hours, the passengers spending a gloomy, cheerless night in the cars. He finally reached home safely on the 11th of April.

Bishop Morris's Fall tour this year embraced the Ohio Conference, which met at Zanesville, September 2d; the Central Ohio, at Greenville, September 17th; and the Genesee, at Batavia, New York, October 1st.

During this year he addressed a letter "To the Younger Classes of Methodist Preachers," through the columns of the Church papers, on "The Study of the Discipline," the substance of which is subjoined as worthy of permanent record, and entitled to serious consideration from all classes of Methodist preachers:

"1. Do not rely upon second-hand information; but go to the fountain-head, the Discipline, and learn for yourselves what is required of you, and how to perform it. 2. Do not read the Discipline merely as a history, or treatise on morals, but study it as an ecclesiastical code. Study it consecutively. When you take up one topic, never leave it till you learn all the book contains in relation to it. For example: You wish to know something respecting the qualifications, duties, and appointment of stewards. Turn to the index, find the word 'steward,' and then examine carefully every page of the book where reference is made to the subject, comparing one point with another, and you have, in comprehensive form, the whole matter. Having mastered it, pursue the same course in regard to the duties of trustees, class-leaders, exhorters, local preachers, preachers in charge, presiding elders, and bishops; also as to rules respecting Sunday-schools, Missionary Society, and other benevolent institutions, not omitting the circulation of religious books and periodicals. In the same way ascertain the business of leaders' and stewards' meeting, of quarterly, annual, and General Conferences, and so of all the rest.

"Again: Do you wish to know how Church members are received, what are their privileges, duties, and responsibilities, and how they are to be tried for various offenses? the whole process is clearly laid down in the Discipline, and easily understood. In this way you may obtain more reliable information, without neglecting other duties, in one year, than you could acquire by correspondence in twenty years. Then, too, you will have the satisfaction of feeling somewhat independent, and ready for any case which may come up in your charge. Instead of having to write and wait for information, you can proceed with a case understandingly at once.

" 3. Such knowledge as may be thus readily derived from the study of the Discipline, is highly valu-

able in many respects. It would greatly increase
your efficiency and usefulness in the pastoral office,
and secure an improved condition of the work, and
by consequence you would have better charges. It
would vastly augment your influence both with the
ministry and the laymen. It would save the bishops
the labor of writing, annually, hundreds of letters in
answer to questions on rule and administration, and
leave them more time for other duties. To know
how to enforce our rules properly, is a material part
of ministerial qualification. Though a brother could
preach like an angel, yet if he possess no business
tact or governing faculty, he will leave every charge
to which he is sent, in confusion, which will render
him unacceptable generally among the people.

"4. Finally, exhort the members, offical and private, to obtain, read, and study the latest edition of
our Discipline, that they may understand their own
rights and duties. Some of them have obsolete editions, and others have none. Some who own the
book seldom read it with care ; so that many of our
members know nothing of the rules except what they
learn incidentally, by occasionally witnessing their
execution. Shame on any Church member who remains willfully ignorant of the rules of his own
Church. And double shame on any pastor who
encourages such ignorance by his example. Time
spent in exhorting members on this duty is not lost ;
for the more knowledge they have of our rules, the
more easily they are governed by them."

In 1863, Bishop Morris presided over the Kentucky Conference, at Covington, February 26th ; the

Western Virginia Conference, at Fairmount, March 18th; the North Indiana, at Wabash, April 9th; the North Ohio, at Mount Vernon, September 2d; the Indiana, at Washington, September 16th; and the North-west Indiana, at Michigan City, September 30th.

He also, during that year, communicated to one of the Church papers his ideas on the subject of "Pulpit Force," saying, among other things:

"So far as I can see, our chief deficiency is at this point,—*we lack force* in our pulpit performances. The orthodoxy of our ministers is but little questioned; our educational advantages are considerable, and increasing; we have comfortable Churches, well filled with auditors who appreciate and support the Gospel. In all these respects we are more highly favored than our fathers were. Yet in practical usefulness they excelled us; their preaching was more successful than ours is. As pulpit orators we are but children, compared to our fathers in Christ. Many of our early Methodist ministers spoke with such wisdom and power as their enemies could not gainsay or resist. Now, if we would be alike successful, we must aim to wield the same power which our fathers did, and for the same purpose; that is, to glorify God in the salvation of men, women, and children. In order to do this, we should have respect, first, to the choice of subjects, selecting such as plead directly to the heart and conscience of our hearers. Here we often fail. A well-put, logical argument, on a speculative question, may interest the curious, and elicit a little praise or censure, according to the notions of critics respectively; but few are permanently benefited by it. The great truths of the Gospel—such as human depravity, the atoning sacrifice of Christ, the agency of the Holy Spirit, and man's personal salvation—are the most effective pulpit topics.

"Secondly, we should preach those doctrines in faith, nothing doubting. When we faithfully execute the commission which God has given us, why should we doubt his blessing upon his own word? But, to maintain full confidence in the Gospel message, we must ourselves be living examples of its power to save. Then our preaching will be 'in demonstration of the Spirit, and of power.' Thirdly, let us not burden ourselves with notes to look at in the pulpit; they are worse than useless. Who would think of moving a multitude by reading a manuscript, with his finger on the lines, and his eyes on the words? He might as well attempt to box with his hands tied, or to run with his feet hoppled. Away with all such incumbrances. Give us a clear field, with head and heart full of the subject on hand, with faith in vigorous exercise; let us look our auditors fully in the eyes, and watch to see where the word takes effect, where the sword of the Spirit strikes, and repeat the blows till the sinner yields to be saved by grace."

In 1864, Bishop Morris presided over the West Virginia Conference, at Parkersburg, March 16th, and the North Indiana Conference, at Knightstown, April 6th. At the session of the West Virginia Conference the following paper was adopted:

"*Whereas*, we have been permitted once more to

have our beloved and venerable senior bishop, Rev. T. A. Morris, D. D., preside over our annual session; and *whereas*, his presence and counsel here have been of inestimable advantage to his brethren and sons in the Gospel, on whom, in this his native State, it has devolved, in these days of darkness and rebuke, to stand in the breach and sustain the banner which God has given us for his cause and truth; therefore,

" 1. *Resolved*, That we express our gratitude to the great Head of the Church for permitting us to meet Bishop Morris again in an annual conference.

" 2. *Resolved*, That we rejoice in that grace which has brought our beloved bishop to the completion of half a century in the work and ministry of the Lord Jesus Christ and his Church.

" 3. *Resolved*, That we tender to Bishop Morris assurances of our hearty sympathy with him amid the growing infirmities and disabilities of age, and our continued prayers that, if it be God's will, he may long be spared to occupy the exalted position which he has so long sustained in the Christian ministry, and to bless the Church and the world with his advice and prayers.

" 4. *Resolved*, That a certified copy of these resolutions be presented to Bishop Morris.

" ALEXANDER MARTIN,

" JAMES DRUMMOND.

" PARKERSBURG, WEST VIRGINIA, *March* 21, 1864."

With the session of the North Indiana Conference Bishop Morris closed his sixth quadrennial of episcopal labor.

CHAPTER XIV.

THE General Conference of 1864 assembled in Union Church, in the city of Philadelphia, on Monday, the second day of May. Bishops Morris, Janes, Scott, Simpson, Baker, and Ames were present. The Conference was composed of two hundred and sixteen delegates, representing forty-nine annual conferences. The opening religious services were conducted by Bishop Morris. After the organization of the Conference in the usual manner, the following preamble and resolutions, submitted by Rev. E. Thomson, D. D., were adopted unanimously, by a rising vote:

" *Whereas*, our beloved senior superintendent, Thomas A. Morris, has completed his half-century of ministerial service, a service scarcely interrupted by sickness, and rendered in various relations— pastoral, editorial, and episcopal—and with uniform acceptance, and which brings him to his seventieth year with a reputation unsullied, an eye undimmed, and a natural force which, though abated, is still strong ; therefore,

" 1. *Resolved*, That we recognize with gratitude

the hand of God in prolonging the life and preserving the health, the mind, and the fair fame of our venerable superintendent.

"2. *Resolved*, That Bishop Morris is hereby respectfully requested to preach before the Conference, at some period convenient for him, a discourse noting the progress of the Church during his past ministerial life, with such observations and counsels as the review may suggest to him."

A resolution was also adopted, on the first day of the session, requesting the trustees of the church in which the Conference held its sittings, to display the flag of the United States over the building during the sessions of the body.

As the country was now in the very crisis of the great Rebellion, we are not surprised to find a further resolution adopted, on the motion of Rev. Granville Moody, D. D., that " Friday, May 6th, be set apart as a day of fasting and prayer to Almighty God, on behalf of our country in this hour of her peril ; and that the occasion be observed by appropriate religious services, morning, afternoon, and evening, in the several Methodist churches of this city ; and that our people throughout the country be requested to observe similar services on that day, in their several places of religious worship."

Early in the session, an address to President Lincoln was adopted, expressing to him the loyalty of the Church, her earnest devotion to the interests of the country, and her sympathy with the Chief Magistrate in the great responsibilities of his high position.

"In this present struggle for the Nation's life," says the address, "many thousands of her members, and a large number of her ministers, have rushed to arms, to maintain the cause of God and humanity. They have sealed their devotion to their country with their blood, on every battle-field of this terrible war.

"Our earnest and constant prayer is, that this cruel and wicked rebellion may be speedily suppressed; and we pledge you our hearty co-operation in all appropriate means to secure this object. Loyal and hopeful in national adversity, in prosperity thankful, we most heartily congratulate you on the glorious victories recently gained; and rejoice in the belief that our complete triumph is near.

"We honor you for your proclamations of liberty, and rejoice in all the acts of the Government designed to secure freedom to the enslaved.

"The prayers of millions of Christians, with an earnestness never manifested for rulers before, daily ascend to Heaven, that you may be endued with all needed wisdom and power. Actuated by sentiments of the loftiest and purest patriotism, our prayer shall be continually for the preservation of our country undivided, for the triumph of our cause, and for a permanent peace, gained by the sacrifice of no moral principle, but founded on the Word of God, and securing, in righteousness, liberty and equal rights to all."

The address was conveyed to President Lincoln by a Committee of five distinguished members of the Conference; namely, Bishop Ames, and Reverend

Doctors Cummings, George Peck, Charles Elliott, and Moody. The reply of the President will ever be regarded as among the most eloquent and beautiful utterances of that great statesman. He said:

"GENTLEMEN,— In response to your address, allow me to attest the accuracy of its historical statements, indorse the sentiments it expresses, and thank you, in the Nation's name, for the sure promise it gives.

"Nobly sustained as the Government has been by all the Churches, I would utter nothing which might in the least appear invidious against any; yet, without this, it may fairly be said that the Methodist Episcopal Church, not less devoted than the best, is, by its greater numbers, the most important of all. It is no fault in others that the Methodist Church sends more soldiers to the field, more nurses to the hospitals, and more prayers to heaven than any. God bless the Methodist Church! Bless all the Churches! And blessed be God, who, in this our great trial, giveth us the Churches!"

During the session of this General Conference, a memorial was presented from Union Chapel, Cincinnati, complaining of the administration of Bishop Morris in their case, and referred to the Committee on Episcopacy. Union Chapel was organized, in 1849, by a number of active and influential Methodists of Cincinnati, with the avowed object of promoting certain changes in the polity of Methodism. The property was held by trustees, in trust for the society; the rule then existing, requiring "men and women to sit apart," was ignored; and a resolution was adopted by the "Official Board," declining the responsibility of furnishing the customary support to the presiding elder, on the ground that the services of such an officer were useless. The position assumed by this charge, in opposition to the usages of Methodism generally, produced more or less irritation ; but appointments were made to it, from time to time, of such ministers as the Official Board selected without consultation with the presiding elder of the district, and generally from other conferences.

In the Fall of 1859, Rev. George C. Robinson, of New York, a young and brilliant minister, was appointed pastor of Union Chapel. Under his ministry the Church was greatly prospered, and he became much endeared to the people. Very soon, however, in consequence of failing health, he was compelled to relinquish his pulpit, and desist from active labor. Under the directions of his physicians, he went abroad, and sought by travel in Europe to repair his broken constitution ; the congregation meantime continuing his salary, and securing as a supply for their pulpit the Rev. W. A. Snively, who held a supernumerary relation to the East Baltimore Conference. The relation of Mr. Snively as pastor of Union Chapel was duly legalized by the proper authorities ; and he continued to fill the pulpit acceptably during the unexpired term of Mr. Robinson.

On the 5th of August, 1861, the Official Board appointed a Committee of three to address Bishop Morris on the subject of a ministerial supply for the ensuing year ; and in this communication to the bishop a request was made that Union Chapel be left "to be supplied," with the understanding that Mr. Snively would be employed for another year. The letter to Bishop Morris closed with these words:

"We will only add that Union Chapel is essentially Methodist, and has not the remotest idea of ignoring its relationship to the Methodist Episcopal Church, whatever may be said to the contrary; and we therefore beg your attention to our own statement, and compliance with our request, unless it be absolutely impossible, in which case we desire to be informed, in order that we may take action in regard to some other course."

Bishop Morris, for reasons that will appear hereafter, declined acceding to the request of the Board, and appointed Rev. George C. Crum, D. D., one of the leading ministers of his Conference, as pastor of the charge. Soon after the adjournment of the Cincinnati Conference, the Official Board of Union Chapel was convened, and a resolution adopted declining to receive Dr. Crum as their pastor. This action was subsequently indorsed by a meeting of the congregation. In view of these facts, Bishop Morris advised the presiding elder of the district to drop Union Chapel from his plan, and hold no quarterly-meeting there, nor furnish any supply, until the brethren of that society conformed to law and order.

On the 28th of October, 1861, at a meeting of the Official Board, a resolution was adopted "that Bishop Morris be, and he is hereby, requested to transfer, or to secure the transfer of, Rev. W. A. Snively to this [Cincinnati] Conference, and appoint him to Union Chapel, as a final disposition of this entire question." This resolution, with others relating to the presiding eldership and the loyalty of Union Chapel to Methodism, having been duly forwarded to Bishop Morris, he sent the following reply:

" SPRINGFIELD, O., *November* 11, 1861.

" *To the Official Members of Union Chapel, Cincinnati:*

" DEAR BRETHREN,—Your resolutions of the 4th and 7th inst. are before me; the first and second of which refer chiefly to the office and administration of your presiding elder, who is responsible to the Annual Conference for his administration, as I am to the General Conference for mine. Presuming that he understands his official duty, and is aiming to perform it as best he can under the circumstances, I need not enter into the special pleadings in his case. I find it enough for me to meet and sustain my own official responsibilty.

" You request me to transfer, or secure the transfer of, Rev. W. A. Snively to this Conference, and appoint him to the pastorate of Union Chapel, as a final disposition of this entire question.

" I am obliged to decline compliance with this request, for the following reasons:

" 1. It would be a violation of official instructions given to the bishops by the General Conference of 1860, namely:

" '1. *Resolved*, That while we cheerfully accord to our excellent superintendents their constitutional right to supply the general work by transfers when necessary, we respectfully request that transfers may never be made solely at the personal solicitation of the preacher desiring to be transferred; nor yet to gratify the wishes of any one charge, between whom and the proposed appointee, negotiations have been previously made.

"'2. *Resolved,* That negotiations for special appointments in the pastoral work between individual ministers and societies, prior to the exercise of the regular appointing power in our Church, is contrary to our economy, and injurious to our itinerant system.'—*Journal General Conference,* 1860, *pp.* 224, 398.

"No comment is necessary to show that to comply with your request would be a palpable violation of this instruction, for which I would be justly held responsible. This alone would prevent my compliance.

"2. The crowded state of the Cincinnati Conference. Not an individual was admitted or readmitted, at its last session, for want of room. Dr. Crum is still without any place, and some half-dozen members of Conference, now in the army, should they return, would find themselves without any field of ministerial labor; and for me to add to the burden, by transferring more ministerial force to this Conference, would be an unreasonable impropriety.

"3. The practice of certain charges negotiating with individual ministers to become their pastors, and then merely asking the bishop to ratify their own proceedings, is embarrassing to the appointing power, and, in my judgment, contrary to the rules and regulations of the Methodist Episcopal Church; and should be discouraged by all concerned, as far as possible. For these very sufficient reasons, I respectfully decline compliance with your request in the case of Mr. Snively.

"As this may be my final response, I wish to say

a few other things. As to the legitimate exercise
of the appoining power, and the motives which influence it, you will please observe that we profess to be
governed by the Discipline, and not by the local
regulations of Union Chapel, or any other charge,—
however pleasant it might be to gratify personal
friends. . . . When churches are not conveyed
to the Methodist Episcopal Church, according to the
Discipline, she claims no legal right to enforce her
authority. Such Churches can only be supplied with
her preachers by consent of parties. While such
Churches secure to our ministers the free use of
their pulpits and the right to administer the Discipline, and will receive and support them on such
terms, we may supply them with pastors, and good
may be done ; but when such Churches cease to
comply with these terms, all we can do is to with-
hold the supply of pastors, and let them fall back on
their own resources. As to the terms on which
Union Chapel can hereafter be recognized (as stated
in my fourth reply, of October 28th), after a careful
review, I find no cause to change. It will be observed that I said nothing about a new deed, believing, as I did, that all these terms could be met under
your existing title. They who assumed and exercised
the rejecting power could at any time adopt the
opposite policy, and receive the preacher sent ; and
he who locked the door on us could unlock it, or
they who directed him to close the door could direct
him to open it ; and the trustees who secured the
pulpit to ministers of their own choosing could
secure it to our ministers if they would. I therefore

kindly, but firmly, adhere to the terms laid down in my said fourth reply. Whether Union Chapel shall again appear on the Minutes of the Cincinnati Conference, is contingent on her coming to the terms of the Discipline—at least, so far as my administration is concerned.

"From the time that Union Chapel received the first pastor from the Cincinnati Conference, in 1852, I tried for years to conciliate good feeling, and to obliterate all unpleasantness that had arisen between her members and the Conference, and to accomplish which I favored certain measures of accommodation in regard to transfers, beyond what some brethren considered consistent with my official obligation, hoping that in due time things would settle down into a regular course, and that Union Chapel would receive pastors from the Conference as other charges do. But in this I am disappointed. She still claims the right to select her own pastors, and so general is the dissatisfaction of other charges on account thereof, that the peace of the Church requires our strict adherence to rule and order.

"It is not in anger that I say these things, 'but speak the truth in love.' I have no pleasure in your d stitution, and at any time when you choose to signify your acceptance of the above terms, we will at our earliest convenience furnish you a pastor from the Conference whose physical capacity to do the work of Union Chapel charge will not be questioned.

"Yours, very truly,   T. A. MORRIS."

The fourth reply, of October 28th, referred to in this letter, contains the condition laid down by the bishop, on which he would consent to restore Union Chapel to its place in the Minutes of the Conference, and appoint a pastor, in the following words:

"When the brethren of Union Chapel shall give satisfactory assurance that they will receive and support such preacher as may be appointed by the proper authorities to serve them, either as presiding elder or pastor, and that such regular appointees shall have full use of the pulpit and the right to administer the Discipline of the Methodist Episcopal Church, as in other regular Methodist Churches, then they may expect to have attention and supplies equal to those of other city charges, and not before, from me."

Instead of complying with these terms, the Official Board of Union Chapel, at a meeting held September 22, 1862, resolved to "refer the questions involved in this controversy" to the General Conference of 1864.

This was accordingly done, as we have already stated; and on the 21st day of May, and the seventeenth day of the session, Rev. J. M. Trimble, D. D., Chairman of the Committee on Episcopacy, presented the following report, which was adopted:

"Your Committee have examined the memorial of Union Chapel, Cincinnati Conference, complaining of the administration of the bishops in their case, and also the official correspondence which it occasioned.

"They find the facts to be, that, in 1861, the minister appointed as pastor of Union Chapel was rejected by the officiary, not because of any thing personally objectionable in the appointee, but because the officiary aforesaid had not been consulted in the

matter of the appointment, they desiring to retain
the services of a man who had already been regularly
appointed to them the preceding two years. Further,
that they not only voted to reject the pastor appointed, but advertised in the daily newspapers that
Union Chapel was without a pastor, and locked the
doors of the Church on Sabbath morning, thus exclud-
ing the pastor and presiding elder, claiming for
themselves the right to do so because of the peculiarity of their deed. Under these circumstances,
Bishop Morris released the minister appointed to
Union Chapel, and notified the Official Board that he
could not consent to the appointment of another
preacher to the charge, except upon the following
conditions, namely: 1. That the official and private
members should jointly agree that hereafter they
would support such ministers of the Methodist Episcopal Church as her regular appointing authority
should from time to time appoint to the pastorate of
Union Chapel; 2. That they should receive such
presiding elder as should from time to time be appointed to the district including Union Chapel, and
pay their proper proportion of his claim, according
to Discipline; 3. That the trustees of Union Chapel
should guarantee to such regular appointees, whether
as pastors or presiding elders, the free use of the
pulpit.

"He further stated to them as follows: Union
Chapel is in a state of insubordination, and if it
remains so till next Conference it will be left off the
list of Conference charges, and cease to appear in our
official Minutes.

"In accordance with this, Bishop Morris gave special instruction to the presiding elder to give certificates of membership to all loyal members desiring to remove their relation to some other charge.

"At the session of the Cincinnati Conference, in 1862, these terms not having been complied with, Union Chapel was stricken by the presiding bishop from the list of Conference charges.

"In all this, so far from seeing any thing to censure, the Committee believe the administration to have been wise and just, and that Bishop Morris is to be commended for the firmness with which he maintained the Discipline and order of the Church.

"J. M. TRIMBLE, *Chairman.*
"T. M. EDDY, *Secretary.*"

On the 26th of May, the Committee on Episcopacy submitted the following preamble and resolutions, which were adopted :

"*Whereas*, our honored and beloved senior superintendent, Rev. Thomas A. Morris, has for nearly half a century rendered valuable and effective service in various important relations to the Church, and for nearly thirty years has officiated acceptably and usefully as a general superintendent ; and *whereas*, his advanced age demands a respite from his arduous labors ; therefore,

"*Resolved*, That whether Bishop Morris shall continue to travel and perform episcopal duties during the next quadrennial term, and, if so, to what extent, shall he be left to his judgment and that of his episcopal colleagues.

"*Resolved*, That our satisfaction with the eminent and highly useful services of our venerated senior superintendent is recorded with profound gratitude to God, and with fervent prayers that we may long enjoy his presence and counsels, and that his path may 'shine more and more unto the perfect day.'"

On the 20th of May, the Episcopal Board was strengthened by the election of Davis W. Clark, Edward Thomson, and Calvin Kingsley, and on Tuesday, the 24th, they were solemnly ordained and set apart to the work of bishops of the Methodist Episcopal Church in the United States of America.

In compliance with the request made by the Conference on the first day of the session, Bishop Morris preached his semi-centennial sermon on the 10th of May. Before commencing his sermon, the bishop said that, to prevent misunderstanding, he would make a brief explanation. In the resolution requesting this service, allusion was made to the completion of his fiftieth year in the ministry; nearly two of these years, however, had passed before his reception into the Ohio Conference in 1816. He then proceeded to deliver the following:

SERMON.

"As for me, this is my covenant with them, saith the Lord: My Spirit that is upon thee, and my words which I have put in thy mouth, shall not depart out of thy mouth, nor out of the mouth of thy seed, nor out of the mouth of thy seed's seed, saith the Lord, from henceforth and forever."—ISAIAH LIX, 21.

"A covenant is an agreement between parties, with certain stipulations by which the parties are bound. The parties in this case are the Lord and his believing people. 'And the Redeemer shall come to Zion, and unto them that turn from transgression in Jacob, saith the Lord. As for me, this is my covenant with them, saith the Lord.' 'This is my covenant' with the members of Zion—with God's believing people—'saith the Lord: My Spirit that is upon thee and my words which I have put in thy mouth, shall not depart out of thy mouth, nor out of the mouth of thy seed, nor out of the mouth of thy seed's seed, saith the Lord, from henceforth and forever.'

"Our blessed Lord, when about to leave his disciples and ascend into heaven, promised that he would give them 'another Comforter, that should abide with them forever.' And in another place he said: 'But when the Comforter is come, whom I will send unto you from the Father, even the Spirit of truth, which proceedeth from the Father, he shall testify of me;' so that the Holy Ghost, vouchsafed to the Church of God through all the successive ages of the Christian dispensation, is given to believers. We think that the Spirit spoken of in the text, however, has reference to the disposition of the new hearts of God's believing and saved people, and which is to be perpetuated among them and their posterity to the end of time. This promise is not restricted to any one branch of the Christian Church. I am very far from believing that all the good people in the world are in our Church. I believe there are many as good in other denominations. We make no opposition to any living branch of the Church of Christ. Yet we shall take the liberty, on this occasion, to speak more especially of our own denomination as being more immediately identified with it, and best acquainted with its history.

"The first Methodist society was formed in England in 1739, nearly one hundred and twenty-five years ago. Since that, the society has branched out all over England, Ireland, Wales, and Scotland, and, by missionary enterprise, has reached some of the heathen nations of the earth. The first American society was organized in 1766, ninety-eight years ago. In two years from this time we shall be celebrating the Centenary of American Methodism, and we hope and pray for a time of refreshing from the presence of the Lord.

"Methodism has become a great power on both sides of the Atlantic; and it is well worth while to inquire what is the secret of this great success. To take in the whole subject in one brief discourse, is simply out of the question. We propose to speak to-day on one topic; namely, *the Spirit of Methodism*. That is our topic.

"I. AND, IN THE FIRST PLACE, THE SPIRIT OF METHODISM IS THE SPIRIT OF TRUTH.

"Pilate, the Roman Governor, said to our blessed Lord while under examination, 'What is truth?' Of course, our Savior did not condescend to answer the question in that connection; but he did answer it in another connection. When praying for his disciples, he said, 'Sanctify them through thy truth; thy word is truth.' Here it is, brethren: the Bible is truth— the basis of civil government, the standard of morals, of doctrine, of experience, and of practice; the standard from which there is no appeal. And the

view of Bible truth received and taught by the
Methodist Church is at once brief and comprehensive. It embraces all that is essential to salvation.
The doctrine of the fall of man, of the redemption
of the world by our Lord Jesus Christ, of the gift
and operations of the Holy Spirit, to enlighten us, to
ennoble us, and to dispose us to the exercise of
repentance toward God and faith toward our Lord
Jesus Christ; the doctrine of justification by faith,
of regeneration by the power of the Holy Spirit;
the doctrine of holiness, or sanctification; the doctrine of perseverance, or continuance in well-doing;
the doctrines of the immortality of the soul, the .
resurrection of the body, the general judgment, and
eternal rewards and punishments in heaven and
hell,—these are the great outlines of the system,
and at the same time it is brief and comprehensive.
It omits, among other things which are merely speculative, the old doctrine of predestination of individuals to life and death, on the one hand; and, on the
other hand, Arianism, and Socinianism, and Pelagi-
anism, and Unitarianism, and Swedenborgianism, and
Universalism, and Mormonism, and all similar forms
of semi-infidelity. Now, the Churches formerly called
orthodox, but now more generally called evangelical, embrace in their creeds the five points of Calvinism, namely: Total Depravity, Particular Election,
Partial Redemption, Effectual Calling, Infallible Perseverance. And, fifty years ago, the Church that did
not subscribe to these points of doctrine was scarcely
recognized as a Church of God.

"But Methodism came along, and shed light upon

these dark points. She presented her five points, which we think are better than theirs; namely, first, all men are sinners; second, all men are redeemed; third, all men are called; fourth, as many as obey the call are chosen; fifth, of those chosen, such as endure to the end shall be saved.

"We do not propose to discuss any of these five points of either system; but we name them only to reach general results. And we say that Methodist doctrine has fixed a deep and lasting and general impression upon the Protestant Christianity of the times, and has greatly modified the views of other branches of the Christian Church. Allow us here to inquire, Do you know any Church, in these days, in which the five points of Calvinism are plainly and pointedly and fully taught? If you do, you know more than we do. But, on the other hand, the five points of Methodism, in substance, are preached in most of the evangelical Churches; and the people joyfully receive them, and subscribe to them generally.

"II. The Spirit of Methodism is the Spirit of Revival.

"That is, the spirit of reanimation. To revive is to reanimate, to bring to life that which was dead. A state of sin and unbelief is a state of spiritual death; but a state of faith and salvation is a state of spiritual life. And, hence, the apostle to the Ephesians said, 'And you hath he quickened,' brought to life, 'who were dead in trespasses and sins.' And again: 'The law of the spirit of life in Christ Jesus hath made me free from the law of sin and death.' But, brethren, when we speak of revival in this connection, we have no reference to the revival of dogmas and rituals, but to a revival in the sense of spiritual life. And, in this regard, Methodism has taken an advanced position, and is leading on the sacramental host of God's elect.

"Before we had the light of Methodism, if a man spoke of knowing that his sins were forgiven, he was called ignorant, deluded, and fanatical. But now there are thousands who can bear witness to this truth without fear. Before the light of Methodism dawned upon the Churches, you might have selected many who were regarded as good men from those denominations deemed orthodox; but what could they tell about their religious experience? They usually said, when questioned upon this subject, If I was converted, it was because I could not help it; if I enjoy religion, I do not know it; if I have it, I can not lose it; and if I lose it, I never had it. This was about the sum and substance of their religious experience. But it is not so now, brethren. There are multitudes of men, not only in our own Church, but in all the evangelical Churches, who can give a clear and Scriptural account of their conversion. Most of them can tell you the time when, the place where, and the circumstances under which, they passed from death to life. They will inform you that they were converted, not because they could not help it, but when they desired this great blessing. When they earnestly prayed to the Lord Jesus Christ to bestow it upon them, they received it; and, having now obtained it, they can say: 'Whereas I

was blind, I now see;' 'We know that we have
passed from death unto life, because we love the
brethren;' 'He that believeth on the Son of God
hath the witness in himself.' Because they are sons,
they can say, 'God hath sent forth the Spirit of his
Son into our hearts, crying, Abba, Father!' and that
'the Spirit itself beareth with our spirit that we are
the children of God.' Here, then, is advancement in
the spirit of revivals, and we rejoice in it.

"III. The Spirit of Methodism is the Spirit
of Enterprise.

"We did not wait for the people to become
Christians, and to organize themselves into Churches,
and to erect houses of worship, and then call us to
their pulpits; but we went out into the highways
and hedges, into destitute places, both in the rural
districts and the suburbs of cities. We went not
only where Christ was *named;* but we went to the
regions beyond, and pointed sinners to the Lamb of
God that taketh away the sins of the world, and
warned them to flee the wrath to come. The Word
took powerful effect. We saw streams of water
break forth in the dry places, and the wilderness
blossom as the rose. There was a terrible shaking
among the dry bones, and they became covered
with sinews and flesh, and lived; and, in thousands
of instances, they who were not a people became the
people of the Lord. We tried to execute upon the
broadest practicable scale the great commission of
our Lord Jesus Christ, 'Go ye into all the world,
and preach the Gospel to every creature.'

"In order the better to do this, we formed as

many congregations as possible, and called them circuits ; and sent out laborers two by two, as Christ sent out his disciples. One was the preacher in charge, and the other was his colaborer and assistant. The circuit usually consisted of from twenty-four to forty congregations.

"The first three circuits which I traveled embraced from twenty-eight to forty appointments, all of which were to be reached every twenty-eight days. To do this required a journey of at least three hundred miles on each of these circuits ; and this journey was not performed by railroad, nor in the mail-coach, nor in the private carriage, gliding smoothly over the graveled pike, but upon horseback, and over roads that would now be generally regarded as almost impassable ; and yet, so far were we from curtailing these plans and endeavoring to relieve ourselves of these burdens, we were continually on the lookout for chances to enlarge our work. If we heard of any neighborhood that was destitute of the Gospel, we went directly to it and talked with the people ; and, if one man in the settlement would open his house for preaching, we made it an appointment, and the next time we came around we were there. When we had an appointment we filled it ; not if it was *convenient*, or if the weather was pleasant, and we could do it without sacrifice, but *always*, unless providential circumstances, over which we had no control, prevented us. If we wanted to *gather* a congregation, we had to be punctual ; and if we wanted to *hold* a congregation, we could not disappoint them. When the streams were swollen, we sometimes found great difficulty in crossing them. If we could find a bridge or a boat, it was well; but if we could not, we committed ourselves to Providence, and, plunging in with our horse, forded or swam the stream. This is what we mean by the spirit of enterprise.

"IV. The Spirit of Methodism is the Spirit of Sacrifice.

"Ours was a citizen ministry, called forth from different avocations. Some were lawyers, some physicians, some teachers, some mechanics, some merchants, and some were farmers, who were converted and called of God to the work of the ministry. They were received and educated, not *for* the ministry, but *in* the ministry; and connected the study and practice of theology together. These men, coming from the people, were sent back to the people, to preach, not the technicalities of the schools, but the Gospel of the grace of God, in plain, unvarnished language, which the people well understood; and the effect was glorious.

"But where was the sacrifice? asks one. I answer, They sacrificed, first, their secular calling. Whatever they depended upon for the support of their families they relinquished, whether it was commerce or law or agriculture, or whatever it may have been. They had to promise to devote themselves wholly to God and his work.

"In the next place, they were called upon to sacrifice their homes. We do not say their homes were spacious or elegant; but they were *homes* nevertheless, and contained all of earth that was dear to them ; and, much or little, they had to be sacrificed for this itinerant ministry, and we became pilgrims and sojourners, as all our fathers were. And all this under the old quarterage rule, with small prospect of a support.

"No provision was made for houses for the preachers. There was no estimate for family expenses, and no claim was recognized but the quarterage claim, and we were fortunate if half of that was received.

"For the first twelve years of my itinerant ministry, with my wife and two children, I kept an exact account of my expenses and receipts, and the controlling rule with us was, not to buy what we wanted, but only what we could not do without. I credited the Church not only what I received from the stewards, but also all I received for marriage-fees and in private presents. At the end of the twelve years I struck the average, and found that during that time I had received one hundred and sixty-six dollars, sixty-six and two-third cents per annum. With this I had to buy horses, pay house-rent, meet all expense of feeding, clothing, and educating the children, and pay all our charities ; that is to say, in so far as these receipts came short of meeting our bills, the balance came out of our private means. We say, then, that the spirit of Methodism is the spirit of sacrifice.

"V. The Spirit of Methodism is the Spirit of Progress.

"I allude more particularly in this to numerical progress. When I joined the Methodist Episcopal Church, in 1813, the aggregate of her communicants in all the States and territories and in Upper Canada,

and upon the whole Continent of America, was less
than one quarter of a million. I think it was about
two hundred and thirty-six thousand. Now our organization proper, after deducting our brethren in
Canada, who left us quietly and for good reasons
connected with their civil institutions ; and the Protestant Methodists, who left us for reasons satisfactory
to themselves ; and the 'True Wesleyan' organization, who left us on account of slavery ; and our
brethren in the South, who left us on account of the
'irrepressible conflict,' and who took away nearly
two thousand preachers and near a half-million of
members,—after deducting all these, we have now,
in our own organization, a fraction less than one million. Then we have a little problem for the mathe-
matician : If one quarter of a million of Methodists
produced during the past fifty years one million of
members, what will one million produce in fifty years
to come ? The answer is, *four millions*. But this is
only a part of the question, as you will perceive ; for
the quarter of a million of fifty years ago was the
nucleus not only of our own denomination, but of
all the Methodist organizations upon the continent,
which now, taken with our own denomination, will
probably approximate two millions. This taken into
consideration, the question will assume this form :
If a quarter of a million in fifty years has produced
two millions, what will two millions produce in fifty
years to come ? The answer is, *sixteen millions*.

"'But, pray,' says one, 'how do you know that
this will be so ?' I answer, I did not say that we
know it will ; but in this calculation we follow the

example of the statesmen, who will take the official record or census, and, ascertaining what was the population at a given time, will compute the increase for each decade, and tell you what population may be expected, say at the end of the century. Now, what we claim is, that our figures are just as reliable as theirs; and if they can give the proximate number of the population, we can do the same of Methodism.

"VI. THE SPIRIT OF METHODISM IS THE SPIRIT OF IMPROVEMENT.

"I know of no better word to cover the numerous items I wish to name. For example, the general style of living among our people has greatly changed. I know most about the Western States, where I was born and brought up, and from whence I have hailed for seventy years; and I speak that I do know, and testify that I have seen, when I say that, fifty years ago, in all the Western States, our people, as a general thing, lived in log-cabins of rude construction, with clapboard roof and puncheon floors. These cabins generally had but one apartment, which answered for kitchen and dining-room, sitting-room and parlor, library and dormitory, class-room and chapel. I have gone into the loft of these cabins many times in the severest Winter weather, where there was no fire, and slept with nothing overhead but the thin roof, and a few logs around me, with large openings between them, and with the covering very scant, and have often arisen in the morning to find my bed covered with snow. I have, in many instances, taken my pillow and placed it across my feet, and placed my coat over that, not merely to prevent suffering from cold, but to keep from freezing stiff. Now our people live in large and commodious houses, conveniently arranged and well furnished. When we look back fifty years to our puncheon floors and clapboard roofs, tin cups and pewter plates and spoons, and then look at the carpets and side-boards and cushioned chairs and silver tea-sets which we now have, we hardly know ourselves; yet our consciousness tells us that we are the same people, though under different circumstances.

"How was it with regard to our churches? There were none hardly deserving the name; and what we had were mostly built of logs, and these were 'like angels' visits, few and far between.' Now we have as many and as comfortable churches as any denomination in the land. Indeed, the statistics of the census credit us with more money invested in church property than any other denomination. How about our Sunday-schools? I answer, fifty years ago we had none. It may seem strange to you, but it is true as preaching, that I had been a traveling preacher four years before I had seen a Sunday-school. The first I saw was at Zanesville, Ohio, and was in connection with a Presbyterian Church. I visited it, and thought it a good thing; and, as we had none, I took my little daughter, now in heaven, and led her to the superintendent, who kindly welcomed her to the school. Now we have these schools by thousands, teachers by tens of thousands, and scholars by hundreds of thousands. But how about our tracts in those days? I answer, we had none, or next to none.

Now they are scattered broadcast through all the land.

"How about our periodicals? I answer, we had none. Now we have many, and our religious weeklies are scattered from the Atlantic to the Pacific. Then we had but few books, except such as were imported from England; but now we are not ashamed to compare our Methodist Book Concern with any publishing-house in America.

"How about our educational institutions? I answer, we had no public institutions of learning. Private members may have taught private schools, but we had no schools under the control of the Church. Now we have about thirty colleges for young men, two Biblical institutions for young ministers, while of seminaries and academies we have more than a hundred.

"But what about our missionary cause? I answer, we had no missionary society in those days. In regard to this, I beg a little indulgence, and to be heard with some degree of particularity. When I was on the Marietta Circuit, from 1816 to 1818, I had in my society, in Marietta, a colored man by the name of Stewart. He was an exemplary man, and prayed in our prayer-meetings. He was industrious and economical, and had earned the means to buy good clothes, a horse and saddle, and had pocket-money besides.

"In the Fall of 1817 he suddenly and mysteriously disappeared. He was not in debt or in trouble, that we knew of, and we could not, in any way, account for his disappearance. Early next Spring he returned, and came straight to my house, and gave an account of himself during his absence. In the Fall of 1817 it was impressed upon his mind that it was his duty to go in a north-west direction from Marietta, and deliver a message to some people, he knew not to whom. At first he tried to shake off the impression; but, failing in this, he mounted his horse and started. He went on until he reached the Wyandot Indians, at Upper Sandusky, in Ohio, when he said at once this was the people to whom he was sent. He went straight to the Indian agent and told him he had a message from God to the Indians. The agent, as was very proper, demanded his credentials; but he had none, as he was only a private member of the Church, and had not even his certificate of membership with him. Of course, he received no encouragement from the agent; but he went to the Indians and talked to them privately, and they agreed that he might address as many as would come together. Several came together in one of their wigwams, and among them another colored man. His name was Jonathan Pointer, and he had formerly lived with my uncle on the Big Kanawha River, and was captured in childhood by the Indians, and had learned the Wyandot language. He served as Stewart's interpreter, and while he talked the Indians wept. And when he was through, they came around him and said, '*Preach more,*' and he did so, and an adjoining Quarterly Conference took cognizance of him, and licensed him to preach, and, by the blessing of God, he had a great revival among the Indians.

"At the session of the Ohio Conference at Steu-

benville, in 1818, a report of Stewart's revival among
the Indians was presented, and Bishop M'Kendree,
who was there, said, 'We must have a mission among
the Wyandots.' But the question was, Where shall
the money come from? We had no flowing treasury,
but the brethren said, We will raise the money here,
and now. We raised the money entirely among the
preachers; for we then sat with closed doors. Some
gave five, and some ten dollars; and in a few moments money enough was raised to send a missionary
to the Wyandots. In the Spring of 1819, the news
of these things had reached New York, and the
brethren there formed the Missionary Society of the
Methodist Episcopal Church. They formed it upon
a good and broad basis, making all the annual conferences auxiliary societies. When the Ohio Conference met at Cincinnati, in 1819, it approved the
organization of the Missionary Society, and ordered
collections to be taken in the several charges. And at
Chillicothe, in 1820, they had a report of the moneys
raised for the missionary cause, and I recollect that
a member inquired, 'What shall we do with this missionary money?' After some discussion, it was voted
that T. A. Morris be appointed to receive it and forward it to New York. This gave me an opportunity
to know how much there was of it. Let it be remembered that the Ohio Conference then embraced
the whole of the States of Ohio and Michigan, as
well as parts of Indiana, Virginia, and Kentucky.
From all this region the contributions for the missionary cause were to be aggregated, and all came
into my hands; and what do you suppose was the

amount? It was *nineteen dollars*, and a fraction over. Now, compare this with the present, and behold the difference! In 1863, the treasurer of our Missionary Society received over four hundred thousand dollars; and, my brethren, I shall be greatly disappointed and excessively mortified if, in 1864, our contributions do not reach half a million dollars. That is the lowest amount that will sustain the missionary work now undertaken.

"VII. THE SPIRIT OF METHODISM IS THE SPIRIT OF LOYALTY TO THE CIVIL GOVERNMENT.

"It is the doctrine of our Church and of the Scriptures, that we should revere and submit ourselves to the civil authority. This is in our Articles of Religion. It was put there in the year 1784, when the Church was first organized, and there it stands, as a monument of our loyalty, to this hour. But we are taught this duty by higher than human authority. Paul says: 'Let every soul be subject unto the higher powers. For there is no power but of God; the powers that be are ordained of God. Whoever, therefore, resisteth the power resisteth the ordinance of God; and they that resist shall receive to themselves damnation.' Now, if we understand the teaching of the Holy Scriptures, rebellion is a crime of a high order, one expressly forbidden by the Word of God; and any man who is guilty of it deserves to be expelled from the Church of Christ.

"VIII. THE SPIRIT OF METHODISM IS THE SPIRIT OF PATRIOTISM.

"After the Southern Rebellion had developed itself in such magnitude that our President became satisfied that there was not power enough in the army, as it then existed, to put it down, he called for volunteers. And who responded? I answer that, so far as we know, all Churches did nobly; but it is true, nevertheless, that we have more than any other denomination who are in the service of our country. We have at least one hundred thousand Church members who have been mustered into the service of the United States. And many of our preachers, also, have gone—some as privates, some as captains, and a great many as chaplains; probably twice as many as from other denominations. There are three members of this General Conference, regular ministers, who have done service for their country as colonels, moving at the head of their regiments amid showers of leaden and iron hail, leading the van of the host, amid the shouting and tumult of battle. These are unfailing indications that the spirit of Methodism is the spirit of patriotism.

"IX. The Spirit of Methodism is the Spirit of Liberty.

"I do not mean liberty for a man to do what he pleases without answering to any body. We do not mean, either, liberty for a man to do what he pleases with the rights of other men with impunity; but we mean the spirit of liberty, in opposition to slavery. Slavery has been the great difficulty and bone of contention for years. It has divided our Church, and now it seeks to divide the country. We have had, for years, this standing question in our Discipline, 'What shall be done for the extirpation of the great evil of slavery?' but we could not answer the question. Philosophers tried, and were bewildered; statesmen tried, but were overwhelmed and confounded; ecclesiastical bodies sought its answer, but found dismay and failure; but God has interposed, and furnished the answer in the present war for the Union.

"The leaders of the Rebellion in the South, while fighting *for* slavery, have done more for its extirpation, in the last three years, than Congress and all the State Legislatures could do in thirty years; and although slavery has not been *extirpated*, it is prostrate and bleeding, and has received a blow from which it can never recover. It has already upon its brow the cold sweat of death; and we pray that it may speedily give up the ghost!

"X. THE SPIRIT OF METHODISM IS THE SPIRIT OF LIBERALITY.

"Now, whoever supposes (and some have so supposed) that the Methodist polity is a narrow and contracted one, and who publishes that supposition, simply proves that he knows not what he says, nor whereof he affirms. When were ever the plans and operations of Methodism contracted? Our illustrious founder took the world for his parish, and we are trying to follow his example. We never have seen the day when we did not preach *free grace* and a free communion; and what Church has done or could have done more? We pray, with the apostle, 'Grace be with *all* them that love our Lord Jesus Christ in sincerity!' We cordially believe, with Paul, that 'it is a faithful saying, and worthy of all acceptation, that Christ Jesus came into the world to save sinners,' even the very chief of sinners. We believe that Methodism will live to accomplish its grand mission, to spread Scriptural holiness over these and all lands. Some have said that the world is soon coming to an end; and some have gone so far as to fix the year and the day; but, thank God! the world still moves, and we believe that many things will come to pass before the end comes. One thing is, that the Word will be preached to all nations. We believe, also, that the Southern Rebellion will be crushed, slavery abolished, the Union of the States restored, a permanent peace established; and last, though not least, after all this, we shall have such a revival of the work of God as the world has never seen. We have the dawning of this glorious day already; and we believe the sun will soon arise in full splendor, and from every hill and valley go up the shout, 'Halleluiah! the Lord God Omnipotent reigneth!'"

CHAPTER XV.

SUPERANNUATION—CLOSING YEARS OF LIFE—DEATH AND
FUNERAL SERVICES.

BISHOP MORRIS returned from the General Conference of 1864 to his home in Springfield, Ohio, in comfortable health, but physically unable to take part with his colleagues in the active work of the Episcopacy. He remained during the next quadrennium in the forced retirement which his health absolutely demanded. But in May, 1868, we find him at the seat of another General Conference—Chicago—and assisting in the opening exercises of that occasion. He called the body to order, and directed the secretary of the last General Conference to call the roll. When that was done, Bishop Morris said, in substance:

"This is the twelfth General Conference, in regular, consecutive order, at which I have been present,—at four as a delegate, and at eight as a bishop; and I have no recollection of ever hearing so many delegates answer to their names on the first day of any session as at this."

Besides Bishop Morris, Bishops Janes, Scott, Simpson, Ames, Clark, Thomson, and Kingsley were present at the opening of this General Conference.

Bishop Baker was detained by ill health, but was present after the first week.

A correspondent of the Cincinnati *Gazette*, describing the bishops as they sat together on the platform, says of the senior: "The central figure of the group is the venerable Bishop Morris, once and for many years a resident of Cincinnati. His portly mien, placid countenance, imperturbable equanimity, and rare good sense, are as noticeable in his old age as at any former period of his long, laborious, and glorious life."

Although not able to preside often over the sessions of this General Conference, Bishop Morris was seldom absent from his seat among his colleagues, and was an attentive and deeply-interested listener to the proceedings. The first question which elicited much interest or discussion was on the admission of provisional delegates, who had been sent up as representatives of mission conferences, organized mainly in the South, under a special provision of former General Conferences. The debate on this question was exceedingly animated and able, and while the legal arguments were very clear and strong against the constitutionality of the proposed measure, yet the *argumentum ad hominem* on the opposite side was still stronger, and the provisional delegates were admitted to seats as members of the Conference by an immense majority.

The next question of general interest was the subject of Lay Delegation. The General Conference of 1860 had submitted this question to a vote of the male membership, and it had been lost by a large majority. In the mean time, however, the subject continued to be agitated. The *Methodist*, an independent paper published in New York, advocated the measure with great zeal and ability, but several of the *Advocates* were scarcely less earnest and no less able in promoting the measure. Evidently a great change had come over the Church in regard to this question since the negative vote a few years before. The subject was now brought before the General Conference by a large number of petitions, of which an overwhelming majority were in favor of lay representation. The discussion was long, warm, and eloquent on both sides. Bishop Morris took no part in this debate, of course ; but he had openly and warmly espoused the cause of lay delegation, and in private conversation advocated it.

The final action of this General Conference was the submission of a plan to a vote of the people, and then to the annual conferences. The result was an affirmative vote in both cases by decided majorities, and the plan was consummated at the ensuing General Conference, held in Brooklyn, in 1872.

A very pleasant episode in the quiet life of Bishop Morris, during this quadrennium, was the celebration of his seventy-sixth birthday, which occurred April 28, 1870. About thirty persons, representing various Churches and interests were present, on invitation ; those having the matter in charge deeming a larger company unadvisable, owing to the feeble health of Mrs. Morris. After a generous lunch, C. M. Nichols, Esq., Editor of the Springfield *Republic*, read the following paper, prepared by Bishop Morris :

"BIRTHDAY REFLECTIONS.

"I was born in Kanawha County, Virginia, April 28, 1794, and am this day seventy-six years old. Unbroken forests, the homes of wild beasts and scarcely less wild and savage men, have disappeared before the march of civilization. Where once stood the log meeting-house, now appears the spacious Church, with lofty spire pointing heavenward. In place of the rude wooden school-house of former times, we have now the amply endowed college. Where we once traveled on horseback, through forests and almost impassable roads, we now go at our ease in palatial cars, at the rate of twenty-five or thirty miles per hour. Once our homes were log huts; but now we have pleasant houses, well furnished with all needed conveniences and comforts. The United States have increased in population from three millions to thirty-five millions, and from thirteen to thirty-seven States; and still they come.

"Only a few years since, millions of our people were slaves, who are now free to enjoy life and engage in the pursuit of happiness, equal before the law with others.

"In Church matters great changes have taken place, and in none more than in our own denomination. When I was born, the 'Methodist Episcopal Church in the United States of America' was ten years old, a feeble and persecuted band. When I joined her communion, in 1813, all the Methodists in the United States and territories, including those of Canada West, numbered less than a quarter of a million. Now, including all branches of Methodism, there are, in the above limits, between two and three millions of communicants.

"These are great changes to occur in one man's life-time ; and yet I see nothing in the general aspect of affairs to warrant the anticipation of less success in the future, but much to encourage the hope of still greater prosperity. We are better provided with churches and school-houses than heretofore, and are better able to sustain our missions, both foreign and domestic, than we ever were, both as to men and means. The general revivals now in progress will be followed, it may be presumed, by greater activity in our missionary work.

"It is true, indeed, that depraved human nature remains the same, amid all the boasted improvements of the times, and requires the same power to renew and control it as formerly. But Jesus is 'the same, yesterday, to-day, and forever.' He is our only hope. We are fallen, miserable, and helpless ; but Christ is mighty to save, and strong to deliver. Let us look to him.

"I have attended twelve quadrennial sessions of the General Conference—four as a delegate, and eight as one of the presiding officers ; though at the last one I was little more than an interested spectator. Whether I shall ever attend another is very uncertain ; God knoweth. Two of my beloved colleagues, much younger and stronger than myself, have quite recently died at their posts of duty ; they rest from their labors, and their works do follow them. May we follow Bishops Thomson and Kingsley as they followed Christ !

"If Methodists prove faithful to God and true to their trust, they will accomplish the object of their mission, which is to spread Scriptural holiness over these lands. Let them adhere to the doctrines and polity of Methodism—to class-meetings, love-feasts, congregational singing, free sittings, and, above all, cherish the experience of a heart-felt religion,—and all will be well. Brethren, pray for me.

"THOMAS A. MORRIS.

"SALUBRIA, *April* 28, 1870."

At the close of the reading of this paper, a hymn was sung; after which, Hon. E. G. Dial, of Springfield, came forward, and presented the bishop an elegant gold watch, the gift of a few friends, in the following words:

"DEAR BISHOP MORRIS,—We are here to-day, with hearts overflowing with kindly feeling, to greet you. You have experienced the joys and sorrows of more than three-quarters of a century; and we come to join hearts and hands with you and your beloved consort, on this your seventy-sixth birthday. You enjoy at least usual health to-day. You have more than ordinary elasticity of spirits for one at your time of life. For these blessings we devoutly thank God. And, now, these brethren—ministers and lay-men of Springfield, your friends and neighbors—have directed me to present you, as a token of their love and esteem, this beautiful watch. Their affection for you and your wife is at least as pure as this refined gold. Accept it in the spirit in which it is given. It will keep the hours for you, well and truly, until angel hands shall mark you the time on the dial-plate of eternity."

The bishop was quite surprised, and greatly affected. He briefly and touchingly expressed his gratitude for the valuable and unexpected gift.

Mrs. Morris was then made the recipient of a handsome present at the hands of E. C. Middleton, Esq.; after which, the venerable Geo. Brown, D. D., of the Methodist Protestant Church; Rev. A. H. Bassett, D. D., of the same Church; Rev. A. Lowrey, D. D., Presiding Elder of Springfield District; Rev. Reuben Miller, Rev. J. W. Gunn, and others,—were called out, and responded in very happy remarks and reminiscences of the past.

These somewhat private and domestic matters may not be of great importance, or of general interest; and yet, after all, they go to make up a faithful history of a public life. Though taciturn to a fault at times, there was, notwithstanding, a personal magnetism about Bishop Morris which attracted all classes to him. In the community where he last resided—Springfield, Ohio—he was greatly beloved by all denominations; and his neighbors and friends embraced every suitable occasion to give expression to the high regard in which they held him.

In the following year—1871—Mrs. Morris, who had long been an invalid, suffering at times the severest pains, died in great peace; but her gain was unspeakable loss to her husband. In a communication to the *Western Christian Advocate*, soon after this bereavement, Bishop Morris said:

"Lucy Morris was born in South Carolina, May

27, 1800. She was converted while praying in secret, at the age of nine years. She united with the Methodist Episcopal Church, in Louisville, Kentucky, in August, 1819. She was married to the writer, June 25, 1844, being at that time the widow of Dr. Merriweather.

"During her illness, which was long and severe, she was wonderfully sustained by grace, showing herself resigned, peaceful, and happy. On Thursday, October 5th, she received a signal baptism of the Holy Spirit, which caused her to rejoice aloud with all her remaining strength. She said, among other things, 'Last night I was so happy in Jesus that my bed was made to feel soft as downy pillows.' Sunday, November 5th, was her last Sabbath on earth, which she passed in the company of her family, who remained to commune and worship with her in the sacred sanctuary of home. On Monday afternoon, November 6, 1871, at about three o'clock, she slept in Jesus.

"She was a genial, kind-hearted, Christian lady. She was scrupulously honest. Her early opportunities were good, for the times. After leaving school, she made considerable efforts to improve her knowledge. Her favorite study was history, both ancient and modern; but, of all books, she preferred the Bible, which she read daily. She became well versed in the Holy Scriptures, especially the historical parts. She excelled in the management of household affairs."

Rev. Dr. Lowrey, long a neighbor and friend of the family, writing of Mrs. Morris, said:

"She will be remembered as a cultivated lady—comely in person, graceful in manners, gentle and pleasing in address, amiable in disposition, refined in feelings, polite in social intercourse, prudent and chaste in conversation, generous and sympathetic to all, especially to the needy. As a Christian, she was sincere and profoundly conscientious. She had a rich spiritual experience."

For more than a quarter of a century had this excellent lady shared the itinerant bishop's lot. She had made his home a happy retreat from the cares of the world and the perplexities of official life—the abode of order, quiet, and love. It was therefore a peculiarly severe blow, now in old age and feebleness, to be separated from one whose life had contributed so much to the comfort and happiness of his own.

In the Spring of the year 1872, the bishop, with the assistance of a traveling companion, made the journey to Brooklyn, New York, where the Sixteenth Delegated General Conference of the Methodist Episcopal Church assembled, on the first day of May. At all but three of these General Conferences Bishop Morris was present, as delegate or presiding officer. And although he performed no official act at the last, except to call the body to order on the first day, yet he was seldom absent from his place on the platform, and was a deeply interested observer of the proceedings.

During the quadrennium now closed, death had made sad havoc in the ranks of the Episcopacy. Four of these honored and beloved chief pastors of

the Church—Baker, Clark, Thomson, and Kingsley—
had fallen. On the sixteenth day of the session,
very solemn and appropriate services were held in
memory of the lamented dead. The opening devo-
tional exercises were conducted by Rev. J. M. Reid,
D. D.; after which, Bishop Simpson read brief
sketches of the lives and characters of the deceased
bishops.

We quote the closing paragraphs only of these
sketches. They very happily bring out the salient
points of the characters described :

"Bishop BAKER was a man of deep and consistent
piety, of unusually quiet and modest deportment, a
clear thinker, a successful teacher, an accurate writer,
a sound theologian, a good preacher, and, as a bishop,
careful and systematic in all his work. For his
sweet and gentle spirit and his amiable manners, as
well as for his learning and talent, he was beloved
by a large circle of friends, and enjoyed the confidence and esteem of the Church. He died at Con-
cord, New Hampshire, December 20, 1871, in the
fifty-ninth year of his age.

"Bishop CLARK was a man of decided views, and
great firmness of purpose. As a preacher, he was
able and successful. His sermons were carefully
prepared, and full of instruction. As a writer, he
was clear, forcible, and exact ; as a bishop, he was
careful in arranging the details of official duties,
prompt in his decisions, and commanding as a presiding officer. His religious experience was clear
and triumphant. As he approached the close of life,
his expressions were both consoling and encouraging

to his family. He rejoiced in Christian song, and the music of hymns soothed his pain and restlessness. He repeated, many times, 'The Lord is my refuge and strength, a very present help in trouble. Amen ; amen.' He died at Cincinnati, Ohio, May 23, 1871, in the fifty-ninth year of his age.

"Bishop THOMSON was a man of decided convictions, and of deep piety; tender and gentle as a woman, but firm and unwavering as a hero. His reading was extensive and varied. As a speaker, he was eloquent ; as a writer, he had few equals for aptness of expression, and simplicity and beauty of style. In every position, as pastor, teacher, editor, and bishop, he worked successfully, and more than met the expectations of the Church. He died as he lived, in calm and peaceful trust and confidence in God. He died at Wheeling, while on his way from the West Virginia to the Pittsburg Conference, March 22, 1870, in the sixtieth year of his age.

"Bishop KINGSLEY was a clear and accurate thinker, a sound theologian, a ready and skillful debater. As a preacher, he was forcible and convincing ; as a writer, strong and logical. He was a man of earnestness of character, deep piety, great devotion to the Church, and of unwearied activity. Of apparently strong and vigorous constitution, the Church expected from him long life and great usefulness; but in a moment, in a strange land, the chariot came down, and he ascended from the summit of Lebanon, on which he had just been gazing. He died at Beyroot, Syria, April 6, 1870, in the fifty-eighth year of his age."

After the reading of these sketches, addresses were made by Drs. Curry, Thayer, Hitchcock, and Moses Hill, commemorative of the lives and services of the deceased bishops.

On the first day of this session, immediately after the calling of the roll, Bishop Janes stated that the bishops were ready to report the vote of the several conferences on the change of the Second Restrictive Rule, providing for the introduction of lay delegates into the General Conference. Whereupon, at the request of the Conference, Bishop Simpson presented the following:

" DEAR BRETHREN,—The last General Conference devised a plan for lay delegation, which they recommended to the godly consideration of our ministers and people. In connection with this plan, they directed the bishops to lay before the several annual conferences a proposed alteration of the Second Restrictive Rule, and to report the result of the vote thereon to this General Conference.

" In compliance with said action, we laid before each of the annual conferences the proposition to alter the Second Restrictive Rule, by adding thereto the word 'ministerial' after the word 'one,' and, after the word 'forty-five,' the words, 'nor more than two lay delegates for any annual conference.' Each conference voted on said proposition, and the aggregate result is as follows :

For the proposed change, ... 4,915
Against the proposed change, . . . 1,597
Blank, ... , ... 4

"Should the General Conference desire it, we are prepared to report the vote by conferences.

"In behalf of the bishops,   M. SIMPSON."

After the reading of this report, a paper, signed by Drs. J. T. Peck, W. L. Harris, R. S. Foster, G. Haven, and T. M. · Eddy, was presented and read, ratifying the change of the Second Restrictive Rule, declaring the Plan for Lay Delegation adopted, and inviting the lay delegates elected under it to take their seats as members of the General Conference.

The vote on concurring with the annual conferences in changing the Second Restrictive Rule, was as follows :

Ayes, ... 283
Nays, ...   · .   .   . 6
Absent or not voting,   .   .   · 3

The vote on ratifying and adopting the plan was 252 to 36, and that on admitting the lay delegates to seats, 288 to 1. And thus was consummated, with wonderful unanimity, a most important change in Methodist polity—a change which Bishop Morris, with that rare sagacity for which he was remarkable, foresaw years before as inevitable, and to which he gave his unqualified approval.

The wisdom of the measure was clearly apparent at a later stage of the proceedings of the General Conference, when it became necessary to take up and adjust certain matters of difference between the Agents of the Book Concern at New York. For the happy settlement of that most unfortunate strife, which was wholly one of financial management, the

Church is largely indebted to the business skill and training of the lay delegates.

At this General Conference there could be no question, as there had been at the preceding one, of the necessity of re-enforcing the episcopal body. Accordingly, eight additional bishops were elected, increasing the effective force to twelve. The newly elected bishops were, Thomas Bowman, William L. Harris, Randolph S. Foster, Isaac W. Wiley, Stephen M. Merrill, Edward G. Andrews, Gilbert Haven, and Jesse T. Peck. With a view to distribute this large episcopal force as equally as possible throughout the work, and to secure the presence and influence of the bishops where they were most needed, the Conference, with great unanimity, designated the special location of each. Although this action looked directly to special and local oversight, it was not intended to destroy or impair the unity or general superintendency of the bishops.

Soon after the adjournment of this General Conference—that is, on the 6th day of June, 1872—Bishop Morris was married to Miss Sarah Bruscup, a lady of suitable age, of thorough culture, of high social standing, of earnest piety, and well adapted to be an agreeable companion and a helpmate.

About a year later—April 28, 1873—on his seventy-ninth birthday, we find another social gathering in the pleasant home of the venerable bishop. Friends were there from Delaware, Cincinnati, and elsewhere, to join their congratulations with those of the bishop's more immediate neighbors and fellow-citizens of Springfield. Judge Dial read a biograph-

ical paper, addresses were delivered by Bishop Wiley
and Rev. Dr. Moody, and a poem, written for the
occasion, was read by Mrs. Bishop Thomson. Bishop
Morris responded to all these earnest and eloquent
words of congratulation in suitable and very touching
language. This occasion was of more than ordinary
interest to the bishop, as an assurance that, although
now on the "retired" list, he was not forgotten.

The last annual conference which the bishop was
able to attend was the Cincinnati. Its session in the
Autumn of 1873 was held in Springfield. Bishop
Ames presided, and was entertained at "Salubria."
He came into the conference-room on the morning
of the last day of the session, bringing intelligence
that Bishop Morris was extremely ill, and might not,
and probably would not, recover. The bishop, however, rallied, and for a twelvemonth longer was in
comparatively comfortable health.

His last official act was to administer the sacrament of baptism to a grandchild of his friend and
former colleague, Bishop Clark, a son of E. W. and
Katie Clark Mulliken, at their home in Springfield.

On Thursday, August 27, 1874, while the Cincinnati Conference was in session at Wilmington, Ohio,
a communication was received from Bishop Morris,
and read as follows :

"SPRINGFIELD, OHIO, *August* 24, 1874.

"*To Rev. Bishop Foster and the Cincinnati Conference, in Conference
assembled.*

"DEAR BRETHREN,—I wish to say a few things
to you in regard to my health, and some other matters. The 28th of last April, I entered my eighty-

first year. I have but little pain or sickness for one
of my age. I sleep well. My digestion is excellent,
and, apart from the infirmities incident to my time
of life, I am very comfortable. I, however, take but
little part in the active duties of life, and, having
served my day and generation as God has given me
ability, I am now resting in the quietude of my
home. True, I am no longer able to go in and out
before you, to sit in your councils, and take part in
your deliberations, yet my heart and sympathy are
with you; and for Zion's prosperity my tears shall
fall and my prayers ascend until my release is signed,
and I go to join the Church triumphant in the skies.

"As to my religious enjoyment, it is not increased
by exemption from labor, but rather the contrary.
This, however, is what I expected; and I find it
requires more grace to suffer than to do the will of
my Heavenly Father. But, although this is the case,
I am by no means destitute of enjoyment. No, dear
brethren; I find the religion I so long preached to
others is able to bring peace and assurance to the
heart in retirement, as well as when in the heat of
the battle, leading forth the conquering hosts to certain victory. Thank God for the Christian's hope!
It comforts and sustains amid all the vicissitudes of
life, and to the trusting heart makes bright the future.
In reviewing the past, I have only this to say, that
God has been very good to me. Most of my associates in the ministry, as well as many loved ones, have
passed away. I yet linger on the shore, and soon
expect to cross the river. I am nearing the Jordan,
and in the course of nature can not stay here much

longer; but beneath me are the everlasting arms, and, through riches of grace in Christ Jesus my Lord, I hope to anchor safely in the harbor of eternal rest. In all probability, this is the last time I shall address you. Before another session of your Conference I may be safely home. Therefore, in conclusion, permit me to say, dear brethren, live for God; preach Christ and him crucified; seek not the applause of men, or the honor that cometh from the world; but so live that, in the great day of accounts, you can say, 'Here am I, and the souls thou hast given me.' Praying the Great Head of the Church to direct in all the deliberations of the present session of Conference, I am, dear brethren,

"Yours, fraternally,   T. A. MORRIS."

A Committee, consisting of Rev. J. F. Wright, D. D., and Revs. M. Dustin, E. H. Field, and J. F. Marlay, was appointed to prepare and report to the Conference a suitable response. On Monday morning the Committee reported the following response, which was adopted by a rising vote:

"WILMINGTON, *August* 28, 1874.

"BISHOP T. A. MORRIS,—*Reverend and Dear Brother:* The undersigned have been appointed a Committee to respond to your letter of fraternal greetings addressed to the Cincinnati Conference, and read at the opening of the present session.

"We assure you that your communication was received by your brethren of this body with sincere pleasure, and listened to with profound emotion.

"We congratulate you that, in the good providence

of God, your life has been spared so long to the Church and the world, and that now, at fourscore years of age, you enjoy so comfortable a state of health.

"Our common and fervent supplication for you is, that God may still have you in his holy keeping; that he may continue to bless you with bodily health, and keep your soul in perfect peace.

"We need hardly assure you of our high appreciation of your long and faithful services to the Church. In performing the various, and oftentimes difficult and responsible duties assigned you, you have made a record of which the whole Church feels justly proud.

"No man living, probably, whose life has been so active and public, has spoken or written fewer words which, dying, he could wish to blot.

"Dear and venerated Father,—we do most earnestly commend you to God and the word of his grace, which is able to build you up, and to give you an inheritance among all them which are sanctified.

"Pray for us, that we, who have entered into your labors, may be worthy sons and successors in the Gospel.

"The grace of our Lord Jesus Christ, the love of God, and the communion of the Holy Spirit be with you always!

"Signed on behalf of the Cincinnati Conference.

"JOHN F. WRIGHT,   M. DUSTIN,
"E. H. FIELD,   J. F. MARLAY."

The letter of Bishop Morris was dictated two days before the Conference convened. On Wednesday, August 26th, he awoke in his usual health, and expressed a desire to ride out; but, while the preparations were being made, he suddenly grew worse, and from this attack never rallied. He did not seem, however, to realize his nearness to eternity until Friday morning, when he inquired of Mrs. Morris if she thought he would die before night. She said that she had no such thought; but added, "We can not tell what a day may bring forth." He replied, "Whatever the result may be, all is well—*all is right.*" He afterward said to his wife that he wanted her to tell him frankly whenever she thought the hour had come.

On Saturday morning, he was observed to draw his bed-quilts closely around him, as if cold. On being asked by his wife if he thought it was a chill, he said, "Why, no, wife; it is a death coldness." On the following day—Sabbath—Philip Phillips, accompanied by a few friends, spent an hour with him in singing and prayer. He greatly enjoyed this service, and frequently, during the singing, exclaimed, "How sweet! how beautiful!" During the prayers, too, he seemed much engaged, responding frequently and earnestly. On Monday evening, when his wife expressed a fear that he might soon be called away, he said, promptly, "All is right; all is right!" She asked him, then, how the future looked, and his cheerful, ready response was, "The future looks bright!" And in this frame of mind he lingered until Wednesday, September 2d, at noon, when he slept in Jesus.

The funeral services were held in the High-street Methodist Church, Friday, September 4th, at two

o'clock P. M., under the direction of the pastor, Rev.
L. Clark, and Rev. W. I. Ellsworth. The attendance
was very large, embracing many ministers of the
Cincinnati and Ohio Conferences. The pall-bearers
were Rev. J. M. Walden, D. D., Rev. W. Herr, Rev.
W. L. Hypes, Rev. J. W. Cassatt, Rev. T. H. Pearne,
D. D., Rev. T. H. Monroe, P. P. Mast, Esq., and
Judge E. G. Dial.

After the singing of the 1086th hymn, prayer
was offered by Rev. W. Herr. A biographical sketch
of the bishop was then read by J. F. Marlay; after
which, brief remarks were made, as follows:

ADDRESS BY REV. J. M. TRIMBLE, D. D.

"My first meeting with Bishop Morris was in
June, 1824, at Athens, the seat of the Ohio University. He was returning from General Conference,
which was held that year in Baltimore. He spent
several days with us, visiting his brother Calvary,
and preached on Sabbath. I next met him at Urbana, during the session of the Ohio Conference
held in that place in September, 1829. This was
his first meeting with the Ohio Conference after his
transfer from Kentucky. He was greeted with great
cordiality by the senior members of our body, and
heartily welcomed back to their fellowship. His
sermon at this Conference, on Sunday afternoon, in
the Presbyterian Church, I shall never forget. His
subject was, the Resurrection of Christ; and the
effect was thrilling, resulting in a general outburst
of praise all over the house. In 1830, during his
pastorate at Columbus, he visited Chillicothe, and

preached several times very acceptably; the understanding at the time being that my colleague, Rev. John H. Power, would aid him in a meeting in Columbus, appointed for April, 1831. Sickness in my colleague's family prevented him from going, and he sent me.

"I left Chillicothe on Friday, reached Columbus on Saturday, and, being a stranger, went directly to the parsonage, a little frame building with two small rooms, in the rear of the Church. Brother Morris insisted on entertaining me, and I was their guest for six days. Their home was a very pleasant, though a contracted one. Mrs. Morris—one of God's noble women—made sunshine every-where in their humble domicile. During that week ninety persons were added to the Church, most of whom were converted. I next met him at a camp-meeting held by the circuit and Columbus Station, a few miles north of the city. Bishop M'Kendree was there, with twenty or more preachers, on their way to the Ohio Conference, soon to assemble in Mansfield. This occasion was a memorable one, on account of the presence and ministrations of Bishop M'Kendree.

"In 1833, I was stationed in Cincinnati, with Rev. J. B. Finley as my senior colleague, and Rev. T. A. Morris as presiding elder. Here my acquaintance with him became more intimate, and my love for him increased. It seemed impossible not to love him, he was so kind and brotherly in his intercourse with his preachers. In April, 1834, he was appointed editor of the *Western Christian Advocate*, and brother Finley was placed in charge of the district. The death of Dr. Sargent, and the failing health of brother J. M'D. Mathews, left the station work to John Collins and myself. Five preaching-places, with preaching three times every Sabbath in two of them, made the work onerous, and it became necessary to call on the Book-room officials, editors, agents, and clerks, as well as our local preachers, for help. The work of procuring supplies devolved principally on me; and I have it to say that I never asked brother Morris to preach without receiving a cheerful and prompt affirmative response: but I can not say this of all to whom I applied.

"His family was in my pastoral charge; and I was frequently in their home, to receive cheer and encouragement from sister Morris. Her record is on high; and her devotedly pious daughter, Jane, a *facsimile* of the mother in every thing good, joins her in the rest that remains for the people of God.

"Bishop Morris was possessed of a good mind, well disciplined by his own efforts in self-culture. He was so amiable in his manners, and so affable in his intercourse with his fellow-men, that he made many friends, and few, if any, enemies. I loved to hear him preach. He always quit when he was done, and generally when there was a most blessed sense of the Divine presence manifest in the audience. But he has passed to his heavenly home, where we hope to meet him.

"O, that God may graciously minister comfort to these bereaved ones! Look up, ye sorrowing ones, and beyond the river; your beloved is there to join his brethren, who have passed on before him, in the delightful employments and enjoyments of heaven, in their song of salvation to God and the Lamb!

"And you, my dear brother, son of my venerated friend,* you will not be separated long from the dear ones who await your coming in the home of the blest. That sainted mother, who nursed you, who clasped you to a bosom glowing with pure affection for her child, will hail you; with outstretched arms she will welcome you, and leading you up to the Throne, will say, Here, blessed Savior, is the son for whom I wept, prayed, and labored in yonder world, washed in thy all-cleansing blood,—I present him now to thee, to be crowned an heir of everlasting life! O Lord, gather all the family at last to share the bliss of heaven!"

ADDRESS BY REV. JOHN F. WRIGHT, D. D.

"The itinerancy of Thomas A. Morris and myself in the Methodist Episcopal Church was long contemporaneous. I was admitted into the Virginia Conference, February 20, 1815; and he into the Ohio Conference, September 3, 1816. In the Fall of 1821, when I was received by transfer into the Ohio Conference, brother Morris was transferred to the Kentucky Conference, where he spent seven years—laboring three years on circuits, two in stations, and two as presiding elder on the Green-river District. In 1824, we were both delegates to the General Conference, held in May, in the city of Baltimore.

"Our first acquaintance, personally, was formed

* Rev. F. A. Morris, D. D.

at this General Conference, which to me was agreeable, and very pleasant. Five years later, he was transferred back to Ohio, and appointed to Lebanon, in the Lebanon District, of which I was then presiding elder. We were thus brought into close association ; so that our acquaintance soon ripened into friendship, which culminated in an intense fraternal love, that never ceased.

"In the Fall of 1829, I invited him to meet me at a quarterly-meeting held at old 'Union Church,' near Xenia, and assist in the labors of the pulpit. The meeting was a success throughout, but the love-feast was glorious ; and the effect, under the sermon of brother Morris, was remarkable. His text was, 'The poor have the Gospel preached to them.'

"We have just heard, from Dr. Trimble, of a sermon preached by brother Morris during a Conference session at Urbana, and the effect it produced. No one could describe that scene. All we can say is, It was the Lord's doings, and it was marvelous in our eyes. We had the aid of brother Morris at several other quarterly-meetings, and at some camp-meetings, while I remained on the district, and always found him not only an efficient laborer, but an acceptable and successful minister of Christ.

"In May, 1832, the General Conference sent me to Cincinnati as Assistant Book Agent, with the Rev. Charles Holliday as my colleague. It was not long until a weekly religious periodical, in connection with the Western Book Concern, was urged, as a matter of necessity, by many of the preachers and people in the West.

"After being much talked about in private circles, it was finally laid before the Western Conferences; and it is believed that they were unanimous in petitioning the authorities of the Church to establish such a paper. The Book Committee and the Agents in Cincinnati laid the matter before the authorities of the Church in New York, and they gave their cordial consent and co-operation to the publication of a paper under the name of *Western Christian Advocate.*

"The next thing was to find a man well qualified to edit such a paper, and the authorities in Cincinnati selected Thomas A. Morris as, in their judgment, competent to do the work. This choice was ratified in New York, and I was appointed to communicate the result to the editor elect, who was serving the Church at that time as presiding elder of Cincinnati District, and residing at Madisonville. About two months later, the first number of the *Western Christian Advocate* was issued, May 2, 1834.

"Brother Morris was as acceptable and useful as an editor as he had been as a preacher and pastor. He served the Church in this position two years, to the satisfaction of the patrons and readers of the paper. As editor, he was regarded as wise, judicious, and careful to conform his views to the doctrines, government, and Discipline of the Church he served. His editorials were strikingly characterized by perspicuity, brevity, and force.

"As an associate and companion in labor for the cause of Christ and the Church, brother Holliday and myself found him to be very agreeable and pleasant.

It may be safely affirmed, I think, that no three officers of the Church ever associated and worked together with more harmony, peace, and brotherly love than we did.

"In May, 1836, the Quadrennial Session of the General Conference was held in Cincinnati. It was decided to strengthen the Episcopacy by the election of three additional bishops. The election was made the order of the day for May 24th. At the appointed hour, when the order of the day was called, Rev. W. Winans, of Mississippi, said: 'As the brother is not present, I will take the liberty to nominate Wilbur Fisk, of the New England Conference, for the office of a bishop.' On the first ballot, Beverly Waugh and Wilbur Fisk were elected, while T. A. Morris lacked but one vote of an election. After one or two other ballots without an election, brother Morris arose and said, 'Mr. President, I earnestly desire to withdraw my name from this canvass, and beg my friends to cast no more votes for me.' Very soon, however, it was announced that he was elected a bishop of the Methodist Episcopal Church.

"At the close of the General Conference, Bishop Morris immediately entered upon the duties of his new office and sphere of labor. My associations with him, however, did not cease with his elevation to the Episcopacy. As Book Agent, I had occasion to visit many of the same annual conferences, and often to travel with the presiding bishops. I kept an account one year, and found that I traveled with one bishop that year more than eight thousand miles, principally in steamboats and mail-coaches.

"I was frequently thrown into the company of Bishop Morris, and I have no doubt we traveled together many thousand miles during the eight years I remained in the Book Agency, after he left the editorial chair. We had many opportunities to commune together, and we had a great variety of subjects for conversation. It gives me great pleasure now, while I linger a little behind him, to retrospect the past, and recall many of the interviews we had in the journey on earth, some of which he adorned with plain, practical, luminous truths, as with jewels. These I have stored away among the richest and sweetest memories of my life.

"His first wife, a daughter of Nathaniel Scales, of Virginia, was raised within a few miles of the place of my nativity, in North Carolina. I knew her well. Two children—Jane and Francis Asbury—were the fruit of this marriage, and they both experienced religion in their youth. I knew and felt a deep interest in them while they were seeking salvation. Jane, some years later, married Mr. Joseph G. Rust, of Cincinnati. After a short but happy married life, she died, leaving a son and a daughter. Asbury entered the ministry, and is now an honored and useful member of the Missouri Conference of the Church South. God bless the descendants of my lamented friend, and may religion never wear out in the family!

"Since Bishop Morris's partial retirement, on account of repeated and severe shocks of paralysis, we have not been much together. I have visited him occasionally, and sometimes we have met at conferences and other meetings. We, however, kept up a correspondence. After his second stroke of paralysis, I wrote him a letter of sympathy and comfort. Though I did not expect an answer in his own hand, as he had been paralyzed on both sides, yet he replied with unusual promptness, saying that, although both hands were affected, he was not entirely helpless in either.

"I inferred from the closing words of this letter that he was impressed it would be the last he would write to me. He closed it as he had not done any previous one. These were his words:

"'And when the great reunion takes place above, may we all be there, complete in Christ Jesus our Lord! Yours, as ever and forever,

"'T. A. Morris.'

"I close this address in some of the words of David, in his lamentation at the death of Jonathan. They accord well with my feelings at this hour: 'How are the mighty fallen in the midst of the battle! O, Jonathan, thou wast slain in thy high places. I am distressed for thee, my brother; very pleasant hast thou been unto me.'"

ADDRESS BY REV. F. MERRICK.

"And now it remains that we perform the last office of friendship left us, to our departed and venerable friend and pastor, that we bear his remains to the grave, there to rest until the morning of the resurrection. But not with unmingled sadness do we perform this office. Death, it is true, is a sad event.

'Yea, though promises and hopes strive to cheat its sadness;
  Full of grief, though faith herself is strong to speed the soul;
  For the partner of its toil is left behind to endure the ordeal of
      change.'

"And it is sad to be separated, though but for a season, from those we love. And yet, in the case of our departed friend, how much there is to relieve this sadness,—the past, full of pleasant memories; the present, of precious consolations; the future, of glorious hopes! A life so simple, so pure, and so true, can not be recalled but with pleasure. As a son, a brother, a husband, and father; as a citizen, pastor, and bishop, he met with the utmost fidelity, and performed with singular propriety the duties which these relations impose; with what fidelity and propriety, those who knew him best will the most highly appreciate. As a writer and preacher he will long be held in grateful remembrance. And who would wish to forget the quiet humor which, as a subtle aroma, ever pervaded and enlivened his private conversation and public discourse? or the no less subtle and quiet pathos with which, at times, he melted all hearts, while he impressed upon them the great truths appertaining to their spiritual well-being?

"To know Bishop Morris was to respect and love him. Few had more friends—who fewer enemies? Pleasant, indeed, is the memory of such a life and character. And the present, with all its sorrows, is not devoid of consolation. That body, worn by disease and oppressed with the infirmities of age, is at rest; and the spirit, which for years had increasingly felt the limitations of its earthly environs, is now free, and, without doubt, unspeakably blessed in the activities and associations of its heavenly home. Absent from the body, present with the Lord. Escaped from earth, at home in heaven.

"And the future! What a vista opens to the eye of faith, as Revelation, piercing the veil, sheds its light upon things to come! How pleasant to know that for our departed friend there is to be eternal progress in knowledge and virtue; deeper and still deeper insight into the character and works of God, and especially into the mystery of sin and redemption, as an unfolding of that character, in the most wonderful manifestation of its wisdom and love; and higher and still higher attainments in all that is ennobling and God-like; and for us, his relatives and friends, who to-day mingle our tears in a common sorrow, reunion with him amid those scenes of ever-increasing light and glory!

"Let us, then, as we bear these remains to the tomb, mingle with our tears the thanks of grateful and adoring love to Him who gave to us and to the Church one so worthy to be enshrined in our affections and memories, and through whose mercy the grave becomes the portal to endless joys.

"To the bereaved family circle I dare not approach, even with words of sympathy and consolation. Your sorrow, dear friends, and your consolation, are alike too sacred for the intermeddling of a stranger. You know who appoints the sorrow, and from whom comes the consolation. The only office becoming me is to commend you, as most sincerely and devoutly I do, to Him who is an ever-present help in time of trouble, and in whom all grace abounds.

"For us all, this hour has its lessons. Life, death, immortality. What means life? In what consists its true significance? How terrible the fact of probation!

Life, a probation for eternity! This cold form reminds us that our probation will soon be closed, our accounts sealed up, our destinies fixed. Who can mistake the lesson?

" Brethren in the ministry, the time left us for proclaiming the great salvation is short. Those lips, once so persuasively eloquent in its proclamation, are now mute in death. Ours, too, will soon be silent. Upon some of our heads these reverend hands once rested, as we took upon ourselves our solemn ordination vows. Around this coffin let us renew those vows. Henceforth, with increased earnestness, let us preach that Gospel he so delighted to preach, and preached with so much fidelity and success. Upon us may his mantle fall, and to us may there be given of that holy anointing by which his ministrations were made so rich in spiritual results.

" The night cometh. Let us work while it is day. And when the last hour shall come to *us*, may it, like his, be peace."

The choir then sang very beautifully the favorite hymn of the bishop:

"My latest sun is sinking fast!"

after which, a long and solemn procession slowly wended its way through the streets of Springfield to Fern Cliff Cemetery, where the impressive burial-service of the Church was read, and all that was mortal of Bishop Morris was consigned to "the house appointed for all living."

CHAPTER XVI.

AN ESTIMATE OF BISHOP MORRIS—PERSONAL APPEARANCE—
CHARACTERISTICS—RELIGIOUS EXPERIENCE.

AS one of the last in the long line of Methodistic heroes, and as perhaps the very last of the pioneer bishops, the subject of this memoir must ever hold a high place among the leading men of the Church. He belonged emphatically to that class of men who are content to be known by their fruits— whose lives are made up of deeds rather than words. And no one, certainly, who has followed the writer through these pages, will deny that Bishop Morris was as faithful and abundant in performance as he was modest and quiet in profession. It seems fitting, therefore, that a little space in his biography should be devoted to a nearer personal inspection of the man, as well as to an analysis of a character so beautiful and symmetrical.

Bishop Morris was not, perhaps, what would be called a man of commanding personal appearance, though, in his prime, he was by no means destitute of the noble mien and dignified bearing which are popularly associated with high position. His portly *physique*, placid countenance, paternal manners, and perfect self-control, as well adorned the presidential chair of a deliberative body as if he had been born to lead. His natural *embonpoint* increased in later life to decided corpulency, of which he was a little sensitive, as will be noticed in his article, inserted in the body of this work, entitled "Lean *vs.* Fat." But his complexion was so fair, clear, and beautiful, his face so kindly and gentle in its expression, and his personal habits so scrupulously neat, that he was, upon the whole, and even to extreme old age, a man of attractive appearance.

His health in early life seems to have been frail and uncertain. It was mainly on that account that he hesitated so long about entering the itinerant ranks; and it was apparently an unsettled question in his own mind, for years, whether he would be able to go on in the regular work after he had entered upon it. It seems surprising that he was physically equal to the severe hardships and dangerous exposures of his long and laborious life. To a modern itinerant, the story herein related, of horseback journeyings through trackless forests, of nights spent in cold and cheerless swamps with no roof but the sky, of swimming swollen streams, of hunger and want, of incessant labor for the public good with very little appreciation or support from the public, seems almost incredible. And yet, when it is considered that Bishop Morris, while performing this excessive labor, was much of the time a sufferer from some form of disease; and that his immense circuits of travel required very long separations from a delicate and invalid wife; and that, for many years, he almost literally paid his own way in the ministry out of a slender private income,—it seems, indeed, almost

utterly inexplicable that he was so sustained in
health, and that he was able, through it all, to maintain so equable a spirit. It is, however, but one
more chapter in that wonderful book of Providence,
illustrating and confirming the words, "As thy days,
so shall thy strength be."

In the matter of mental culture, Bishop Morris
belonged to a class of men whose exact _status_ it is
difficult to define. A scholar he certainly was not,
in the popular sense of that word, and yet he was
by no means an unlearned man. He was what
might be called, in the best sense of the much-
abused expression, a self-made man—as, indeed, were
many of the moral giants of those days. We have
seen that schools were few in number and poor in
quality in the region of country where his school-
days were passed; and yet it was his good fortune
to be a pupil for some time in the best school accessible—a grammar-school, taught by a thoroughly
educated Englishman, near his father's house. In
this school young Morris acquired no doubt the
elements of a good English education, and, probably,
some knowledge of the ancient languages; for, years
afterward, he pursued the study of Greek with good
success on horseback, while passing around his circuits. He was always a student; and his sermons,
essays, and editorials furnish abundant evidence of a
wide range of reading, as well as of a mind of rare
natural endowments. His style was epigramatic,
clear, and forcible. In this respect, a very competent
critic has said that no minister in our Church has
more nearly resembled Mr. Wesley than Bishop

Morris. His printed sermons are characterized by the same simplicity of style, the same pith and directness, the same lucid arrangement, and the same earnest and practical enforcement of the truth.*

It was one of Bishop Morris's most remarkable characteristics that he could, while displaying on all occasions immovable firmness of purpose in what he believed to be right, so demean himself as to give no offense. It will be recalled how he passed through the stormy days of the so-called radical controversy, and the still fiercer antislavery agitation, as well as the great conflict in the Church which culminated in the separation of the Church South, with decided opinions, firmly held and fearlessly expressed, yet with the sincere respect and confidence of all parties. It was this rare characteristic which secured for him, in a very marked and unusual degree, the love of the whole Church, throughout his entire life. He was as free, perhaps, as any man could be, from offensive self-assertion and mere dogmatism. The respectful deference he paid to the opinions of others, and the modesty with which he dissented from his brethren, could not fail to win the admiration of an opponent even. That men were sometimes aggrieved at the course he felt it his duty to pursue, is certain ; but it is equally certain that Bishop Morris was incapable of treating his ministerial or other brethren with disrespect. And this trait of his character deserves to be carefully noted by those who are called to exercise episcopal functions. Men may possess learning, genius, eloquence, so as to speak with lips which

* *Ladies' Repository*, November, 1874.

seem touched almost with celestial fire ; and yet they may be, at the same time, characterized by such faults of temper and manner as to excite the prejudices of their fellow-men, and so destroy their influence and usefulness utterly.

The apostle Paul took especial pains not to give needless offense, and, so far as he could do so with a good conscience, he became "all things to all men ;" not for the purpose of gaining popularity, but that he might win souls to Christ. It can hardly be questioned that, in this respect at least, Bishop Morris was in the line of "apostolical succession." In matters not affecting the great interests of religion, he was exceedingly pliable and conciliatory, and easy to be entreated. It is doubtful whether any man ever had, or could have, more perfect mastery of his tongue. Who ever heard him, under the greatest provocation, say an ill-tempered or bitter word? Who ever saw him, amid the vexations or annoyances of the chairmanship of an annual conference, lose his temper or self-control? He never made a profession of Christian perfection ; and yet, if to live Christ-like, if always to exhibit the lovely spirit of him who was meek and lowly, and whose words, actions, and whole deportment were kind, gentle, and attractive, is to have attained to that exalted state of grace, then those who knew him best will concede to Bishop Morris what he did not claim for himself.

As a presiding officer, Bishop Morris has been referred to since his death by a judicious critic, who knew him long and intimately, as "the *beau-ideal* of a Methodist bishop." It is certainly safe to affirm that, from the beginning, the Church has had no bishop whose administration was more universally acceptable. Bishop Morris was a man of rare practical wisdom—it was usual, throughout his life, to speak of him as a man of remarkable common sense—and his judgment of men and measures was seldom at fault, and rarely questioned. He has been referred to sometimes as a man who had few, if any, salient points, and whose character is therefore not easily defined. It is true, doubtless, that he had no gift or grace in marked prominence, because his common sense, or practical wisdom, prevented the cultivation of one grace or talent at the expense of others. He was a symmetrically developed character; he cultivated his mental and moral faculties proportionately, "growing into a perfect man, unto the measure of the stature of the fullness of Christ." And it was this ability to view all subjects periscopically—from every point of view—and to take in the true measure and capabilities of men "for the work," in a practical common-sense way, that made Bishop Morris so successful as a presiding officer in an annual conference. He never departed, in estimating men in the ministry, from the old and safe Methodistic criterion, "gifts, graces, and usefulness;" and no bishop ever succeeded better in putting the right man in the right place.

Methodist ministers always felt safe when they were in his hands; for they knew him to be incapable of using the power of his official position to gratify a personal preference, or redress a private grievance. His quick and accurate judgment of men, his sterling honesty, which made it instinctive with him to do what he believed to be right, his deep and tender sympathy with his brethren in the pastorate, his uniform kindness of disposition, his perfect self-control, and his inflexible decision, were among the qualities which conspired to make him peculiarly the man for the office he filled for so many years, with so much honor to himself, and so much usefulness to the Church. It is highly probable, furthermore, that his popularity as a presiding officer was enhanced not a little by that quiet humor which, in the words of another, "as a subtle aroma, pervaded and enlivened his private conversation and public discourse." As the president of a conference, he was not in the habit of flaunting his authority in the faces of his brethren. He affected no superiority, and was never apparently much concerned about his official dignity. He put on no prelatical airs, indeed, of any kind; for he never felt that his office lifted him above the fellowship and sympathy of his brethren. On this account he was easily approached by preachers and people, and his patience in hearing statements, and sometimes counter-statements, was inexhaustible.

The characteristic of Bishop Morris which, as much at least as any other, accounts for his success, was his unaffected humility. When the apostles disputed among themselves which should be primate in Christ's kingdom, he taught them that ambition and self-seeking and love of pre-eminence, instead of gaining them preferment in his kingdom, would but postpone their preferment. He that desires the office of

a bishop desires a good work, not because it lifts him
above his brethren, but because he is afforded an
opportunity, as Saint Paul did, to "labor more abundantly," and make himself "the servant of all." The
extreme diffidence and shrinking modesty with which
Bishop Morris entered upon the work of the ministry—his painful and embarrassing doubts about his
call to the work, growing mainly out of his deep conviction of his own unfitness for it—the evident reluctance with which he entered upon the office and work
of a bishop, and his desire to resign it at the end of
his first quadrennial term; and, in short, his unas-
suming manner in public and in private, and his whole
course through life, attest sufficiently that he was
remarkably endowed with that rarest of the Christian
graces, humility. As pastor, editor, and bishop, he
held high positions among his ministerial brethren;
but the positions always sought him: he was the
farthest possible remove from an ecclesiastical office-
seeker. And so meekly did he wear his honors, that
it may be doubted seriously whether he ever excited
a feeling of envy in any breast. Bishop Morris was,
in the best sense, a progressive man, not one who
despised old things because they are old, but one
who, carefully studying the signs of the times, could
see, in the mighty movements that are going on in
the world, evidences that the race is yet in the infancy of a glorious manhood yet to be developed, and
that the world's best days are yet to come. While,
in accordance with the universal tendency of old age,
he lingered much in the past, and loved to recall the
heroic times of Methodism, yet he indulged in no

gloomy forebodings of the future, but always expressed himself as confident that still better days were in store for the Church and the world.

In his "Reflections," written on his seventy-sixth birthday, and published elsewhere in this volume, after speaking in glowing terms of the progress of the Church since he entered the ministry, he adds: "And yet I see nothing in the general aspect of affairs to warrant the supposition of less success in the future, but much to encourage the hope of increasing prosperity." In the general progress of the country, in which the Church necessarily participates, so far as regards her material resources and exterior accommodations, changes, more or less important, in matters of mere form and polity, become a necessity. At such times, a conciliatory and progressive policy is the dictate alike of religion and common sense.

Thus when, a few years ago, the question of "Lay Representation" was reopened, Bishop Morris had the sagacity to see that, however premature some former discussions of the subject might have been, yet now the altered circumstances of the Church required such a modification of its government, and accordingly he gave the measure his unqualified approval. Its overwhelming success before the laity and the conferences was due to the influence of no one name more than to that of the senior bishop.

On the question of slavery, also, Bishop Morris was doubtless a conservative in his early life. Born and raised in a Slave State, and for seven years of his ministerial life necessarily in contact with the system in its mildest forms—as it existed in Kentucky and

Tennessee—we are not surprised to find that, while he was in no sense a pro-slavery man, yet when charged with being "an Abolitionist," as he journeyed through the extreme South, he felt the title to be, and spoke of it as being, the reverse of compliment-ary. And yet when the Church South was organ-ized, strong as were the ties that bound him to the section in which he was born, and great as were the inducements held out to him to connect himself with that organization, he did not hesitate or falter an instant in his allegiance to the Methodist Episcopal Church. Like many other wise and good men, by constitutional temperament inclined to conservative views, Bishop Morris was led along by steps and stages to a full realization of the enormities of slavery, and finally to the conclusion that it was indeed, in the language of the wise and illustrious Wesley, "the sum of all villainies."

And from the hour when bloody treason fired on Sumter, through all the dark and gloomy days of the great slavery Rebellion, the Star-spangled Banner floated day and night from the flag-staff of "Salu-bria;" nor did any one rejoice more sincerely in the final overthrow and complete extirpation of slavery than Bishop Morris.

While always open to conviction, and ever on the alert for truth, and never ashamed to modify his views on sufficient grounds, he was, at the same time, a man of remarkable firmness. Always ready to adopt new views if they were supported by reason and sound argument, yet he had no fickleness—no fondness for change—no disposition to take up new things simply because they were new. His opinions were never hastily formed. His belief in the Christian religion, and his opinions on the great themes of Revelation, were the result of earnest and prayerful consideration. His adoption of the creed of Methodism was in consequence of a careful comparison of the doctrines therein taught with the Holy Scriptures; and, although the influence of early training, and the prevailing prejudices of the day would stand as very strong barriers in the way of his doing so, yet he could not do otherwise, with his instinctive honesty, than become a Methodist, when satisfied that it was his duty to do so. He was certainly no bigot. He recognized all Christians as fellow-soldiers in the same great army of Immanuel, and joyfully co-operated with them in every possible way; and yet it was from a very thorough conviction of their truthfulness and importance that he uttered the following words, in 1859, in a sermon on "Methodist Church Polity," preached before the North Indiana and Pittsburg Conferences, and published in the same year, at the request of those bodies:

"Brethren, hold on to your doctrines, especially of general atonement, the witness of the Spirit, and of full salvation. Hold on to your experience of grace. Hold on to your Discipline. Hold on to your peculiar usages, to class-meetings, love-feasts, congregational singing, revival meetings, the mourners'-bench, and to kneeling in prayer. Hold on to itinerancy, and, as far as may be, to the circuit system; to the presiding eldership, and to general superintendency. In a word, hold on to every thing essential to the success of Methodism; for it has saved millions now in heaven, and millions more in Europe and America who are still heading for the world of light and peace above."

As a preacher, Bishop Morris was distinguished for clearness, simplicity, directness, and brevity. His manner in the pulpit was quiet, and yet earnest; while his style was conversational, it was, at the same time, sufficiently animated. In the early days of his ministry, before his health was impaired by repeated attacks of paralysis, he was often very eloquent, and at times would raise an audience to the highest pitch of religious fervor and enthusiasm. Drs. Wright and Trimble both refer, in their remarks made at the funeral, to a sermon preached once at Urbana, during a conference session, the effect of which upon the audience was very remarkable; and it is certain, from the testimony of many others also, that a very unusual power often accompanied his discourses, even when he seemed least to strive after effect. Still, Bishop Morris was never, perhaps, what would be called a popular preacher. The work of the minister was, in his judgment, evidently too high and holy and serious for the employment of meretricious arts. He felt that he had a message from God to the people, and he delivered it with the dignity and solemnity becoming an embassador of Christ. Flights of fancy, flowers of rhetoric, startling and sensational declamation, profundity, in the sense of saying what neither he nor others understood, and originality, in the sense of teaching doctrines contrary to the Word of God, however popular with multitudes of hearers, are pulpit methods which Bishop Morris could scarcely have been tempted to employ. And yet his printed sermons are worthy to be studied as models. His clear, terse style; his short, simple, and pointed sentences; his sound theology and sound sense, constantly remind the reader of John Wesley's incomparable discourses. One peculiarity of the bishop as a preacher, and which might well be studied and imitated by his successors in the Gospel ministry, was his habit of closing when he was done. Often when the interest was at its height, when there was no flagging of attention on the part of his hearers, and with apparent abruptness even, he would close the Bible and sit down, leaving his congregation wondering at the suddenness of the conclusion.

Upon the whole, we may say of Bishop Morris's preaching as we have said of his character,—it lacked the salient points, perhaps, which render characterization easy and obvious. And yet this very lack, so to speak, was in consequence of the fullness and completeness and thoroughness of his preparation. His sermons were symmetrical, doctrinal, practical, and thoroughly evangelical; not by chance, or because he had a *genius* for sermonizing, but as the result of deep and earnest study. If he preached, as he rarely did, a sermon of considerable length, he was in the habit of saying, apologetically, that his discourse was unusually long because he "had not had time to make it short." And although his delivery of sermons was always what is called extemporaneous, no one perhaps was ever more painstaking and conscientious in preparing for the pulpit.

Bishop Morris was a man of very strong local attachments and warm personal friendships, and no estimate of his character would be just which ignored his social and affectional nature. Amid all the long and weary journeyings of life, *home* was always the one dear spot to which his "heart untraveled fondly turned." He had many pleasant temporary homes among the kind and generous people whom he served in various relations; but "Spice Flat Cottage," "Mount Olivet," "Home Lodge," and "Salubria," were especially dear to his heart. The minute and humorous description of the last-named place, given elsewhere in these pages, shows the depth and tenderness of his attachment to the home of his old age. While the bishop was reticent, almost to a fault, in general society, he was a delightful companion in the circle of his intimate personal friends. A vein of pleasant humor often ran through his fireside talks which made them exceedingly agreeable, and he had an inexhaustible fund of anecdotes, personal and otherwise, with which he almost always spiced his conversation. But, while an occasional flash of wit indicated latent stores of that dangerous weapon, and while his quick and keen appreciation of the ludicrous would sometimes raise a laugh at the expense of another, he was the last man in the world to wound the feelings of any one by a mere wanton use of such powers. Indeed, the humor of Bishop Morris was not of the broad, coarse kind. It pervaded his conversation, in the language of Dr. Merrick, already quoted, as "a subtle aroma," and was usually so quiet and delicate in its character that its aromatic flavor was lost by passing through too many hands. For this reason, mainly, there has been no attempt in this volume to reproduce the numerous anecdotes related of Bishop Morris. Many of them, aside from their accessories, and disconnected from the circumstances which gave them birth, would be pointless and unprofitable. Besides, they are not the things, however innocent and proper, for which Bishop Morris would wish to be remembered.

Of his personal religious experience the bishop spoke seldom, and always with great modesty and reserve. In this respect he so nearly resembled another eminent senior bishop—Rev. Elijah Hedding, D. D.,—that the masterly portraiture of the latter, drawn by his distinguished biographer, the late Bishop Clark, would apply equally well to Bishop Morris.

"He was a man of deep and unaffected piety. His religion was not devoid of feeling; but it rested rather upon the basis of principle than of emotion. It was at the farthest remove from asceticism, or that repulsive austerity which so often makes religion itself seem unamiable. In him, trifling and levity found no place; but cheerfulness—the genial sunshine of the heart—diffused its loveliness all around him. There was no self-reliance, no confident nor high professions; but there was what was far better,— piety, silent but incessant, consistent, deep, all-pervading; working out practical results, producing genuine fruits, forming the character, regulating the life. No one can doubt his deep experience of the things of God and of the sanctifying of the blood of Jesus. But of this last he avoided making any public profession. This may have resulted as much from the extreme modesty of his nature, the poor estimate he always formed of himself and of his performances, and his painful consciousness of his errors and imperfections, as from his profound sense of the high responsibility attached to such professions. He may, too, have thought that the profession that he was a sinner, seeking salvation through the blood of Jesus, was more fitting to his condition and more congenial to his feelings than any other."

This paragraph, as we have very slightly modified it, might as well have been written originally for Thomas A. Morris as for Elijah Hedding. Its writer, after a life of distinguished usefulness, died as gloriously as he had lived ; and now his own "Life-story" is a rich addition to the biographical literature of the Church. He, too, had avoided making a profession of great attainments in religion, in explanation of which his biographer, Rev. Daniel Curry, D. D., makes the following statement, which, no doubt, is a fair presentation of the views and feelings of Bishop Morris also: "To the doctrine of Christian perfection, as expounded by Wesley in his best-matured statements, and interpreted by other points in the Wesleyan theology, he yielded a most hearty assent. He contemplated a ripeness of Christian experience that, in a qualified sense, might be called 'perfection,' as not only an ideal toward which Christians should be always pressing, but as a state of still-progressing grace that may be reached. But his deep convictions respecting the infinite majesty and all-consuming holiness of God's law, and of the exceeding sinfulness

of sin, as it inheres in fallen souls—his deep consciousness of his own heart's infirmities, and the
severity of his judgments upon himself"—might
well make one of his sensitive nature and extreme
humility hesitate as to the propriety of a particular
and prescribed form of professing it.

Undoubtedly, that sterling honesty which was
always a conspicuous trait in the character of Bishop
Morris would naturally incline him to great circumspection in making any profession of personal attainments which it was not clearly his duty to make.
He was of that class of men who would rather profess too little than too much in regard to themselves,
and who, while conceding to others of a different
mind the largest liberty as to their forms of profession, are at the same time fully persuaded that a life
wholly given up to the service of God, and regulated
and governed by the precepts of the Gospel, is, after
all, one of the best possible evidences of genuine
Christian character.

Bishop Morris was not a demonstrative man.
His religion exhibited itself as a uniform, active,
holy principle of obedience to the will of God ; and
it permeated his whole life, private and public. He
was "a doer of the Word, and not a hearer only."
It was also characteristic of the man to speak sparingly and modestly of himself. He had, in fact, a
deep dislike for whatever bore even the semblance
of egotism ; and for any thing like mere ostentatious
display or parade he had a hearty and wholesome
contempt. That such a man should be somewhat
reserved in speaking of his religious attainments, and

the exercises and frames of his mind, seems entirely natural. But there were times when he spoke fully and freely concerning his religious experience; and no one, perhaps, ever enjoyed a more uniform, tranquil, and peaceful state of mind.

His letter to the Cincinnati Conference, dictated only a few days before he breathed his last, very beautifully expresses his feelings in view of the near approach of death:

"I find the religion I so long preached to others is able to bring peace and assurance to the heart in retirement, as well as when in the heat of battle, leading forth the conquering hosts to certain victory. Thank God for the Christian's hope! It comforts and sustains amid all the vicissitudes of life, and to the trusting heart makes bright the future. In reviewing the past, I have only this to say, that God has been very good to me. Most of my associates in the ministry, as well as many loved ones, have passed away. I yet linger on the shore, and soon expect to cross the river. I am nearing the Jordan, and in the course of nature can not stay here much longer; but beneath me are the everlasting arms, and, through riches of grace in Christ Jesus my Lord, I hope to anchor safely in the harbor of eternal rest."

This, which may be regarded as the dying testimony of Bishop Morris, is eminently characteristic of the man. While it is pervaded throughout by a spirit of humility as lovely as it is rare, it is, at the same time, the blessed language of the full assurance of faith and hope; an assurance so strong and comforting, even down to the last moment of his life, that he could say, with his dying breath, " The future looks bright."

The life of Bishop Morris is of special interest to the communion he served with so much fidelity and for so long a period of time, for the reason that he is the last of the general superintendents whose personal experience extends far back into what is often and very properly called the heroic period of Methodism. At his birth, the Methodists of the United States, white and colored, numbered less than seventy thousand ; he lived to see them a great and powerful section of the grand army of Immanuel—three million strong. And the reader of this biography will not need to be told that, in promoting this wonderful growth, few men were more efficient than Thomas A. Morris.

His life embraced a most interesting period of the history both of the country and of the Church. His official responsibilities were accepted with the modesty which is always characteristic of real merit, and discharged with the fidelity and courage of a hero. On the episcopal bench a place is vacant which can not be easily filled ; for his wisdom in council was the most distinguishing feature of his long career as a bishop. Always recognized and appreciated by the Church, even down to his extreme old age, this quality of his mind was of special and incalculable service in those early and formative days of Methodism in which he bore so prominent a part.

And now, the story of his eventful life, of his

early struggles and sufferings, of his incessant labors, of his extensive journeyings, of his strange adventures, of his dangerous exposures, will read, even to many of this generation, more like a tale of romance than of reality. And, as we close this record, we seem to have reached the end of one distinct and unique period in the annals of American Methodism; an epoch made memorable for all time, in ecclesiastical history, by names that were not born to die.

THE END.